MW01231700

DANCING

ALONG THE

UPPER MISSISSIPPI

Watch For These Forthcoming Books

from

Popcorn Press

Last Waltz In Goodhue

Creative Autobiography

Publication, Summer 1997

Jim Franklin

County Road No. 9

Novellas, Stories, Personal Essays

Publication, Summer 1998

Jim Franklin

Ragtime Along The Upper Mississippi

Historical Novel: 19th Century Steamboating

Publication, Summer 1999

Jim Franklin

The Capitol, Mississippi River Steamboat

Dancing
Along The
Upper Mississippi

Jim Franklin

1997

Upper Mississippi River
Book Publisher

Popcorn Press
McGregor, Iowa

Dancing Along The Upper Mississippi
© 1997 by Jim Franklin. All rights reserved. No part of this
book may be used or reproduced in any manner whatsoever
without written permission except in the case of a brief
quotation embodied in critical articles and reviews.

Popcorn Press
126 Main Street
P.O. Box 237
McGregor, Iowa 52157

5 4 3 2 1

Library of Congress Catalog Card Number: 97-91758

ISBN 0-9634689-3-6

Printed in the United States of America

Cover background screen photo and Frontispiece:
The Capitol, Mississippi River steamboat passing through the
pontoon bridge at Marquette, Iowa circa 1932.
(Photograph courtesy of Mary Jo Pirc).
Cover inset photo, McGregor, Iowa
(Jim Franklin personal collection)
Author photo, back cover, by Joanne Collins.

Mark Twain quotations are public domain.
General Editor, Mark Twain Project,
University of California, Berkeley

For Anne and Joe

Acknowledgments

Although the writing process itself is a solitary endeavor, the completion of a publishing project of this magnitude was not accomplished without the assistance and encouragement of many individuals. As Father Marquette and Joliet were assisted by the Indians while exploring these great waters, so also did I receive assistance and encouragement along my river exploration.

My thanks to Jerry Haas for leading me to two important Mississippi River books—*Old Times on the Upper Mississippi* by George Merrick, and *Steamboating on the Upper Mississippi* by William Petersen.

To Doug Farley for his help in deciphering the history of the Alexander Hotel.

To the staff of the McGregor Public Library, especially Sue Kroesche and Sue Henkes for their assistance during my researching of McGregor's and Marquette's history, and leading me to Diamond Jo Reynolds.

My gratitude to the McGregor Historical Museum, especially to Jan Williams for her assistance in deciphering McGregor's and Marquette's past.

A special thanks to the staffs of the Western History Library of the Denver, Colorado Public Library, the Mississippi River Museum of the Dubuque County Historical Society, and the Prairie du Chien Public Library.

Heartfelt and warm appreciation goes to riverboat Captain Jack Libbey—Smithsonian Mississippi River folklife consultant—for giving his time to talk with me, endlessly, in the pilot house of the Miss Marquette, about the river, steamboating, Mark Twain, towboats, snags, reefs and four-mile currents. Also, for his reading and proofing of the manuscript to insure accuracy of river and riverboat terminology. Above all, for his special interest in this project and love of the river.

To Joanne Collins for her belief in the project, for her enduring encouragement that this book would, in fact, someday be published. A special thanks to her for believing in me, for pushing me over sandbars, through the narrows and menacing waters.

Finally, to Herb Collins without whose support this project would have been hung up in shoal water like an abandoned steamboat left to decay on the reefs of the great river. A special thanks to him for pushing me over sandbars and reefs into deeper water. Also, to Herb for reading and proofing the manuscript, for getting inside my characters, for offering suggestions, for being a sounding board, but most of all, for believing in this project. For that I offer deep running waters, wind on your stern, my eternal gratitude, and may you reach port before the devil knows you've cast off.

Dancing Along The Upper Mississippi is a work of historical fiction both in characters portrayed and story line. Any resemblance between the fictional characters in this story and characters in McGregor, Marquette and Prairie du Chien is purely intentional.

Contents

Dancing Along The Upper Mississippi

An Historical Novella

The face of the water, in time, became a wonderful book—a book that was a dead language to the uneducated passenger, but which told its mind to me without reserve, delivering its most cherished secrets as clearly as if it uttered them with a voice. And it was not a book to be read once and thrown aside, for it had a new story to tell every day.

—Mark Twain, *Life On The Mississippi*, 1883

A T THE FIRST BLAST OF THE STEAM WHISTLE, HANK'S heart skipped a beat. He heard the bellow even before the acrid black smoke reached his nostrils. That low, rolling, baritone-pitched blast always made his old heart skip. It echoed down the valley around Marquette Bend, bounced off Point Ann, then rattled up Main Street until it dead-ended against the bluff behind St. Mary's church. Every time he heard that deep-throated blast, every time he smelled that coal-burnt smoke, his heart pounded against his chest. But he had been experiencing that thump throughout his entire life, sixty-nine years; he didn't worry about it anymore. It hadn't killed him yet. This steamboat coming around the bend wouldn't either. He laid his bifocals on the rolltop desk, raised his lanky, aching body out of the swivel chair, shuffled to the front door as fast as his old legs and bad hip could carry him, swung the tattered screen door open and walked toward the river. From the levee, a yell . . . "S-t-e-a-m-boat's a comin'."

Regardless of the task he was involved in—writing, editing, setting type on the 1930-vintage Linotype machine, printing the *North Iowa Times*—the powerful blast of a steamboat whistle was irresistible to him and to most villagers now joining him on the trek to the river. Even though he had experienced hundreds of steam-boat passings in his lifetime, it was still an exciting but increasing-ly rare event. Sometimes it stopped at McGregor, but most often it stayed in the main channel, continuing downriver to unload passengers at Dubuque or Davenport. As he reached the levee,

3

catching his first glimpse of the steamboat upriver, he could tell immediately that it wouldn't be docking today—belching too much coal-black smoke through its stacks to be able to stop— because he knew steamboats as well as every variety of trading scow, keelboat, broadhorn, timber raft or packet that had plied this river. And he knew the river itself, intimately, with its deceptive currents, its ever-changing colors, its melodious sounds, its sand bars, points, eddies, reaches and reefs, particularly the waters around McGregor and Marquette. He had lived his entire life in McGregor, this tiny hamlet sequestered between the long sloping bluffs of the Upper Mississippi, but he had probably spent as much time on the river as he had on land, so it didn't take him but a second to determine the speed of the current, to observe the dipping and swaying of the fishing boats fighting valiantly to remain tethered to the dock, to see how far up the boat ramp the waves were being pushed by the steamer before he surmised that it was heading past.

"How you doin' today, Hank? She's a beauty, ain't she?" Bernie hollered from the swaying dock waving his ever-present Chicago Cubs baseball cap, shaggy hair blowing in the breeze.

"Hi, Bernie. Yes, she is that. Looks like the Miss Red Wing from up in Minnesota. Can you read her masthead from here?" Hank said as he stepped gingerly onto the darting dock.

"Nope. Not yet. She needs to come on another couple hundred yards or so before I can read it," Bernie hollered while gulping beer from a long-necked bottle. "I know many boats passing here, but my eyesight ain't as good as it used to be, needs to be closer."

"I understand that. Mine has been deteriorating for several years from too much typesetting, editing columns and reading type backwards. I have to change my bifocals about every two years, but I don't have to rely only on my eyes to identify a steamer. I still have good ears and that blast sure sounds like the Miss Red Wing. We'll know in a couple of minutes. Wait! I think I hear music. A calliope? That's odd. If she's blasting calliope music she can't be the Miss Red Wing, because she doesn't have one. She must be the Delta Queen."

There were twenty to thirty gawkers now lining the levee and standing on the dock, because a steamboat passing was a big event.

Folks liked seeing them even if they couldn't be riding on one themselves. Steamboats were going someplace else, had been someplace else, were a link to the world. Steamers had been plying the Mississippi from St. Paul up north to New Orleans down south since the early 1800s. They had helped this town and other villages along its waterways to grow and prosper. Residents of St. Paul, Red Wing, Lake City, Winona, La Crosse, Lansing, Harper's Ferry, Marquette, McGregor, Prairie du Chien, Lynxville, Clayton, Guttenberg, Cassville, Dubuque, Davenport, Burlington, Muscatine, Keokuk, Hannibal and St. Louis owed their lives to the steamboats plying the Upper Mississippi's meandering currents. These villagers lining the levee today loved living here, but that didn't mean they wouldn't liked to have been riding downriver to somewhere else on that steamboat. Steamboats and the endless river created a wanderlust in them. On a steamboat, they could be children again just like Huck Finn and Tom Sawyer.

"Well, you're right again, Hank. She is the Delta Queen," Bernie said as the Queen's bow pushed waves toward the dock causing the tethered fishing boats to rock violently. "She's a beauty, that's for sure, don't you think?" Bernie said while grabbing the bow of a fishing boat that had broken from its mooring.

"Yes, she is a gorgeous and elegant paddlewheeler, one of the few still plying the river. That single, fluted chimney is very distinctive; of course, her intricate fretwork and filigree along her decks are pure steamboating lore, right out of the nineteenth century," Hank said as he steadied himself on the undulating dock, "and her gleaming white cabins with a blazing red paddlewheel certainly is eye-catching." The Queen *was* a beautiful steamer with white filigree on the upper decks, gilded acorns on the derricks, flags flying from the forecastle, and plumes everywhere. By now the Queen was rapidly bearing down on the sightseers, calliope bursting forth with its strident, raucous steam rendition of *I'm For-ever Blowing Bubbles*. Tiny bursts of steam sprouted, just like bubbles, from the aft deck every time the calliopist depressed a key. And she was filled with merrymakers, most of whom appeared to be on the starboard deck waving and hollering greetings to the landlocked villagers, themselves waving from the levee. The

Queen was now directly abreast of the dock out in the main channel, paddlewheel churning vigorously, thrusting its blades deep into the blue river, propelling the steamer downstream. It was close, not thirty yards away, just a good fishing cast from the dock. The thrashing paddlewheel sprayed gawkers as she roared past. While rounding the Marquette Bend upriver, the Queen didn't appear to be traveling fast, but gawkers could now see her speed, feel her mighty power, sense her massive energy. But all too soon she was past the levee, calliope searing the valley's pristine air with *Cruising Down The River*, steam whistle tearing through the village's peaceful ambiance causing folks to cover their ears as she approached Point Ann. Another few minutes and she would be completely out of sight. Hank felt the river shudder, felt the energy in the waters as the dock settled back to its rightful place, as the river gradually settled back to its regular state of affairs after being adulterated by the passing steamer.

"That certainly was a treat, but I have to get back to my newspaper, Bernie. The *North Iowa Times* comes out tomorrow, so I have to go to press tonight. I have another three to four hours of work before bedtime. I'll see you later. Have a good night," Hank said as he jumped from the dock onto the boat ramp and began walking toward his shop.

"Hell! You're workin' too hard, Mister Editor. Why don't you sit here on the dock with me and have a couple a beers. I've got a six pack needing tending to. Want to help me out?" Bernie shouted as he flipped off the top of another Old Style brew.

"Thanks, but I do have to get the paper printed. A couple of Old Styles would slow me down too much, then folks wouldn't have their newspaper tomorrow."

"Hell! That wouldn't be any loss. You don't put nothin' in that old rag anyway . . . just kiddin', Hank. The *Times* ain't a bad paper. I like reading your River Reflections column, and I like your editorials about things happening around here, even though you do get a bit testy about our mayor. Well, guess I'll just have to finish off this beer myself then. See you, Mister Editor. I'll look forward to tomorrow's exciting edition," Bernie said as he turned back toward the calming river to begin serious work on the six pack.

Hank trudged back up Main Street to his shop, waving and greeting villagers also leaving the levee, invigorated by the passing of the Delta Queen, but wishing the weekly edition was printed. He had finished setting hot type on the Linotype, had set upper and lower case characters into printer's boxes, and was now ready to print. He placed page eight into the printer, inked the rollers, then started the old Ludlow printer. As he watched it pass through the press a thousand times, mesmerized by the pulsating rhythm of the printer, he realized that he was weary, not from editing, writing and reporting events along the river, but rather, from the nonstop weekly schedule of back-breaking press work and endless hours of typesetting at the Linotype. As he saw the counter click number 679, he thought, really for the first time, about retiring. Oh, he always knew he would need to someday, most people did, but he had never actually put a date on it. Charlie up the street at the drugstore had retired last year. Homer at the shoe shop said this was going to be his last year of fixing soles and heels; even Reverend Richards at the Methodist church said he was thinking about retiring from fixing souls and heals.

Maybe it's time for me to take down my shingle, too. I've been editing the Times *for forty years. Golly, has it really been that long? Let's see . . . after serving my apprenticeship while in high school, I purchased the* Times *in . . . was it 1910 or 1912? No, I believe it was earlier than that. It must have been 1909. It's 1949 now so I have been editor for forty years.*

Page one thousand rang the bell on the printer. He replaced the type tray with page seven, set the counter to one thousand, then restarted the press.

Forty years. In a few months I'll be seventy. Me, seventy? I can't believe it. My father would be, yes . . . my fath . . . th . . . whoever . . . wherever?

He toiled until midnight churning out the eight-page paper until the June 19, 1949 issue was completely printed. Although he was bone tired, he was happy the paper was finally finished. He shuffled to the rear of the shop, walked over to the Biedermeir cabinet, opened the door to locate a black-labeled bottle, then poured a hearty glass of Jack Daniels. He shuffled to the overstuffed chair by the potbellied stove and slumped heavily into its tattered, bumpy cushion. A full measure of Jack Daniels and a Harvester Perfecto were his reward at the end of a press run. He bit the end off the cigar, scratched a matchstick across the sole of his shoe, sucked deeply, then blew the tangy smoke toward the dust-laden, corrugated tin ceiling. He lifted the glass ever so slowly to his parched lips, took a generous sip and let the smooth whiskey slide across his tongue. He held it there for a moment savoring the flavor, the bite, the tartness before swallowing it, feeling it coat his throat while burning its way down into his stomach. He set the glass on the printer's table, cupped his hands behind his head and leaned back into his ancient chair.

This chair has been here longer than I have, has served editors before me, and will be here long after I'm in my grave. Another editor will sit here after printing his weekly edition to have his drink and cigar.

He smoked and sipped for an hour, occasionally falling asleep only to be brought back to reality by the sudden jerking of his head as his chin bounced on his chest like the little toy bird on the window sill that dipped its head into the water glass all day long. He had turned out the lights except for one hanging over the printer's table. In the shadowy recesses of the shop, he squinted at the Linotype, the printer's boxes, the rolltop desk, the Norman Rockwell paintings on the wall, the Round Oak potbellied stove with two Windsor chairs, a rocking chair and two overstuffed chairs guarding it, and the wall shelves filled from floor to ceiling with archival *Times* issues. This was his environment, his life. This is where he had spent the past forty years, in this village along the river. He emptied the glass of Jack Daniels, was ready to set it down but on this night decided to have another instead of his usual one. He poured a healthy glass then walked to the desk, sat in the chair, inhaled deeply, sipped gratefully and continued to survey the domain begun by Colonel Richardson before the Civil War, and the one Hank had continued when he purchased the *Times* in 1909. Editing had been a good life, he thought, a good career. He had enjoyed his interaction with folks in Marquette and McGregor as well as neighboring towns—Clayton, Garnavillo, Elkader, Guttenberg, Harper's Ferry, Prairie du Chien, Lansing—up and down the river. He had enjoyed investigating and reporting the hundreds, if not thousands, of stories and reports he had filed throughout his career. There had been some momentous characters, some mo-men–tous stories. But tonight he realized that he couldn't continue much longer, that he couldn't maintain this schedule. He thought maybe it was finally time to retire, to sell out to a cub editor. He needed more time to float the river, to fish for crappies and walleyes in the back waters out on Horseshoe Lake. He needed more time to smell the river, to hear the mournful wail of herons out in the marshes, to listen to the squawking of hawks and bald eagles as they soared from the bluffs along these waters. If he retired, he could still write, still edit, but on his own time, not on this weekly, back-breaking schedule. By the time he had found the bottom of his second glass, by the time the cigar was singeing his fingers, the Regulator clock had loudly struck twice and he was feeling very mellow. He raised his lean, long-legged six-foot frame slowly out of the chair, buttoned his pinstriped vest, placed a summer Stetson hat upon his silvery head, ran his fingers through a white, flowing beard, tugged on the ceiling chain to turn out the light, shuffled to the front door to insert a bent skeleton key, locked the door and walked up Main Street toward home. Reaching the First State Savings corner, he turned impulsively for a look at the river. Moonlight was reflecting off the channel so he could see that it was calm, not a single ripple remained from the Delta Queen, not a soul meandered about, although he might have caught a glimpse of a slumping figure down on the dock. He walked up the darkened street past the shops, turned right and continued walking toward his beautiful Queen Anne home at the foot of Methodist Hollow. By the time he reached the front steps, seeing the night light flooding through red and blue stained glass windows into the street, he had indeed decided to retire.

I'll be seventy in December. That would be a good time. I could write stories again, maybe about life on the Mississippi, my life at The Times.

He slipped into bed, cuddled up to his wife's warm body content with his decision . . . to retire . . . to fish . . . to write.

2

Getting the weekly *Times* printed was always satisfying for Hank, because he could then relax for a couple of days without feeling the pressure of working on the next issue. Today would be a good day—a day to drink coffee at Bruno's Cafe, a day to chat with friends on the street, a day to catch crappies or perch off the end of the dock or along the willows in Horseshoe Lake, a day to smoke cigars, a day to enjoy another Jack Daniels.

"I see you haven't let up on the mayor one bit about buying that new fire truck, Hank," Charlie chided as Hank joined the fellows for morning coffee at Bruno's Cafe. Charlie was one of the regulars, a fixture among the morning coffee group. He hadn't a hair left on his head, a fact which caused considerable chiding among his cohorts, but he tolerated it because he was a man of good humor. He was also kind and always willing to be of service to someone in need, something he had been doing for fifty years. He wasn't one to change his attire, though, as he was usually seen around town in a gray cardigan sweater worn over a plaid shirt buttoned at the neck—his uniform. He wore that sweater daily whether it was a sultry summer day or a cool day in autumn. Clarissa didn't think it appropriate because of his stout stature— made his legs look short she said—but had given up trying to change him. 'That's Charlie,' she said to everyone who would listen, as if trying to offer an excuse for his attire. "You wrote about the mayor last week in your editorial, and you've come right back at him again this week. Don't you think you're being hard on him?"

"We don't need that new fire truck, Charlie. The old one has done well for twenty years now. Purchasing it is like tossing money in the river, foolish if you ask me, and you know what Huckleberry Finn said about fools, don't you . . . 'Hain't we got all the fools in town on our side? And hain't that a big enough majority in any town?' The mayor needs to be taken to task for being so foolish and pushing it through the village council," Hank answered as he sat alongside Charlie and Doc, sliding his gangly legs under the counter. "How about a cup of coffee, Bruno? and fry two sunny-side-up eggs with hash browns, also. I developed a hearty appetite printing the paper last night."

"How long are you going to keep at the newspaper business, Hank?" Bruno asked as he overflowed Hank's coffee cup, spilling it down the sides and onto the counter. "You're getting kind of old, you know, and crotchety, too. Your editorials are getting nastier. It's surprising for an old fart like you. I'll fry those eggs and hash browns now," Bruno said as he walked back toward the steaming grill.

"Retire? Why would I want to do that. If I did I'd only sit here all day drinking your weak coffee, wasting my time and loosing my hair like 'Chrome Dome' Charlie here. Hell! I have things to do yet—editorials to write, stories to report, papers to print. I can't retire and waste away to nothing like you fellows."

"Retirement isn't so bad, Hank. I did it last year, but other than getting too many honey-do's from Clarissa, I kind of like it. I spent forty-four years with Theodore at the drugstore filling prescriptions for Doc's patients, but once out from behind the counter, I've been enjoying myself," Charlie answered while displaying a constant nervous habit of fiddling with the top button of his shirt to see if it was still buttoned, "and you should think about it. You aren't a spring chicken anymore, Mister Editor."

"Charlie's right, Hank. By the way, you haven't been in for a physical exam in over a year, have you? Your cholesterol was high at your last exam, and I see your weight is creeping up. And here you are ordering fried eggs, fried ham and fried potatoes. You had better call my secretary today to schedule an exam . . . and watch those eggs," Doc said as Bruno set a huge plate of fried eggs and ham in front of Doc.

"Talk about me watching my fat and cholesterol! Look at what you're eating, Doc. You have enough food there for next week's editorial—Fat, Cholesterol, Old Age and Old Farts—" Hank retorted, "and my weight isn't so bad. I have a little extra around my belt, nothing like your paunch, though, but I'm only about one-seventy-five. I'd say that's good for my height and age."

"Anyway, Hank, we needed that new fire truck. We just couldn't depend on the 1920 La France anymore ... needed a valve job, new tires, and it didn't have much pressure for the fire hoses anymore ... couldn't depend on it. What with Japan and Germany surrendering a few years ago, we'll soon have more jobs, more money, more manufacturing, more tourists. We certainly needed that truck. Isn't that right, Doc?" Charlie said while slurping coffee and dripping several drops onto his already coffee-stained sweater.

"I don't know. Hank has a point about the fire truck. We need other things like a new library, for instance. Mrs. Newell has been running it out of her home for years. It's time we had a regular library building. And the streets need fixing. We need curbs and gutters throughout the village; we still have dirt roads up at the end of Methodist Hollow and Walton's Hollow, too. I'm in agreement about the fire truck. We could have waited a few years," Doc answered as he finished his coffee and dug into the plate of overflowing fries and sausages. Bruno placed a heaping plate of eggs, ham and potatoes in front of Hank, filled his cup as well as Charlie's and Doc's, set the coffee pot on the counter, wiped his huge, muscular hands on his greasy apron, and leaned on the counter to join the conversation.

"You old farts just keep going on about incidental things. You're not focused. Let me tell you what we should really be doing," Bruno said launching into one of his frequent lectures to his captive audience. Bruno had a way of getting folks' attention being the burly fellow he was, and speaking with a booming voice. He had the size to play linebacker with the Chicago Bears, six-foot-two, one-ninety-five, but never did. In fact, he resembled the Bears outstanding lineman, Leo Nomelini, with his massive shoulders, crew cut and square jaw, although there was some light graying around his temples. Out-of-towners frequently asked him who he had played for, but Bruno just said, "Oh, a pro team down around Chicago." But he liked to display his hulking body, being vainly proud of it at fifty-two years of age. He strutted around the cafe in a white apron over a white, crew neck T-shirt, pack of

Chesterfields rolled into the left sleeve. T-shirts also gave him the opportunity to show off the two tattoos he got while a Chief Petty Officer in the Navy—left arm tattooed with *U.S. Navy* just below the elbow, right arm tattooed with the ample bosom of a voluptuous lady. "Now, I agree with Hank about the fire truck, but I don't agree with you, Doc, never agree with you, that we should have used the money for a new library. I'm of the opinion that we should have saved the fire truck money and used it to build a bigger gymnasium up at the high school instead. When they put up the new school in, what was it, 1931, basketball wasn't a popular sport yet. They built a tiny shoe box of a gym. The floor is too short and narrow, there's not enough seats, and the whole place is colder than ice fishing out on Horseshoe Lake in January. We need to expand it. Isn't that right, Charlie?" Bruno bellowed.

"I don't know, Bruno. My children are out of school, graduated and married. One's up in Lansing working at Lock and Dam No. 9. The other's down in Dubuque butchering steers for the Dubuque Packing Company, but you may have a point there," Charlie said brushing his hand over a bald head, searching for nonexistent hairs like water in Death Valley. "Doc and I and Hank never played basketball because that Naismith fellow didn't get around to inventing it until the early 1890s. We threw balls around in the school on Ann Street, but it sure wasn't basketball . . . more like dodgeball."

"I believe you're correct, Charlie, but even if we would have had the game, you would have been too much of a runt to play. But that gym is small, I'll grant you that, Bruno. Why don't we get something going about the gym?" Doc said.

"Believe I will," Bruno answered as he unrolled his sleeve to get a Chesterfield. "There's a school board meeting Monday night . . . think I'll attend.

What do you think about a bigger gym, Hank?" Bruno asked pouring another round of coffee to the fellows.

"An expanded gym? A new fire truck? A new library? I don't know. That's something I'll need to think about. I don't want to write without researching, but I will consider it. I could write an editorial, after the one on fat and cholesterol and old farts, though.

Fellows, I'd like to converse with you all morning, but I have things to do at the shop. I printed the paper last night, and now I need to outline some ideas for my next River Reflections column; then I want to do some research in back issues on a few special topics. I'll probably see you back here about noon. What are you serving today, Bruno? Is it worth coming back for?" Hank said as he stood and headed toward the door.

"Meat loaf and whipped potatoes with gravy and green peas. Special. Dollar-twenty-five. Take it or leave it," Bruno hollered from the grill.

"So long, Charlie. See you, Doc. Bye, Bruno," Hank said as he bounded through the door.

As he left the cafe, he saw Cletus sweeping trash down the gutter toward the river. "Hello, Cletus. How are you this fine morning?"

"Uh . . . hi, Mister Hank. I . . . I'm do . . . in' . . . doin' jus' fine. You pre . . . pressin' the p . . . paper today?" Cletus said as he continued sweeping trash with a long-handled broom, creating a swirling dust cloud—like locusts devouring a wheat field—covering his lime-green Dekalb feed cap, his unruly black hair, his stained Pioneer Seeds jacket and his Oshkosh Bigosh blue-striped, high-backed bib overalls.

"I printed last night, so I don't suppose you've read my editorial about the fire truck" Hank said as he continued walking alongside Cletus, brushing dust from his sleeve.

"N . . . No. I . . . I'm . . . not so g . . . good at re . . . readin', Mister Hank, but I . . . like the new f . . . fi . . . fir . . . fire truck. It's pretty . . . real red," Cletus said while scooping trash and bottles out of the gutter and shoveling them into his wheelbarrow.

"It is red, Cletus, that's for sure. But . . . well, I'm glad you like it. You can come by the shop to pick up the bundles for delivery now. And, as usual, when you have finished, I'll have a treat for you."

"I . . . I'll do th . . . that . . . M . . . M . . . Mister Hank. I . . . I'll . . . c . . . come right d . . . down for the p . . . p . . . papers just as s . . . s . . . soon as I . . . I f . . . finish the s . . . s . . . street an' empty m . . . my wheelbarrow," Cletus answered through a cloud of dust.

Hank crossed Main Street waving to villagers along the street and in the stores. He was instantly recognizable—tall and striking, dressed in blue pinstriped slacks, navy blue suspenders, an always unbuttoned vest hanging awkwardly from his lanky frame, tie never quite cinched at the collar. He had always believed that a man in his position needed to be dressed; consequently, he was one of the few men, other than Doc, who wore suit pants and tie on a regular basis, but even though he wore a suit, his jacket was usually thrown over his shoulders, and he had a way of defeating the whole purpose of wearing one. Clerks in the bank waved, Samantha Cheuvront, plodding uptown with her ever-present camera swinging to and fro from her neck greeted him; Old Buck, the black Labrador Retriever perpetually ensconced in front of First State Savings raised a lazy eye as Hank petted the dog while simultaneously glancing at the river before reaching his shop. He knew it was going to be a humid day, but his shop was tucked into the bluff, so he would get some cooling from that. The shop was a building typical of the style constructed at the turn of the century along the Upper Mississippi. In fact, many stores in McGregor, Marquette, Guttenberg and Dubuque looked the same, having been built during the 1880s and '90s. They were two-story, brick-faced structures with elongated, arched windows, builder's name emblazoned on the facing. The *North Iowa Times* shop was one of those buildings, built in 1862, a building which had served Hank well enough all these years. It fit like an old glove. He walked past the Linotype to the rear thinking momentarily about lifting a short glass of Jack, but deciding it was much too early for that. Maybe later. Tossing his suit jacket on the printer's table, he sat at the rolltop desk shuffling papers, reaching into the drawer for a Harvester, lighting it then leaning back into the swivel chair thinking about retirement.

Maybe the fellows are right? Maybe I am getting crotchety in my old age. I decided last night to retire, but I awoke this morning having second thoughts, but now . . .

He sat at the desk for an hour, doodling and jotting notes. By ten o'clock he had reaffirmed his decision to retire in December. It was time for a cub editor to take over the newspaper, to let someone else worry about fire trucks, paving streets, a new gymnasium. He still believed in village causes, but he was weary. Yes, it was time to retire . . . to the river.

In the rear of the shop, from floor to ceiling along the back and sidewalls and around his desk, archival issues, every yellowed and tattered copy back to the first issue in 1856 hovered like chicken hawks ready to swoop down on their prey. He was familiar enough with the history of the *Times* to know that after it had been started as a Democrat paper, three years later, the Republicans began a rival paper, *The McGregor News*. Publishers, editors, names changed frequently in those years—*McGregor Press, Pocket City News, Home Journal, McGregor News*—but it was the *North Iowa Times* that had lasted. For at least the past five years, he had been meaning to review the stacks, to organize them for posterity, to secure them in a safer place like that new library Doc had suggested, but he had never got around to the task. It seemed like such a large job. But as he now stood before the stacks, craning his neck to the ceiling, he realized how much history was here, and also what a fire hazard it was. If he were to have a fire, much of the history of the village and its people would be lost. That thought disturbed him as he absentmindedly relit his stogy with a match strike across his left sole.

And I have been smoking these stogies, flipping matches around for years. The whole thing could go up in flames.

He walked along the sidewall, around the potbellied stove and ducked under the rusted and blackened stove pipe.

Sparks from that stove could set this entire building ablaze, and that smoke stack doesn't look safe, either. I had better look into that.

He continued along the back wall where torn, tattered, yellowed and wrinkled issues jutted out from the shelves, some having already succumbed to gravity. Along the sidewall were shelves containing twenty-five feet of newsprint, ninety-three years of the *North Iowa Times*—incidents, murders, drownings, accidents, rapes, incests, illicit affairs, bastard births, fire trucks, steamboat explosions, expected and unexpected deaths—a chronicle of the two villages, maybe even the key that would unlock the mystery of his father. He stretched out in the swivel chair to gaze at the environment he had helped create. They certainly weren't all his issues, as many editors had preceded him, but he was responsible for a large share of it. After sitting for a few moments, he walked to the far wall behind the printer, climbed the rolling ladder to the ceiling and pulled out several issues including the brittle and yellowed first issue.

North Iowa Times
October 10, 1856
F. W. D. Merrell, Publisher
A. P. Richardson, Editor

NORTH IOWA TIMES ESTABLISHES
FIRST NEWSPAPER IN THE VILLAGE

> Today, McGregor has its first, official newspaper. This town is a bustling, thriving river town, and it is high time we had a newspaper. Messrs. Merrell and Richardson are proud to bring this paper to the citizens of McGregor and North McGregor. We will publish every Wednesday, sufficient news notwithstanding.

There was a column about the history of McGregor, a half page about Strawberry Point, a statement by the county clerk indicating that Clayton County was valued at $3,112,074, a couple of ads from G. Hawley & Son's Carriage Works, and Amos Pearsall's Livery Stable, advertisement about Monona, a report of steamboat dockings at the McGregor Wharf: April, 17; May, 116; June, 105; July, 89; August, 65; a short article about the steamboat Effie Afton destroying a railroad bridge at Rock Island, a statement about Mormons leaving Iowa City for Salt Lake City pulling hand carts, and schedules for several church services.

He picked up another issue, this one dated 1875, Colonel Otis, Editor. It was so brittle and faded that he had difficulty reading many of the headlines: Village Builds New Dock at The Foot of Main Street; Alexander MacGregor's Kin Dies in Sabula; Diamond Jo Steamboat Line Plans Headquarters Building In McGre-

gor. He read through the entire issue including a report of President
U. S. Grant speaking in Des Moines, then climbed the ladder to pull
out additional issues. By noon he had retrieved twenty to thirty and
had them spread on the printer's table. He poured over them,
crouching with a magnifying glass to read type that was yellowed
and faded.

*I should pull this together, synthesize much of this material.
I could write my memoirs about my years here. I could organize it
by decades, the significant events of our villages and others along
the river. It would be a good retirement project. It needs to be done
for the village.*

Hank retrieved a match from his vest pocket, stoked another
cigar while being more careful this time where he discarded the
match, and untied his tie completely to spend the next several
hours reading through 1875, '76, '77, '78 and '79 issues. He read
several fascinating stories about early McGregor and North McGregor, later to be called Marquette: Carriage construction, runaway
horses, house construction, ferry boating to Wisconsin, fires,
channel fishing, keelboating, and sawmills as well as a smattering
of headlines about state news: State Normal School Established at
Cedar Falls; Canal Opened on the Mississippi above Keokuk;
Wheat Belt Passing Westward as Iowa Turns to Corn Production;
State Population Reaches 1,624,615. But about three hours into
reading, he noticed a Steamboat Dockings report in a September
1878 issue, back page, lower left-hand column . . .

STEAMBOAT DOCKINGS

Steamboat	Captain	Pilot	Arrival	Departure	Cargo
Diamond Jo	Mr. Harris	Mr. Burns	Th. 1:15 p.	Th. 3:30 p.	Wheat
Winona	Mr. Hatcher	Mr. Tibbles	Sa. 10:20 a.	Sa. 2:10 p.	Plows
John J. Roe	Mr. LaPointe	Mr. Cormack	Su. 2 p.	Su. 5:07 p.	Soap

During the 1870s and '80s, he found that the *North Iowa
Times* reported every steamboat docking at the McGregor wharf
for the previous week. Even though traffic on the Mississippi
wasn't as extensive then as it was prior to the Civil War, it was still
an important mode of transportation and shipping along the Upper

Mississippi while the railroad system gradually established itself, and Iowa painstakingly emerged from the archaic mud and gravel road network to hard-surfaced but narrow roads. Steamboats were unloaded and loaded with a wide array of merchandise—apples, coffee, lard, molasses, tea, beer, tobacco, salt, soap, axes, grindstones, picks, plows, reapers, saws, scythes, shovels, andirons, candles, guns, ovens, pans, pots, powder, stoves, milled flour, wheat—and frequently, cords of wood from the surrounding hills for their boilers, "wooding up," for continued trips up- or downriver. The report stated only name, captain, pilot, arrival, departure and cargo for the Diamond Jo and Winona, but further stated that the John J. Roe crew and passengers had disembarked to refresh themselves by walking along the riverfront, then partaking of sarsaparillas at the H. D. Evans Dry Goods Emporium. The editor indicated that Pilot McCormack was accompanied by two unnamed young cub pilots on a trek along the boardwalks to the Mississippi House hotel for spirits, all three resplendent in their striking uniforms, the pilot wearing a navy blue double-breasted jacket, gold epaulets on the shoulders, over blue pin-striped trousers, head topped with a floppy-billed cap with 'Pilot' imprinted in front for all to see. The cubs were dressed similarly but sported open jackets, buttoned vests and similar floppy caps without an imprinted name distinction, being only cubs. The three dashing figures were admired by sightseers as they strutted down the gangplank, particularly by two young ladies, themselves dressed in their finest Sunday clothes of long-flowing gowns of tucked linen with velvet ribbon belts, straw hats topped with imitation roses, and carrying parasols. The editor stated that steamboat dockings frequently brought out young ladies to gawk at and admire the young cub pilots, steamboat piloting being an honored and respected profession, but he stated that the ladies may be shortsighted in not focusing their eyes closer to home on local men instead of wandering cub pilots. "There are certainly enough eligible young men in the villages," he evangelized, "without having to train wandering eyes on outsiders." And he stated that before the John J. Roe backed out into easy water to straighten up and steam downriver, the two young ladies, unnamed, had spent considerable time spooning with the cub pilots along the wharf. Hank found it interesting that editors in those years frequently interjected personal opinion, sometimes even moralizing "news" reports. He removed his bifocals, placed them on the desk, leaned back in the chair with hands behind his head and gazed at the ceiling while pondering the report. On the surface it appeared incidental, but something made him wonder. There was some unknown element that he couldn't identify at this moment.

He set the issue aside and proceeded to read a July 1879 headline: Samuel Clemens Visits Village. Hank recalled old-timers saying that Samuel Clemens had indeed visited McGregor, but he hadn't thought about it for many years.

My gosh, Samuel Clemens in McGregor? He was a long way upriver from Hannibal.

Hank read further into the story. It said that Clemens had arrived the morning of July 4 for a special celebration sponsored by the village. The mayor had had an association with Clemens in earlier years, and was able to encourage him to visit the village for the celebration. Clemens arrived on the steamboat Minneapolis; in fact, he had piloted it himself all the way upriver from St. Louis. Hank recalled from his Mark Twain readings that Clemens had been a cub pilot on the Mississippi before the Civil War, so this had been an appropriate way to enter the village. The article went on to state that Clemens descended the gangplank to the welcoming cakewalk music of McGregor's Walter Family Band, white hair blowing in the breeze, resplendent in white hat, white suit, three-button white vest, white shoes, full white moustache, and sporting a huge cigar. Villagers were excited to see the famous world-traveled author, and honored that he would take the time to speak at their Fourth of July Ceremonies. A large crowd had turned out for the event on a beautiful but sultry summer day. A special bandstand had been erected in Diamond Jo's Triangle Park for the event. Red, white and blue bunting hung from the railing circling the bandstand. The McGregor-North McGregor Silver Cornet Brass Band was seated on the bandstand behind Clemens serenading the huge crowd with favorite rags, cakewalks and Civil War songs—*Battle Hymn of the Republic*; *Just Before The Battle,*

Mother; Dixie's Land; When Johnny Comes Marching Home. Just
before the mayor introduced Clemens, the band broke into a
rousing rendition of *The Star Spangled Banner* complete with an
unusually long field artillery snare drum roll which seemed to
startle Clemens. He hesitated, momentarily, because he had "retired," according to his own admonition, after a brief spell in the
army. He spoke to the throng about how fortunate they were to live
in McGregor and North McGregor here on the shores of the
greatest of all rivers. He said that in all of his travels in America and
Europe, no river could compare with the Mississippi, ". . . it's a
monstrous big river," and he said that, "its mile-wide tide rolling
along, shining in the sun," was particularly significant, like no
other. He compared it to the Platte River out there in Nebraska and
Colorado, "The Platte was 'up', they said, which made me wish I
could see it when it was down, if it could look any sicker and
sorrier. No place can compare to life along the Mississippi," he
shouted across the platform out into Triangle Park. And although
he liked the entire breadth of the Mississippi, he was especially
fond of it from Hannibal to St. Paul. He had plied it hundreds of
times; of course, much of his writing about Huck and Becky and
Tom and Aunt Polly was set along that stretch of the river. The
congregation listened in awe as he told additional stories about
Tom Sawyer and Huck Finn, episodes that he hadn't put into or
publishers had taken out of *Huckleberry Finn* and the *Adventures
of Tom Sawyer.* Clemens tucked his thumbs into his vest, flipped
the cigar from right to left in his mouth without missing a beat or
word. Once he got to talking there was no stopping him. Folks were
standing in the sun getting hot, tired and thirsty, some even sipping
water from the artesian well, but Clemens talked on and on about
the Mississippi. He told of his own childhood in Hannibal, of his
experiences as a cub editor down in Tennessee, about writing
stories like *The Old Ram*, and the *Man Who Corrupted Hadlyburg*,
and of course everyone wanted to know more about *The Notorious
Jumping Frog of Calaveras County.* Now, by the time he began
telling the story of that famous frog, everyone forgot how much
their feet ached, how hot they were, how thirsty they were. "Why,"
Clemens said, "that frog had so much buckshot in him that he

couldn't have jumped from this stage onto the grass. That had been ol' Jim Smiley's best jumping frog, Dan'l Webster was his name, and Jim was mighty set to bettin' on him," Clemens said. "When that stranger appeared, ol' Smiley set him up for a wager but the stranger outfoxed him. While Jim was off finding another frog for the wager, the stranger filled ol' Dan'l with buckshot, distending his belly so that he was closer to the floor than a low-bellied snake." It was a great story and Clemens delighted in telling it. The article went on to say that Sam talked for three hours, drinking no water, but smoking five cigars. He made up for his parchedness later by sipping several whiskeys at the American House Saloon, ate a scrumptious catfish dinner in the dining room, then retired to his suite where unconfirmed reports indicated that he had "entertained" several young ladies of the village. He boarded the Minneapolis steamer the next morning, then waved to folks from the hurricane deck. Samuel Clemens never set foot in McGregor again, as far as anyone knew, yet Hank felt there might be more to it than that. He pondered over the article as he had with the 1878 article about the John J. Roe cub pilots. After reading for so long, the time had escaped him. He looked up at the ticking, pendular clock as it struck seven times. Muriel would have dinner on the table. He was late.

3

After dinner, Hank retired to the parlor for coffee and conversation with Muriel, his stately, attractive wife of forty-four years, and Catherine, his diminutive ninety-five-year-old mother. He shared the stories he had read earlier in the day—home constructions, ferry boating, steamboat dockings, Samuel Clemens' Fourth of July speech—until he saw that Catherine was becoming weary. She was frail now, but had been extremely sturdy, weathering her ninety-five years with vigor, grace and style. Hank looked at her with new eyes tonight, eyes that had been looking at this indefatigable woman for all of his years. Although she was approaching the century mark, she still had considerable vitality with her long hair rolled in a bun, her vision good enough to read the *Ladies Home Journal*, her ears good enough to hear what she wanted to hear. She had been attentive to Hank while sipping her coffee, although he thought she might have become agitated when he related the accounts of the steamboat dockings, and Samuel Clemens' appearance in town. Suddenly, she was on her feet and walking gingerly toward the stairs. "Thank you for the lovely dinner, Muriel. Good night, Son," she announced as she sat in the chair lift, pulled the lever and slowly ascended the incline to her third-floor apartment.

"I'm very tired, too, Henry. I think I'll retire," Muriel said carrying the coffee cups out to the kitchen.

"I'm sort of wound up with everything I've read today . . . think I'll sit for awhile, maybe read a book, smoke one more cigar. I'll be up shortly," Hank said as he ambled toward the glass-encased barrister bookcases in the parlor.

"All right, dear, but don't stay up too late," Muriel said hanging her apron behind the kitchen door, "because you aren't a spring chicken anymore."

"Spring Chicken? That's the second time today someone said I wasn't a spring chicken," he said walking to Muriel and giving her a peck on the cheek. "Good night, dear, sweet dreams."

He browsed through the bookcase considering several titles until his eyes stopped on Mark Twain's *Life On The Mississippi*.

H'm, I haven't read this book for years. It might be enjoyable to reread.

He tried to remember the last time . . .

It must have been when I was in high school, about 1915. My friends and I simply took the river for granted then. We assumed everyone in Iowa lived along the Mississippi, but, of course, that wasn't true.

He lifted the book from behind the glass door, settled into his favorite overstuffed lounging chair, lit a cigar and began reading.

Samuel Clemens was a product of the river, having been reared in Hannibal, Missouri, a village only slightly larger than either McGregor or Marquette. His childhood was enveloped by the village and the river. His entire character was river. And although he eventually left Hannibal for Tennessee, Nevada, London and New York, Hank knew that Clemens remained a product of his Midwestern community. The book's first section was about Clemens' childhood in Hannibal. Hank was struck by the similarity of that childhood and the life Clemens later described for Tom Sawyer and Huck Finn. Although Hank wasn't a fiction writer himself, he knew that many authors' writings were, in fact, autobiographical. Clemens had even said as much about his own writings. Many of Tom's and Huck's escapades along the river—going shoeless about the village, smoking corn cob pipes, chewing tobacco, skipping school, digging for worms, fishing for bluegills, rafting, keeping a watchful eye on village scoundrels, investigating caves, catching robbers, chiding drunks—reminded Hank of his own childhood, although he had missed several of those experiences himself. After an hour, he placed the book on his lap, removed his bifocals and leaned back on the cushion. Although he was drowsy, his memory had been jogged by reading. He began recalling his own life along the river until his head slumped to his chest; he jerked suddenly to continue reading . . .

Clemens had been fascinated, obsessed with the river, so much so that he thought the greatest calling in the world was to be *on* the river as a steamboat pilot. As a boy, he would scurry to the levee at the first blast of a steamboat's whistle just like Hank and other villagers did yesterday. Clemens and fellow rascals would frequently sneak onto the steamboat, investigating it from bow to stern, boiler deck to Texas deck all the while trying to keep from being detected by the captain, the pilot or the mate. If undetected they would float downriver a couple of miles on the steamer, then dive into the river and swim to shore. Other times they would jump into a scow to follow it downriver until they were finally outdistanced by the speeding, churning steamer. Oh! what a life to be a steamboat pilot, Clemens dreamed every night. There wasn't a greater calling for those boys, even from Providence himself. Piloting was better than doctoring or undertakering or even ministering. A minister could just save souls, if they wanted savin'; a doctor could just save bodies, if they wanted savin'; an undertaker could just save corpses, if they wanted savin', but a steamboat pilot? Well, that was the cat's meow, the epitome of a calling, the epitome of a career, Clemens said. Young Sam was certain, swear it on a dead cat, that he was going to be a pilot when he grew up.

Hannibal isn't that far south of the Iowa border, and although Hank had never been there, he felt an affinity for it.

It must be like any other river town—McGregor or Marquette or Guttenberg or Prairie du Chien. Maybe I should take a steamboat excursion down to Hannibal next summer after I retire. I've been as far south as Keokuk several times, and Hannibal is only about forty miles farther downriver.

Hank read that by the time Clemens was thirteen, steamboat captains were letting him board their boats, even inviting him to the pilot house. Pilots would frequently need to steam back upriver or downriver for short distances around Hannibal to checkout repairs to the paddlewheel or to the boilers during which times they would permit him to ride along. Some pilots eventually permitted him to actually take the wheel for a short distance. Once Sam touched that towering wheel, there was no turning back. He was hooked. He knew he would be a steamboat pilot in a few years.

Clemens became that pilot long before he became an author, long before he wrote about Tom and Huck and Becky and Aunt Polly and Indian Joe and Big Jim and Pudd'nhead Wilson. But those fictional characters were developing in his mind when he took the wheel to pilot steamboats on Hannibal's waters.

Before Sam Clemens became a pilot, his southern neighbor, St. Louis, had been a major river port for westward expansion. At one time it was considered the most westerly city in the country, to Easterners at least, and the principal port to the western plains. Thousands of immigrants traveled from the east down the Ohio river to St. Louis, then up the Mississippi until they forked westward on the Missouri river, eventually joining the Platte across Nebraska to Colorado. Others continued northward to settle in Iowa, Wisconsin and Minnesota territories.

The Lower Mississippi was Sam's primary training river as a cub pilot under crusty, seasoned pilots and captains; in later years he plied the Upper Mississippi. Mr. Horace Bixby "learned" him the power and thrust of the Paul Jones as it churned upriver against the surging current. Clemens eventually learned to recognize every sand bar and point from Hannibal to St. Louis; later, every sand bar and point north to Quincy, Keokuk, Fort Madison, Davenport, McGregor and North McGregor. He became more acquainted with the river than with the ravines, hills and caves of Hannibal. Like Mr. Bixby, he began recognizing its always changing currents and colors—deep azure blue swells, yellow shoal waters, shimmering moonlit surfaces, ripples radiating to the shore, slanting wind sears across the surface, whitecaps as the winds whipped the river into a froth. He learned that azure blue meant deeper waters, yellow tint indicated dangerous shallow water. And he gradually learned the sounds of the river, too. Persistent, slapping waves on the bow meant easy water, but deep-toned waves meant a strengthening, difficult current that required more steam from the red-hot boilers below him. He learned to recognize the tonal 'whoosh' of the paddlewheel as it constantly fought against the current. He watched blackbirds, bullfinches, blue jays, hawks and bald eagles, memorizing their music, their changes in pitch and squawks of urgency as the weather changed. He learned to recognize their feeding habits, and by that, he knew the depths of the channel, the strength of its current. He learned the life of the great river. But most importantly, he learned that the river changed constantly as it surged to the Gulf. Depths, currents, river banks, sand bars, debris and cutoffs were different on each trip. Danger lurked constantly around every bend, on every reach, near every bluff- or sand reef. In spite of the danger, Sam loved every minute, every day of piloting, and he loved river people, too. Folks who actually earned a living on and from the river, and even those who were smart enough to just live along the river were the most important people in the world to him. Why, he couldn't imagine folks choosing to live anywhere else. The characters and scoundrels on the Mississippi were real people. Hannibal, Keokuk, St. Louis were real towns. Landlocked towns were only places for people to survive, and they did a mighty poor job of that too, he thought.

The book slipped out of Hank's hands, falling to the floor as his chin bobbed onto his chest, bifocals settling in his lap. After sleeping for several minutes, he jerked awake, glanced at his watch and realized he had been reading into the early hours of the morning. In bed, he fell asleep dreaming about the river, about Samuel Clemens, about piloting a steamer.

4

"Good morning, fellows. How is everyone today?"

"Well, if it isn't the crusty editor himself. What are you going to do with yourself today now that you've printed that rag of yours? I wish I had the life of a newspaper editor. I would sit in my easy chair to write about anything I chose like the mayor, the fire truck, the library and the streets instead of hearing patient complaints all day. That would be the life. You certainly have yourself an easy job," Doc said as Hank walked to the counter at Bruno's Cafe. One of Doc's great delights was chiding Hank; it had been a game between them for over thirty years. Doc was an institution in the village, having been around forever, or so it seemed. He had purchased the only local practice from the Clark doctors right out of medical school, never intending to stay in one place so long, especially this little burg on the river, but once he became established, he never left. People in the county had accepted him immediately in his early days of practice, even though he looked like a teenager then with a hairline to his eyebrows and fair skin. He certainly hadn't looked like a doctor when he sauntered into town that first day. But Doc had lost most of his hair over the years, the hairline was nonexistent now with only lonesome wisps which he combed judiciously to cover the bare spots, although he had miraculously retained the fair skin and features of a younger man including the inability to grow a decent beard. Even pushing sixty-two, he could pass for a man considerably younger, or so he thought. He might have even been a musician instead of a physician because of his long, slim fingers. He did play a little piano— mostly early Mozart intermezzos and his one memorized piece, Beethoven's little bagatelle *Für Elise*—but those fine, slim hands had served him well as a general practitioner and surgeon. "Charlie here and me are the real workers in this village, isn't that right Charlie? And although Charlie is retired, he still works harder than you, Hank, don't you, Charlie? Of course, I work my hands to the bone trying to keep you aging gentlemen healthy."

"Damn! I didn't realize I would receive such a 'friendly' reception this morning. I expected to be among friends, but maybe I had better move on down to Bert's to hang out with a different crowd. You guys have become testy," Hank said as he flung his suit jacket to a chair and sat next to Doc and Charlie at the counter.

"Don't get huffy, Mister Editor. We're only chiding you. We like you and your paper, don't we, Charlie? But we need to keep you on your toes, keep your mind sharp. You aren't a spring chicken, you know," Doc retorted as he pulled out his chained pocket watch from a vest pocket to check the time.

"And you can kill that 'spring chicken,' Doc. Even Muriel said that to me last night. I know I'm pushing seventy, but I'm not an old rooster yet.

MISTER BRUNO! How about some service? I've been sitting here all morning but still don't have coffee. I might have to take my business down the street to Bert's," Hank hollered to Bruno hunched over the grill.

"I don't mind if you do, Hank. I'm of the opinion that it might be abundantly more pleasant around here without you. You just go on and join that morning whiskey group," Bruno snarled as he stomped toward Hank, steaming coffee pot in hand, Chesterfield cigarette dangling from the corner of his mouth. Bruno had a gap between his two front teeth, a feature which let him blow smoke through it by parting his lips and curling his tongue as if he were going to whistle the *Iowa Corn Song*. It irritated his regular customers, but not enough to stay away. As he poured coffee, he blew a twisting column of smoke directly at Hank, "And when are you going to write about expanding the gym? You have to get off the mayor's back . . . time to move on, to write about a bigger gym. Are you going to write an editorial about that this week? There's your coffee, you impatient bastard."

"I've been thinking about it," Hank responded while waving his hand to dissipate the cigarette smoke, "but I have a couple of days yet to determine next week's editorial . . . it's a possibility; however, I'm considering the riverfront, also. That dock at the foot of Main Street is beginning to look tacky and unsafe. I may need to prod the mayor about fixing it up. It's our lifeboat, you know. Visitors drive over here from Waterloo, Cedar Rapids, even Des Moines. We have to keep it in tip-top shape for those weekend boaters. It may be time to get on the mayor about that.

Fix me an order of French toast, Bruno, and don't burn the hell out of it. I don't want to fight heartburn all day," Hank said as Bruno returned to the grill.

"You'll eat your French toast anyway I fix it, burnt or not, otherwise you can walk down the street and have whiskey for breakfast, and Hank? Lay off the mayor . . . write about a new gym," Bruno snarled as he stuffed his cigarette in a corrugated aluminum ashtray directly in front of Hank, then hulked back to the hot grill like a linebacker searching for someone to hit.

"What are you going to do today, Hank? I have to run errands over in Prairie du Chien for the wife, then wind my way up to Waukon Junction to see my brother. I certainly have a full day ahead of me," Charlie said as he finished his eggs and ham.

"I started reading Mark Twain's *Life On The Mississippi* last night before retiring. I hadn't read it since high school. Didn't we read it in English Class for Mrs. Bergman? Anyway, I became fascinated with Twain's escapades as a cub pilot on the river. I might read a few more pages this morning, but I have also been thinking about reviewing back issues of the *Times* to research a few topics."

"Why would you choose to do that?" Doc asked wisping his isolated hairs into place.

"Well, you see fellows, I've been thinking of re . . . I . . . uh . . . I've been thinking of *researching* our village's history about important events and people that lived here throughout the past one hundred years or so. I don't know, it just seems like time to do it," Hank answered as Bruno plopped burnt French toast in front of him.

"Sounds fishy to me, doesn't it to you, Doc? Hank, are you thinking of quitting? That sounds like a retirement job to me, wanting to go back and see what you've done, wanting to go back and relive your life's work," Charlie answered.

"I am *not* thinking about retiring, Charlie. I just think it's time to compile our history. I began looking at those old issues yesterday, and I became concerned about a fire hazard, too. If my place burned, we would lose much of our documented history. I sure would hate to see that happen," Hank answered.

"You had better stop smoking those old stogies then, and keep your matches away from the papers, too. That would be my suggestion; besides, sucking those Perfectos isn't the best thing for your lungs, you know," Doc snarled while once again retrieving his pocket watch for the correct time and placing a black homburg on his barren head, "and you aren't any spring chicken, Hank."

"Good-bye, fellows. I've had all the talk I can tolerate about chickens. But you see, I'm more like an old violin than an old chicken . . . and let me tell you, fellows, there's a lot of tunes left in this old violin. I'm getting better with age," Hank hollered as he threw his jacket over his shoulder and bounded out the door, Doc on his heels, into the bright morning sunlight.

"Good morning, Cletus. How are you today?"

"G . . . G . . . Good . . . morn . . . ing M . . . is . . . t . . . er Hank. I . . . I . . . 'm do . . . in' okay. Got a lot of sw . . . eep . . . ing to do t . . . t . . . day. Those f . . . fish flies were r . . . r . . . real thick last n . . . n . . . n . . . night, and I've got to get 'em s . . . swept up so the m . . . m . . . mayor doesn't g . . . g . . . get mad at m . . . me," Cletus answered as he swept fish flies and debris through the gutter.

"You're doing a fine job, Cletus, and don't you worry about the mayor. I'll take care of him. You're about the best village worker we have. I appreciate your work keeping the streets swept clean. You keep up the good work, and stop by the shop later today. I still have a present for you," Hank said as he stepped across the gutter toward the bank. Cletus tugged his Dekalb feed hat lower onto his head trying to straighten it, but not succeeding, "O . . . O . . . kay, M . . . Mister Hank. I'll be down for m . . . my p . . . present later in the d . . . d . . . day. S . . . so . . . long."

Hank strutted toward the shop meeting villagers along the sidewalk. "Good morning, Samantha. Are you feeling all right today?" Samantha had just taken a long puff on her signature Red Dot cigar as she met Hank.

"Mornin' . . . [cough] . . . to you, Hank," she said through the billowing Havana smoke. "Shit! My arthritis is actin' up again, what with all this humidity, but I'm not doin' so bad . . . feelin' good enough to motor onto the river today for a photo shoot." Samantha shifted her protruding hips from left to right as she talked, first standing on one leg then the other, an action which reminded Hank of waddling ducks down by the river. "My Scenic Photos business is growin', you know. Folks from Waterloo and Cedar Rapids buy lots o' them. If my old fishin' boat'll take me past the high bridge, I'll take me a six pack along for company, then shoot Marquette and the pontoon bridge from upriver. That swinging railroad bridge has always been a popular shot with folks aways from here." Samantha certainly was a sight to see as she paraded around the village. Out-of-towners usually did a double take when seeing her on the street or at the cafe—duck hunter's cap askew on her head, multi-pocketed fisherman's vest filled with every imaginable camera device, assorted paraphernalia and cigars, bright red flannel shirt covering her busty, bottle-shaped physique, olive-drab Army khaki pants with side button-down pockets stuffed with film and cameras, black Army combat boots—but most villagers accepted her for who she was. Certainly, some turned their noses up and looked away when meeting her on the street, but Hank didn't. He saw a woman under that camouflage, although it certainly wasn't evident by her apparel. Besides, he wasn't deterred by a person's appearance. What was under that clothing, what was inside that heart and soul, what went on in that mind was more important to him than external appearance. And Hank was proud of Sam's persistence in the face of considerable difficulty. She had been supporting herself with her Scenic Photos business since moving to McGregor from Prairie du Chien many years ago, taking pictures from every slough, creek bed, valley, ravine and vista in the area. "Lookin' like a nice sunny day, Hank, after the fog burns off," Sam said standing in front of the post office, formerly Diamond Jo's magnificent home.

"It sure does, but I would be careful about drinking. Drinking and photo shooting don't mix well. You have to keep a clear eye and steady hand to operate your cameras, as you know," Hank said.

"Don't you worry none 'bout my drinkin', Hank. You worry 'bout your smokin', and I know what you keep in that back cabinet, too. I've seen you through the windows, imbibing, and early in the mornin' sometimes even," Sam snapped back.

"Stop by later. I'll share some of what I have in the Biedermeir with you. Have a nice shoot."

"So long, Mister Hank."

"HANK! HEY, HANK! HOLD ON JUST A DAMN MINUTE," Bernie hollered stumbling up the sidewalk from the docks, out of breath. "Ain't seen you since the steamboat passin' yesterday. How you doin'?"

"Good morning, Bernie. How are you? But I can see and smell how you are. You're hitting the bottle sort of hard, aren't you? and it's early to be drinking heavily," Hank said halfway through the screen door.

"Shit! The old lady was gettin' on me last night . . . needed to soothe my innards this morning . . . had to get out of the house before she roasted me again."

"You had better go easy on the bottle, though.

Are you working? It would be good to work regularly, Bernie. You can't simply mope around all day, fishing and drinking. Would you like to do some work for me? I could have you assist Cletus delivering the *Times*, and I also have some trash to clean up behind the shop. I have even been thinking about rearranging the archives, because I'm concerned about a fire hazard. You could help me with that. How about it? I could pay you by the hour, say one dollar?" Hank asked, placing a hand on Bernie's shoulder.

"I don't know, Henry. Me and work don't mix so good . . . tried it several times, but I get bored . . . rather fish and drink on the dock or out in my scow. Fishin's important, Hank . . . ought to do more of it yourself. Fact is, that's what I was hollerin' at you about. Want to go fishin' this morning? Crappies are biting real good down below the bend. How about it? Me and you and some juicy night crawlers, a couple of chicken sandwiches and a six pack?"

"Please do *not* mention *chicken* around me; fishing tempts me, but I have my day planned. I want to read more Mark Twain, then I'm going to begin reviewing the archival issues of the *Times*. So, I don't have time for fishing today, but you go ahead. And think about my job offer. I could use help, and you could use work. You have a wife and children to support. Let me know tomorrow."

"I'll think about it, a little. Goin' fishin'."

Bernie wobbled down the street toward the docks, and although it was only a quarter of nine in the morning, he already had a good start on that six pack. Hank enjoyed his whiskey, but he kept it under control, seldom drinking before five o'clock, whereas Bernie started every day with a beer and a bump. While Hank was having coffee and eggs at the cafe, Bernie was having a couple of Dubuque Stars or Old Styles at Bert's Tavern. Drinking was a way of life with Bernie, but it affected his health, his work, his wife, his children. And he certainly wasn't the only imbiber in town. Many guys and a goodly number of ladies were also heavy on the bottle. Bert's Tavern even had a sign over the bar: "We don't have a town drunk. We all take turns." Most things about living along the river were wonderful, but drinking heavily wasn't one of them. Hank knew it. Doc knew it. Charlie knew it. Cletus drank beer after a day of sweeping. Samantha drank after a day of photo shooting. Bruno drank after a hard day at the grill, and of course, the fellows frequenting Bert's drank to get the day started. It seemed that river life and drinking went together.

Maybe I'll write an editorial in a couple of weeks about excessive drinking, Hank thought as he opened the front door and walked through his shop.

There was a small gas cooking stove in the back corner beyond the potbellied stove where Hank fixed soup and coffee.

This morning, he wanted more and stronger coffee than what Bruno served. He filled the chipped blue enamel pot with coarse grounds, then boiled the coffee to the proper strength. For a fleeting moment, he considered dropping in a touch of Jack Daniels, but remembered his lecture to Bernie only a few minutes ago. He shuffled to the rocking chair, loosened his tie and vest, then opened *Life On The Mississippi* to read for a couple of hours in the homey atmosphere of his shop while drinking strong coffee and chomping on a crusty, two-day-old doughnut. But as the sun slithered through the rear windows slicing across the room, he soon became drowsy, finally stretching out his gangling body to doze off in the chair . . .

> *"Henry? Hello, I'm Sam . . . Sam Clemens. You're Henry from McGregor, aren't you?*
> *"Yes, that's correct. I'm the editor of the* North Iowa Times. *We cover all the news along the river that's fit to print . . . and some that isn't. 'What in the world happened?' is our subtitle."*
> *"That's good, Henry, and I'm glad you're an editor. I did a good bit of editing myself, you know. I started out down in Tennessee as an assistant editor, but I didn't last too long there. The editor I worked for didn't enjoy the humor and satire I inserted into my editorials. Besides, I didn't like Tennessee all that much anyway. Went out to Nevada Territory mining for awhile, but all in all, Missouri was better . . . liked the river better, too."*
> *"Me too, Mister Clemens. I wouldn't live any other place but here. Speaking of rivers, I've been reading your book,* Life On The Mississippi. *It's good. I wish I had written it myself."*
> *"Thanks, Henry, but I've written better material. I'm partial to Tom Sawyer and Huck Finn, and I like my short stories, too," Sam said as he pulled up a chair alongside Henry.*
> *"Make yourself comfortable, Mister Clemens. I'm*

glad you stopped by today. You know, your visit is coincidental, happening as it has just as I began reading your book. Care for a cup of coffee?"

"Don't mind if I do, and you could, ah . . . slip a little something extra in it for me, if you had some Old No. 7, that is," Mr. Clemens said as he placed his hat on the printer's table while settling into a softer chair.

"Yes, I do. Although I don't usually imbibe in the morning, what with you being a guest today, I'll make an exception. Two extra coffees coming up," Henry said as he reached for two mugs and the black-labeled Jack.

"Just call me Sam. I'm only Mark Twain to my readers. I'll call you Hank if you'll call me Sam."

"That's a deal. And here is your Jack Daniel's coffee, Sam."

"Much obliged, Hank."

"You know, Sam, as I just said, I began rereading your book only last evening. It's fortuitous that you would stop in today," Hank said as he settled into his chair and began sipping coffee.

"I don't know, Hank. I have to get out of Hannibal once in awhile. I relish traveling up- and downriver to see river folks. I like running down to St. Louis then up to St. Paul. The river gives me life, you know. Darnation, if I travel only a few miles inland, I get the heebie jeebies, my throat gets parched, I feel landlocked, I begin looking for water. Missouri and Iowa are fine states, but the inlands don't compare with the river lands at all. You've got beautiful land in this valley, almost as good as around Hannibal, but not quite," Sam said as he, too, began drinking coffee.

"We are proud of it, very proud but you've been here before, seen this valley before, haven't you? I was reading an archival issue yesterday when I found a story I had forgotten about. It said that you were here in 1879 to give a speech for the Fourth of July Celebra-

tion. And I might also say, the article said you 'entertained' a few local ladies in your suite that night? Anything to that?" Hank said smiling lightly.

"I do like to entertain, but it was all in good company, in good taste. I travel so much speaking and promoting my books that I get bored just being holed up in a hotel room every night. I frequently entertain ladies when I spend a night."

"Although it's presumptuous of me, would you mind telling me who you entertained that Fourth of July evening so many years ago? I've been wondering about several things in my past, about my heritage, about, oh, about things in general. Would you tell me about your guests?"

"That's much too long and too many guests ago to remember, Hank. I can't remember them all, but what is this you're trying to establish about your past?" Sam said unbuttoning his vest to get more comfortable. "You make a mighty fine cup of coffee, sir, a mighty fine cup . . . think I might have to come to McGregor more often. Now, what is this about your past?"

"I'm attempting to find out a few things about my parents, genealogy, that sort of thing, but more about you. I want to know about your writing, your stories. Tell me about The Old Ram, my favorite Mark Twain short story."

Sam settled back, tipped his mug of coffee toward the ceiling, wiped coffee from his mustache and began telling Hank the story of The Old Ram. "Actually, that story had been passed down for several generations in the Clemens family. My father told the story to me, and he said my granddaddy had told it to him. So, when I got to writing, I just extrapolated a few facts and situations to end up with the published story which goes something like this . . .

Now, ol' Jim Blaine's grandfather had owned that ram for thirty years, or however long a ram can live, *and let me tell you, that ram was a cantankerous old ram . . . had a mind of its own, that's for sure. Warn't much Blaine could do with him 'cept feed him, water him, and fence him. He warn't an ordinary ram 'tall. Got out of the fence one day, he did, and waltzed over to the edge of the Blaine farm to gaze down upon a meadow. Now, the ram had never been permitted out of his fencin,' so he was mighty pleased to be free . . . saw a feller down there in the meadow, farmer by the name of Wilkerson, I believe. No, it warn't a Wilkerson at all. He was a Hagadorn, farmer Hagadorn. Sightin' Hagadorn swathing hay in the meadow pleased that old ram, mightily. Of course, you know rams 's bent to rammin'. That's their nature. They aren't like cows, grazers and all; they're rammers. When that ram saw Hagadorn, he generated only one thing in his mind—rammin'. Well, ol' Hagadorn had his mind on swathing, unsuspecting of the events unfoldin' up on the hill. That ram was rearin' its back, snortin' and diggin' in with its hind feet, gettin' set to charge down the hill. Grandpappy Blaine was fit to be tied to see his ram all loose, but before he could fetch a rope, the ram was snortin' down the hill, chargin' full speed toward farmer Hagadorn. Blaine hollered to Hagadorn. Hagadorn turned, saw the chargin' ram, then scurried toward his hay rack and just in time, too, 'cause that ram, mighty bent on rammin,' hit the rack so hard it knocked the farmer plum out and set that rack to rockin' on two wheels. Now, Blaine was old, but agile and good with a rope, so before the ram could charge the poor farmer flat on the ground, Blaine lassoed the ram around his horns from twenty feet and jerked him onto his back. He tied him up, hog tied him in fact, then went to aid Hagadorn, who I might say, had Prov'dence on his side . . . couple of bruises, but saved from the old ram. Hagadorn was all right, but he never talked to Blaine again. For years after that episode, the ol' ram perched himself on top of the hill, tied to a long and sturdy rope, lookin' down at Farmer Hagadorn.*

Yes, sir, my pappy and grandpappy used to tell that story every chance they got. It made a good story for me, too, Hank. Other than The Notorious Jumping Frog of Calaveras County, The Old Ram *is one of my most successful. Glad you like it."*

"HANK! WAKE UP! You've knocked your coffee over, your book's on the floor, your cigar's burnt itself to a stub," Bernie hollered stumbling into the shop. Bernie had a way of showing up at anytime, intruding in fact, but Hank had become used to his and other people's intrusions. It was a way of life in the shop, in the village. Bernie was basically a good person even though slovenly, a heavy drinker and exceedingly lazy. Mostly, he sauntered around town sporting his ever-present tattered Chicago Cubs baseball cap dressed in faded, torn jeans which hung exceedingly low over his pot belly, and wearing scruffy white tennis shoes with holes through which his big toes protruded. He usually sported a three-day black stubble on his face, "And you're liable to set this whole place a fire. You was snortin' like an old ram, too."

"A . . . what, an old ram? No, it couldn't be," Hank murmured as he shook the sleep from his head and sat up.

"You must a been dreamin'. When I walked in you was fussin' and movin' around so. You been dreamin', Henry?"

"I guess I must have been. I must have dozed off reading Twain's Mississippi book, and then that old ram . . ."

"See! Told you so, talking about a ram. Shit! I need a beer," Bernie said snorting to the door. "See you later."

After Bernie banged through the screen door, Hank reheated the coffee to shake the sleep from his head then resumed his search through the archives. He hoped this second session would shed additional light on the mystery of his unknown father. On the long side brick wall, rolling the ladder along the track toward the early issues, he realized he couldn't go through every one . . .

Maybe I'll just pick a few at random for now. I can always go through in more detail later, after I retire.

He climbed to the top of the ladder, reached far to his left and carefully pulled out more issues from 1878 and 1879. Cradling the dusty copies under his left arm, he descended the ladder and carefully placed them on the rolltop desk where he began leafing through the delicate and brittle issues. Much in the '78 and '79 papers was difficult to read as both the paper and ink had faded; also, the type used in those years was archaic and washed out making it difficult to read.

As an editor himself, he was interested and fascinated with the tone of the articles as well as the types of reports the editor had chosen. Even now he made several mental edits as he scanned headlines to see what caught his attention, hopeful that a word, a name would catch his eyes helping him to solve the riddle of his long-lost past, the past his mother was reluctant to . . . no! downright unwilling to reveal. He leafed through the papers for half an hour while sipping coffee and drawing deeply on his cigar. The news was mostly about council meetings, fishing excursions, local gossip, and runaway carriage horses, but as he was about to close the September 1878 issue and return the copies to the stacks, he again noticed a Steamboat Dockings Itinerary report . . .

STEAMBOAT DOCKINGS

Steamboat	Captain	Pilot	Arrival	Departure	Cargo
Dubuque	Mr. Beebe	Mr. Tibbles	Tu. 11:17 p.	Tu. 4:33 p.	Wheat
Keokuk	Mr. Holcomb	Mr. Cushing	Fr. 11:21 a.	Fr. 2:10 p.	Wax, oil
John J. Roe	Mr. LaPointe	Mr. Cormack	Sa. 10:00 a.	Su. 5:07 p.	Tea

Three steamboats graced our wharf during the past week helping to keep the river traffic at a good current for our local economy. The Dubuque carried wheat and sorghum but few passengers. The Keokuk docked briefly to unload candle wax, oil and milled flour, then loaded 3,000 sacks of grain for its continued trip upriver to St. Paul. The John J. Roe made a second docking, returning after an absence of three months. Roustabouts unloaded tea, flour, sugar, candle wax and axle grease, then loaded 200 barrels of beer from the McGregor Brewery. All three steamers "wooded up" before continuing their journeys, but this editor observed, once again, the presence of several local, fair-haired ladies conversing with the crew of the Roe. In fact, the young folks were even more brazen at this docking, seen to be spooning right in public view. Now, this behavior may be tolerated in St. Paul and St. Louis or even Dubuque, but we don't condone it in our villages. As we welcome steamers to our wharf—they being a lifeline for our commerce and transportation—we do want to protect our villages against vagrants and riffraff that occasionally ply the river. With steamboat landings becoming more frequent, every citizen is asked to be aware of unusual or indecent behavior. We of this community hope the young ladies will be more discrete in the future.

This was the second report of young ladies meeting cub pilots along the wharf. Still, no names were reported. He pondered . . .

The time would be about right. H'm?

He set the issue aside, then returned the others to the stacks, climbing back up the ladder to retrieve additional issues. He would go back and read other 1878 and '79 issues more closely at a later time. Maybe he could find something that would lead to an answer. After all, he was born in 1879.

I sure would like to know before I die. I'm no spring chicken!

He pulled out six issues from 1920 to 1925, descended the ladder, poured more coffee, opened the shades wider on the back windows to let sunshine filter through, then walked back to the desk. By 1920 the type had improved, the newsprint had improved, the editing and stories had improved. Of course, he himself had started reporting in 1909, but those early assignments were mostly obituaries and local gossip. There were articles about rutted Main Street, the building of a new church, a carriage which had overturned on Market Street with the team subsequently running helter-skelter through the village, the arrival of the Ida Fulton steamboat with the Bix Beiderbecke-Frankie Trumbauer Jazz Band aboard, and an article he had written in a 1925 issue about the drowning of Patrick O'Reilly, proprietor of O'Reilly's Fish and Bait Shack. Hank had forgotten about O'Reilly's death even though it had happened only twenty-five years ago. He read the long, detailed article, because, as he recalled now, Patrick had been a well-liked and personable character in the village, and a riverfront fixture for many years. Hank recalled that no one knew, for sure, how he had drowned, only that his body had been found washed up against the shore downriver from his Fish and Bait Shack, his fishing boat farther downriver broken in two, lapping against the riprap around Pictured Rock.

Hank laid his bifocals on the newspaper, hoisted his spindling legs onto the desktop, ran his fingers through silvery hair, stroked a pure white flowing beard and recalled the times and experiences of Patrick O'Reilly. He hadn't thought about him for many years, but he had known and liked him, even spending innumerable hours in his shack listening to stories by the locals. But Hank was startled out of his reverie by a pounding and stomping at the front door. He swiveled to see Cletus bounding past the Linotype machine. "Hi . . . M . . . M . . . Mister Hank. I . . . I've c . . . c . . . come f . . . for m . . . my p . . . p . . . p . . . present."

"Hello, Cletus. It's nice to see you this morning," but as Hank greeted Cletus he looked at the pendulum wall clock to see it was already past noon. He had been reading for several hours without realizing it. "Present, did you say? Sure, that's right; I told you to stop by, didn't I?"

"W . . . w . . . what . . . do you h . . . h . . . have f . . . f . . . for m . . . m . . . me?" Cletus stammered as he sat in an overstuffed chair by the potbellied stove. Hank walked to the cabinet, captured the Jack Daniels bottle, grabbed two tumblers and placed them on the printer's table by Cletus. "I have a little touch of Jack for you. I know you enjoy it, but you don't have much money to buy any for yourself, do you?" Hank said pouring two fingers of Jack into each tumbler.

"T . . . Th . . . That's r . . . r . . . r . . . right, Mister Hank. I do like J . . . J . . . Jack b . . . but the m . . . mayor doesn't p . . . pay m . . . me enough t . . . to buy s . . . some," Cletus said lifting the tumbler to his lips, throwing his head back, cap falling to the floor, drinking heartily. "T . . . Th . . . That's r . . . r . . . real . . . [cough] . . . good."

"I'm glad you stopped for your present; besides, it gives me an excuse to join you even if it isn't five o'clock. Let's have a little toast," Hank said as he clinked his glass with Cletus', both men then tipping their tumblers toward the dusty ceiling.

Cletus enjoyed coming to the newspaper shop to talk with Hank, to hear his stories, because as he had told Hank earlier, he wasn't good at reading. If the truth be told, he couldn't read at all, but he enjoyed looking at the headlines of the *North Iowa Times* and the morning *Register* at Bruno's through his bottle-thick eye glasses, trying to understand their meaning, even attempting to sound out the confusing characters. But mostly, he liked photos, especially those in the *Life* magazines scattered around Hank's shop. He had had considerable difficulty learning to read while in grade school; consequently, many of his classmates had made fun of his inability to read even the simplest of words and short sentences in the Dick and Jane books. They had also taunted him unmercifully because of his extraordinary size—obese, big as a ninth-grader towering over his smaller fourth-grade classmates. But he had kept a smile on his face, seldom becoming angry with the children who chided him. For the past thirty-eight years he had maintained his pleasant disposition in the face of adversity.

Cletus was a regular fixture around the village sweeping the gutters and streets, pushing his lawn mower down Main Street searching for the mayor's grass. Most townsfolk respected him, although many ignored him. Not Hank. He saw a person in that massive, blubbery body, under that tilted feed cap, inside those tent-sized Oshkosh overalls and tattered Red Wing boots. Hank liked and admired Cletus.

"I have been reading early issues of the *Times* this morning, Cletus. I'm thinking about retiring, but don't say anything to anyone, particularly the fellows at the cafe. I can't keep up this pace much longer. At any rate, I read an old story this morning about Patrick O'Reilly's drowning in 1925. Do you remember that?" Hank asked as he settled into his favorite chair by the stove.

"I . . . I . . . remember P . . . P . . . Patrick. I . . . I used t . . . t' visit with him at his Bait S . . . Shack. H . . . He'd let me clean fish sometimes then g . . . g . . . give m . . . m . . . me some for supper," Cletus said as he quickly emptied his tumbler. Hank rose to refill it, then topped his own off with a finger or so.

"Patrick's drowning surely was an unfortunate accident. I remember how the villagers were so stunned and upset about it, but I'm surprised I haven't thought of him in many years until my memory was jogged by reading this article. He was quite a guy, 'Sure an' begorra, an Irishman he was.' I'm still surprised he drowned, though. It just doesn't make sense; in fact, no one could understand it, what with him being such a fine riverman. Patrick could pilot a fishing boat, any kind of boat as a matter of fact, as well as anyone on this river. I went fishing with him many times in the main channel, in Horseshoe Lake, in the sloughs around Prairie, at the confluence of the Wisconsin and Mississippi down by Wyalusing Park, and I watched him handle that boat in the worst weather the Mississippi could throw at him—wind, rain, snow squalls, gales, whitecaps. Oh! He was a riverman, Cletus. I still can't figure out how or why he drowned.

You know, he operated his bait shack for many years, the only bait shop around until that guy in Marquette opened. Sometimes Patrick would get out in his fishing boats even before the sun came up, motoring one and pulling another a couple of hours before the rest of the villagers were out and about. He would float the main channel and sloughs searching for schools of minnows and small fish to sell for bait, because that was before he could buy bait from suppliers in La Crosse. But that wasn't simply a business for him. No, sir, it was his life. He felt better on the river than anyplace else. Oh, he was courteous enough to the fishermen who bought bait and rented his boats, but being on the river by himself—floating under sweeping willow trees along the shore, watching hawks and eagles soaring over these bluffs, dipping his line into the deep blue waters of the river's lakes and sloughs, floating red-topped bobbers for bluegills, perch and crappies, dropping stink-bait for river-bottom catfish, trolling the channel for walleyes, fly fishing down in Sni Magill—that's what his life was about. Anytime he could escape from the fellows at the Bait Shack to get onto the river, he would do it. Sometimes, he would even ask me to watch his place for an hour so he could go fishing, alone. He preferred solitude . . . said he could think better that way . . . said he couldn't think clearly when people were around.

I remember one day, Cletus, I had newspaper business down in Clayton. After I had finished and was eating a fish sandwich at The Lite House on the bank of the river, I looked through the window to see Patrick floating past with his tell-tale two fishing boats. I was surprised because Clayton is downriver several miles from here, but that didn't make any difference to Patrick. He was following his river instincts, analyzing the current, the changing hues of the water and the lapping against the shore for signs indicating fish or bait. He had so many minnows, walleyes, crappies and catfish in his boats already that they were floating low in the water. Later that evening, after I had returned to print the paper, I walked to the docks to see him chugging upriver toward his shack. He had been gone all day, but had two boats full of bait and fish." As Hank talked on and on, he failed to notice that Cletus had been slipping lower into the cushions, eyes glazed, marginally awake, but listening.

"T . . . Th . . . That's a good story, M . . . M . . . Mister Hank. I . . . I remember P . . . Patrick t . . . too."

"How about a topper? One finger?"

"S . . . S . . . Sure 'c . . . 'cause I'd like to hear m . . . more about P . . . Patrick." Hank rose to pour Cletus and himself each a finger of Jack, then settled back in his chair.

"Have you ever been into Spook Hole, that cave out at Beulah Falls?"

"N . . . N . . . Nope. I . . . I . . . get kind of scared in c . . . caves."

"Well, Patrick heard there was a special small minnow species living in great quantities deep inside that cave. Not one to miss a business or fishing opportunity, he prepared for a journey into it. He rigged a miner's cap and light, trucked two canoes out to the cave, squeezed his canoes and himself through the narrow, boulder-guarded opening to invade the darkness of the river cave, by himself, as usual. At that time, no one knew how far back into that hill the waters flowed, but Patrick was determined to find those minnows. He paddled into the cave using only his miner's hat for light. I told you, Patrick knew waters—Bloody Run, Sni Magill, the Wisconsin, the Mississippi, the Turkey, the Upper Iowa—but even he wasn't prepared for Beulah's meandering dark waters and . . . getting lost. Patrick O'Reilly, the Upper Mississippi's riverman *par excellence* got himself lost . . . got turned around and confused concentrating too much on the water searching for bait that he couldn't find his way back out. And if that wasn't bad enough, after a couple of hours of searching, his miner's light burned out. There he was, in total darkness, 'whoosing' noises swooping through the cave, bats swarming all around him— whining, whistling, squeaking—bumping his head on stalactites, canoe bumping against stalagmites . . . lost." He admitted to me later that he was preacher-praying-scared."

"W . . . W . . . Wh . . . at d . . . d . . . did he d . . . d . . . do then?"

"He attempted to calm himself then began paddling with one hand, feeling the walls of the cave with the other. He was a smart Irishman, that Patrick, even though skeptics around here said that wasn't possible for an Irishman. He reasoned that the walls closest to the cave opening would retain more heat from the sunlight of the day, so he took off his glove to run his hand along the wall. He told folks later that he rowed for about half an hour in one direction in pitch-black darkness while feeling the wall, but it got colder and colder. He turned the canoes around to paddle in the opposite direction, again testing the temperature of the wall with his fingers. He changed hands frequently, paddled with the right, felt with the left until he thought the wall began to feel warmer. He told me later that he was scared to death, and although he had never depended on other people, he had wished someone were there to help him escape. Sure, it was a good Irish Lord, he was, looking out for Patrick that day, because the walls did get warmer. Patrick knew he was paddling toward the opening then. He saw a dim light ahead of him, the opening to the cave. Cletus, he never found the minnows, but he was a free man. From that day forward he stayed off Beulah's waters. He decided he was a riverman, not a caveman.

Patrick was a drinking man, too. Have you ever met an Irishman who wasn't? He had a hand-painted sign—a big decaying wooden oar—hanging over the entrance to his Fish and Bait Shack:

Give an Irishman lager for a month,
and he's a dead man.
An Irishman is lined with copper,
and the beer corrodes it.
But whisky polishes the copper,
and is the saving of him.
—Mark Twain

And he believed that sign, too. His Fish and Bait Shack was just that, a shack, but fishermen and would-be fishermen loved congregating there. The place was hot and sultry in the summer, drafty and cold in the winter, but that's where you would find them—mostly infernal scoundrels they were—tipping the bottle, too. When the waters were muddy, when the fish flies invaded the river valley, when the waters were too high, fish wouldn't bite. That's when yarns were spun around the shack like a spider's web. Patrick wasn't a story teller himself, and not much of a talker either, but the other fellows were; besides, Patrick enjoyed their stories. Stories, a beer and a bump made an otherwise long day palatable.

I myself happened by one day for 'two fingers' after I had finished printing, you see. As I ducked under the Irish sign, churlish Mac McIntosh was spinning a web about Indians who had lived in these hills and bluffs hundreds of years ago. Now, Mac was a master story teller, but when he didn't know the facts, well, he simply concocted them. Mac had farmed up there north of Marquette on Pleasant Ridge for years. He said that every spring while plowing he would turn over Indian artifacts—arrowheads, clay pot remnants, stone cutters—items like that. He said he even found the remnants of a teepee one day, although none of the fellows believed him, being purebred skeptics, you see. Villagers had heard that yarn before, but Mac never showed proof. He said he had locked them in his barn, because he was going to open an Indian museum after he retired from farming. The fellows laughed from deep in their potbellies at the museum idea. They told Mac he was a farmer, that he didn't know anything about running a museum. But Mac was a persistent and stubborn Scotsman. He said he *would* build a park and museum someday along the river above Marquette to display his artifacts, and to honor the Indians. He said he wasn't that much of an Indian lover himself, but he liked history and wanted to preserve his farm and the Indian heritage in northeastern Iowa. He said there were many old burial grounds closer to the river and down over the bluff from his eighty acres, and that the government would probably make a park out of it someday. There were scores of bear effigies along the river, he said. Now, Mac was a story spinner of immense proportions, so he couldn't let it go at that. He said that one day while planting corn he looked up to see two Indian braves galloping out of the woods straight toward him. He grabbed the steering wheel of his rusty International Harvestor until his hands turned blue. He said he was ready to die. They were riding so fast that he didn't even have time to call out to his wife up at the house. The braves raced right up to him, reined their horses on their hind legs, reached out with their flashing hands, but to his immense surprise and relief, only touched him gently on the face before galloping back into the wooded hills. He sat on his tractor, stunned. He had expected to be dead by now, but all they had done was to achieve a coup on him. They had touched a white man, even if he was a Scotsman. Well, Cletus, you probably know that the fellows didn't believe that story either, but it made for a good one, and it helped pass the time of day. Mac McIntosh, to his dying day, said it was true. Two Indian braves achieved a coup on his grizzled face."

By now Cletus had slumped into the bowels of the chair, his massive body filling it to overflowing, cap slipping over drooping eyelids, trying valiantly to listen. The Jack Daniels had loosened Hank's tongue and his mind. He was having a grand time relating to Cletus the tales of Patrick O'Reilly and the scoundrels at the bait shack. He considered pouring another 'two fingers,' but decided against it; instead, he wobbled to the coffee pot to pour a burnt cup of coffee into his stained mug. "Do you want a cup of coffee, Cletus?"

"N . . . No . . . s . . . s . . . sir, M . . . Mister Hank. Don't drink c . . . coffee."

"Carl Schwartz was not to be outdone by Mac's Indian tale. Carl launched into a story about his grandfather trapping beaver on

the east channel near Prairie du Chien. Carl said that even he, as a
boy, trapped beaver with his father; of course, the skeptics didn't
believe that any more than Mac's Indian yarn. They said beaver
had all been trapped out of this region long before he was born, but
that didn't deter Carl at all. He just patted his beer belly, sucked a
Dubuque Star dry in two gulps and continued his beaver tale. He
said his great-grandfather had helped establish Prairie du Chien
when it was a trading center for beaver hides, assorted furs, and
timber. His grandpappy had even helped build the Villa Louis
mansion over there along the flood plain; of course, the fellows
knew that wasn't true, but they were enjoying his tale. Carl said his
great-grandfather had ridden deck passage on the Belle Of The
West upriver from St. Louis to trap beaver along the tributaries of
the Upper Mississippi, then sold the hides later to buyers in Prairie.
He said trappers over on the Missouri worked the river all the way
west until it joined the Platte in Nebraska before diverting into two
branches in Colorado, but his great-grandfather didn't want to
trade with those western Ute and Arapahoe Indians; Iowa's Sac
and Fox were cantankerous enough when trading. Carl said his kin
set beaver traps all around Crawford County, and over here, too, in
Bloody Run and Sni Magill. Carl said the Mississippi was a lot
different in those days, back in the 1850s, not looking anything like
it does today. He said it was always changing course, always
cutting new channels, sometimes even cutting entire towns off.
Why, one day a village would be in Iowa, he said, and the next it
would be in Wisconsin because that river was continually shifting
alluvial muds and sand around. The fellows laughed when he said
alluvial, but they continued listening and sipping. Carl said changing channels made steamboating and beaver hunting dangerous,
made it hard to find beaver, too. But beaver, mostly, don't like the
main channel anyway, he said. They like to get off into smaller
rivers and streams like the Yellow or Turkey rivers to build their
dams and lodges, and to raise their kits. His great-grandpappy
would leave the Mississippi's main channel to portage along those
smaller rivers and streams where there were sufficient saplings for
beaver feeding. He would trek for weeks on end until he found
lodges, until he acquired a bale or two of hides to sell to the buyers

in Prairie. Carl went on and on about beaver trapping in the region until the guys were worn out with so much beaver talk. Even Patrick was tired. They laced their boots, hitched up their britches and trudged out of the shack. Patrick pulled the chain and shuffled home to his hotel room.

No, sir, Cletus, I cannot understand Patrick O'Reilly drowning of his own accord. He was much too good of a riverman for that to happen. Something else must have happened. It wasn't like him to lose control of his fishing boat, and even though he liked to imbibe, he was careful about not drinking when working the river. I think something spooked him. Mac McIntosh always said Patrick might have seen a couple of Indian braves whooping from the shoreline. Carl Schwartz always said that beaver had bitten through his boat causing it to sink. I never believed either of those suppositions, but *something* spooked Patrick." Hank looked at a snoring Cletus, then gazed out the window to see that it had grown dark, that he'd been talking all afternoon and into the early evening. He threw a blanket over Cletus and placed his feed cap on the printer's table before Hank cinched his suspenders, locked the door and walked home.

5

"How was your day off, Hank? I wish I only had to work three days a week, but then I wouldn't be able to keep everyone healthy working so little. How do you manage to edit a newspaper in three days?" Doc challenged from the end of the counter.

"Something confuses me, Doc. How is it that you say you're working so hard all of the time, but every time I arrive, you're here before me. You take more coffee breaks from the Clinic than Cletus does from sweeping and mowing. He works harder than you do. Shoot! Cletus is the guy *really* keeping this village healthy by sweeping up germ-infested trash," Hank retorted as he placed his summer Stetson on the adjoining stool and sat next to the sartorial doctor. "Cup of coffee here, Bruno? Throw on a couple of eggs and hash browns, too. I'm hungry this morning, and in spite of what Doc says, I do have a heavy day of work ahead."

"Good morning, Hank. Coffee and eggs coming up, but I doubt what you said about work. You old farts talk about working hard, but you don't do it. You ought to stand behind this hot grill all day like I do. Now, that's work," Bruno said pouring coffee to everyone. Besides Hank and Doc the congregation included Charlie in his habitual gray cardigan, Samantha Cheuvront in her camouflaged duck hunter's cap tilted back on her stringy, gray hair, sitting alone at the end of the counter sucking on a Red Dot, slurping coffee and reading the *Des Moines Register*. Michael Mc–Taggart, sporting his perpetual tam-o'-shanter, was slouched over a cup looking directly into the bottom for more coffee, and Bob Burdick, Pioneer Seed cap awry, silent as ever staring into space. A couple of obvious strangers, devoid of caps, had straggled into town and were reading the stained menu, trying to understand the conversation at the counter.

Hank liked coming to Bruno's Cafe for breakfast—Muriel had reluctantly given up fixing it for him years ago, eventually accepting his desire to start the day with his cronies—where he enjoyed, usually, the good-natured chiding from Bruno and the regulars. It kept him on his toes, kept his mind sharp, he thought. He had started his day this way at Bruno's Cafe for the past twenty years. Bruno's hadn't always been Bruno's, but there had usually been a cafe in the hotel. When built in 1899 it had been christened The Lewis Hotel—seven colonnades gracing the front along Main Street—but Hank had seen its name changed to the Pocket City Hotel, the Zimmerman Hotel, and the Scenic Hotel over the past fifty years. Bruno had been running the cafe for the past four years since being discharged from the U.S. Navy after the Battle of Midway, as he was fond of relating to anyone within listening range.

"Now, don't burn those eggs," Hank yelled to Bruno hunched over the sizzling grill.

"It doesn't make any difference if I do. That's the way you're going to eat them; that or join the whiskey group down the street.

I know that your wife gave up fixing breakfast for you years ago," Bruno responded while blowing cigarette smoke through his gapped teeth.

"Sunny-side up. That's how I like them."

"Shoot, Hank, you just scramble them anyway. I'm of the opinion you're getting fussy in your old age, and you know, you aren't a spring chicken anymore," Bruno snipped as he flipped Hank's eggs on the grill.

"That will be enough talk about spring chickens. I told you yesterday there are a lot of tunes left in this old violin," Hank said as Bruno plopped a side order of greasy hash browns in front of him.

"Have you written that editorial about the new gym yet?" Charlie asked.

"No, sir, I have not, but neither have I forgotten about it. I've been researching early issues of the *Times* and finding out interesting things that happened here before the turn of the century."

"That's dusty, boring historical stuff, over and done with, Hank. I'd like to see you get going on the gymnasium editorial, isn't that right, Bruno?" Charlie responded.

"Come on, Hank. We need a new gymnasium. As Charlie said, write the damn editorial," Bruno snarled.

"We'll see, fellows. I'll get around to it, but I have a few more things to research today before I start editorializing. But to quiet you antagonists for awhile, maybe I will walk up to the high school to look it over if Bruno ever serves my eggs."

Ten minutes later he had finished his over-hard eggs, "I'll be getting on my way then . . . see you all for lunch if you old farts aren't too busy," Hank said, absent-mindedly slipping into his suit jacket instead of tossing it over his shoulder.

"Good morning, Cletus. I see you're at it bright and early. How did you sleep last night in the chair?"

"M . . . M . . . Morning, Mister Hank. I . . . I . . . let myself out this m . . . morning then walked home. Th . . . Th . . . Thanks for covering me with a b . . . blanket."

"You're welcome. Enjoy the day."

Hank decided to walk to the high school before going to the shop. He enjoyed long walks, but hadn't been doing enough of them lately; besides, it would be good for stretching his ailing hip and for walking off the eggs and hash browns. Doc was right; he needed more exercise to burn off creeping cholesterol. As usual, a heavy fog hovered near the top of the bluffs surrounding McGregor on three sides, but once the sun rose higher it would burn off filling the sky with billowing white clouds. He walked up Main Street admiring the valley he had lived in for so long—towering bluffs covered with a blanket of walnut, elm, maple, evergreen—the valley he had periodically taken for granted. When driving Muriel and Catherine through the prairies of central Iowa, he would be startled by the flatness of the land, but here the bluffs rose as much as four hundred feet above the river where, this morning, they painted the valley a lush, emerald green, an overture to the pallet of ambers, reds, rusts, burnt ochres and vibrant yellows that would blind his eyes in a couple of months. Autumn along the river, in these hills, was downright spectacular. Once that first frost invaded the valley these trees would begin their joyous, exploding, blazing dance . . . dancing along the Upper Mississippi.

As he shuffled along he was aware of a special sound, a sound different from towns out on the prairie where a conversation or a whistler's tune floated across the plains to the endless horizon. He had realized, years ago, that these bluffs contained sound. A person could hear so easily that it was almost like living inside the old Sullivan's Opera House. In fact, he needed to be careful what he said on the street, because the conversation could easily be heard by someone else a hundred yards away. It was a close sound, an enveloping sound, a soft, warm sound—sounded like home.

He stopped at the drugstore to see Theodore, not being in such a hurry that he couldn't chat for a few moments. Folks in this valley were never in that much of a hurry. "Good morning, Theodore. How is business today?"

"Greetings, Hank. How are your old bones this morning? Do you need aspirin for your hip, or some of my cure-all for your consumption?" Theodore asked peering over his bifocals from behind the ornate antique prescription enclosure. Hank could hardly see him because of the extensive paraphernalia around the enclosure and hanging from the walls. Theodore was fond of telling customers he had inherited the drugstore from his father who had purchased it in 1879 from Ramage and Peterson, the original owners who had started the business a few years earlier in 1872. It was obvious Theodore wasn't one for fixing up the store with fancy doodads, as he told most customers. It still had the same 1872 worn, undulating counter from years of customers pushing coins across it, the same glass-covered cases holding a variety of ominous looking drugs in bottles, the same smell. With all the drugs behind the counter—chloroform, ether, alcohol, boric acid, tincture of iodine, peroxide, carbolic acid, chlorine, ammonia, quinine, castor oil, Epsom salts—there was a nose-tickling odor not found in other merchant's stores on Main Street. That odor blended with the dusty, dank odor of the ancient floors, walls and ceilings to attack Hank's nostrils, flaring them wide every time he walked in the door.

"No, sir. I'm pushing seventy, my hip bothers me periodical-ly, cholesterol is a tad high, but no arthritis or consumption. Mother has arthritis, though, and it gives her considerable trouble, partic-ularly in humid weather, but today looks like it's going to be nice and dry. But as long as I'm here, I could take some aspirin home for her."

"How is she doing? She used to come in, but I seldom see her anymore," Theodore said as he hooked a bottle of aspirin from the second shelf with a long wooden staff.

"She's doing quite well, but can't walk downtown anymore. Some hearing loss and periodic breathing difficulty but golly, I hope I'm doing that well at ninety-five. She's a tenacious lady."

"You don't say. Is she really ninety-five? I had no idea she was that old. Darnation! You've good genes, Hank. You'll probably live to be ninety-five or one hundred yourself. Your mother's genes certainly are good, and your fath . . . er . . . you . . . that . . . I . . . I'm sorry. You never knew your father, did you?"

"No, I didn't. Catherine is a sweet lady but stubborn. She has never been able to talk to me about my father. It has upset me all these years, but I have never succeeded in getting her to confide in me. I hope she does, though, before she dies, or I do. I sure would like to know who my father was," Hank said as he shuffled toward the door. "I'm walking up to look at the gymnasium. Bruno says we need a bigger one, and he wants me to write an editorial about it. Thanks for the aspirin."

As Hank reached the sidewalk, he was greeted with a horn blast, a duotone sound his old ears hadn't heard before. It blared a second time. He turned to see Walter Browning III honking at him from a new auto. Hank walked to the curb as Walter parked carefully to avoid stubbing the tires.

"Walter! What on earth are you doing in that car, and what kind is it?"

"I just bought it, Hank. Isn't it a beauty? It's a new 1949 V-8 Ford. They arrived a couple of weeks ago. I saw a picture in the *Telegraph Herald*, and as soon as I saw it, I knew I had to get one," Walter shouted as he stepped out of the new car.

"Lawyering must be good to buy a car like that," Hank said enviously.

"It didn't cost that much, but lawyering has been pretty good; of course, it doesn't hurt to have the only shingle in town. No competition, you know," Walter said as he reached into his vest for a cigar. "Care for a King Edward?"

"Don't mind if I do. Thanks. That sure is a fine looking auto. Forty-nine, you say? V-8, you say? Let's have a look under the hood." They stepped carefully off the high curb, curbs built many years ago to contain flood waters rising up, and gully washers sweeping down Main Street. Walter raised the hood to proudly display a huge engine, one which looked considerably different from Hank's Chevrolet engine. It wasn't square-blocked, but rather, a V-shaped engine.

"It has four cylinders on each side. That design saves space and generates additional horsepower, too," Walter said pointing to the engine block.

"How many horses does it have?"

"One hundred eighty, I believe. I don't know for certain. I've only just driven it from Dubuque."

"You had to go all the way to Dubuque to buy it? Aren't there Ford dealers closer than that?"

"Yes, but they didn't have the new models in yet, and I couldn't wait. What do you think of it? Do you want to go for a ride?" Walter asked as they walked entirely around the car, admiring it from every angle. By now other villagers had noticed the car, and several were gathering in front of the drugstore . . .

"What kind of a car is that?

How many horses under her hood?

What'll she do on the straight away?

What kind of mileage does she get?

How much did she cost?" . . . asking questions that flowed faster than a spring runoff in Sni Magill. Walter tried to answer as many as he could while simultaneously trying to keep grubby young hands off the sleek, rounded hood, fenders and trunk. "I would like a ride, Walter, but I'm going to the high school to look it over. Come by the newspaper office tomorrow. Let's take her up to the prairie to see what she will do. Thanks for the cigar," Hank said as he left Walter at the curb with a growing cadre of admirers.

A pleasant aroma reached Hank as he passed Peder Torsrud's Meat Market. Hank was a sucker for Peder's fresh homemade sausage smoked with a mixture of hardwoods from the trees on the bluffs. Peder had been cranking out hundreds of sausages every week for as long as Hank could remember. Peder prepared newly-smoked sausages as well as hams and dried beef every week for Saturday shoppers. This being Saturday, Hank could tell a new batch had just come from the smokehouse, the hickory-smoked flavor attacking his nostrils twenty feet from the door. He walked into the Market.

"Good morning, Peder. I tried valiantly to walk on past, but that hickory aroma grabbed ahold of me like a number ten fishing hook hooking a walleye out in Catfish Slough. By the way, have you been fishing lately? We used to fish together frequently, but haven't done that the past couple of years. When are we going again? We aren't spring chickens, you know."

"Good morning, Henry. Ya, I don't have fishing time so much anymore, but I would if Ole and Per would do more stuffing of der hog casings and stoking of der smokehouse for my sausages and hams. That and waiting on der customers takes up my times, but you're right about that; we need to do that again like when boys we were. Maybe next week, then. I'll stop to your shop in some days."

"You have yourself a date. And while I'm here, how about it if I take along two big sausages and a pound of your sliced dried beef. Muriel and Catherine love your meats," Hank said pointing into the meat counter.

"Just so! Coming up. These sausages are made from grandfather's recipe in der old country, but I've put my own recipe in them over der years with changing amounts of beef, pork, and seasonings. Been experimenting with der smoker wood, too," Peder said as he reached for two long amber-colored sausages.

"I know that because I can smell your smokehouse all the way down to my shop. Sometimes I catch a particularly sweet aroma, other times it's more spicy, more tangy. I know when you're experimenting," Hank answered, "besides, you know how smoke hangs in this valley. It doesn't escape these hills anymore rapidly than a whispered conversation."

"You betcha. I like to experiment, though I need to graduate it otherwise der customers get smarmy. Most of der river folk don't want changin'. They like things stayin' just so."

"*Smarmy*? Have you been reading your English-Norwegian dictionary, Peder? But you're right about change. Anytime I write about something new in my editorial or River Reflections columns, I receive letters about it the following week. Villagers tell me to let well enough alone. I know some things should be, but we also need change. It's 1949, the war has been over for four years, many things in the village need changing, updating. Shoot! Only a few minutes ago I saw Walter Browning's new V-8 Ford. It has rounded fenders and a sloping windshield, designs we've never seen before. And it has fat tires with whitewalls, a sloped trunk, and you ought to see the dash . . . speedometer goes all the way up to eighty. Hell! Peder, there aren't any roads in Clayton County where you can drive eighty."

"Valter Browning has a new Ford? *Uff da!* That der ol' codger of a lawyer must be making lots of money from us if he can buy der new car. I can't be doin' that from these meats," Peder said while wrapping them in white waxed paper, tying each with coiled string hanging from the ceiling.

"Lawyers do make considerable money. I was reading Mark Twain's *Life On The Mississippi* a fortnight ago. I have the book right here. He writes . . . 'They all laid their heads together like as many lawyers when they are gettin' ready to prove that a man's heirs ain't got any right to his property.' Incidentally, do you know where that quote first appeared? The *Iowa Journal of History and Politics* in 1929. He also said this of lawyers . . . 'To succeed in the other trades, capacity must be shown; in the law, concealment of it will do.' That's what Twain thought about lawyers, but Browning is a good guy; he's fair and he's an excellent supporter of the village, even though he wasn't a very good mayor, but now, as I recall, he was better that our present mayor."

"*Fortnight?* Who's been reading der vocabulary, then? But I read where you've been hard on der mayor, Henry. I think you'd best lay off for awhile. Isn't such a bad job he's doing, could be worse."

"He might do a better job if he didn't spend so much time fishing and hunting. Shoot! You and I like to fish and hunt, too, but we tend to our business, don't we? And speaking of work; I have to get on my way. Bruno's chiding me about writing an editorial for an expanded gym. I'm walking up to take a look," Hank said as he slipped the bag of meats under his arm.

"So! Taste this week's sausages before you high tail it out of here," Peder said handing him a large chunk of sausage. Hank slipped the meat into his mouth and tasted the freshest, tangiest hickory-smoked sausage he could remember. There was just enough bite, just enough briny flavor to the seasoning to tingle his tongue, yet the smoky flavor made his mouth water.

"That's wonderful. You're getting better all the time even if you aren't getting rich. Thanks, and stop by so we can go fishing."

"'Hellos' to der ladies, Muriel and Catherine."

"And 'hello' to Sörinne."

With hickory aroma clinging to his nostrils, Hank once again resumed his trek, passing a brick Victorian-era house converted to the village library, the upholstery shop, the furniture shop, and the undertaker's shop while greeting villagers walking downtown for Saturday shopping. Most still purchased groceries and dry goods on Saturday even though they could have done it during the week. Saturday was simply the traditional shopping day . . .

"Good morning, Mrs. Stoneman. Nice to see you today."

"Hello, Mrs. McDonald. My, what a pretty bonnet."

"Top o' the mornin' to you Daugherty. Ah, sure and I didn't know it was that Irishmen rose so early."

"Aye, go on with you. It's the truth, Henry."

"Howdy, young man. What a bright red tricycle you have," until he finally reached the school at the Buell Park grounds. He hadn't actually devoted much attention to it once it was built about twenty years ago. The community had been so proud of it then, because it was very modern compared with the ancient, but sentimental structure he had attended. He walked in a side door to the gym to look it over. It didn't seem as small as Bruno made it out to be, but enrollment was growing, basketball was becoming increasingly popular; Bruno may have a point. He walked around the basketball floor, up onto the stage, then squeezed his lanky legs between the narrow seats to ponder the structure. As it was summer, the building was devoid of students; however, the chatter and shrieks of children echoed, from somewhere, in his ears. He was momentarily transported back to 1898, the year he graduated from *his* Ann Street school. He recalled that three-story structure had wooden stairways and dry wood everywhere, a real fire trap, in retrospect. His classmates had speculated how it was likely to burn. It did in 1930. Zigzag fire escapes had adorned the west side which students were supposed to use in an emergency. Little did they know that one day the stairs would be used for a real fire instead of fire drills. After twenty minutes of reminiscing and pondering this gym, he concurred with Bruno.

He's right. It is small. We have fine children here, as good as anyplace else in Iowa. Parents believe in a good education. They want the best for their children whether it's athletics or math or English or literature or music. Our children deserve a larger gymnasium. I'll write a couple of editorials to prod the community.

___ 6

After dining on roast chicken, dumplings, green peas and apple pie with Muriel and Catherine, Hank loosened his tie and slipped off his wing-tips to continue reading *Life On The Mississippi*. He was enjoying the episodes of Twain's life on this great river. Also, he had neglected pleasure reading the past several years; it felt good reading fiction or semi-fiction again. "Now, don't stay up late, dear. You need your sleep," Muriel preached as she kissed Hank on the cheek.

"I won't. I'm only going to read for about an hour," he said as he kissed her good night. Adjusting the pedestal lamp over his left shoulder, he lit a final cigar, drew deeply into those old lungs and began reading Chapter VI: A Cub-Pilot's Experience about Clemens' steamboat training in 1857, only a few years after Alexander MacGregor had ferried across the Mississippi from Prairie du Chien to establish a landing on the Iowa shore, a landing later used by soldiers trekking inland on the Old Military Road to Fort Atkinson, the ancient limestone fortress guarding the Turkey River.

It was difficult to imagine Samuel Clemens floundering early in his life, particularly in light of his later distinguished international reputation, but Sam had had difficulty "finding himself," as Catherine was fond of saying about people who meandered through life. Before he settled on writing books he had been a rascal, a steamboat pilot, a reporter and a miner. But Hank knew that much of Tom Sawyer's and Huck Finn's characters were autobiographical, containing characteristics of Clemens' own Hannibal childhood, a childhood he would draw upon in his later writings.

Sam had meager beginnings in the Missouri town. Born in 1835, he was but a boy when steamboating was the primary mode of transportation in the country. It was an era before railroads crisscrossed the Middle West, a time before the Wrights flew at Kitty Hawk, a time before state commissioners brought the people of Missouri and Iowa out of mud-rutted roads. River travel was the *only* decent transportation, and to be a steamboat pilot was the highest possible calling for a young man, particularly Sam Clemens. A pilot was the *freest* person in the world, not answering to anyone—kings nor presidents nor God. No one was as important and free as a river pilot. On the river, standing behind a five-foot spoked steering wheel, his word *was* God. Even the captain deferred to him. Sam realized this early on, because from the time he was a shoeless toddler plying the waters of Hannibal, he watched pilots at their trade by spending most of his youth along the river on minuscule rafts, scows and boats, tubs steamboat pilots scoffed at, vessels Sam himself would scoff at years later as he piloted ornate filigree and gingerbread steamboats to St. Louis, Memphis and New Orleans. Lowly keelboats without steam engines could only float downriver with the current, needing men manning twelve-foot poles to get them back upriver; barges were helpless without a paddlewheel, trading-scows and log rafts were scum, a terrible nuisance to steamers. But Sam and his cohorts would raft into the main channel to get as close, even on the magnificent floating palaces. He just knew that someday he would pilot a steamer instead of a raft.

As much as the youthful Clemens had dreamed about piloting, he wasn't prepared for it when the opportunity arrived. He was overwhelmed with what he needed to know and remember. In the 1850s, seasoned pilots trained cub pilots before they could become full-fledged pilots. There were no pilot schools in New Orleans or St. Louis; instead, on-the-job learnin' was the order of the day, the same type of on-the-job training budding jazz musicians like Louis Armstrong and Kid Ory experienced forty years later when developing their skills sitting in with old-timers—Buddy Bolden, King Oliver, Jelly Roll Morton—in New Orleans' Storyville District's brothels, and on northern-bound steamboats.

Sam was taken on as a cub pilot aboard the Paul Jones, Mr. Horace Bixby, pilot, but he wasn't ready for Bixby. Sam thought piloting would be easy, having spent his childhood daydreaming about it on the levee, watching steamboats churning past Hannibal. Someday, he would stand behind the huge varnished spoked-wheel steering the magnificent Paul Jones up- and downstream shouting commands to deck hands on the main deck, "Heave ho there on the larboard side!" . . . hollering down to the boiler room, "Fire those boilers, and be quick about it!" . . . shouting commands to the steward in the galley, "A spot of tea here, for the pilot. Don't dally now!" It would be easy as falling off a raft in mid-stream. Oh, he would have a grand time piloting and receiving the adulation he justly deserved. After ringing the bell thrice for docking, Sam would saunter down the gangplank into Hannibal, men, women and children stepping aside, deferring to his magnificence as he swaggered up Main Street. He was mistaken, dead wrong. Learning to be a pilot was the most difficult thing he had ever attempted. Mr. Bixby saw to that.

Bixby threw a different kind of schooling at Sam than what he had previously experienced in that little log cabin school. Now Sam, like Tom and Huck, had never been one for schoolin'. Anytime he could escape its shackles, he did. Fishing, rafting, cave exploring and treasure hunting were his exploits. But skipping school eventually caught up with him; it slowed his learnin', his mem'ry considerably. When he first took the wheel of the Paul Jones, he wished he had worked harder in school, because Mr. Bixby fired facts at him port and starboard as they ran upriver past Keokuk . . . "That's nine-mile point to starboard.

That's Eagle Point fore one mile.

Mark that snag jutting from yonder bank.

That's ten-mile point.

We're approaching Point Ann below MacGregor's Landing."

Why, Sam couldn't see any sense in Mr. Bixby's running on so. He was a steamboat pilot now, surely someone else would remember that gibberish. If Mr. Bixby chose to remember it, he could; Sam was only interested in steering the gilded queen upriver. Coming downstream a couple of days later, he found out how wrong he was, because Mr. Bixby began firing questions at him this time . . . "How much shoal water below nine-mile?

How far does the eddy jut out below Point Ann?

How many fathoms off Eagle Point?"

Sam didn't know. He hadn't tried to remember those things while steering upstream, but he learned a powerful lesson, because Mr. Bixby didn't retreat. He advanced like Grant storming Vicksburg, tearing into him, chiding him up to starboard, down to larboard, fore and aft until Sam was reduced to a sniveling deck hand, a roustabout, not yet a full-fledged scoundrel, but certainly less than a distinguished river pilot. Bixby harangued all the way back to Hannibal pointing out how important it was to know the river and how Sam wasn't along for a joy ride. Passengers and freight shippers depended on his skill. The captain sequestered himself below in his Texas-deck cabin depending completely upon the pilot. If Sam wanted to be a pilot, he would have to notice and remember everything about the river, day and night, and not only once. The river was constantly changing; he would need to know it as it changed for hundreds of miles. Point Ann would look different at night than during the day. Nine-mile would measure less twain coming down stream than going up. Sand bars, eddies and islands were constantly changing, constantly shifting. Sam didn't think he would be able to remember all the river's secrets—points, bars, shoal water, landings, reefs, twains, quarter-twains, half-twains, soundings. When rafting with his boyhood chums, they just floated lazily upon the river, going where the current took them, letting it make their destination decisions, not realizing then that a steamboat pilot needed the memory of a king, a river king. But after several days behind the big wheel, Sam knew he would need that memory. He knew he would need to "see" when it was pitch-black below Quincy. He knew he would need to "read" boiling water off Point Ann or Fire Point. He knew he would need to recognize shoal water below Burlington, Davenport and Keokuk. He knew he would need to "read" the deep waters below Guttenberg and Dubuque while steaming upstream or downstream. He knew he needed to, but was sure he would never learn all of that.

Ashes from Hank's cigar had fallen onto his lap, the cigar hung limply in his mouth, his bifocals sat askew on his nose as the book fell to the floor. He was sleeping, dreaming . . .

"So, you think you want to be a river pilot, do you, Henry?"

"Yes, sir, I would like that very much. My school chums and I always admired the steamers passing McGregor. Sometimes we paddled out to them, even tried to board, but they went much faster than we could paddle. It was exciting and dangerous, too."

"I know, because I did the same as a boy, and then I actually became a pilot before the war."

"What's your name, mister? You were a pilot?"

"Name's Clemens. Sam Clemens. You remember me, don't you. We talked once before about The Old Ram, *your favorite short story?"*

"Of course ... Sam! Sorry I didn't recognize you."

"Listen, I've got a steamer wooding up down at the wharf right now for a run to St. Paul. Would you like to come along? I could drop you off on the way back downriver," Mr. Clemens asked as he reached for one of Hank's cigars, lighting it and letting the smoke curl around his heavy mustache.

"Would I? Sure as you're a lightening pilot, I would. I've been setting type and breaking my back printing the newspaper for so many years that I need to get out of the shop, get back on the river where I spent my childhood, like you," Hank said excitedly. *"When do we leave?"*

"We can leave right now. Let's shove off. I'll even let you take the helm when we get upriver."

From the pilot house, Sam shouted orders ...

"Ahoy there! Stand by to cast off!

Lend a hand there! And be quick about it. One hand for yourself and one for the ship!

Fire those boilers, gentlemen. Red hot and be quick about it!" Then bells to the engineer for slow astern. Sam backed her away from the wharf into easy water then straightened her up. *"Fire those boilers with pitch! Let those chimneys burn black for the folks along the levee!" More bells to the engine room for full speed ahead. With the bow straightened up in the channel, the Gem City churned upstream toward North McGregor as the powerful paddlewheel left the wharf frothing in its wake. Hank sat on a high bench behind Mr. Clemens in the pilot house during cast off watching the frenetic activity of the deck hands below. This was his first ride with a famous river pilot.*

Mr. Clemens steered the steamer with imperceptible movement of the wheel; he appeared to be on a pleasure cruise, first standing to starboard steering one-handed while searching the shoreline, watching waves lap against sand bars and islands, then to larboard while squinting under his bushy eyebrows. The river was calm as the steamer chugged past Flemming's Sawmill at North McGregor toward Lansing, paddlewheel persistently thrumming against the surging downriver current. The view was extraordinary, inspiring for Hank—expansive breadth, island-dotted river, towering rock-ribbed bluffs, cottonwood, oak and maple trees enveloping the surrounding hills and bluffs—one which looked considerably different than from his fishing boat. Mr. Clemens demonstrated the skills of a master pilot, sometimes even maneuvering the steamboat sideways to slide through a crossing. And he continued shouting commands like a king. Oh! to be a king, a king of the river. Several miles above North McGregor he asked for a sounding, because he was concerned about the depth of the river out from Effigy Point near a mid-channel reef. He knew there had been shoal water over that reef on his last trip upriver. Three deck hands jumped into a sounding boat and paddled out in front of the steamer. They began sounding the river by dropping lead lines into the blue waters, measuring its depth in several places while hollering back to the steamer. . .

"No bottom!

Quarter twain!
Half twain!
Quarter twain!
Mark twain!"

Sam steered the steamer toward the sounders, following closely the course they were charting. He steered to starboard then to larboard all the while shouting commands, and sending bells to the engine room . . .

"How does she head?" . . . three bells, slow ahead . . ."Hard astarboard! Steady as she goes!" . . . two bells, slow astern. "Starboard handsomely, and keep her so!" . . . four bells to the engineer, ahead full. The chimneys bellowed black, swirling smoke; all three decks shuddered as the red-hot boilers forced pent-up steam through the gauge cocks and thrusters to the paddlewheel. She hit the sand, creaked and groaned, but eventually slid over the sand bar out into deeper, easy waters. The sounders returned, lashed their boat on the boiler deck as Sam shouted, "Full speed ahead!"

"That was a superb job of piloting, Mister Clemens. Why, that was lightening piloting if I ever saw it," Hank shouted admirably from the high bench.

"Weren't so much, Hank. You have to know the river if you're going to be a pilot, and I remembered that boiling water over the Effigy Point reef. You have to remember everything, not once, not twice, but every time, daylight or coal-black of night. This river will look much different when we steam back downriver during the night. It won't even look like the same river. You'll think you were steaming on the Wisconsin or the Missouri instead of the Mississippi. Come over here now. Take ahold of the wheel and steer her while I catch a cup of coffee," Sam said as he walked away from the helm.

"I . . . I don't know, Mister Clemens. I have never steered a steamer before," Hank said nervously.

"Just keep her in the middle of the channel . . . water's deep here, almost four fathoms. Pick out a point upriver and steam straight toward it." Hank gingerly stepped off the bench and limped toward the imposing wheel. He stood behind it, hardly able to see over its top, then placed both hands on the magnificent, sparkling wheel, spokes radiating out like a sunburst. It felt strange as he nervously fingered the jutting spokes. Piloting had looked so easy for Sam as he steered one-handed, looking everywhere about the steamer and the river, but it wasn't easy for Hank. He didn't move his hands, didn't turn the wheel. He didn't stand to starboard or larboard like Sam. He didn't shout commands to the boiler deck. He stared at the point—a sheer-faced cliff—he had selected upriver; however, the steamer began drifting, coming dangerously close to an eddy.

"Fast to starboard, Hank! Keep her in the main channel." Hank quickly spun the wheel right and felt the steamer come back away from the eddy. After that scare, he began making minute adjustments, began feeling the magnificence, the power of the steamer, but he still focused only on the cliff. He was concentrating too much to look at the beautiful scenery he was passing through. He was much too concerned with snags, menacing trading-scows, keelboats cordelling up the river, timber rafts attempting to engulf the entire channel, coal barges, broadhorns and lazy fishermen floating dangerously close to the paddlewheeler to be sightseeing. After several miles, Sam relieved him, but Hank didn't sit on the pilot's bench this time; instead, he walked to the window to now admire the river, the river he had suddenly acquired a new appreciation for—its grandeur, its power, its majesty, its danger. A few miles above Harpers Ferry, he saw Sam steering strongly to starboard as the river bent sharply toward Wisconsin, diverting into three channels. It was a wonder Sam knew which was the deepest, which was the main

channel, but that was the job of a river pilot. He had to know.

Approaching the bend below Lansing, they saw innumerable islands and sand bars. Sam rang the engine room bell for more steam, because the current was extremely powerful in this reach, at least a four-mile current. Hank could see several miles to the Wisconsin bluffs as they approached the bend. When not steering, he could now enjoy the grandeur of the valley with its pallet of deep blue waters, emerald green forests in ravines and draws between the bluffs, sand-colored limestone cliffs jutting from high precipices; also, the sounds of waves sloshing against the bow, water splashing over the paddlewheel creating a pulsating roar as it dug deep into the blue river; black birds squawking as they swooped around the steamer picking up bits of discarded food, the clanging of the steamer's bell when riverboats drifted too close. And he saw eagles soaring from cliff tops, diving toward the river in search of food. He saw channel bass and sunfish and schools of minnows surging to the river's surface, gulping air and insects. He saw deer, rabbits, squirrels, even a lone beaver waddling along the bank searching for cottonwoods. He saw folks along the shore fishing, talking, sitting. Like Sam, Hank felt important and proud as he waved from the pilot house. He felt like a river king.

In three days and two nights they had reached St. Paul, unloaded their cargo and had begun the run back downriver. As Sam had said a couple of days ago, steaming downstream was much different than steaming upstream. The pilot had less control, in fact, making it difficult to steer, because the river's four-mile current pushed the steamer in many directions. The boilers, however, burned less wood. Sam let Hank take the wheel again as they approached Red Wing, a quaint Minnesota town nestled below Barn Bluff, and he still had the wheel as they churned past Frontenac and Maiden's Rock—the rock guarding the long standing river legend of Winona, the Sioux Indian maiden who cast herself off the sheer precipice of the soaring bluff to the jagged rocks below because she wanted to marry a hunter instead of a warrior as her parents wished. Sam said if you listened closely, you could still hear Winona's death song near the rock. Hank didn't hear it, but was in awe of the towering five hundred-foot bluff and the width of the Mississippi at Lake City where it was as much as five miles wide, so wide it was called Lake Pepin. As the river again narrowed below the lake at Wabasha, Sam took the helm through the narrows.

Sam was certainly correct about night steaming. It was so pitch-black that Hank couldn't even see the bow from the pilot house; he wondered how Sam knew where he was. But Sam had told him that a pilot must know the river, day or night, upstream or downstream. He had to know it more in his mind's eye than with his real eyes, because on a swarthy night like this, he had only his memory to navigate by. Piloting by memory didn't make Hank feel good, though; he was nervous the entire night. But he found that Sam was indeed that lightening pilot. With the steamboat shrouded with canvas to contain all light—nary a cigar nor burning embers of a pipe permitted—he piloted the Gem City through the narrows at Wabasha sighting on Chimney Rock jutting up out of the bluff like a smokestack on a steamer, sighting on the pyramid-shaped moonlit Queen's Bluff; through the reefs at La Crosse, around the bend at Lansing, through the slip at Harper's Ferry, along the effigy bluffs above North McGregor, and slid her up to the wharf at McGregor.

"Henry! Wake up. You've burned a hole in your trousers, and you have ashes all over the rug. Heavens! You're a mess," Muriel said shaking him vigorously in the chair.

"Muriel? What are you doing on the st . . . steamer?" Hank said as he straightened himself in the chair.

"You've been dreaming again. And it's two o'clock. Come up to bed now."

___7

"Top o' the mornin' to you, Daugherty.

Morning, Peder. I can't stop to sample your sausages. I have an editorial to write, but I'll stop on my way home. Muriel and Catherine love your sausages and dried beef.

Hello, Theodore. Those aspirin are doing Catherine just fine . . . can't stop because I have a 'meeting' with the fellows.

Good morning, Cletus. How are you today?"

"M . . . M . . . M . . . Mornin', M . . . M . . . Mister Hank. I'm d . . . doin' jus' . . . fine. Have to mow lawns t . . . today."

"Stop into the shop when you'd like another present."

"S . . . S . . Sure will. G . . . G. . . Good-bye."

"If it isn't the 'city council' drinking coffee and hard at work as usual," Hank intoned entering the cafe while throwing his suit coat over a chair.

"Look there, everyone. It's our distinguished editor. What have you been doing with yourself? Doc and I haven't seen you for days," Charlie said as Hank sat next to him.

"Good morning, Bruno. I smelled your greasy grill up past Peder's. Are you using lard again, that cheap stuff?" Hank taunted as Bruno approached with the menacing, hot coffee pot, once again filling his cup to overflowing.

"Morning, you old fart. I'm in business to make a profit, and if I can make more using lard, I use lard. That other shortening costs too much; besides, your copper-lined stomach wouldn't know anything different anyway.

Have you started that gym editorial? You're slowing down in your old age, Hank. The 'council' here wants action. Are we going to read that editorial this week or not?" Bruno asked as he refilled mugs around the counter.

"Speaking of old age? I do believe I'm seeing more graying around those temples, Bruno. Better touch it up with some of that formula from the drugstore. You wouldn't want your out-of-town customers thinking you've passed middle age, would you?

But, concerning the editorial, I believe you will see it this week. I'm busy, though, because I have considerable researching yet with the early issues of the *Times* and the *News*. Did you know there was another newspaper here shortly after the *North Iowa Times* began? First, it was called the *Pocket City News*, then about 1877 the name was changed to *McGregor News*, a Republican paper."

"Nope, and I don't care . . . don't enjoy history like you do. I live in the present, for the present. Are you going to write that editorial or am I going to have to write it for you?" Bruno snapped as he placed his face directly in front of Hank's.

"I'll write it. Be patient. Possibly this week, maybe next. Quit prodding and serve me a Danish. I don't have much time."

"Hell! You've got nothing but time, Hank, nothing but time," Bruno snarled as he reached into the cardboard box for a day-old Danish.

Hank drank coffee, ate a dry Danish, chatted with Doc, Charlie, Michael and Samantha for only ten minutes before going to the shop. He was anxious to get back into the stacks, anxious to find out more about those cub pilots spooning with the young ladies. "I have to leave, fellows. Your enlightening conversation is overwhelming, but I have important things to do. Have a good day.

Put my coffee and roll on my account, Bruno. I'll pay you later in the day," Hank hollered as he flipped the suit jacket over his shoulder and bounded to the door.

"Yes, and I'll send the marshal out for you if you don't, mister editor, because you're running a pretty big tab here. You're into me for five dollars already," Bruno hollered, wiping lard onto his dingy apron.

"Maybe you will get it and maybe you won't. It doesn't seem to me like you need money anyway, Bruno, as much as you charge us. But I'll pay . . . probably."

As he left the cafe, Hank looked to the top of the bluff toward McGregor Heights, noticing for the first time this season, soft coppery reds and shaded yellows breaking through the green blanket covering the bluff. These hills would explode with vibrant colors in the following weeks. He loved autumn when the valley's pallet changed from summery green to autumn ruby reds, piercing yellows, burnt ochres and rusts. Villagers anxiously awaited their arrival, momentarily forgetful of the long, harsh, bleak Iowa winter that followed, winters that had been growing more difficult for Hank. Charlie now wintered in Florida, but Hank hadn't reached that point yet. Muriel and Catherine just didn't want to leave the village and their friends for several months, but now that he would retire soon, he might be able to convince them.

When he entered his shop, a sense of foreboding suddenly rushed over him like tumbling waters in Bloody Run. The seasons were changing—summer creeping into fall, himself creeping into old age, Catherine approaching the century mark—waters were rushing through his life. His hip ached, his eyes had weakened, he slouched more. While trimming his beard this morning, he was startled by the hollow-eyed haggard man in the mirror, noting especially the furrowed crow's feet around his deep, dark eyes. Weariness had accompanied autumn. He limped toward the desk tugging on his suspenders while looking around the shop. Suddenly, he shivered realizing he wouldn't be here much longer; it was time to let go, to read, to write his memoirs, to float on the river. He climbed the rolling ladder to retrieve additional newspapers from 1878 and '79, then descended the precarious ladder to the desk. Even though he was primarily searching for clues to his father's identify, as a life-long newspaper man, he was fascinated with the content and style of the articles, the typefaces used before the turn of the century, the ink, the printing and editorial styles.

A week ago he had found a second Steamboat Dockings report about young ladies cavorting along the wharf with cub pilots from the John J. Roe. Although names were not printed, he felt an urgency to investigate further, hoping to find another report providing more detail, maybe even names. He flipped the pages slowly, being extremely careful not to tear them as there was only one copy of each *Times* issue prior to 1900. He studied the advertisements, many made from primitive woodcuts. He read a fascinating article about the King of Italy's murder and the gruesome sentencing of the killer—ten years in a coffin-like chamber twelve feet below the prison floor. The condemned man was required to stand, there not being enough room to lie down in the chamber. He "lived" on bread and water. Prison officials didn't want to kill him; rather, they wanted to torture him.

How cruel, how antiquated, how medieval.

Hank placed the issue in the wire basket and picked up the March 1879 paper containing much news about North McGregor. The paper now included River Ramblings, a community column about activities throughout the week . . .

RIVER RAMBLINGS

Mrs. Benton's three children from Giard visited her at her home on Garnavillo Street Sunday afternoon.

John McLenahan's Holstein broke through its fence last Friday afternoon requiring three hearty runners to catch the sprinter.

Gregor MacGregor sprained his ankle stepping from a carriage in front of Pearsall's Livery Stable.

Margaret Odell served tea to the Pocket City Bridge Club on Saturday afternoon. Members from as far away as Froelich, Giard and Farmersburg attended. Thelma Boyle poured.

He flipped to the back page, ready to place the issue in the basket when he found what he had been searching for, another Steamboat Dockings report . . .

STEAMBOAT DOCKINGS

Steamboat	Captain	Pilot	Arrival	Departure	Cargo
Ida Fulton	Mr. Bates	Mr. Harlow	Tu. 11:15 p.	Tu. 1:30 p.	Casks
Keokuk	Mr. Holcomb	Mr. Cushing	We. 10:20 a.	We. 2:18 p.	Flour
John J. Roe	Mr. LaPointe	Mr. Cormack	Sa. 3:14 p.	Su. 11:37 a.	Syrup
Diamond Jo	Mr. Harris	Mr. Burns	Th. 1:15 p.	Th. 3:30 p.	Wheat

STEAMBOAT TONNAGE
INCREASES DURING PAST WEEK

The Port of McGregor has seen considerable activity this past week with four steamboats gracing our wharf. The activity has increased the tonnage being handled here, inturn meaning increased revenues for our village.

The Ida Fulton with Mr. Bates, captain, Mr. Harlow, pilot, docked for a few hours on Thursday unloading beer casks for the McGregor Brewery. She then wooded up for her continued downriver trip to St. Louis.

The Keokuk with Mr. Holcomb, captain, Mr. Cushing, pilot, steamed in the following day unloading flour shipped from the mills in Cedar Rapids. She also wooded up for her final leg. The John J. Roe with Mr. LaPointe, captain, Mr. Burns, pilot, docked on Saturday afternoon carrying corn syrup as well as a bevy of passengers traveling from St. Paul to St. Louis. The Roe departed on Sunday after wooding up.

Lastly, the Diamond Jo owned by McGregor's Diamond Jo Reynolds, Mr. Harris, captain, Mr. Burns, pilot, stopped briefly to wood up, but even that brings revenue to our port. We certainly like to see our wharf busy, because each mooring brings goods, passengers and money to our village. Even when docking for only a few hours, crew members and passengers usually spend freely. We are concerned, however, with the continued inappropriate behavior of some crew members as well as ladies of our community. The John J. Roe made an infrequent overnight docking during which time crew members, specifically cub pilots, were seen once again cavorting with two young ladies of the community. On overnight dockings, passengers and crew normally stay on board, sleeping in their cabins; however, we have recently noticed crew members frequenting our local hotels. This was such a case. It is not our intention to document the activities of crew and local ladies, but we couldn't help noticing the activity late into the evening along the wharf and subsequently, at the American House. As we have stated in previous reports, the ladies would do well to look more closely at our local gentry instead of casting their eyes on wayward cub pilots. We don't condone such brazen behavior, but in the interest of editorial decorum, we are withholding the names of the ladies. We hope there will be no repeated behavior.

Overnight stay? American House?

Leaning back in the chair, he bit the end off a Harvester, spat it into the brass cuspidor, struck a flaming wooden match, thought momentarily about accompanying it with a finger of Old No. 7, but changed his mind as it was only half past nine. The report captured his attention for a long time as he sat pondering, wondering . . . Maybe he would attempt to talk with Catherine after dinner.

Could it have been?

Even though he needed to begin editing next week's issue, he was distracted, maybe even obsessed with his search, but additionally, he was enjoying reading the old papers. As he had told Bruno, early in the settlement of the village there had been two newspapers. Part of the reason was to provide an opportunity for editors and readers to promote political views through the press. The early *North Iowa Times* had been a Democrat paper; the *McGregor News* promoted the Republican political viewpoint. The *Times* won the war of the newspapers over the years; however, the *McGregor News* had been a significant publication. Pulling out an issue of the *McGregor News* dated December 11, 1878, he saw an article about McGregor's first school structure and a second superstructure school building. Because of Bruno's prodding about expanding the current gymnasium, he decided to read the ancient article. He descended the ladder, settled into the swivel chair, adjusted the pad to relieve pressure on his aching hip, and began reading the brittle 1878 copy of the *McGregor News* . . .

In the winter of 1874-'5, a destructive fire swept away a number of buildings on the east side of Ann Street, between Second and Third. Among these small buildings was the first school-house this district ever had. It was a small brick structure, 12 x 16, of one story, with small windows and door. It was built about 1850, by Alexander MacGregor. Previous to that date this coulee between the hills was only known as MacGregor's Landing, and consisted of a couple of cabins and Mr. MacGregor's house at the landing, which was large enough to accommodate the adventurous traveler who touched on these shores in that early day. This was the second school north of the Turkey River.

Following the fire, a new school building was completed at the end of 1878. Colonel Otis, editor, stated that it had been constructed by the H. F. Hyde Company of Dubuque with a foundation of heavy masonry, walls of red pressed brick, floor and ceiling joists anchored and bound with iron, the facade finished off with cut stone from "the beautiful cream-colored limestone quarried near the city." The tall imposing tower on the side of the three-storied structure had been ornamented with "large plates of cut stone, and very heavy sills and caps of single pieces."

Shoot! We always believed that tower was where the teachers sent kids to be "tortured" when they hadn't completed their studies.

He read where some of the stones had been quarried near Clermont west of McGregor. The building was constructed to "hold about 700 students with fourteen rooms and twelve wardrobes."

On the first floor are the A, B, C and D primary grades; on the second floor, A and B grammar, high school and two recitation rooms; on the third floor is the C grammar. There is also one room for music teaching, and one large room for the superintendent, as well as a small one for the library.

I'll write an editorial this afternoon to get the ball rolling about expanding the gym.

He puffed deeply and thoroughly on his long cigar, drawing the tangy smoke deep into his ancient lungs, coughed heartily, then carefully placed the brittle paper into his overflowing wire "In" basket.

Time was escaping. He needed to start next week's paper, but this new found archival interest was becoming an obsession. Two hours had already passed and he hadn't started the gymnasium editorial, composed type on the Linotype nor summarized notes from the village council meeting. Yet, the archives were tugging at him like a five-pound bass caught on a number eight hook and ten-pound line.

I'll read just a couple more then get to work.

His hip had become stiff while reading causing him to wince as he climbed to the top of the dusty stacks. 1879 seemed to be a significant year in his search, so he leaned far to the left for an issue, then to the right for a random 1939 copy. As he reached the floor, a piercing pain shot through his hip and up his back.

I had better stop at the drugstore for aspirin on my way home.

The 1939 copy wasn't as yellowed and brittle as the 1879 paper; in fact, he had edited it. But there had been so many editions during the past forty years that he certainly didn't remember them all. He scanned the headlines of the torn 1879 issue: McGregor Growing Like Wildfire!; Girls' Industrial School Established at Mitchellville; Meat Packing Plant Opens at Ottumwa; John J. Roe Sinks, 98 Repor . . . the remaining headline and accompanying article torn away. As he picked up the 1939 issue, he briefly pondered the sinking of the Roe, but was distracted by a headline.

LUDWIG BIERSDORF DIES FROM RATTLESNAKE BITE

Ludwig Biersdorf, a life-long resident of Marquette, died Friday evening from a rattlesnake bite received when hunting in the bluffs north of Marquette. Although he had received several bites throughout his hunting career, sub-sequently recovering, this particular bite proved fatal. After receiving antitoxins in the McGregor Hospital for two days, Mr. Biersdorf succumbed late Friday evening.

Mr. Biersdorf was one of the area's interesting characters, and certainly a recognized man of the community. He had several occupations throughout his life—rattlesnake hunter, rattlesnake guide, fisherman, fisherman's guide—and unconfirmed sources said that he also supported himself by gambling in back rooms of various hotels and saloons up and down the river. There are no known relatives. Services will be held Monday morning at McGregor's Undertaker's Shop. Interment will be held at the Pleasant Grove Cemetery. Interested folks are encouraged to attend.

Hank recalled writing the article, but hadn't thought about Ludwig in years. Most people had known Lud, as he was known in this area, or at least knew of him, because he was hard to miss as he pedaled his massive body on a fat-tired bicycle wearing bib overalls, a long-billed Chicago White Sox baseball cap tugged down to his eyebrows, and silver-tipped black cowboy boots. He was regularly seen pedaling his Schwinn through the lower streets and benches of Marquette, on the highway between the villages, up Bloody Run on his way to trout fishing, even north of Marquette to the Yellow River bridge to hunt rattlesnakes in the towering bluffs.

"Mornin', Hank. You printed the paper yet? I was wonderin' if I could get a couple o' pictures in this week's rag," Samantha said as she waddled like an overweight, unbalanced duck toward Hank, banging her right hip on the printer's table, her left on the Linotype machine. Hank's shop was simply too confining for Sam's bottle-shaped physique. "And you oughten to move these damn machines so's a body could walk through."

"Hello, Samantha. I'm happy to see you. No, ma'am, I don't have it done; in fact, I'm delinquent. I've become involved in reading these old papers, so I am behind. I'll get to it in a couple of hours, though.

You said you have pictures? Show me," Hank said as he raised his aching body slowly out of the stuffed chair.

"Been up north o' Marquette takin' photos for my Scenic Photos business. Rowed out to an island just off the main channel last night as the sun was settin' to get a new shot o' the pontoon and suspension bridges. Think you could run 'em this week? They're good, and hell! . . . it wouldn't hurt my business none, either."

"Let me see them." Hank looked at the photos and was impressed. Photography talent had passed him by, but he certainly appreciated it in others, particularly Samantha. "They are nice. Sure. We'll run at least one on the front page, because I'm short on news reports anyway."

"Much obliged, Hank. You're a good fella."

"Don't mention it. I'm happy to help you out."

"What'cha readin'?" Samantha asked, glancing at the yellowed paper.

"I have been reviewing past issues, thinking I should pull them together before something happens," Hank said as he walked to the coffee pot. "Do you care for a cup of coffee?"

"Don't mind if I do, but no sugar or cream. I drink my coffee like my booze," Samantha said as she settled into a Windsor guest chair near the potbellied stove, "straight."

"Would you like a little 'sweetener' in your coffee? It's too early for me as I need to write an editorial on the gym, but you could have a spot," Hank said as he poured cold well water into the pot.

"Don't mind if I do, but just a touch . . . need to take more shots up on the Marquette bench, today. I'll need a steady hand.

Anythin' interestin' in these old rags you call a newspaper? By the way, what's this about pullin' your archrivals together. You plannin' somethin', Henry, like retirin'?"

"*Archives*, Samantha, *archives,* but I don't know. The crowd at the cafe chides me about it of course, I deny it but between friends, I am going to be seventy in a few months. I have been editing the *North Iowa Times* for forty years; did you know that? I guess I've decided to retire at the end of the year. Don't go spreading that around town, though. It's not time yet to make an announcement."

"Won't . . . seventy, you say? Didn't realize you was pushin' that golden age. Shoot! I'm fifty-four. Those years do catch up with us, now don't they?" Samantha said as she hoisted both boots onto the weathered hassock. "What's in those old rags?"

"Fascinating reports and articles I have forgotten about. Last week I read an article about Patrick O'Reilly drowning down below Pike's Peak. Do you remember him?"

"Hell, yes. Remember 'im well. Never understood how as good a riverman as he was could get hisself drowned."

"Nor I, Sam. I still don't understand it. Something on the river surely spooked him.

Do you remember Ludwig Biersdorf? As you walked in, I was reading an article I wrote about him ten years ago when he died from a rattlesnake bite," Hank said as he turned the flame down under the boiling coffee.

"Ever'body remembers Lud. He was a real character, that man. Hell! Me and him . . . ah . . . Lud and me had some dealin's? I even went with him rattlesnake huntin' a few times. That was an experience, I tell you."

"I never knew that. You went rattlesnake hunting?"

"Hell, yes. Oh, he did the actual snake catchin', but I was with 'im climbin' those bluffs lookin' for rattl'rs. Then sometimes after an afternoon of snakin' we'd go to his shack up there in Bloody Run for a ronderview."

"Do you mean a *rendezvous*, Samantha?"

"Whatever. Folks 'round here thought Lud was just an ol' rundown bachelor . . . thought he was only a worn out drunk ridin' his bicycle 'round town pickin' up trash, but let me tell you, there was a lot of life in that man . . . a lot of life. He weren't the same man in his shack as you saw ridin' 'round here—not the same man at all."

"That is fascinating, Samantha. Please tell me more about the rattlesnake hunts you went on," Hank said as he poured two coffees, one with "sweetener."

Samantha sipped long and deep on her coffee, settled back into the chair, chewed off the end of a long Red Dot cigar, spat it into the spittoon, fired it with a flaming wooden match and began telling Hank about rattlesnake hunting, and other things with Ludwig Biersdorf.

"Well, was this way . . . The first hunt was purebred happenstance. I'd been out with my camera shootin' shots of the river

above Marquette, me bein' 'bout five years into my photo business
then, just developin' a file for folks who'd begun comin' here 'bout
'35? Things had been pretty damn hard during the Depression, you
know that, Hank, but after ol' FDR got hisself into office—after
gettin' Heebert Hoover out o' office—things began improvin'.
Folks had a little more cash in their pockets to jingle so's they could
do things like drivin' up here for fishin' and pleasure boatin' and
sightseein'. I had me a few postcards on display over to Bruno's
Cafe and up to Theodore's Drugstore. Hell! Folks from Oelwein
and Waterloo and Cedar Rapids liked 'em, so I expands my
business some. Anyways, one day I was north of Marquette there,
just startin' to climb a bluff for a couple of wide-angled downriver
shots when I see's this giant of a fella 'bout a hunnert feet above
me standin' on a precipert, hollerin' at me not to climb 'cause
there's rattlesnakes on these cliffs. Shit! I'd climbed them bluffs
many a time, Henry, and never'd seen hide nor rattle of a rattl'r, but
this fella hollerin' at me—couldn't make out who he was—caught
my ears. He climbed down the rocks and as he got closer, I could
tell right off it was Lud Biersdorf 'cause they's nobody that big
'round these parts. Now, he was scowlin' . . . was angry and mighty
testy as he tromped closer towards me. 'You're Samantha Chevrolet, aren't you?' he says. 'I've seen you around town with your
camera box. You shouldn't be in these bluffs, Miss Chevrolet . . .
ought to know better because there are a lot of rattlesnakes in here,'
Lud snarls as he sidles up to me, stickin' his hairy face right in front
o' my eyes, 'and they don't like folks, specially women-folk.' I
says, 'Shit! First off, Old Man, my handle's Cheuvront, not
Chevrolet, you got that straight? And secondly, rattl'rs don't scare
me none, but you're scarin' me what with that crazy look on your
face and that long-handled somethin' over your back.' Lud settles
a mite then and says, 'I don't mean to scare you, ma'am . . . just
want to protect you from getting bit, that's all.' Well, Lud slowed
hisself down considerably then and I settled some, too. We set on
a big rock 'bout fifty feet above the river road and jawed some.
Can't say we actually knowed each other at that time, but we'd
seen t'other 'round the villages, greetin' t'other from time to time,
but that was all. Anyways, as we set on that rock we started havin'

an . . . oh, hell! . . . an attraction to t'other what with both of us bein' single and all? I'd been an old maid all my life, like folks 'round here like to say; 'course most thought Lud was weird, not all together you know, but that weren't the case at all. He was a good ol' boy, and those later ronderviews at his shack up in Bloody Run still haunt my mind some. . . haunt me terribly."

Samantha removed her duck's cap, laid her head back onto the cushion, closed her eyes and said nothing for several minutes. Hank was aware that she was remembering old times. He honored the moment by silently sipping coffee, looking around the shop, caught for a moment in his own thoughts . . . of his mother, his father.

"Anyways," Samantha resumed, sitting up suddenly and startling Hank, "Lud says that as long as I was there, maybe I'd like to go snake huntin' with an expert, bein' hisself, and that if we climbed higher, I'd also be able to take some shots from a couple o' hunnert feet up, 'if you can climb that high, Miss Cheuvront,' he says. Well, Henry, I doubts my talent to climb as fast as him, but he was a real gentleman, specially after comin' on so strong first off; folks didn't know that, you know. He helped me up those cliffs climbin' over and 'round dangerous hangouts, juttin' boulders and preciperts same as fellers danced me over to the Spit and Whistle. He was smooth as top-shelf whiskey skirtin' those rocks. Now, it was regular gossipin' amongst folks that he was smooth with a fly rod, but he was smoother'n a hog on ice skatin' across those boulders huntin' for rattl'rs. Hell! He was more t'home on those cliffs and in the cool waters of Bloody Run than he was on flat land. Folks 'round here thought he spent all his time ridin' that big bicycle pickin' up trash. Shoot! They should've seen him climbin' rocks, should o' seen him wadin' in Bloody Run or down in Sni Magill flickin' that line across them rushin' waters. He'd stand in the middle o' the stream, whip that line high behind his head, then skim it over the water without as much as makin' a ripple, landin' that fly right where he wants, smack in the middle of a blue swirlin' pool where hearty trouts was feedin'. He was a master, that man was . . . and in his shack up there in Bloody Run? He was a master there, too, but I probably shouldn't go into all o' that with you.

Anyways, Lud guides me left and right . . . 'Step here, jump there, Miss Cheuvront,' always holdin' my hand. When I got short o' breathin' we'd sit on a rock for a spell; he'd wait patient-like till I could go on. And the camera was bangin' 'round my neck, punchin' me in my tits, so Lud reaches for the camera, brushes me some—kind of on purpose I was thinkin'—and puts it 'round his own bull neck. Then we climbed higher. Lud was in his domain, I see'd that. He talked, too, 'bout everythin' on the bluffs and down along the river; talked like folks 'round here didn't know he had a knack for. He loved them bluffs, that's for sure. He'd stop climbin' and pullin' on me, turn 'round to look at the river all the way over into Wisconsin. He pointed out Point Ann and Pike's Peak . . . said that Pictured Rocks was right below the Peak and that they's some kind o' legend 'bout it which he couldn't remember; then he pointed out sand bars and Bergman's Island on the river far below us; even show'd me where the Wisconsin joined the Mississippi—called it a Confederate— 'course I already knew that. Says that's where ol' Father Marquette and that Joliet guy canoe'd into the Mississippi sometime back in the 1600s, or something like that, to stake out this land. He said to look upriver towards the Indian eulogies . . . said someday he'd take me up there to hunt rattl'rs. He talked nonstop climbin' the cliff. Hell, Hank, I couldn't get a word in edge-wise or from any other direction 'cause he was so happy tellin' me 'bout his territory. He held my hand firm-like, pullin' me further up till we stood on the very summit just like that priest and Joliet did. Lud then says to me, 'Miss Cheuvront, you could get some nice pictures from up here.' When I caught my breathin', I looked down on Marquette and saw zig-zaggin' streets in ravines and draws along the river and up in the benches . . . saw them like I'd never seen 'em before. They wasn't no order or sense to the layout of those roads at all. And I could see where Bloody flowed down out of a draw an' dumped itself into the Mississippi. It was a pretty sight from up there, Hank. I'd taken high shots before, but never from such a good vantage point as what Lud had pulled me to. The suspension and pontoon bridges looked mighty different from there, too. Lud hands the camera back to me so I shoots an entire roll of film. He was patient as a church mouse whilst I snapped one picture after another. Why, once when I stepped too close to the precipert to get a better angle, he even held me 'bout the waist so's I wouldn't fall. Felt good, too, and I think it felt good to him 'cause he held me for a long time, even after I didn't need no holdin'. I reloads my camera, then he asks me if I'd like to hunt some rattl'rs. I said I'd be game for that, so he led me by the hand down and 'round the south side o' the cliff where the sun was beamin' on us and heatin' up those rocks like a fryin' pan. Lud said rattl'rs, bein' cold blooded and all, liked to sun themselves on the hot rocks. He said that's where he usually found 'em. Even though I was scared, I had confidence in him and his skills, and Hank, I have to tell you, that man started lookin' mighty good to me, me being an old maid and all. Anyways, we descended 'bout fifty feet down the south side before Lud stops, edged his way to the overlook and whispers . . . 'Rattlers just below us . . . see three of them.' I felt my skin tingle 'cause I'd never encountered a real rattl'r in the wilds. Hell! I'd seen 'em in cages downtown Marquette where Lud and his fellow scoundrels used to show 'em off in front of the Standard Oil Station, but a rattl'r in a cage and a rattl'r sunnin' hisself on the rocks is two different circumstantials. Anyways, Lud grabs my hand harder, says not to worry, says to follow him. We skirted the boulders an' comes up on three rattl'rs from below. Lud was leadin'; I was followin'. Lud whispers, 'Stay here, Miss Cheuvront.' I caught that. He reaches 'cross his back to grab a long-handled snake fork. He steps slow as molasses in January towards them coiled snakes till he's 'bout three feet from 'em. Now, I knowed those rattl'rs saw Lud comin' 'cause their rattles began singin' their deadly song . . . never heard such a sound in my life as when them rattles drummed that hauntin' sound into my ears, Hank; t'was a desperate, dry, lonesome death rattle, kind of like that raspy gurgle my grandma made when she was croakin' back 'bout '99. Why, it stung my ears, caught in my throat so, but Lud had heard it a hunnert times . . . says to me he was slyer'n those dumb snakes and that they was just fakin' with those rattles. Before they could strike, Lud hooks two of 'em from the side, had 'em danglin' in the air, and had stomped his cowboy boot on the remainin' snake's neck, pinnin' it on the rocks. Those fang biters didn't stand no chance. Before they or even me knew what was happenin', Lud had whipped a gunny sack over his shoulder, stuffed two rattl'rs inside, whirled a string around it faster than a cowboy wraslin' a rodeo steer, and had reached down grabbin' the booted snake behind the head till his fangs spouted out o' his mouth like a river frog catchin' flies. He whirls to show the flarin' rattl'r to me, and from six feet I could see it spewin' deadly poison towards me. I steps backwards several times, but Lud says not to worry 'cause, 'rattlers can only spit three feet; besides,' he says, 'they have to bite you to cause any serious trouble.' I had my doubts."

"Do you care for another 'sweetened' coffee?" Hank asked as he raised slowly out of the chair. "Ouch! Darnation! I'll have to see Doc about this hip. It's been aggravating me something terrible lately."

"Don't mind if I do. Your coffee goes down mighty well this mornin'.

Know what, Hank? I hadn't thought all that much about Lud in a couple o' years, but what with you findin' that article. Hell! It's brought back old memories, good times," Samantha said, unbuttoning her fishing vest because of the warm coffee.

"I didn't know, don't think anybody knew that you and Ludwig were lovers, but that's nice. Everybody needs a friend. Here's your coffee. Any more tales about him?"

"Sure as shootin',' he loved snake huntin' and trout fishin' and gamblin' and he liked; you know, Hank, you bein' a married man and all. He was a big man in so many ways—ridin' that bike, kind of overpowerin' it what with him weighin' over two-hunnert pounds, 'course he liked his beer, a real guzzler he was. Anyways, after that first snake huntin' day, I went with him a couple more times; mostly, he hunted alone though . . . said it was too dangerous havin' somebody else with him . . . said he could catch more snakes alone. He caught 'em mostly for the excitement and danger of it, but he made some bucks sellin' 'em, too. Snake meat and snake hides kept hisself in beer money, that and gamblin'."

"Did he ever get bitten before the fatal bite?"

"Said he'd been bit innumerantable times, but they's no

snakes that could kill him, that's what he said. Should o' seen his hands. They's all swollen from bites; looked like night crawlers, and he had two-pronged snake bites on his legs, too. I saw 'em."

"And he never had any serious problems with those attacks?" Hank asked leaning closer toward Sam.

"Lud was a tough ol' cuss. Ornery in some ways to folks on the street, but mighty gentle up in his shack. He always carried knives with him when huntin' . . . said that when bit he'd simply slice his skin open, suck the poison out and spit it back at those damn snakes. He was crusty, that's for sure."

"That is hard to believe; of course, I suppose if I were bitten by a snake and knowing the eventual outcome, I would do the same.

Did he usually hunt on the cliffs above Marquette?"

"Moved 'round lots o' places like along the river above Marquette, and top of Bloody Run draw up there by the McIntosh farm. Sometimes he'd throw that snake catcher and gunny sack over his shoulder and bike downriver to Sni Magill, tryin' his luck there. Other times he'd bike all the way upriver to those Indian eulogies . . . said they was some great caves and huntin' spots up there. He mostly liked catchin' snakes sunnin' on the rocks, though, rather than crawlin' into the caves to get 'em. Caves was too dangerous, he said. Lud knew most everythin' 'bout snakes like where and when they sunned, what they et, where they hibernated, how many feet they could travel in one jump, things like that."

"What do you think happened that day he was bitten?" Hank asked as he sipped his cold coffee and lit his first cigar of the day. He noticed that Samantha was mellow now, enjoying reminiscing about Lud. He thought it was good for her. He had known her, as well as most people in the village, for most of her life, had liked her, but had felt sorry for her living and being alone all of these years, an Old Maid as she had said.

"Don't know. Perplexes me even today. I'd seen him at the Marquette Hotel that very mornin'. I was goin' up to Harper's Ferry for a photo shoot in their slough, so I stopped in for breakfast with the river gang. I'd been to his shack the night before, you know, for some friendship and a few beers. He was in fine spirits that mornin' . . . said he'd won a couple hunnert dollars a few nights before playin' poker up around Harper's, and the day was gonna be hot, just the right weather for snake huntin'. He's gonna catch a mess of snakes and make some bucks selling 'em, he said. He'd get five dollars a snake, and on a good day he'd catch ten, twenty diamond backs. He'd bat the shit out of 'em in that gunny sack, then hang 'em on hooks outside his shack. Sometimes folks would even want a live rattl'r. He'd make more money on them, although the game wardens frowned on that activity. Anyways, back to the hotel. We finished our breakfasts, then made plans for meetin' later in the day over to the Burke Saloon. Next time I saw him was in the McGregor Hospital, eyes glazed over, starin' at the ceiling, in a comma . . . never talked to me again . . . never heard that big, gruff voice one more time."

Samantha began crying, tears rolling down her ravine-laced cheeks. Hank walked over, placed a hand on her shaking shoulders, but said nothing. "I'm sorry, Hank. He's a crusty old cuss, but he was good to me, he sure was," she said dabbing her eyes with a big red handkerchief.

"Don't know what happened. He was such an expert at snake huntin' . . . best there was around these here parts. Can't explain it even today. The bite was on his left arm just below his elbow 'cause I saw it in the hospital, but he could have cut hisself, sucked out the poison and spat it right back at that damn snake. Doc said there weren't no cut marks. I didn't see none, either. Don't understand it. His knife was still holster'd when a couple o' hunters from Waukon Junction found him sprawled down by the roadside. Maybe that poison worked too fast on him this time. Maybe he was gettin' old and loosin' his reactin' time. He wasn't drinkin' when I left him at the hotel, so that weren't a factor unless he fired it up later. On the other hand, he said he never drank before huntin', only afterwards. Don't understand it, Hank . . . never came out of the comma. Doc filled him with antitexans, pumped out his system best he could, but that didn't do no good. We buried him three days later.

Lud didn't have no relatives. Always said his Austrian ances–

trals died in a tornado up there in Minnesota someplace when he was a young'n. He never wanted to jaw about it. Me, and I remember you was there, and 'bout ten other folks planted him up there in Pleasant Grove Cemetery on a nasty, cold and rainin' day so's Lud could look down on Bloody Run forever. I put up a tombstone a year later, after I sold more photos, some even from that first day I shot pictures with him."

Ludwig Biersdorf
1889-1939
Snake hunter, Fisherman, Friend

Samantha leaned back in the chair, closed her eyes, whimpered softly as tears trickled down her cheeks like a gully washer in Bloody Run. Hank limped to the coffee pot to turn off the burner, then shuffled back to her placing both hands on her shoulders. He could feel her heaving, shuddering as she remembered Lud. She reached up and grabbed Hank's hand and held on tightly as she had done years ago when Lud pulled her up the bluff going rattlesnake hunting.

She was silent for several minutes, but then opened her eyes, and a broad smile flashed across her grainy, drawn face as she recalled more pleasant moments. "We sure enough had some good times together, huh! Up in his shack on a mornin' when fog covered the whole holler, Lud would fry up eggs and raw fries and fresh brook trout for breakfast. Now, I wasn't much for eatin' fish as mornin' vittles, but with them bein' fresh out of the cold stream, and the special way he had o' fixin' 'em, well, he alterated my mind some. We'd sit outside on log benches eatin' those greasy fries and tangy fried trout and drinkin' Lud's bitter, pot-boiled coffee just listenin' to the stream burblin' an' tumblin' over rocks, polishing 'em smooth as Bloody rushed on down towards the big river. And we'd watch the first golden rays o' the mornin' slice through the fog so's we could see the river, and the bluffs above Prairie du Chien. Folks 'round here didn't even suppose Lud and I were friends, at least I don't think they'd knowed, but I suppose somebody did. Don't make no mind anyways.

Oh, how he loved to fish. If it wasn't rattl'r huntin' he was doin', if it weren't playin' five-card stud, it was fishin'. Maybe of all the things he liked to doin', other than you know what, he loved trout fishin' the best. Hell! Sometimes, before I even got my ass out o' bed, Lud would have got up and caught hisself a big Brown or Rainbow trout. He was somethin' with a fly rod, a real master, I tell you. Only couple of times did I go fishin' with him, though, 'cause that was somethin' he liked to doin' by hisself, but when I did, I knew 'nough about fly fishin' to know I was in the presence of a real artesian. Well, he'd set me someplace easy like along the bank of the stream, then he'd either move upstream or downstream, away from me . . . said it was to give me enough room to cast, but I knowed it was 'cause he wanted to fish by hisself. I'd see him standin' on a rock up there beyond the Bloody Run campsite, pick a particular fly from his cap, tie it on the line, then cast that line ever so easy, so graceful-like into the tricklin' stream. He'd flip the line couple o' times . . . out . . . back . . . out . . . back . . . that line skimmin' couple o' feet above the water, whippin', flashin' in the mornin' sunlight. On the third cast he'd lay that fly in just the spot he chose. If he didn't catch no trout in the first two or three casts, he'd pick another fly, always experimentin' until he'd catch one. Hell! I just threw my line out there *hopin'* to catch a Rainbow, but Lud, he *knowed* he'd catch a trout. Luck had nothin' to do with it. Then I'd see him wade into the stream, sometimes with waders on, sometimes without. One time, believe it was late in the fall when the trees along Bloody had changed their colors, I saw him hook a big Brown an' follow him right upstream. Bloody was rushin' mighty fast that day, but Lud had hooked him good . . . he wasn't about to loose 'im. He hooked him while casting from a big boulder, but Lud was soon in the stream, rod arched like a bent willow, tip dippin' so low that I thought it was gonna break, but he was smart. He give that Brown slack, stayed right with that fish. Couple o' times, Lud was in so deep o' water that I thought he'd of drowned . . . lost his hat—came floating downstream to me—but he stayed with that fightin'-mad trout. Lud knew when to give the Brown line, knew when to tug at him. Five minutes later, Lud was on the other side of Bloody, standin' on the bank, soaked from head to boots, but he had the Brown. Lud whipped his net out, held his fly rod high in the air then scooped the big Brown out o' the tumblin' stream. He hollered to me to look at his prize. Well now, Hank, I don't think I'd ever seen him lookin' happier. But then do you know what he went and did? Why, he let that Brown back into the stream. I was flabbergusted. After all that work, he let the fish go. I asked him about it later at breakfast, but he just shrugged . . . said somethin' about catchin' bein' the important thing, not keepin'. He said somethin' about fish needin' a life, too. I didn't understand none of that, but, Hank, Lud sure loved the waters. And he loved bein' on the Mississippi, loved catchin' Rainbows down in Sni Magill, but mostly, he loved fishin' Bloody Run. I think that Lud was mighty haunted by those waters.

I've been ramblin' on long enough, Hank. You need to get this week's rag to press, and I need to get to Marquette for that photo shoot. Thanks for listenin'. I didn't know this was gonna happen, but what with you finding that article, well, it just brought back lots o' mem'rys. Hope you didn't mind my ramblin' on so," Samantha said as she slowly rose from the chair, tossed her dead cigar into the spittoon, buttoned her vest and waddled toward the door.

"Not at all, Samantha, not at all. You're a friend. Anytime you would like to talk more, just come on in. And, Samantha? I'm glad that you and Lud were friends. I'm glad to know that he had something other than snake hunting and fishing in his life, even if for a short time."

"I'll see you, Hank. Thanks for the grounds."

___8

After the long session listening to Samantha, Hank's hip ached. He needed to walk and clear his mind, too. Limping down the sidewalk toward the river, always the river, he approached the boat ramp to stand for a moment looking out over the waters to the Wisconsin shore, the shore from which Alexander MacGregor had ferried over one hundred years ago, 1837, from Prairie du Chien to establish this landing which eventually flowered into this town. Were it not for MacGregor, Hank wouldn't have spent his life here.

"How you doin', Hank? I ain't seen you around for couple a days," Bernie hollered from the end of the dock. "Want a beer?"

"Afternoon, Bernie. No, thank you. I have to write an editorial yet this afternoon. I'm only walking out an aching hip."

"Ah, come on, Hank. I've got most of a six pack left yet. One little beer won't hurt your old head none. Might even help it," Bernie taunted as he stood and staggered toward Hank, bloodshot eyes glowing like a river beacon in the fading afternoon.

"I appreciate your intended hospitality, but another day. And I need to keep walking. Stop into the shop sometime and we'll share a beer." Hank walked unsteadily on the undulating dock back to solid land then headed upriver along a path toward Marquette. Normally, he enjoyed talking with Bernie, but right now, he wanted to be alone. If he had stayed, Bernie would have talked nonstop; in fact, most villagers talked extensively when they saw Hank out and about because he was a good listener. Townsfolk frequently overwhelmed him with concerns about arthritis, gout, consumption, school buildings, fire trucks, city council meetings, church suppers, street cleaning, fishing, births, deaths, hernia operations, hog prices, milk prices, corn prices, and frequently, gossip. It was one of the hindrances of being editor, because people assumed he was interested in everything, but he had his own thoughts, his own concerns today.

A narrow dirt and pebble path ran adjacent to the railroad tracks along the river. For several years he had thought the two villages should collaborate on constructing a permanent walking path here. He had even written several editorials proposing it a few years ago, but the mayors and village councils had never supported it. They retorted that if people wanted to walk, they could either trek along the highway or the tracks. But Hank liked walking here even without a smooth pathway, because, although though it didn't happen often, he periodically liked to escape.

The river was displaying soft hues this late afternoon, not like the brilliant, vibrant colors to be showcased up on the bluffs in a few weeks. People seldom noticed the river's shades, but he did. He looked into its depths to see a pallet of blues: azure-blues near the surface, smoky-blues just below, steely-blues a couple of layers lower, and midnight-blues on the bottom. The river was also streaked with greens especially closer to shore where bluish-green swirls blended with moss-green algae. The hues contributed a special character, one which changed daily, hourly. Sam Clemens said a river pilot needed to memorize the river if he were to be a good pilot . . . needed to know its colors and currents by day, by night. Hank knew its sounds, its music, also. Today, it was singing a gentle euphonious melody more like a brook than a river . . . no waves, no cacophonous splashing, no discordant harmony, only deep blue waters with pleasing harmony flowing like a Rogers and Hammerstein melody, gently, persistently toward the gulf. Other days, though, stormy, windy days when the river was angry, the music was angular, discordant, sounding like a steamboat calliopist gone mad as white caps created foot-high waves—foaming, crashing violently against hulls, tearing violent gashes into the soft shorelines, its melody more Wagnerian than Dvorakian. And the odors and aromas of the river were imbedded into his brain like the melodies. In spring, after the harsh winter had finally loosened its grip, waters flowed freely with a fresh, sparkling, ice-tinged aroma. Later, when floods swept through the valley, it carried a murky, dusty, mud-tinged odor; during the dog days of summer the odor was like a cesspool, but Hank knew it changed constantly, refreshing itself. Odors and aromas were part of its natural cycle. Today, it was zestful, musky.

Autumn would soon explode on the Upper Mississippi. Ducking under golden tree limbs reaching over the river, he skirted around rocks, crept under overhangs, hopped over a trickling creek meandering to the river and shared the path with rabbits, squirrels collecting nuts, a lone beaver, a raccoon, and several sandpipers foraging for food. In a few weeks the leaves would reach their highest glory, the entire valley exploding with vibrant artist's colors. Samantha would attempt to capture it on film, sightseers would attempt to capture it with box cameras, writers and poets would attempt to capture it in verse, composers would attempt to capture it in melody, but none would. A photograph, a beautiful melody, a watercolor or a poem was a poor substitute for the real thing. One could only experience it by being with it, here. And even though he tired of the swarm of weekend sightseers who descended on the valley like fish flies during a summer deluge, he knew he needed to share *his* season, *his* land, *his* river.

As he sighted Marquette, his encounter with the river had replaced Sam's story in his consciousness. Leaping over a small boulder, a piercing pain raced through his hip and up his back. As a boy, he had walked, ran and jumped along the river; dove into it, and swam its menacing currents with nary a pain nor ache, but those activities were now only memories. He wondered how many jumps there were from boyhood to retirement when he hoped to have a few good years, because he had seen several friends and colleagues live only two or three years after quitting, stroke or heart attack striking them down. He knew he wasn't any different from John Coard or Willard Williver or Mac McIntosh, or even Ethel Hawley who toppled over last March in front of Pilkington's Undertaker Shop—massive heart attack. Village cynics said she made it easy for the undertaker, having saved him hearse money what with her dying in such a convenient place.

The path was barred abruptly by a two-ton boulder which he recalled had toppled from the bluff about ten years ago lodging itself near the shore; he skirted around it up to the railroad tracks to continue his trek where he had often walked as a boy—suddenly, he *was* a boy again skipping on black, creosoted ties and walking the endless rail, arms flailing wildly . . . what child hadn't walked the rail balancing one foot in front of the other, sometimes even playing "chicken" with an oncoming freight only to jump off at the last moment as the coal burner roared past spewing coal-black, menacing smoke. Boys think there is no end to life. An old man knows there is. All too soon, he was walking on cinders again.

"H . . . Hi, M . . . Mister Hank. W. . . Wh . . . What'cha doin'?" Hank was startled and slightly embarrassed to see Cletus sweeping cinders along the shoulder of the road, peering at him from under his feed cap.

"What are you doing? You don't need to sweep the highway."

"I . . . I . . . like s . . . sweeping—jus' goin' to M . . . Marquette, Mister Hank." Hank walked toward Cletus, grabbed him firmly by the shoulders, turned him around and pointed him back downriver. "Back to McGregor with you, Cletus, and watch out for cars."

"Okay, M . . . M . . . Mister Hank. B . . . B . . . Bye."

As he watched Cletus sweeping the roadside back to McGregor, Hank glanced across the road and saw the remains of the McGregor Brewery tucked into the bluff. Only jagged remnants of a limestone wall remained, but he remembered when it was still producing thousands of barrels of brew each year for this area and beyond. He and his pals had played among these ruins, searching the deep, cool caves in the bluff after the big Milwaukee brewers had forced the collapse of John Hagensick's enterprise, the building finally collapsing sometime after World War I. Because of his historical interest in the valley, he recalled that the brewery had been a successful enterprise for about forty years, generating brew from steam-powered boilers in what had been an impressive three-story building topped with an eye-catching cupola, not unlike the ornate pilot houses topping the great steamboats passing a hundred yards from its front. As he walked past the ruins, he fondly remembered the attempts of his high school friends at getting free samples from the brewmaster. And he recalled Catherine talking about evenings spent at the adjoining beer garden.

Reaching Marquette, Hank saw a towboat rounding the bend about a half mile upriver, whistle searing, echoing throughout the river valley signaling the pontoon bridge to swing open. The river was so wide at this point—west main channel, east channel, backwaters, lakes, sloughs—that after the horrendous expenses of the Civil War, it was financially prohibitive to construct a long suspension-style railroad bridge from mid-channel to Marquette. In 1874 engineers had elected instead to construct a floating, swinging bridge, what would be the first pontoon bridge on the entire Mississippi. The towboat was churning around Marquette Bluff when Hank saw the bridge begin to open, a slow process taking about ten minutes. It swung in a gentle arc, opening wide for the encroaching tow. The opening had been an exciting event for him as a boy, but even now, as an old man, it still held a child-like excitement. The tow was only an eighth of a mile away when the pontoon bridge opened completely, the tow still searing the valley with piercing tones from its whistle. The Hawkeye State was pushing twelve barges, probably loaded with either wheat or corn to ports downriver in St. Louis or Memphis or to sea-going ships at the Port of New Orleans. After the Hawkeye State slipped through the narrow bridge opening while spewing diesel fumes to the top of the bluffs, the pontoon bridge slowly closed, connecting its tracks once again to the Iowa shore. Hank turned around and headed back along the tracks toward McGregor, once again attempting to walk the rails. On his return walk, he planned the editorial about expanding the gymnasium. By the time he sat at the typewriter to begin his two-fingered key punching, the editorial flowed magically through his warped fingers. By half past five, he had finished.

___9

"Hello? Anyone home? Muriel? Mother? Where are you two?" Hank hollered as he entered the foyer and hung his suit jacket on the hall tree.

"We're upstairs, Henry. Mother isn't feeling well, so I've put her into bed. I'll be down shortly," Muriel called from the stairs.

"Mother not feeling well? I'll be right up." When he entered the bedroom, out of breath from the long stairs and sixty-nine years, Catherine was sitting in bed, propped up with several pillows. Muriel was helping her sip water through a straw. "Hi, Mother. What's the problem?" Hank inquired as he walked to the bed and kissed her on the cheek.

"Land sakes! 'Tain't nothing at all, Son, just a little cough," Catherine said as she adjusted the bun on the back of her head.

"Mother was having trouble breathing, so I brought her upstairs," Muriel said, adjusting the pillows behind Catherine's back.

"Say! I've only caught a little cough and cold," Catherine huffed, "and I'm too old and obstinate to let it get me down," she said, leaning back into the bed pillows. "I'll be out of this bed quicker than you can say 'Jack Sprat.'"

"Well, I hope you'll feel better tomorrow. You have hardly been sick in all of your ninety-five years, have you?" Hank said squeezing her wrinkled hand.

"That's right, Son, and I don't plan on being sick for the next ninety-five, either.

Now, what have you been doing with yourself today . . . drinking coffee with your cronies at the cafe?"

"Actually, I have been writing an editorial about building a bigger gymnasium. I only finished it before walking home."

"Bigger gym?" Catherine said, grimacing slightly as she twisted in the bed. "Why on earth would we need a bigger gymnasium? It seems fine to me. Land sakes! It's good enough for these kids." Catherine coughed and wheezed as she tried to recline. Hank and Muriel lifted her forward so she could breath better. "Give me a spoonful of that consumption medicine, Muriel."

As Catherine began breathing easier, Hank told her and Muriel about Samantha Cheuvront's experiences with Ludwig Biersdorf, then he casually slipped in a comment that he had also read several 1878 and '79 Steamboat Dockings reports. He told them about cub pilots cavorting with attractive young ladies along the wharf and later at the American House Hotel. Then he stopped suddenly, not speaking for about a minute. He watched his mother—chest heaving, shallow breaths, gasping for air—letting her absorb what he had said. He watched her eyes. Catherine betrayed nothing, only the imperceptible sound of clicking eyelids, soft as a butterfly in flight, caressed the quietness. Breaking the silence, he whispered, "I know it has been many years, Mother, but do you recall that incident?"

"Goodness gracious! No! Why would I remember such a story as that? We were proper young ladies in our time, not like these young whippersnappers today. Shenanigans such as that weren't talked about, weren't discussed," Catherine said as she shifted uncomfortably in the bed. "May I please have more water,

Muriel?" Catherine asked coughing several times. "Why would you ask me about that?"

"Oh, curious, that's all. You would have been about nineteen then, and I'll bet you were an attractive young lady yourself," Hank said as he stroked Catherine's hand.

"Heavens! I don't know if I was attractive, but I do know that young men would take a second look my way when I was fixed up for church, you know."

"You never heard about cub pilots cavorting with young village ladies then? I thought maybe you might have seen or even talked with the young steamboat pilots yourself. Just curious." Hank raised out of the chair and walked around the bed looking directly into her eyes. He looked deeply, pleadingly, wanting her, at last, to share the great secret she was holding inside her frail body, wanting her to release the secret of his unknown father. Hank needed to know his name. The days were getting short, he was getting old, his mother was . . . she was having a coughing spell. "Did you know the cub pilots, Mother?"

"Why . . . why would you ask me that? Of course I . . . [cough] . . . I . . . [cough] . . . didn't. Muriel, give me more consumption medicine, please."

"Would you care for more pork roast, Henry?"

"Thanks. It is delicious.

I'm concerned about Mother. Do you think it's only a cough, only minor consumption?" Hank inquired as Muriel served more roast, whipped potatoes and gravy onto his plate.

"I'm not certain. We were enjoying tea in the parlor this afternoon when she began having difficulty breathing. She believes it's only a cough, but I'm worried, too. I'll watch her closely tonight then see how she is feeling in the morning. If she isn't better, I'll call Doc to come over.

But you know, dear, you shouldn't be pressing her about your father, not in her present condition. I know how it troubles you, but this is not a good time to be bringing up the past."

"I understand but I read that report, and somehow, I don't

know, somehow I feel Mother's presence in it. I have a suspicion that one of the unnamed young ladies was Mother. I sure wish she would release her secret. It's getting late, you know," Hank said as he poured additional gravy over the potatoes.

"I know how much you want to know who your father was, but she's old and frail. She's held that secret for seventy years in spite of your pleadings. I don't believe any living person in Clayton County knows the answer to her secret. Her friends of those years have long since passed away. Why don't you let her be at peace with it? Be glad you've had a mother for all of these years, even if you didn't know your father."

"Maybe you're right, Muriel. Maybe you're right."

____10

"That editorial coming out tomorrow?" Bruno inquired as Hank joined the coffee group at the counter actually wearing his suit jacket this morning, tie cinched tightly.

"Yes, sir, it's in this week's edition. Now, I'll have my usual cup of coffee and an order of French toast."

"Thank heavens. Fellows? He finally wrote the editorial. Hallelujah!

French toast this morning? You worried about your cholesterol? You're a little old to start cutting back on fried foods; they've already done their damage. You aren't worried about getting older are you, Hank?" Bruno asked as he reached deep inside the refrigerator for maple syrup.

"Old? Of course not, but I see you've been to the drugstore for some of that new hair formula . . . toning down those temples are you? Can't a guy change his ways once in a while? I've been eating your greasy foods for so many years now that I'm tired of them. In fact, I might even start eating breakfast up at the Marquette Hotel. I could use a change of place, a change of face. I'm getting sort of tired of you old codgers," Hank said, smirking to everyone.

"That'll be fine and dandy with us, won't it, Doc? I'm of the opinion that Hank's getting too churlish for me anyway," Bruno retorted while flipping thick bread onto the grill.

"*Churlish?* Where did you learn such a pretentious word? Have you been secretly studying the *Reader's Digest* vocabulary list again?" Hank taunted.

"Hell! I know some big words, mister fancy editor. How about *smarmy?* I'll bet you don't know what it means. Use that in your newspaper. Editors aren't the only people who can use fancy words you smarmy, churlish, irascible, infernal old fart."

"Say, Doc, Mother wasn't feeling well last evening. Would you stop by the house today to check on her? She said that it's only a cough or consumption, but Muriel said Catherine has been short of breath lately. Do you think you could work that into your hectic schedule today?"

"Short of breath, you say? Certainly," Doc responded as he checked the time on his pocket watch. "I've time before I go to the clinic. She's tough, though. I've been doctoring her for forty years and haven't seen anything get her down yet. You have good genes, Hank."

Hank finished his French toast, caught up on the latest gossip, bid his farewell then ambled toward the shop. He would finish printing the weekly edition by noon, then review the archives for the remainder of the day. He realized they were becoming more important to him than putting out the paper. Editing was becoming an interruption.

By noon the one thousand issues of the paper were printed, bundled and stacked by the front door ready for Cletus' distribution. Hank was happy to have completed the printing, but he was also tired. Hours of typesetting at the hot Linotype, printing, binding and bundling were taking their toll.

The leaves on the bluffs will be turning colors soon. I'm turning grayer—the seasons are changing, Hank thought as he shuffled to the cabinet, reached for the Jack Daniels, poured a hearty glass, lit a cigar and slumped into his chair by the stove.

Another edition completed. How many more do I have left before December?

He sipped and smoked for an hour, then set his head back—tired but relaxed—for a short nap this early autumn afternoon.

Mellow from the hearty Jack Daniels, he slept for an hour before Cletus banged the front door off the spring as he barged in. Seeing Hank snoring, he loaded the papers into his two-wheeled cart behind his bicycle, totted some to the post office, then distributed the remainder door to door throughout McGregor and Marquette. Cletus thought he might return later for a "little treat" which Hank usually offered him after completing the delivery.

Cletus' rumblings had wakened Hank. He rubbed the sleep from his exhausted eyes and weathered face, ran a comb through his white, long-flowing beard—*Muriel has been after me to shave it off, but I've worn it for thirty years . . . would feel naked without it*—and stretched his creaking bones as he slowly stood up. He took one step when his hip momentarily gave way. It was becoming an increasing problem, frequently aching and feeling weak.

Maybe I'll have Doc take a look at it one of these days.

He reheated the coffee, splashed cold water onto his face, then limped toward the ladder. Climbing it was getting harder; everything was getting harder these days, but he was determined to find a clue to his father's identity. He had previously reviewed 1878 and '79 issues, the 1925 issue on Patrick O'Reilly's drowning, and the 1939 issue on Lud Biersdorf's death. Today, he would review some 1930's issues. Steadying himself on the uncertain rolling ladder, he located the 1930's bin and pulled out several brittle issues, almost missing a rung while descending. After pouring a cup of coffee, he began reviewing the papers. Actually, these were newspapers he had edited, so as he scanned the type and layout, he was pleased with what he found. It had been many years since he looked at these particular issues, if ever, but they looked good. He saw that the type was still crisp with sharp edges to the characters, particularly in the body of the copy, and the ink was still deep black. Throughout his editing years, he had experimented with several brands of ink to find one that had a rich quality. 1931 looked good. It had held up well for the past eighteen years.

Several articles were devoted to joblessness and hard times in Mendon Township and Clayton County as the early thirties had been the height of the Great Depression. Thousands of men had been out of work—the Chicago, Milwaukee, St. Paul & Pacific Railroad had reduced employees, the river shipping industry had reduced its work force, farmers had difficulty getting fair prices for crops, milk and cattle, merchants' stock didn't move—times had been extremely difficult for everyone. Hank recalled his own difficulty trying to keep the *North Iowa Times* afloat. Local merchants had little money for advertising, thus greatly reducing his revenue. He recalled how his household had to cut back on groceries, travel and entertainment to withstand the onslaught of the Depression. He shuddered, even now, remembering how close he had come to loosing the paper. Carrying on the long tradition of the *Times* democrat philosophy—himself being a staunch, unrelenting Democrat—he blamed Iowa's own President Herbert Hoover for most of the Depression, but as a loyal Iowan, he had hoped Hoover would get the country rolling again. *Hoovervilles* had sprung up throughout the country including Clayton County, one even under the suspension bridge in Marquette. Hobos throughout the state and the Midwest hitched rides in boxcars, then jumped off at villages to try their luck. They camped in tents and cardboard shacks or simply, under the stars. During the day they would walk door to door through the villages asking for food, work, handouts . . . anything. They weren't bums, but rather, men and families down on their luck. Hank leaned back in the chair recalling how FDR had finally replaced Hoover in the White House to begin the New Deal program which put men and women to work through the Civilian Conservation Corps (CCC), and Works Progress Administration (WPA) programs building parks, dams and roads. Roosevelt pulled the country, Clayton County, too, out of the Depression.

He laid the 1931 issue aside then began leafing through a July 1935 *North Iowa Times*. On page two he found an article recalling a long-forgotten incident . . .

AREA BLUES SINGER MISSING: SEARCH CONTINUES

Ethel Matters, resident of Prairie du Chien, well-known blues singer and piano player, has been missing for two weeks. She was last seen performing at the Roundhouse Bar in Prairie du Chien on Friday evening, the 29th of May. The proprietor said that she didn't appear, as scheduled, for the Saturday evening performance. He didn't report her absence to the police, because, as he stated, "That was a common occurrence for Ethel. She wasn't exceedingly dependable, but she was talented." After not appearing at the bar for several days, he did notify local police. To-date, her whereabouts are a mystery. Neither the owner of the Roundhouse, friends nor acquaintances have heard from her. If any citizens of the area have any information concerning Ethel's disappearance, please notify the Prairie du Chien police department immediately.

Leaning back in his chair, Hank laid his bifocals on the desk and reflected upon the mysterious disappearance of Ethel Matters. He realized, at this moment, that her disappearance remained unsolved almost twenty years later. How a three hundred-pound black woman could disappear so suddenly in this region without leaving a trace remains a mystery. For several weeks after her disappearance, people reported sightings up and down the Wisconsin shore in Lynxville, De Soto and Cassville, and also along the Iowa shore. One eagle-eyed citizen even said he saw her sitting in a back booth at the White Springs Restaurant in McGregor chomping down an entire barbecued chicken dinner. All reports were unconfirmed. Ethel Matters was never seen, in this area, again.

The tinkling of the front doorbell perked Hank's ears. He swiveled his chair to see a tall, distinguished looking gentleman standing at the front counter.

"Hello, sir. My name is Mister Slocum, Slade Slocum from Prairie du Chien. You remember me, do you not? I have previously placed advertisements in your excellent newspaper; now, my good man, I would like to place additional advertisements for a special event I am promoting. Do you perchance have space in your next several issues?" the suave, derby-hatted-pinstripe-suited-silk-tied gentleman said as Hank limped toward the counter.

"Good afternoon, Mister Slocum. Of course I remember you, but I haven't seen you in a long time. How are you?"

"I am quite well, thank you, but I must say, sir, that you are appearing older since last I saw you. However, it has been several years as you do not frequent my clubs, do you? I presume you are not the night life, sporting type?" Slade said as he tightened the knot on his hand-painted blue silk tie, and brushed lint specks from his suit jacket.

"No, I'm not much on night life, although Muriel and I do eat out occasionally. We enjoy dining at the White Springs—the old Klein Brewery west of town—and periodically stop into the Highway Inn, too. And when the wind is blowing from the west, we drive over the bridge to Prairie to dine, frequently at Kabers, but we don't go bar hopping as the youngsters like to say. I know your place on Black Hawk Avenue in Prairie, though. I hear music when you have the door open; however, I don't care for Western music. Your establishment isn't for the ladies and me, although Catherine said she used to kick up her heels at the Dousman Hotel along the river when she was a flapper girl back in the Twenties."

"You might consider stopping into the Roundhouse Bar, however, my good man. I operate a proper establishment devoid of rowdiness. In the early years, we possibly catered to some undesirables; however, our current clientele is considerably improved. We do offer Western music and dancing on Friday and Saturday evenings, certainly not music of my own choosing; nevertheless, the local clientele loves it. I hire jazz and swing bands for some of my other clubs. Next time you are motoring through Prairie, consider stopping. I will offer you a cocktail, on the house.

But I'm here on business, always business. I own and operate several nightclubs along the Wisconsin shore—the Roundhouse Bar and Beyond The Blue Horizon in Prairie, Clyde's Fish and Dish in Lynxville, Fred's Feed and Read in Cassville, and two clubs in East Dubuque. I hire bands and singers from Milwaukee or the Twin Cities, sometimes Chicago. I then schedule them on a rotating circuit of my clubs. One must have entertainment to attract today's clientele. They also desire fine cocktails, hearty brews, exquisite food, and sociable dancing.

For a special forthcoming promotion, I have contracted Doc Evans' band from Minneapolis for three weeks to play my clubs. They certainly are an extraordinary traditional jazz band which should draw well. I have previously prepared a camera-ready advertisement copy for you. Are you prepared to run it during the next two weeks?" Slade asked, placing the half-page ad on the counter.

"Sure, no problem, Slade. I'm happy to have your business."

"Now, sir, I must depart. I am driving to Guttenberg to place an advertisement in the *Guttenberg Press*, also; then I am on to Dubuque to contact the management of the *Telegraph Herald.* I am canvassing the entire river valley, from La Crosse to Dubuque, because I know these good people will enjoy listening and dancing to Doc Evans."

"Wait a minute, Slade, before you go. I was reading an old issue of the *Times* when you walked in. It's an article about Ethel Matters' disappearance in 1935. Do you remember her?" Hank asked as Slade was halfway out the door. He stopped, turned, and with a startled look, walked back toward Hank.

"Do I recall her? My good man! I am the gentleman that hired her when first she arrived in Prairie du Chien. Heavens! I have not thought about her for several years. She was never located, was she? I recall officials dragging the East Channel, Pickerel Slough, Catfish Slough and Sawmill Slough near the Wisconsin shore for several weeks without finding a clue to her whereabouts. Goodness gracious! Even if they had hooked her they would have had considerable difficulty hoisting her into the boat, as she weighed over three hundred pounds. Search parties also combed Wyalusing State Park thinking perchance she had been picnicking there and had inadvertently toppled off a cliff; however, they never located her. It was a mystery. It still is."

"You said you hired her? Come on back and sit a spell, Slade. You have time to tell me more, don't you? Guttenberg and

Dubuque have been around for one hundred years; they aren't going anywhere. I'll fix us a couple of Jack Daniels, *cocktails* as you say, then you can tell me her story."

"I absolutely should be continuing my business trip, but, my good man, I assume one Mister Daniel's would not delay me excessively."

Hank fixed two generous Jack Daniels highballs, *perceiving* that Mr. Slocum could afford to loosen up a bit. Handing one to Slade, they retired to the easy chairs by the stove. The two men certainly were a contrast—Slade displaying the demeanor of an English gentleman, resplendent in a three-piece, pinstriped navy blue suit, hand-painted silk tie over a gleaming white dickey, diamond tie tack, highly polished Oxford shoes . . . impeccable. Although Hank was dressed in his usual dress slacks, suspenders, white shirt and tie, he could never quite get his ensemble together. His clothes were formal; he wasn't. Slade clinked his glass with Hank's, "To Miss Ethel Matters, blues singer *par excellance*, friend, wherever she may be." The two disparate men drew deeply from their drinks.

"When did you first meet her?"

"I believe, sir, it must have been approximately 1930. I was then becoming established in the nightclub business, having recently purchased the Roundhouse Bar, my first club. I was attending the bar when she wobbled through the door, and I reiterate *wobbled,* late on an overcast autumn afternoon prior to Thanksgiving, snow flurries already appearing in the gray sky. She added many pounds to her hefty frame over the next few years; however, even that afternoon, she was already a hearty woman weighing in excess of two hundred fifty pounds from my estimation. Regardless of her obesity, Henry, she was light on her feet. She didn't move like a heavy woman. Subsequently, after I offered her gainful employment, she would occasionally dance with the clientele, tossing and twirling men around the dance floor as if they were butterflies. She was lighter on her feet than the one hundred fifty-pound men she danced with. However, as I was previously discoursing, I was attending the bar, only two gentlemen drinking boilermakers, the evening patrons not yet having arrived, when this obese black woman saunters into my establishment. Oscar and Bert took a double take as she waddled directly to the bar and inquired of me if I was the owner. I responded affirmatively. She rejoined, 'Honey, I'm a blues-singin'-piano-playin' mama. You hirin'?' I retorted, 'I am always inquisitive of new talent, ma'am. Do you have any?' She placed her fleshy arms on her extended hips, thrust her jaw directly at me and responded, 'Damn right! I got talent . . . best you eva' heard. You got a piano in this joint? I'll show your sweet ass just how much I got.' When she retorted with 'sweet ass,' Bert and Oscar glanced at each other, guffawed, gulped their boilermakers and followed her to the piano. Henry, over the years I had had many musicians seeking employment; therefore, Ethel appearing and desiring to sing and play was not out of the ordinary. I was not expecting any significant display of talent from her. I momentarily considered dismissing her; however, with her sassy approach, I did permit her to audition, nonetheless. She bounded around the bar dislodging bar stools from their moorings, bounced off the bar, and scattered tables and chairs in every direction on her sojourn to the upright piano. She placed her ample physique on the piano bench, extended her arms over the keyboard, placed a fleshy left hand on the bass keys and proceeded to play the liveliest boogie-woogie I ever had the pleasure of hearing. Her left hand was magical. For the duration of one minute she did not place her right hand on the keyboard, electing instead to manipulate her fuzzy hair, her dress, her dangling earrings all the while playing that extraordinary, astounding eight-to-the-bar boogie-woogie. After she had that piano rocking and rolling with her left hand, she subsequently began playing melody with her right, syncopating and driving it upward to the extremity of the keyboard. She now had both hands flying over that old eighty-eight, and Henry, that was not all that was flying . . . the three of us were standing behind her with an excellent view of her flying posterior. I had doubts that the piano bench would maintain its integrity. And the more she pounded, the more she perspired. Sweat rolled down her round temples, dripped from her weighty arms, and before she completed that boogie-woogie, her dress was soaking wet, thereby displaying every lump and fold she possessed on her prodigious physique. Oscar, Bert, I and several other regulars who had entered listened and watched in astonishment. We had never heard anyone play with such extraordinary energy and fire, with such salty, earthy, pulsating rhythm. She finished with a flourish—both hands scrambling up and down the keyboard. She played that final chord with such extreme force that the entire piano rocked on its casters. She turned, looked me in the eyes and said, 'Is that hot 'nough for you, sir, mister what's yo' name?' 'Mister Slocum, Slade,' I rejoined. 'Well, Mister Slade, honey. You gonna hire me or not?' she said as she walked up to me laying her ponderous arms on my shoulders, her round, perspiring black face not six inches from mine, her abdomen pushing me slightly off balance. She was drenched, and by now, radiating an odor—tart and saucy—but I responded affirmatively, 'Miss Matters. I am prepared to offer you a contract. If you elect to accept my offer, you may commence tomorrow evening here at the Roundhouse. I am offering you employment through the holidays, from now through New Year's Eve. We will evaluate your continued employment after that date.' Then she inquired, 'How much you payin,' 'cause I don't come cheap?' 'Seventy-five dollars per week,' I responded, 'shows on Friday, Saturday and Sunday evenings. Mondays, Tuesdays, Wednesdays you will have off; however, you might elect to assist me tending bar on those days?' She said, 'I'll take it, honey, but ain't doin' no bartendin'. I'm a pro . . . didn't spend my time up in St. Paul practicin' piano and singin' to do no bartendin'. Seventy-five it is then, but Mister Slade?'—she now had placed her sparkling brown eyes only inches from mine—you ain't even heard me sing.' Releasing me from her vise grip, she wobbled back to the piano and launched an earthy, up-tempo rocking stomp . . .

> *Come on up some night, my castle's rockin',*
> *You can flip your wig 'cause everything's free.*
> *On the top floor, the third door to the rear,*
> *That's where you'll always find me,*
> *Stuff in there the chicks want to see.*

She possessed a deep, husky voice much like Bessie Smith's,

somewhat like Billie Holiday's but heavier, and she had that piano rocking now, that's for sure, rhythm oozing out of her . . .

Don't worry about a thing,
'Cause I'm paying the cops for protection,
Tell them cats downtown they can let their conscience be.
Oh, come on up, bring your friends,
And we'll start the ball a rollin,'
My castle's rockin', come on by and see.

I was overwhelmed at my good fortune. I knew she would attract and hold a clientele. Oscar and Bert were dumbstruck. I had found a gold mine in Ethel Matters . . . and something more."

Slade leaned back in the chair, drained his cocktail, gazed around the newspaper shop for a moment, then hoisted his glass. "Mister Daniels is quite tasty, sir. I believe I might accept a second." Hank fixed two more drinks then settled once again into his chair, by now completely engrossed in Slade's story. "How did she happen to be in Prairie du Chien in the first place?"

"Several weeks after arriving she informed me that she had been driving to Kansas City to see if she could strike the big time there. Kansas City was wide open with gambling, prostitution, bootlegging, narcotics and racketeering in the early Thirties under T. J. 'Big Boss' Pendergast and his juggernaut political machine. Pendergast did not recognize prohibition, electing instead to run Kansas City in the manner he chose—what was good for Kansas City and Pendergast was good for musicians, particularly big black jazz bands and blues singers. At one time there were over one hundred nightclubs and forty dance halls operating around Eighteenth and Vine, each supporting live music. She said she wanted to sing like K. C. blues singer Julia Lee. Ethel hoped to join up with Count Basie's Band or Benny Moten's Band or Walter Page's Blue Devils or Andy Kirk and his Clouds of Joy Orchestra at The Reno or the Subway or the Chesterfield. She did have monumental plans.

Ethel had grown up in St. Paul, Southside down by the Stockyards, I recall. She had been a successful club singer there, but she wanted a wider venue, wanted to obtain a recording contract. She was bound for Kansas City when she stopped in Prairie," Slade said as he tilted his highball to the ceiling, quickly emptying his second drink.

"Do you care for another, Slade?"

"I certainly would accept your hospitality, Henry. Mister Daniels has lost none of his fine quality since I have last partaken."

"Why did she ask you for work then if Kansas City was her destination?"

"Ethel had prodigious talent, but she attracted trouble. I sensed immediately that it was following her. And I believe she was also broke. I believe she was operating from town to town, earning only enough money to get closer to Kansas City. Her hop-scotching might have worked, but as I discoursed earlier, trouble followed her closely. By the time she had finished a one-week stand at a club up in La Crosse, she retained only sufficient money to drive to Prairie where she found me . . . and I found her. For five years, Henry, she was great for my business. Singing and playing boogie-woogie piano kept her in booze . . . and men. She never arrived in Kansas City, at least not alive as far as anyone knows.

An obese black woman like Ethel stuck out like a sore thumb in Prairie du Chien. People in 1931 and '32 were not accustomed to seeing black women around our town. In fact, I don't believe there was a single black family living in town, then along comes Ethel . . . ebony-black, obese, sweaty, sassy. Citizens didn't know what to think of her as she waddled down the sidewalk, but she paid no attention to them; besides, she always had that big smile on her face, a smile that spread from ear to ear. She was easy to like, hard to dislike. If anyone looked at her disparagingly on the street or in the Roundhouse, she disarmed them by sauntering up to them, putting her three hundred-pound arms around them, hugged the living breath right out of them, and saying, 'Honey, you ain't half bad at all, you're all right. Come on up and see me sometime.' Then she would dance away leaving the poor guy dumbfounded, gasping for breath and wiping his brow. She could handle herself.

She began performing at the Roundhouse three nights per week. Once the word spread around town that I had hired a new and talented singer, my business quadrupled. She most assuredly could attract a crowd. The heartier she sang, the heartier they drank. The bar would be three deep by ten o'clock. In fact, I hired two additional bartenders to service the clientele. She would play and sing for hours on end. Men would buy her so many drinks that the entire top of the piano would be lined with bottles, and she could empty them, too. I don't know how she managed it, but she could sing the blues, accompany herself with mournful piano, chat with customers, drink beer and pound out eight-to-the-bar all night without loosing a beat. Of course, that prodigious body was capable of absorbing considerable liquor, but even so, it began to concern me. Sometimes she would leave after the last show, about two in the morning, with two or three men hanging on her arms like puppets on a string. I would see the entourage staggering down the street singing, slapping each other on the back, laughing. Trouble, Henry. Trouble followed Ethel. Frequently, the next evening, I would observe bruises and scratches on her arms and face, but I never asked her about them. I reasoned that she was good for my business . . . I should stay out of her's.

About a year later, I purchased Beyond The Blue Horizon up the street where I then also scheduled her. She was now working for me six nights a week, Thursdays off. She had rented a small apartment above the Coast to Coast store on Black Hawk Avenue. Occasionally, after I had cleaned up at the Roundhouse and was driving home, I would see dim lights and darting shadows up in her apartment. I knew she was entertaining, but I reasoned that was her choice. But I was concerned." Slade reached for his glass to take a healthy drink. He wiped his lips, then set the glass back on the table. With the momentary pause, Hank joined him.

"One night at Beyond The Blue Horizon, late, a drunken redneck from Boscobel taunted her about her singing. He wagered five dollars that she didn't know *Just A Closer Walk With Thee* all the way through. She looked at him, spread that famous grin from ear to ear and said, 'Honey, ya'll may have made your move too soon,' then turned around to play the most mournful hymn-like dirge I had ever heard. This wasn't the style of music she usually played and sang, but something touched her big bones that evening.

I was aware that she had been drinking heavily, but even so . . . a *Closer Walk* was fantastic. She played so slowly, sung so earthy that I didn't think she could continue the tempo . . .

> *I . . . am . . . weak . . . but . . . Thou . . . art . . . strong,*
> *Jesus, keep me from all wrong;*
> *I'll be satisfied as long,*
> *As I walk, let me walk close to Thee.*

> *Just . . . a . . . closer . . . walk . . . with . . . Thee,*
> *Grant it, Jesus, is my plea,*
> *Daily walking close to Thee,*
> *Let it be, dear Lord, let it be.*

Everyone in the club ceased what they were doing—the bartender stopped pouring drinks, the waitresses stopped serving food, the customers stopped eating . . .

> *In this world with toil and snare,*
> *If I falter, Lord, who cares,*
> *Who will all my burdens bear,*
> *None but Thee, dear Lord, none but Thee . . .*

> *Just a closer walk with Thee,*
> *Grant it, Jesus, is my plea,*
> *Daily walking close to Thee,*
> *Let it be, dear Lord, let it be.*

When Ethel arpeggiated that last chord throughout the entire breadth of the keyboard letting those lonesome bent notes float toward the blue, twinkling ceiling starlights, several moments of silence enveloped the entire nightclub before everyone burst into applause. Henry, to this day, I have never heard anything so moving. Ethel reached my soul that night. The Boscobel redneck staggered over to her, took a five-spot out of his billfold, tucked it in her prodigious cleavage saying, 'Honey, you sure 's hell can sing,' and staggered out the door.

Even though times were hard around here in the early Thirties, people needed to get out occasionally; consequently, my business was good; of course, the new Marquette suspension bridge made it much easier for you Iowans to come over instead of having to ferry across on the Rob Roy. People didn't have enough gas money to drive to La Crosse or East Dubuque. About all they could afford were a few beers and dancing on Friday or Saturday night close to home. I realized a golden business opportunity developing in spite of the hard times; therefore, I began purchasing more clubs because Wisconsonites like their beer and brats. I realized I had a pure gold mine in Ethel, too. I knew she might eventually burn herself out living the hard, fast life she did, but I wanted to experience the wildfire while I could. I hired her to sing in all of my new clubs, rotating her schedule so that every two weeks she would appear at each club. It was good while it lasted, until Ethel disappeared, but I'm getting ahead of myself.

I purchased a dive upriver in Lynxville in '31. It was a run-down joint when I first saw it, but people then weren't interested in fancy clubs anyway. I bought it for a dime, fixed it up with new linoleum-topped tables and wood chairs, scrubbed the bar and washed the walls and floors to eliminate the dead fish odor, because it had been primarily a fishermen's bar. They would clean fish on the back deck then walk in for a few brews. I retained the name—Clyde's Fish & Dish—because I reasoned that the local clientele would feel more comfortable with a familiar name. It was a good purchase. I attended the bar myself for a month, then hired a young man from Seneca to operate it full time. The place didn't have a piano; consequently, I transported one up from Prairie. I brought Ethel in on a Saturday evening for her first appearance; I believe it was the night after Thanksgiving, cold and snowing. We drove north from Prairie in my auto because, by now, her's was giving her considerable trouble; she was a horrible driver anyway, even on dry roads. It was a hell of a night to be driving, Hank. We shouldn't have even been on the road. Highway 35 north was icy and treacherous. The snow whipped over the Wisconsin bluffs, blowing and swirling in my headlights; I thought we would never arrive safely, but we did. All the way up I was thinking, 'What an unfortunate evening to introduce Ethel,' but I already discoursed to you that Wisconsin people are hearty—weather has little affect upon them. Prior to opening night I had placed advertisements in the Seneca, Eastman and Gays Mills newspapers announcing that a famous blues singer and barrel-house piano player from St. Paul would be appearing Friday night at Clyde's Fish & Dish down by the river. Henry, you can imagine my surprise when Ethel and I slid into the parking lot to find it filled, and in that snowstorm. I walked in, Ethel on my arm, and every eye in the place popped out of its socket. They certainly were not expecting a singer looking like Ethel. I believe every Old Style bottle in Clyde's rushed toward dry lips and stunned, parched throats. But Ethel wasn't fazed at all. She was used to staring whites. Remember, I said she was sassy? She released her grip from my arm, sauntered to the bar, grabbed an Old Style right out of the hands of a toothless old fart, then waddled around tables and chairs on her way to the piano, bouncing off startled customers right and left saying . . . 'How ya'll doin', folks? And what are you doin' out on a stormy night like this? Don't ya'll have 'nuff sense to stay home? Damn! As long as ya'll are here, might as well have a good time, don't you think? Drink up now while I see's what this ol' upright can do. I'm gonna lay it on you. We gotta get in the groove."

She tugged her corset higher, sucked half of that Old Style in one gulp, placed her ample posterior on the piano bench and proceeded to pound out a fast and vigorous rocking boogie-woogie just as she had done for Oscar, Bert and me the first day she sauntered into the Roundhouse. Now, Clyde's had not been constructed sturdily—only wood plank floors over high water stilts, clapboard walls and tar paper roof—so when she put her three hundred pounds to boogieing, the piano rocked, the floors rolled, the tables swayed, beer sloshed, everything tilted a couple of inches toward the river. She sent quakes right through the clientele. She hadn't played sixteen measures before the entire place started rocking with people swaying, clapping and jumping up to dance. The one waitress and one bartender I had hired couldn't keep up with the drink orders. Then they began singing along with Ethel. Let me tell you, Henry, she kept those revelers entertained for a couple of hours before she stopped, even once. By nine o'clock the top of the piano was lined with Old Style bottles like ducks waddling toward the river. Those white Wisconsin Scandinavians and Czechs, even a few Irishmen, crowded around this black woman at the piano, completely entranced by her performance. They brushed her hefty frame, now completely soaked with sweat, because all of that energy needed to be released somewhere. She pounded out *Pine Top's Boogie*, then sang a lonesome blues for a change of pace. My goodness! She could sing the blues. I recall how she moaned *Downhearted Blues* that evening . . .

> *Gee, but it's hard to love someone,*
> *When that someone don't love you.*
> *I'm so disgusted, heart broken, too,*
> *I've got the downhearted blues.*

> *Once I was crazy about a man,*
> *He mistreated me all the time.*
> *Next man I get, he's got to promise me,*
> *Be mine, all mine.*

> *Lord, he mistreated me,*
> *And he drove me from his door,*
> *Yes, he mistreated me,*
> *Drove me from his door,*
> *Ah, but the good book says,*
> *Gonna reap just what you sow.*

She sang with extraordinary vitality and meaning in her lyrics. Lonesomeness, hurt and pain dripped from her . . .

> *Lord, I walked the floor,*
> *I rang my hands and I cried.*
> *Yes, I walked the floor,*
> *I rang my hands and I cried.*
> *I had the downhearted blues,*
> *I just couldn't be satisfied.*

I ain't never loved a free man in my life,
I said I ain't never loved a free man in my life,
But my father, my brother, and a man that wrecks my life.

But I got the word of a judge,
Yes, I've got the sucker in my hands.
I got the word of a judge, sucker in my hands,
And the next man that gets me,
Have to come on down to my command.

Most of those folks had never heard a black blues singer
before. Certainly, they had heard white blues singers in La Crosse,
but a white singer doesn't emote like an ebony St. Paul songstress.
They had never heard someone sing with so much emotion, so
much feeling, so much earthy energy. When she unleashed her
lyrics you absolutely knew she had lived every word herself. As
noisy and rowdy as those folks had been when she was pounding
out the boogie-woogies, they stopped talking, stopped shouting,
only listened when she began singing *Downhearted Blues*. They
sat around the tables, closed their eyes, absorbed her blues. They
began feeling what she felt as she bent straight notes into blue
notes, as she slid into *downhearted* and *lonesome*. Henry, she was
crying notes by the time she finished, and had people dabbing there
eyes, too. But as soon as her last blue note evaporated through the
ceiling, she attacked those ivories again, got Clyde's rocking and
rolling all night.

Ethel was special, I'll tell you. To this day, I have never met
a woman like her . . . and up in her apartment? . . . well . . . she was
special there, also."

"Slade? Are you telling me you . . . too?"

"Hell, yes, Hank! I had four wives over the years, but with the
business I'm in—nightclubs, late nights, beautiful ladies—temptation, Hank, temptation," Slade rejoined as he reached the bottom
of his drink once more, "and it started that night up at Clyde's,
because while she was seducing my clientele with her songs, the
snow kept falling, furiously. By one o'clock there must have been
two feet in the parking lot. My Seneca and Eastman clientele were

hearty folks accustomed to driving snow-packed roads in those coulees along the river; besides, they only had four or five miles to drive home, but I didn't want to drive twenty back to Prairie on icy roads, so Ethel and I stayed at Clyde's throughout the evening. There were two cots in the storeroom and . . . we had had an excellent night at the bar . . . as I said, Ethel was quite a woman.

I now had booked her at Beyond The Blue Horizon on Sunday and Monday nights, Clyde's Fish and Dish on Tuesday and Wednesday nights, and the Roundhouse Bar on Thursday, Friday and Saturday nights. She certainly was a singing machine, but she also managed to find time for herself. There were many late nights I saw that dim light flickering in her apartment as I drove home. It made me lonesome, Henry . . . Ethel was special.

About the first of December in '31, I purchased another bar downriver in Cassville. The other clubs were doing well, Ethel was drawing significant crowds, so I was riding the riverboat special. The place was called Fred's Feed and Read, or some such moniker. A balding, toothless old fart served brats and fish sandwiches on weekends, only beer during the week. He also had a few books stacked along the wall beside the bar for free reading—Mark Twain's *Tom Sawyer*, *Huckleberry Finn*, *Life On The Mississippi*, *Roughing It*, I recall now; Charles Dickens' *The Old Curiosity Shop*, Hamlin Garland's *Main Travelled Roads*, O. E. Rolvaag's *Giants In The Earth*—books mostly about the river, Iowa, Minnesota and Wisconsin pioneers. A man at the Roundhouse mentioned to me one evening that this Cassville fellow wanted to sell out and go fishing for the remainder of his life. On a sunny, early December day, I hopped into my Chevy for a drive to Cassville."

Slade had become increasingly relaxed telling his story of Ethel. The Jack Daniels had slackened his mind and tongue to the point that he was dangerously close to becoming a commoner instead of a gentleman. Hank could tell he was relishing the moment, though, recalling earlier times with Ethel.

"To digress for a moment or two, friend, I wasn't born in Prairie du Chien, but I was reared in another 'Prairie' town— Prairie du Sac, an inland village near Madison—then when I moved westward to the Mississippi, I became extremely attached

to this river valley. Now, December wasn't the best month for me
to be driving, but the sun was shining so brightly through the
crystal-clear skies, snow glistening from the tops of the bluffs, a
light layer covering the trees along the river road, a crust of ice
forming on the river's shoreline that I knew the drive would be
breathtaking, and it was. Eagles were soaring from the bluffs,
walleyes were sprouting through the ice-tinged surface in search
of insects and oxygen, crappies were feeding near the surface on
whatever they could find before the next hard freeze closed the
river. I even saw deer trekking down the hills to the river's edge.

The drive was easy because the road was clear and dry from
the piercing December sun. I was soon skirting the evergreen-
covered limestone bluffs of Cassville searching for Fred's Feed,
but it didn't take long, Cassville being so tiny. My heart sank when
I located the dilapidated structure on the riverbank below the
Denniston House Hotel, but I knew what I had accomplished with
Clyde's. This place could be fixed up, also. I purchased it for a
second dime, cleaned it up and two weeks later imported Ethel.
When I escorted her in on my arm that Saturday evening before
Christmas, the reaction was the same as in Lynxville. Those gray-
haired, toothless old farts and dowdy ladies certainly weren't
anticipating a hefty black woman to be singing in their village, but
Ethel performed her act once again. Within five minutes she had
them eating out of her hand like pigeons pecking seeds. Once she
began singing, her looks were unimportant, although those folks
weren't any more accustomed to black people in their town than
the people in Prairie or Lynxville. They loved her. They knew
immediately that she was a pure gold nugget, because she played
and sang from her heart. She sat at the piano and hollered, 'I'm
gonna lay it on you, now. We gotta get in the groove—talk to me,
talk to me now." She began with *Suitcase Blues*, a rollicking
boogie-woogie, pounding and rocking that piano until I thought
she would snap the strings or break off the ivories. She flipped her
left hand up and down the bass keys playing eighth-note octaves
as fast and hard as she could for at least five minutes without
playing a single melody note. She could play a bass line and drink
beer from a bottle simultaneously. And the rhythm she generated?

You have never heard anything like it. She played with so much energy, so much fire that it would make a corpse get up out of his coffin and start dancing along the Mississippi. And you should have seen her body rocking and rolling, too. It moved in a fluid motion like waves upon the river, Henry, and I'd told you earlier she had a lot to move. Her left hand rolled, her left arm flailed, her meaty shoulders heaved, her knockers bounced, and her derriere . . . it put on a show all by itself. I'm telling you, it troubled me watching all of that movement, but business is business. She laid down such a powerful bass line that folks had difficulty remaining still. Then she would put down her Old Style to launch into a syncopating, surging melody with her right hand rolling out tremolos on the top of the keyboard. Both hands were now flailing across the keyboard—pulsing, pushing, rocking, boogieing—head pumping up and down like a cooing pigeon. Customers sitting near her got a bath, because sweat beads flew in every direction, but they didn't care. They were experiencing something they had never seen or heard in Cassville, or anywhere for that matter. That evening they stopped worrying about the Depression for a few hours. Then she stopped suddenly, changing the mood. She began playing low, mournful, soulful, lonesome blues chords. She closed her eyes, threw her head back and in a deep, gravely voice began moaning low, so soft you could hardly hear her . . .

Every day, I have the blues,
Every day, I have the blues,
Every day, I have the blues,
'Cause I'm still in love with you.

Nobody loves me, nobody seems to care,
Nobody loves me, nobody seems to care,
Bad luck seems to follow me, Baby everywhere.

But then she gradually raised her voice, singing the blues that were so deep in her soul . . .

Feelin' low in spirit with no place to go,
Feelin' low in spirit with no place to go,
My baby left me, 'cause I'm goin' down slow.

Every day, every day, every day I have the blues,
Every day, every day, every day I have the blues,
'Cause I'm still in love with you.

She touched everybody's soul that night. Even though I had heard her sing *Every Day* many times, I would have to stop serving drinks when she sang it. I don't know, Henry, if I loved her or not, but she was an extraordinary woman. She touched my soul that night.

But there was a troubled side to Ethel, also. Anyone who sang the blues with that much feeling had to have lived the blues. After performing until two o'clock, then sloshing whiskey night after night until the sun came up, I could see the fast life was taking its toll on her. Many evenings, when I was fortunate enough to accompany her to her apartment instead of her usual bar leeches, I would help her up those long, steep stairs, Ethel wheezing fiercely by the time we reached the top. Then she would say to me, 'Slade, honey, believe I needs some o' that whiskey to catch my breathin'. I would fix her a highball or two, then if she didn't pass out on the sofa, she would usually say, 'I'm so low and lonesome, honey, that I sure could use some lovin'. She was lonesome, Henry, I could see that. Afterward, I would heave and puff and flop her onto her bed before I trekked back down that lonesome stairway.

I mentioned earlier how overweight she was? All of her drinking and eating didn't help. My goodness but she loved to eat, especially barbecued chicken and ribs. We would leave Fred's or Clyde's about two o'clock, then eat at an all-night diner, getting back to Prairie at four or five. She could eat an entire chicken or slab of ribs in one sitting. She was getting heavier by the day, even needed to buy new dresses because of split seams.

I grew increasingly concerned about her. I sensed that troubles had followed her from Minnesota, but she never wanted to talk about them . . . said she had left them in St. Paul, but I knew that wasn't true. In Prairie she attracted some of the most extraordinary 'infernal scoundrels', to quote Mark Twain, that I had ever seen. Men usually hung around after her show, sometimes two or three accompanying her out the door. I was concerned with what could happen with those scoundrels hanging onto her like leeches, sucking the life out of her. Of course, I had a significant business investment and personal interest in her, also."

"Let me fill your glass one more time, Slade. You're getting dry talking on so about Ethel," Hank said as he reached for the glass.

"You're right about that. I hadn't realized I had been talking so long. Apparently this Jack Daniels has loosened my tongue. Sorry about that," Slade said as he stood to stretch.

"Don't worry about that. It's good for you to talk, and I'm fascinated with your story. I told you that Muriel and I aren't much for going to nightclubs, so although I knew of Ethel, I had never heard her sing. Many folks around here did, however. Here's a fresh cocktail.

What happened shortly before she disappeared?" Hank asked as they both relaxed in their overstuffed chairs with fresh drinks.

"Ethel had first appeared at the Roundhouse Bar in late 1930. The last time I saw her was on a Friday night in July of 1935. I remember how hot it was that week. She had been performing nightly in that muggy weather with her usual energy. She stayed to the task, not letting the excessive humidity slow her down one iota, because once she began singing, the rest of the world disappeared for her. She could perform in a snowstorm, in a Mississippi flood or on the most sultry day Wisconsin could throw at her. That night settled in my mind because I noticed something different about her face—the smile wasn't as wide, the eyes weren't as bright— something different about her singing. I remember turning to listen from the bar. I had been listening to her for five years, Henry, so I knew her songs, her style. She was an improviser, a creative blues and jazz singer who never sang a song the same way twice. That's one reason she was such a good musician. People heard her moan *Downhearted Blues* or *Empty Bed Blues* a hundred times, never once sounding the same. One night she would sing *Downhearted* with an earthy moan, the next night with a lilting sense of hope. She could pull and stretch the melody, improvising little notes above and below it, always reaching, pushing while accompanying herself with new chords, substituting rich chords for old, dried, hackneyed ones. But on that last night I heard something I had never heard before. I can't describe it, but it was sadder, deeper, more distant, more blue-lonesome than I had ever heard before. During a break when she waddled to the bar, I leaned over to ask her if she was all right. She said, 'Hell yes! Slade honey,' but there was forlornness in her eyes that I had never seen before.

About an hour before closing, as she was singing *I Gotta Get Back To My Used To Be*, I noticed a tall, heavy, surly-looking black man wearing coal-black sun glasses swagger through the door. The Roundhouse was so crowded that he had to push his way through my clientele standing three-deep around the bar. But he didn't stop at the bar; instead, he moved silently, steadily toward Ethel until he found a vacant corner table. He ordered a martini—that was different because my customers were not martini drinkers—but I prepared it, extra dry with only a sniff of vermouth, three olives, and sent it with the waitress. He sipped slowly, never taking his eyes off Ethel who had her back to him, nor looking at anyone else. For her last song of the evening she sang *Nobody Knows You When You're Down and Out*, her favorite closer. As she turned slightly on the piano bench to adjust her clinging dress, she caught a glimpse of him out of the corner of her eye. I was watching; suddenly, the quality of her voice changed from round, warm and soulful to agitated and edgy. I knew she was startled to see him, but she finished the song like a real pro. People clapped for an encore, but she was done for the evening. The man finished his martini, rose from the table, walked straight to her then leaned down to speak something into her ear. As they shoved through the crowd around the bar, Ethel leaned over to me and said, 'I'll be leavin' now, Slade. My friend here's gonna take me home . . . see you tomorrow night.' I didn't feel good about it. I wanted to hurtle the bar to put my arms around her, to protect her, but of course I was too old to clear the bar anyway. She walked out willingly with the man, appearing to be enjoying his company. I never saw Ethel again. She didn't show up the next evening nor the evening after that. I went up to her apartment, once again trekking those long stairs. It looked about the same with clothes in disarray on the couch, dirty dishes in the sink, but no Ethel. I notified the police. They never found her in Prairie du Chien. Kansas City police had never heard of her. She had vanished from my life. I'm telling you, Henry, for many years afterward, I had those *Empty Bed Blues*."

Slade slumped lower, not speaking for several moments. He reached for his glass, lifted it to his quivering lips, drained the last drop of whiskey, slowly placed it on the printer's table as he brushed his eye with an embroidered linen handkerchief. Hank watched, but said nothing. Slade looked around the shop for several minutes, finally getting out of the chair. He walked over to the rolltop desk and noticed the newspaper article about Ethel: Area Blues Singer Disappears. He dabbed his other eye, then turned to Hank, "She was one hell of a singer, one hell of a boogie player, one hell of a woman.

Now, I must be departing, my good man. I would be honored if you would stop in to the Roundhouse sometime to partake of my hospitality."

_____11

"Good morning, Hank. It was good to read your editorial about a bigger gym. There has been considerable talk around town, too, not all positive but that's to be expected," Doc said as Hank sat next to him at the cafe's counter.

"Hi, Doc. I knew I would receive a strong response but that's fine. At least we'll get the community talking. It will take some time for everyone to absorb the idea, though, what with it meaning a bond issue and higher taxes.

Good morning, Bruno. Thanks for the coffee."

"Morning to you, sir. Nice job on the editorial. We'll get people riled up now, that's for sure. It will probably take a couple of years, but you've started the process, put the gears in motion so to say.

How are your aching bones this morning? That hip still giving you trouble? I noticed a limp as you walked in," Bruno said as he once again overfilled Hank's cup, floating the saucer in coffee.

"It is bothering me. I suppose I'll need to take advantage of Doc's services here to check it out. It seems to be getting weaker and I have pain every day now, not serious, though. It's hell getting old, isn't it, fellows? I feel as if I'm becoming a maintenance problem. I was walking on the tracks to Marquette the other day, trying to walk the rails like we did when we were boys. Fifty years ago I could balance-walk the rail from McGregor to Marquette, an entire mile, but now? Shoot! I couldn't take but one or two steps on the darn thing before falling off. But then if I've gotten older you fellows aren't far behind. You know what Mark Twain said about aging, don't you? Gentlemen, I quote . . . 'It takes some little time to accept and realize the fact that while you have been growing old, your friends have not been standing still in that matter.' I read that a couple of nights ago in his *Life On The Mississippi*. So you see gentlemen, you're aging right along with me. Speaking of age, where is Charlie this morning?"

"I believe his wife coerced him into driving to Mason City for a couple of days . . . visit relatives or something like that. Charlie didn't want to go, but he didn't have a choice in the matter," Bruno hollered from the steaming grill. "What'll you have for breakfast? French toast or eggs?"

"Make it eggs with a side order of hash browns. And sunny-side up on the eggs, not your usual over-hard variety."

"Coming right up. Two eggs, over-hard!"

"I stopped at the house to see your mother yesterday, Hank. Do you have a moment to talk about her?" Doc said slurping coffee, then tucking his fingers into his vest pockets while turning to face Hank.

"Sure, Doc. What did you find out? How is her cold?"

"She doesn't have a cold. I've been doctoring her since I opened my clinic, so I know every ache and pain she has had. This doesn't look good, Hank. I think we have trouble," Doc responded while twisting his coffee cup with those fine, slim surgeon hands. Doc's words caught Hank off guard. He had gone about his usual morning routine, then walked to the cafe recalling Slade Slocum's story about Ethel Matters. Catherine's consumption hadn't entered his mind. Suddenly, his face flushed, his hands tingled.

"Trouble? What do you mean? Mother has always fought off sickness. This is just something normal, something she can shake, isn't it?"

"I'm afraid not. She has congestive heart failure. Her lungs are filling up with fluid making it difficult for her to breath. Those lungs and heart have worked for ninety-five years. The condition causes a slow deterioration of the lungs in which they eventually fill with fluid; the heart loses its ability to pump efficiently. It looks, Hank . . . well, it looks bad," Doc said as he diverted his eyes from the empty cup directly into Hank's worried, haggard eyes. Hank didn't respond for a few moments, staring instead out the window while sipping cold coffee. Bruno overheard the conversation from the grill, but he respected the moment. He placed Hank's eggs in front of him, then hulked back to the grill without saying a word— highly unusual for Bruno. After a couple of minutes Hank turned, placed his hand on Doc's arm, "How long, Doc?"

"At her age, three months, six at the most. She'll probably acquire pneumonia and that will hasten her condition." Bob Burdick sauntered in and sat at the counter, placing a dime on the counter for a cup of coffee. A couple of minutes later Michael McTaggart followed giving "Top o' the mornings" all around, but Hank didn't respond to either fellow. He didn't even notice Samantha sneak in the back door and sit by herself in a corner booth. He whispered to Doc, "I'm almost seventy and Catherine has been around all of those seventy years. I have never known a time *without* her, and I have never known a time *with* my father. It's odd, isn't it? Live your entire life with one, not even knowing the other. I cannot imagine her not being here. Isn't there anything we can do? Isn't there medicine she can take to improve her condition? Should I take her to Arizona's drier climate? There must be something we can do," Hank pleaded as he nibbled at his eggs, eventually setting his fork on the counter having lost his appetite.

Bruno's over-hard eggs and greasy potatoes no longer appealed to him. He pushed the plate away.

Doc pondered for several moments before responding to Hank's pleading. He was a talented physician with those wonderful hands, but he was equally as sensitive and talented with human emotions. Regardless of the years of chiding and barbs thrown between he and his friend sitting next to him, this was a tender moment, difficult for both of them. "I'm afraid not, Henry. She's simply wearing out. Her heart is loosing its energy, like your car did last year. Only thing is, you could get an overhaul to regain compression, but medicine doesn't have an overhaul procedure yet for failing hearts and lungs. Drier Arizona air might help her head, but it won't help her heart. It's time, Hank. It's just time."

"I've lost my appetite, Doc. Thanks for looking in on Mother. I'll stop by the clinic later this afternoon to pay on the bill.

Bye, Bruno. I'll see you later," Hank said as he flipped two dollars on the counter and walked toward the door without bidding farewell to anyone. Bruno didn't chide him. Even he had sense enough to keep his mouth shut this morning.

Hank trudged toward the shop without noticing Cletus sweeping the first fallen leaves of autumn in the gutters. Cletus took off his cap and waved to him, began stuttering a greeting, but saw that Hank was distracted. Cletus was confused. He reached into his bib pocket and pulled out two sticks of Juicy Fruit gum. Other people frequently didn't greet him, but Hank always did. Hank shuffled toward the office, but absentmindedly walked past to the docks. The sun was rising later over the Wisconsin hills these mornings and farther to the south; a remnant of the evening's chill still enveloped the valley, greenish mist shrouded the river. He walked onto the dock to the end, pulled his suit collar up around his sagging neck to ward off the morning chill and dampness, then stood looking out over the fog-shrouded river. No one was on the dock yet which gave him an opportunity to be alone with his thoughts. He was greatly saddened by Doc's news, greatly saddened by the thought of loosing his mother.

Is this what getting old means?

But he suddenly felt self-centered, realizing he was thinking more of himself—how his mother's impeding death would affect him—than of Catherine's pain. And he thought about his unknown father, too.

Will I ever know?

He grabbed a three-legged canvas stool from a fishing boat, opened it and sat on the dock as the sun fought its way through the fog, periodically cutting through to dazzle his moist eyes. The sun's energy startled him into realizing that he should think about his mother instead of feeling sorry for himself. He shuffled off the dock with a quicker pace, resolving to be the best son he could be during her remaining time. He vowed to do whatever he could to make these final months, happy months for Catherine.

As he stepped from the dock to the boat ramp, a grizzled, mustachioed man wearing a nautical-braided cap and fishing vest stepped onto the dock. Hank was several steps up the ramp when the man hollered, "Ahoy there, mate! Aren't you the editor of the local newspaper?" Hank turned slowly when he realized the man was speaking to him.

"That's correct. My name is Henry, but folks call me Hank. Do I know you?"

"No, mate, I don't believe you do, but I recognized you from your picture in the *North Iowa Times* . . . moniker is Thomas Merrick. I reside on the island in Guttenberg, but I'm a towboat captain, so I steam through here quite often. I seldom get an opportunity to be here, on shore that is, but I'm meeting a fishing mate this morning. He said the crappies are biting well on the back side of Sturgeon Lake in a hidden cove just beyond the West Channel. I seldom pass up an opportunity to catch good-frying crappies," Thomas said stroking his long handlebar mustache.

"Towboat captain? Which one?"

"The Hawkeye State out of the Port of Keokuk. As I said, I reside in Guttenberg but I have to drive downriver to Keokuk to get my towboat, but that isn't so bad because in the tow-shipping business I work an entire month, six-hour watches, twenty-four hours a day, then I have a month off. It's an odd schedule, but I love the river . . . wouldn't trade it for anything, especially landlocked work," Thomas said, setting his tackle box and rod on the dock.

This chance meeting of Thomas momentarily distracted Hank from Doc's disturbing report. He had wanted to be alone to contemplate Catherine's illness, but he was perked with Grant's demeanor. Thomas didn't let him go; he continued. "I have many long hours to fill when I'm on duty, so I try my hand at writing prose, and I read a great deal—novels, history of the river, newspapers—it's a hobby, particularly newspaper editions from Guttenberg, Monona, Garnavillo, Dubuque, Prairie du Chien, even your *North Iowa Times* just to keep up with the goings-on along the river. I know you are a riverman at heart, mate, even if you are landlocked here pushing your typewriter most of the day. I've read many of your editorials—sort of hard on the mayor, aren't you?—as well as your River Reflections essays about the Upper Mississippi Valley; you have a good way with words.

I've spent most of my sixty years piloting boats of one kind or another in these waters," Thomas said sweeping his arm in a wide arc toward the river. "Say, mate! How would you like to accompany me on the Hawkeye State towboat sometime? You could join me on a shipping trip, then write a modern-day account of your journey just like Mark Twain did in the 1880s when he gathered information for *Life On The Mississippi*. I know you admire his writing and wit, because you quote him often in your River Reflections column. You've certainly read *Life On The Mississippi*?"

"Of course I've read it. Do you read Twain also? But I guess that's a forgone conclusion; any riverman would read him. I read *Life* in high school; coincidentally, I'm re-reading it now."

"How about it then, sir? Does that not sound like an excellent idea? You would be experiencing the river first-hand. After the trip, you could write essays about the experience; additionally, we could have enlightening conversations instead of my usual unintelligent meanderings with deck hands. Although I have navigated these waters hundreds of times, always enjoying them, the company aboard is frequently less than inspiring.

Have you ever ridden on a towboat?"

"No, sir, I haven't, but it is something I would enjoy. I've seen tows passing our levee for most of my life. I piloted fishing boats, scows and rafts as a boy, and I've ridden the Delta Queen on excursions up to Lansing and down to Dubuque, but no, I have never steamed on a towboat. I might accept your offer in the future, Thomas, but I . . . ah . . . I have just received some bad . . . well, some disturbing news concerning my mother's health. The future is uncertain at this moment. And, of course, I would have to get a substitute to edit the paper while I was away, something I've never done before. What length of trip are you suggesting?"

"There are several options, sir, depending on the amount of time you would have. Until the main channel is closed by ice, which is usually about the end of November, I'll primarily be shipping wheat between St. Paul and St. Louis, cruising past here about every three weeks. I assemble my tow in Keokuk, transport corn and wheat from there to St. Louis, unload, then reassemble a salt and fertilizer tow for the upriver trip to St. Paul. On arrival I exchange the Louisiana salt for Minnesota and Dakota wheat before running back downriver, loading additional grain ship- ments at Red Wing. We unload the grain at St. Louis for shipment by rail to the East and West coasts. The round trip takes about fourteen days depending on weather and river conditions. You could join me for all or part of one round trip. There is a nip in the air today, so I suppose I have about only four trips before Old Man Winter socks this river in. Shipping begins again after the ice releases the river from its vise grip around mid-March."

"That does sound exciting. I'm pleased with your offer, but my future is . . . well . . . with mother's condition, uncertain. But I would like to do it, someday," Hank said as the two men walked toward the bait shop on shore. "Give me your phone number in Guttenberg, and I'll get back to you when I know more. You can always call me at the shop."

"Aye, aye, sir!

Do you want to come fishing with us today? Those crappies will be flashing white water out there, chomping at any bait we throw at them."

"Not today. Thanks. I'll call you," Hank said as he trudged up the boat ramp toward Main Street. He waved to Thomas as he reached the sidewalk, and as the sun finally broke through the green mist flooding the valley with sunlight, he found himself battling mixed emotions—sadness about his mother's heart failure, a sense of excitement about steaming his beloved Mississippi on a towboat.

On the way to the shop he thought about the impending river trip next spring. He had often wondered what it was about this region, this river that attracted him. He wondered if it were only a matter of a known environment, that he had simply been born, raised and lived sixty-nine, soon to be seventy years here. He had never had a desire to move to larger inland Iowa cities like Iowa City or Des Moines or Waterloo. He had never had a desire to live in the central or western Iowa farm belts, either. They held no attraction for him. He believed that if he had been raised in inland, landlocked towns such as Mason City, Osage or Spencer that he would have eventually migrated eastward to the river. The extra–ordinary beauty of the river valley was an obvious magnet, but he wondered about the magnetism of the river itself. He believed there was a connection with his soul, his spirituality in those waters. The expansive river offered a sense of openness, a sense of excitement. When he periodically drove Muriel and Catherine fifty or sixty miles inland, even though he enjoyed driving through the sprawling prairie to gaze upon waving fields of golden grain and endless, horizon-stretching verdant fields of corn, he would feel a sense of confinement, lonesomeness creep over him. Emerald corn to the horizon was pure gold to farmers, but to a riverman like Hank, it was to be enjoyed on a Sunday afternoon drive, not for an eternity. Passing field upon field of quavering tassels, he often thought of Huckleberry Finn . . . 'Other places do seem so cramped up and smothery, but a raft don't. You feel mighty free and easy and comfortable on a raft . . .' Hank always enjoyed returning home, to the river. He had often pondered these feelings, had written several essays about it for the River Reflections column, yet he had never truly understood these feelings. Maybe it was impossible to put the Mississippi into words as Mark Twain had attempted, and for the most part, succeeded. But even as great a writer as he was, Twain couldn't fully capture its character, either. Maybe that was the point. Writing stories about the river, poetry about the river, even taking photos of the river was like trying to experience God—the attempt was good, the result was failure. *Being* on the river, *feeling* its waters splashing against your face, *hearing* its music was the way his soul was one with the river. As he reached the front door of the shop, he turned to look over the main channel, feeling the warm sun strike his face. He was glad Catherine had brought him to these waters.

The shop was warm and cozy as he entered, sun splashing through the windows. He was intent on continuing his archival search. He lit the gas stove to reheat yesterday's coffee, walked toward the stacks, but stopped suddenly with his foot on the first rung. He shuffled back to his chair and slumped heavily into its lumpy cushion and protruding springs. Today, he didn't have the motivation to search and read. Catherine's condition was having a significant impact on his mood; he sat, brooding about his mother . . . and father.

"HANK! What in hell you doin' just sittin' there?" Bernie shouted as he banged his paunch on the Linotype and printer's table on his walk to the back. "You ought to be out fishin' or somethin'. It's a great looking day, not one to be sitting here in the dark. We won't have many more like this before snowflakes start blowin' over the bluffs. Want to go fishin' with me, have a few beers?"

"Hello, Bernie. Thanks for the offer. I'll join you one of these days, but my hip is bothering me too much today to sit in a boat," Hank answered as he was startled out of his melancholic reverie.

"Somethin' wrong, Henry? You ain't your usual self. You down or somethin'?" Bernie asked.

"I'm all right. My hip is aching, that's all. Would you like a cup of coffee? It's yesterdays but it's hot," Hank asked as he slowly rose and ambled toward the stove.

"I'd prefer a Dubuque Star, but I guess coffee'll do if you ain't offering beer," Bernie said slumping heavily into the rocking chair. A couple of minutes later, Cletus entered carrying two long-handled brooms. He shuffled to the back banging the brooms off the counter and the Linotype, finally leaning them against the printer's table. "M . . . M . . . Mornin' . . . M . . . Mister . . . Hank.

M . . . M . . . Morning, B . . . Bernie," Cletus said as he pulled up a Windsor chair and sat with a thump and cloud of dust.

"Good morning, Cletus. It's nice to see you. Would you like a cup of coffee? It's yesterday's but it's hot," Hank asked.

"S . . . S . . . Sure. I . . . I'd like s . . . some c . . . coffee."

"Thanks for delivering the papers. I have your pay here in the drawer. You do a good job of distributing the *Times*. I appreciate it as does everyone else in the villages."

"Y . . . Y . . . You're welcome," Cletus answered while attempting but failing to cross his massive legs.

"How you doin' there, Cletus?" Bernie said slapping him on the back causing dust to fly onto the chair, Bernie and the printer's table.

"I . . . I . . . I'm d . . . doin' jus' f . . . fine. G . . . G . . . Got to sweep the street to the boat ramp yet t . . . today. Lots of l . . . leaves."

"You're one hell of a sweeper, I'll say that for you . . . ain't much of a job, though, if you was askin' me. HEY! HANK, you want to slip some Jack Daniels in that coffee?" Bernie hollered to Hank standing at the stove.

"I don't believe so. Let's have only strong coffee instead of strong booze. And, Bernie? I have to take you to task about Cletus' job. He has a good one and he does it well. He is dedicated, consistent, responsible, and does the village a great service. I would like to see you get a responsible job, too," Hank said while serving coffee to both visitors.

"I know, Henry, but work and me don't seem to get along so good. I get a job selling worms and minnows at the bait shop, or hosing down the docks after fishermen clean their catch, but after a few days, I get myself all bored; rather be just sittin' on the dock fishin'," Bernie said accepting the hot mug from Hank.

"That's all right for you then, but I wouldn't berate Cletus for sweeping the streets."

"Sorry, Cletus. I apologize. You're a hell of a sweeper."

"T . . . T . . . Thanks, B . . . B . . . Bernie."

"What you gents doin' just sittin' and sippin'?" Samantha said as she joined the congregation around the stove. "Mornin', Cletus . . . Bernie . . . Hank. You got more o' that bitter coffee, Hank? I could use a cup," Sam said plopping her camera onto the printer's table.

"Good morning, Samantha. How nice to see you. Hot coffee coming right up."

Sam, Bernie, Cletus and Hank sat around the potbellied stove for a couple of hours chatting. Samantha told about taking sunset photos from Indian Isle. Bernie told about fishing for catfish in the main channel, and Cletus told—stuttered the best he could—about sweeping the streets clean of leaves, cigarette butts, and empty beer bottles. Hank listened. On other coffee klatch days he talked considerably, because the gang liked hearing his stories. He was as good of a story teller as he was a writer and editor, but not today. He had wanted to be alone—to think, to brood—yet this distraction was good for him.

After a couple of hours of coffee and conversation, the klatch broke up leaving Hank alone once again. A blustery gray cloud had swept over the bluff behind the shop as the group was chatting, so by the time he locked the front door and walked home, a cold, damp wind had invaded the valley. He knew it wouldn't be long before snowflakes began sticking to his beard on his walks.

____12

Over the next two months, Hank and Muriel watched Catherine closely. There was no sudden, drastic change in her condition, but rather, a gradual, persistent evidence of entropy. Her breathing became more shallow, her appetite more diminished, her disposition more quiet, withdrawn. At Thanksgiving dinner she hardly touched her turkey, mashed potatoes and pumpkin pie. She no longer liked sitting in the straight-backed dining chairs, preferring instead the sofa or better yet, her bed. Watching his mother deteriorate greatly troubled Hank, but he knew it was a natural process. After all, she was ninety-five. After dinner, he and Muriel assisted Catherine up to bed, then he went for a walk and a smoke in the neighborhood to walk off his dinner. Even though the weather had become overcast and cold—usually snowed by Thanksgiving in the valley—he liked walking, especially after a full meal. He slipped on a topcoat, hat and gloves before walking out into the blustery night. Instead of heading toward the river, he walked away from it through Methodist Hollow. It was dark now, no one else on the street, making it a good time to be alone with his thoughts. Through stained-glass windows, he saw other families still dining on Thanksgiving fare. He was happy for them, but saddened knowing this would probably be the last Thanksgiving with Catherine. The old Grim Reaper waited for no woman, no man. He pulled the collar higher around his neck and tugged his hat lower as a brisk wind whirled from the top of the hollow. Walking the incline to the end of the street, he stood for a long time—pensive, melancholy—looking over the houses below him. He knew he should be giving thanks for his own tolerable health, for a loving wife, and for sixty-nine years with a warm, kind and loving mother. Once again, he realized he was feeling unduly sorry for himself instead of thinking about Catherine.

It's time to get out of this pitiable mood. It's time to make the best of her condition.

By the time he walked in the door, he had resolved to be upbeat for his mother's remaining time.

"Don't you think the village could use new Christmas decorations?" Bruno asked as Hank joined the klatch for breakfast, "and maybe you could write an editorial about that," he suggested while once again overflowing Hank's coffee into the saucer.

"You never stop, do you, Bruno? If you aren't harping about a new gym or the pot-holed streets or the decaying docks, it's the Christmas decorations. Why don't you run for mayor? then I could criticize your policies in my editorials. You hold forth here in the cafe and agitate. That's what you are, Bruno, an agitator," Hank snarled as he burned his tongue on the steaming coffee.

"Damn right, Hank. I am an agitator. This town needs agitation. It's too complacent. We've set a pine tree in the middle of

Main Street for twenty years now, stringing a few measly lights on it and calling it a Christmas decoration while the rest of the village is dark and depressing. We should have lights strung on the docks and all the way up Main Street from street light to street light. We ought to showcase our town. Folks would then come sightseeing for the holidays just like they do when the leaves turn colors. We got to sell this town, Hank. A measly old pine tree in the middle of the street with a couple of hardware-store-variety blue lights on it, traffic hazard at that, doesn't do it, does it, Doc?" Bruno said while blowing Chesterfield smoke through his gapped teeth at the congregation.

"You might be right, Bruno," Doc responded while hanging his suit coat over a chair, "but people don't go sightseeing much at Christmas anyway. They stay home with families. Now, what I would like to see is for someone to build a ski run and lodge on top of one of these bluffs, maybe up there on McGregor Heights. You know, at one time there was a lodge and a one hundred foot tower up there from which you could see four states . . . brought lots of people to the village. A ski lodge would bring people and make us economically stronger during the winter months to balance out the loss of summer boaters. Why don't you write an article about that, Hank?"

"You guys sure are scheduling the work for me, but I'm getting tired. I have a birthday the twenty-ninth of next month; I'll be seventy. I'm going to retire to let a younger editor take over and write those editorials."

"Did I hear him correctly, Doc? Did he say retire? I never thought I'd hear him say that word," Bruno said placing the coffee pot on the counter directly in front of Hank and Doc while leaning down to look directly into Hank's haggard eyes.

"I believe you did," Doc answered. "None of us can go on forever. I'm sixty-two and have been thinking about retiring, too. Charlie left for that Florida winter retirement community a couple of days ago, so we won't see him again until spring. I'm thinking about becoming a Florida 'snowbird' next winter myself," Doc announced as he chomped into one of Bruno's dried cinnamon rolls.

How is Catherine, Hank?"

"She gets weaker every day, Doc, slowing down. I'm terribly disturbed about it, but I'm resolved to make her remaining days as comfortable as I can. At least she doesn't seem to be suffering, just wearing out. I only hope we can have a pleasant Christmas."

"Give me a call if she gets too uncomfortable. I can always stop by the house," Doc answered checking this watch.

"Thanks, Doc."

___13

On Christmas Eve Hank had a long, personal tradition of presenting gifts to less fortunate people. He had had a good life, so he wanted to share food baskets with those who had a harder time. He had a standing tradition of inviting Cletus, Bernie and Samantha to his shop for an afternoon toast and food baskets, then visiting some folks having hard times. This year he drove to Methodist Hollow to deliver a basket to Olga Torgelson, up Walton's Hollow to drop off a basket to Claus Baumgartner, back to Prospect Street to chat with Adolph and Norma Kurz, drove around the bluff to the Marquette bench to share baskets with Margaret O'Day, and finally, to the Marquette Hotel. It was the hardest stop of all, because he had to climb the rickety stairs, walk through the narrow, dark hall past the stinking toilet all the way to the end to find Elizabeth Grant where she lived in a ten by ten dilapidated room, alone. He stepped on the creaking boards, out of breath, and knocked on her door. He heard a rustling noise—the door opened slowly. Two blood-shot, drained and gaunt eyes glared at him around the partially opened door. "Elizabeth? It's Hank from the newspaper. I have a Christmas basket for you."

"Hello, Henry. Won't you please step in?" Hank was apprehensive about entering, as in previous visits, but he couldn't avoid it. He carried the basket into a one-room cell with only a single brass bed, dresser, chair and tiny plastic radio playing Burl Ives'

Frosty The Snowman. The room was littered with cigarette butts, wine bottles and paraphernalia Elizabeth had picked up on the streets, paraphernalia she sold for her meager existence. The odor was dank. He didn't sit.

"I've brought fresh fruit, Elizabeth—apples, bananas, grapefruits and melons. You'll also find cheese, sausages and crackers in here. Merry Christmas!"

"Thank you, Henry. You're a kind man. You never forget me at Christmas; other folks do, but you don't," Elizabeth said touching him lightly on the arm.

"I wish I could do more. Stop into the shop if you need anything." He reached out to shake her bony hand, but impulsively reached around her thin shoulders to give her a hug, "Merry Christmas, Elizabeth. Merry Christmas!" He walked rapidly down the catacomb hall, bare light bulb burning fiercely, wiping tears from his eyes. By the time he had stepped outside into the cold, fresh air, it was snowing. He looked back up to the curtain-less window in Elizabeth's room. She was standing there waving . . . "Merry Christmas, Elizabeth."

After a Christmas Eve dinner of oyster stew and crackers, Muriel, Catherine and Hank adjourned to the parlor to open gifts. The stew had been a tradition with Catherine's parents, one that had been accepted into Hank and Muriel's life, also. Hank had been apprehensive throughout the day about opening gifts, painfully aware that this would probably be his last Christmas with Catherine. But by the time they retired to the parlor, he was determined to be cheerful—a couple of hearty brandies would help. He went to the cupboard to pour two snifters for Muriel and himself. "Would you like a little brandy, Mother? It would make you feel nice and warm on this cold night," Hank asked as Muriel helped Catherine to the sofa near the Christmas tree.

"Yes . . . believe I will what with it being Christmas Eve and all, but just a touch," Catherine said as she eased her tiny, frail body into the corner of the sofa. Muriel made her more comfortable by placing a pillow behind her back. As Hank handed Catherine and

Muriel brandy snifters, he proposed a toast . . . "Merry Christmas! Mother. Merry Christmas! Muriel. To the women I love most in all of this world. To this Christmas and to many more." The three raised their glasses in toast, then sipped the tangy brandy as all eyes simultaneously looked to the twinkling tree.

"Merry Christmas! Son. Merry Christmas! Muriel. Of course, I don't know how many more Christmases I'll be around. This is probably my last before passing on . . . [cough]. This . . . brandy, [cough] . . . is tart."

"Merry Christmas! Catherine. Merry Christmas! Henry. And Mother, don't be talking that way. You'll outlive both Henry and me."

They exchanged gifts for the next hour while sipping brandy and snacking on a fluffy cheesecake Muriel had prepared. Hank played Christmas records on the new 45-rpm player—Bing Crosby's *White Christmas*, Perry Como's *Oh, Holy Night*, Gene Autry's *Rudolph The Red-Nose Reindeer*. After a couple of snifters his melancholy had lifted somewhat. He was enjoying this night with Catherine and Muriel, not thinking much about the future. They finished opening gifts then sat for a long time watching the candles flicker, wicks burning slowly and dripping wax onto the candle holder. Catherine looked content having emptied her snifter, coughing periodically, even asking Hank for a "touch" more. He poured another two fingers into her snifter then placed the Waterford cut-glass decanter on the coffee table. They watched the candles flickering, casting dancing shadows on the ceiling. Silence—warm, comfortable, peaceful—enveloped the room.

"Your father? . . . he was . . . [cough] . . . Heavens to Betsy! . . . I should talk to you about your father before I go," Catherine whispered shattering the silence like breaking glass.

"Go? Where are you going?" Hank blurted, ears suddenly pierced by Catherine's words.

"Oh, for heavens sake! You both know I'm dying. I know I'm passing on. It's all right. We all have to do it. Actually, I'm looking forward to it. Sometimes I wake up in the morning disappointed that I'm still alive. After you've lived ninety-five years like I have, the prospect of dying isn't so bad. I've had my time," Catherine said as she twisted on the sofa to get more comfortable. Hank sat across from her in the wing chair, Muriel to his left in an over-stuffed chair. "I need to talk to you about your father, Henry. I want you to know before I pass on. It's difficult for me, as you well know, but it isn't fair to you not to know about him. My time is coming."

Hank couldn't believe what he was hearing. Adrenaline surged through his body, but he remained externally calm, not wanting to deter Catherine. He looked at Muriel. She returned his look with wondering, questioning glances, but remained silent also, electing to let Catherine speak at her own pace.

"Your father's name was John Dalton. Your suspicions of a few days ago were correct, Son; I *was* one of the young ladies cavorting with the cub pilots. We had several rendezvous' back in '78 and '79, and let me tell you, they were wonderful. But my pride over the past seventy years has caused me to hold it all in. I know I should have talked to you—I tried many times—and to others years ago, but I just couldn't bring myself to it, but now that I'm dying . . . [cough] . . . I want to tell you.

John was a cub pilot on the John J. Roe steamboat. As you know, Henry, being the historian you are, steamboats docked frequently at the Port of McGregor in those years. Land's sake! It was an exciting time in the village when a stern-wheeler or side-wheeler glided into our wharf. Mother and father didn't want me to mingle with the riffraff from the steamers, but you know I have a mind of my own. I would dress in my finest to stand on the levee as the steamers slid into port. It was in the summer of 1878 that John first descended the gangplank, tipped his cap to me, intro-duced himself and asked if I would like to join him for a sarsapa-rilla. Of course I was interested, but I didn't show it too soon. I opened my parasol to shade my face from the sun, looked out over the river for a few moments, then when I could see that he was properly agitated, accepted his offer. We walked up the boardwalk to the American House Hotel—Mother was aghast later from this news, saying it was a bordello and certainly not a proper place for her daughter to be seen—where he purchased two sarsaparillas. We enjoyed them on the veranda while he talked on and on about steamboating, as I recall, what with him being all excited about being a full-fledged pilot someday. Goodness gracious! but he was a charming and attractive young man in his blue uniform. We just didn't have any young men like that in the village, and to be a pilot in training? Well! There wasn't any higher calling . . . [cough].

"Mother, may I get you some consumption medicine?" Muriel asked as she hurried to Catherine.

"Never you mind, Muriel. Tonight, I'd prefer more brandy. Hank? As I was saying, we enjoyed our chat; John said he would be steaming through McGregor on another trip later in the fall before ice closed the river, and that he hoped I would be at the wharf to meet him. Land sakes! I was impressed with that handsome young man, but I was coy . . . wasn't born yesterday, you know, so I didn't play my hand out too rapidly. I said that if my social calendar wasn't filled, I would be at the wharf for the next docking of the John Roe. He brushed my cheek lightly with his lips then raced up the gangplank, waved to me from the pilot house as the Roe backed out into the main channel, chimneys billowing pitch-black smoke. The captain rang that big bell, the steam whistle pierced the valley and John was gone. That's how it began, Son. That's how I met your father."

Hank had so many questions. He had wanted to interrupt Catherine, but knew it would be best if he simply let her talk. He drank heartily from his snifter trying to calm the fire burning in him as she adjusted the pillows and resumed her tale. "He kept his word, good as gold it was, and returned that fall. Of course I was there to meet him, in spite of mother's objections. John was terribly excited to see me, so much so that he hugged me right there on the wharf in front of everyone. A few eyes skittered and glared at me from the milling crowd, but I didn't mind. I wasn't as Victorian as some folks around here would have you believe. My lady friends weren't either. Heavens! I even used to go dancing Saturday evenings at the Dousman Hotel along the river front in Prairie, and I also attended performances at the Athenaeum Opera House in McGregor, unescorted mind you.

John was training under a Mister LaPointe, I recall, running freight and passengers from St. Louis to St. Paul. Then the bitter winter of '78 and '79 closed the river until the middle of March in

'79 when the Roe made its third docking in McGregor. It had been a long, bleak winter, Son. I was mighty lonesome . . . [cough] . . . in love and terribly anxious for him to return. I have to tell you, well . . . it's hard speaking about it, but . . . but when John docked it was . . . you two know . . . it was hard staying apart. As fate would have it, the steamboat had an overnight stay . . . and . . . well . . . two young persons in love? . . . you know . . . I . . . we . . . [cough] . . . [cough]." Catherine reclined into the pillows and tried to breath deeply, but her breath was coming only in short, spasmodic spurts. She hadn't talked this much in a long time. Hank and Muriel could tell it was tiring her, but Hank couldn't, didn't stop her. He had waited too long to hear her story.

"The next morning before the Roe left port, as we were standing on the wharf, John proposed. He said he would have a ring for me on the next trip upriver. I accepted his proposal while hugging him there on the wharf, in spite of old maid, spinster eyes burrowing into me. He kissed me directly on the lips, raced up the gangplank and waved furiously as the steamer backed out into easy water. I was the happiest young lady in McGregor.

The Roe's next trip was downriver to New Orleans, so I wasn't to see him for a couple of months. In the meantime . . . Henry? . . . [cough] . . . I became "pg" with you. And in 1879, in this conservative village, that was the worst of sins. Mother wanted to send me to the Benedictine Convent in Dubuque for a year to have the baby, but I put my foot down on that. I loved my mother, but I was persistent about staying here. I loved John. He was going to marry me. So what if we weren't yet married. I told you before that I wasn't all that Victorian. We would be married, at least engaged, on his next trip upriver. Only . . . only . . ." Tears welled up in Catherine's eyes, her frail body shaking; she wheezed and coughed vigorously . . . "one day I picked up the *North Iowa Times* to read of a disastrous explosion north of St. Louis in which the John Roe's boilers exploded one black night causing her to sink immediately. Ninety-eight passengers and the entire crew were lost. The pilot, Mister Cormack, and cub-pilot John Dalton were listed as dead along with ninety-eight passengers . . . [cough]. I was devastated, and "pg." Mother consoled me the best she could, but

I thought my life was over. John had written a letter indicating his love and intention to marry me on the next trip upriver. I showed it to your grandmother which quieted her heart, somewhat. I still have the letter upstairs. Mother supported me, graciously, courageously for the next seven months. She stood firmly by my side while withstanding blistering, withering sarcasm from 'well-intentioned' ladies in the village. You were born December 29, 1879 to Catherine Brandenburg and John Dalton."

The silence in the parlor was deafening. Catherine reclined on the pillows; Muriel wrung her hands nervously as Hank slouched lower, sipping his brandy and staring at the flickering Christmas candles. After all of these years, he finally had a name, he finally had a father he could identify. He rose slowly from the chair, walked over to Catherine, leaned down and kissed her on the cheek. He took out his handkerchief and wiped the tears streaming down her face, "Thanks, Mom, I love you. John . . . John Dalton."

After Catherine composed herself, she continued. "He was an honorable, handsome, intelligent, witty, gentle and kind man. I'm sorry you didn't get a chance to know him, but you look like him, Son. Every day for the past sixty-nine years, I've seen him in you. I lost a husband, but I gained a son.

I'm tired now. Please help me up to bed?"

After helping Catherine upstairs, Hank returned to the parlor. He poured one final brandy, lit a cigar and a couple of fresh candles, then turned out the reading lamps to sit in the warm glow of the flickering candles and twinkling Christmas tree lights. He had difficulty comprehending what he had just heard. For so many years, he had felt he was a bastard. Children in grade school had made fun of him, taunted him because he didn't have a father. They said he was the son of Injun Joe who lived in the caves above Marquette. They said he wasn't any better than Huck Finn, uglier and dumber, too. Hank had had to endure those taunts, that chiding. Even in adult life some villagers continued to look askance at him. But tonight, he finally had a father. He wasn't a bastard anymore. He was a son.

____14

Because of Christmas and New Year's activity, Hank's birthday on the twenty-ninth usually crept up on him. And this was a big one, too . . . seventy. Was seventy old? His fiftieth hadn't bothered him. Even turning sixty was easy enough, but he wondered if now he would begin feeling like an old man. He hoped not. Other than his aching hip, he felt fine.

Although Hank had momentarily forgotten his approaching birthday, Muriel didn't. After a day of editing at the shop he had returned home to find the dining room and parlor gaily decorated with banners and balloons, and Benny Goodman's *King Porter Stomp* flowing from the record player. Muriel was sensitive to his feelings—turning seventy wasn't too old for a festive birthday. She had prepared his favorite meal of baked chicken with half-baked potatoes, topped off with a birthday cake filled with sixty-nine candles, a larger seventieth directly in the center. Catherine was feeling well enough today to join them at the table. As Hank huffed and puffed on the candles, Muriel offered a toast. "To Henry, my dear husband. May you have the happiest of birthdays, and may you have many, many more." Catherine rose slowly from the table, grasped her wine glass, raised the shaking goblet elbow high to offer her toast, "I'm not going to have anymore birthdays, but to you, Son, Happy Birthday! from your old mother . . . and from your father, John."

"Thanks, Mom. Thanks, Muriel. I've been blessed spending so many years with the two loveliest woman I could ever know. "Happy New Year! to both of you," Hank answered as they clinked glasses in a toast. "Let's adjourn to the parlor, Mother, for Muriel's angel food cake. It is my favorite, you know," Hank said holding Catherine by the arm and leading her to the sofa. As Catherine settled into the soft cushions, breathing easier today, she said, "It's difficult for me to believe that in a couple more days it will be 1950. Why, I was born way back in 1854. I won't make it to one hundred, because that's five years down the road."

"Of course you will, Mother. You have good genes. You will probably outlive both Muriel and myself. I'll bet you will be having parties here after we're gone, singing and dancing the night away. You'll go on forever, if you ask me," Hank said tipping his wine glass toward her.

"I doubt that . . . [cough] . . . Son. I doubt that very much. I'm tired now. Help me upstairs. It's been a nice birthday party."

"I will in a moment, Mother, but first, I have an announcement to make before you go up. Muriel . . . Mother? I've made the decision to retire at the end of the year. This seventieth birthday is an appropriate time to do it, don't you think? I have made arrangements for a new editor to take over on January 1 so that I may spend more time with the both of you."

"Why, Henry. I think that is absolutely wonderful. I've actually been hoping for several years that you would do it, but I knew you needed to decide in your own sweet time. Congratulations," Muriel said as she walked over and hugged Hank.

"She's right, you know, Son. You're no spring chicken; now if you'll both help me up to bed."

"Good morning, Doc. Good morning, Michael. Good morning, Samantha. Good morning, Bernie. Good morning, Cletus. Why are all of you here so early?"

Happy Birthday to you,
Happy Birthday to you,
Happy Birthday, dear Henry
Happy Birthday to you.

For he's a jolly good fellow,
For he's a jolly good fellow,
For he's a jolly good fellow,
Which nobody can deny.

Bruno walked from the storeroom carrying a chocolate-covered cupcake, corrugated paper wrapping still encasing it, single candle stuck askew in the center. He placed it in front of Hank at the counter, then for the hundredth time, overflowed his cup. "Happy Birthday, you old fart. Glad you made it to seventy."

"HAPPY BIRTHDAY, HANK!" everyone in the cafe hollered.

"Thanks everyone. You sure caught me by surprise, but I'm glad you're here. You're my best friends. Thanks for the . . . ah, cake, Bruno." Everyone walked over to Hank to wish him a personal "Happy Birthday," and to shake his hand. He was deeply touched.

"Now, here is some real food for you, Henry." Bruno placed a heaping plate of eggs, pork sausages and country-fried potatoes in front of him. "On the house today, mister editor . . . not charging you anything, but today only."

"Happy birthday, Hank," Doc whispered, "and how is Catherine making it through the holidays?"

"She's slowing down, Doc, that's for sure, but her spirits are good. The ladies gave me a birthday party last night, but we put her to bed early. She can't sit up very long. Stop up to the house to check on her whenever you can," Hank answered as he attacked his heaping breakfast.

"I'll do that.

It looks like snow. I think we're in for a hard winter . . . feel it in my bones. When those storms begin howling down the valley, I'll wish I was wintering in Florida with Charlie. Maybe next year.

I have to see patients at the Clinic, Hank. Have a good birthday. Bye, Bruno. Bye everyone," Doc said slipping into his suit coat and ambling to the door.

___15

Indeed it was a hard winter. No winter in this valley was ever easy; however, the winter of 1949-50 was especially bitter. The high bluffs held the cold in the ravines and coulees in a vise grip, neither permitting it to escape nor periodic warmer southern winds to enter. January had been especially hard with temperatures falling to as much as twenty-five degrees below zero on star-studded clear nights. Like most villagers, Hank had a head bolt heater in his car to warm the oil on freezing evenings; even so, there were days his auto wouldn't start, so he would walk downtown. Muriel didn't think he should traipse out when it was bitter cold, but he had difficulty adjusting to retirement, not needing to go to the shop everyday. He had needed to get out of the house, almost daily, and once his lungs acclimated to the cold air, walking in below zero weather felt good. He even persuaded Muriel to accompany him on neighborhood walks occasionally; that is, if the sun broke through enough to warm the valley to ten or fifteen degrees above zero. On cold but sunny days in early February he had frequently walked to the riverfront to gaze out over the frozen river. For all practical purposes life had stopped here, but not completely. It existed underneath the waters as fish dove deeper to protect themselves from the ice near the surface. Heartier animals survived to be rejuvenated by the spring sun and warming waters, but he also knew that some river life wouldn't survive the winter. He had also enjoyed walking up Methodist Hollow, Walton's Hollow and along the river path listening to snow crunching under his boots, listening to the silence on the river and in the valley. The valley had a close, warm, enveloping sound in the summer months, but during the winter, it was harsher with every foot step, every conversation snapping and bouncing off ice-crusted surfaces.

To Hank, winter was a season to be enjoyed, not one to be

avoided. The river valley took on such a different hue—grayness swept over the valley for days, if not weeks, but the sun would periodically break through the bluff-to-bluff overcast sky to indicate that all was not desolate. The warm, golden colors of fall had been blown to the wind, replaced by the bitter, leaden colors of winter. And like the autumn-winter change, his own seasons were changing. Catherine's illness wasn't one he wanted, but like the ending of a golden fall, aging and illness were inevitable; his seventieth birthday and retirement were significant changes. He knew that life couldn't be all golden anymore than year-long burning yellow and red leaves bathing the valley. Sure, winter brought bleakness, grayness, bitter, howling winds, sixty to seventy inches of snow and ice to the valley, conditions which virtually isolated McGregor and Marquette at times, but he knew these conditions were less terrible than when hearty Norwegian, Swedish, Czech, Irish and German immigrant pioneers had homesteaded this country during severe Iowa winters before the turn of the century. Those folks had survived in soddies out on the prairie with only dirt walls and thatch roofs to protect them from the howling winds which roared in from the Dakotas carrying Alaskan nor'westerlies, ripping crops and hearts out of men, women and children. And centuries before pioneers broke sod in the territory, Indians had survived winters along this river. Certainly, 1950 winter conditions weren't anything like that.

By mid-February Catherine's breathing had become shallower, her color had grown ashen, and Hank had become increasingly concerned, and melancholy. After one particularly long and difficult evening sitting up with her, he had intended on going to his shop the next morning to assist the new editor, but had walked past to the levee instead. He had been fearful that Catherine, like much of the wildlife over and under these waters, wouldn't survive the winter. As he stood on the levee gazing at the frozen river that morning, he had looked upriver toward Marquette to see a strong, gray squall rolling down the river valley towards him. The suspension bridge was already shrouded in swirling clouds; he could see the squall was moving fast. It would follow the river downstream picking up snow and razor-sharp ice pebbles, whirling them into his weathered face. He had pulled his coat tighter around his neck to face the encroaching storm. As a boy he had relished the elements brought on by the varied seasons, liking nothing better than to be in the middle of a winter storm to feel the ice sting his face, or to skip along Bloody Run in the spring when the snow began melting, rushing cold and crystal clear to the Mississippi, or to hunker down in a fishing boat, perspiring in the sultriness of July and swatting mosquitoes from his face out on Horseshoe Lake, or to walk these hills during the fall feeling the warm, embracing sun shower his face as it slipped lower to the south. But as a man, in the face of the storm, he had retreated to the warmth of his old shop.

The new editor had several logs burning in the potbellied stove, but was nowhere to be found. He was probably at the cafe having his morning coffee, starting another long association with newer, younger fellows just as Hank had done so many years ago. He was grateful for the warmth of the stove, but melancholy that this season had changed, too. He had been replaced. The old cast-iron potbellied stove had been an enjoyment for years, having been here for as long as he could remember, even from the first day he worked as a cub reporter. It was a meeting place, too, especially during the winter when it radiated warmth to those drawn to it, but even in the summer it was a "talking" place. That morning, however, had been for Hank and his thoughts. He had momentarily considered searching the archives, but hadn't been compelled to review them after Catherine had delivered her long-held secret on Christmas Eve. He had thought he would continue at another time to find out more about his father, a father that had emerged from the depths of the Mississippi with a name . . . John. He had fixed a cup of coffee, plopped his feet on the hassock, then watched the red and blue flames dance along the slow-burning logs. He had hoped, desperately, that Catherine might have one more spring.

But it wasn't to be. Catherine simply hadn't had any more time left. Ninety-five years of living had used up her heart, her lungs, her will to live. Each day had found her growing weaker. By the third week of February she had been confined to her bed with Muriel and Hank alternately tending to her throughout the evenings. They had sat by her bed holding her hand, talking to her, gently lifting her bony, emaciated back for better breathing, giving her water and food. She had hardly eaten for a week, drinking little, wasting away to nothing. Doc had stopped in every couple of days to listen to her heart and lungs, but he would simply shake his head at Hank and Muriel. They would talk later in the hall. Catherine's days had been numbered. Yet, those final days had been surprisingly pleasant for Hank. He had been so close to her throughout his lifetime. She had been so kind, so patient, so supportive of him during the years, even when he was a little rascal; in turn, he had dedicated himself to making her life the best he could. When he and Muriel had married, Muriel accepted Catherine as her own mother. It had been a good life, the three of them in that big house.

On the evening of February 28, Catherine had drawn her last breath. Hank and Muriel had seen it coming for several days as Catherine was near a coma, drinking only a drop or two of water, eating no food. Hank had heard the dry rasp in her throat, heard the weak little coughs during her last days. Periodically, her eyes would open slightly, but she hadn't recognized him. But he had stayed by her side, wanting to be there at the end. He had watched closely, fearing her last breath, wondering how it was possible to live ninety-five years, to have taken in millions of breaths in that lifetime to then have it come down to only a few, then five, then two, then the last. He hadn't been able to comprehend Catherine breathing her last breath. It had come as he looked at her gaunt but loving face. He nearly missed it, it being so shallow, but he knew— her last breath, the last chord in Catherine's song. He had stood by the bed holding her hand, helping her cross to the other side, not wanting her to cross it alone. He couldn't. But holding her hand, seeing the last vestige of life in the person who had given him life had been important. And although he had watched death approaching for several days, he hadn't been fully prepared for it when it actually happened. He had thought it would be logical. It wasn't. There isn't anything like it. Dead is dead. Dead is no more. Existence is gone. He had looked down at Catherine expecting her to take another breath, whispering, "Take one more breath, Mother, please?" She hadn't. He reached down to close her eyelids, then sat in the chair for a long while gazing at her face. Downstairs in the dining room, Muriel had realized how quiet it had become upstairs. When she entered the bedroom, she knew. She had walked to him, putting her arms around his shoulders.

Catherine Brandenburg was buried March 2, 1950 on a brisk but sunny morning in the Pleasant Grove Cemetery on a bluff overlooking the Mississippi River not far from the ancient Indian burial grounds. She didn't live to be one hundred, but she came close. As a life-long resident of McGregor, she had many friends, although most had preceded her to the cemetery. It seemed as if everyone in both villages had attended her funeral. A few lingering snowflakes swirled over the bluff's edge as Catherine's casket was lowered into the grave. Mourners greeted Hank and Muriel offering condolences—Bruno, Bernie, Doc, Michael, Samantha, Theodore, Peder, Charlie passed in single file. The line stretched around the pine trees and down the gravel road to the cemetery gate. Hank and Muriel had greeted each one until the last person wearing an over-sized blue, rumpled gabardine suit and floppy top hat finally stumbled toward them—Cletus. "I . . . I . . . I . . . I'm s . . . s . . . sorry, M . . . Mister Hank about y . . . y . . . your m . . . mom," He had grabbed Hank's arm awkwardly, then stumbled back down the gravel pathway.

Hank had soon found that anticipating death and experiencing it were not the same. Catherine's death had put him into a deep melancholy such as he had never experienced. He had considerable difficulty accepting her death, her absence from his life. The void of retirement troubled him, also. For the next month, as winter's grip gradually relaxed, he had been in a quandary neither reading, writing nor reviewing the archives down at the shop; in fact, he hadn't even stopped into Bruno's Cafe with any regularity. During March when valley winds were desperately attempting to blow away the last vestiges of winter, Bruno would look out the window of the cafe to see him shuffling, head down to the *Times* shop or to the riverfront. Hank had wanted to be alone, mostly walking along the muddy river path, or along the railroad tracks as the snow and ice gradually released the valley from winter's hold. Bruno was concerned about him. And Muriel had seen him slipping deeper into his melancholy, loosing interest in most things he enjoyed. A month after the funeral she had felt it was time for him to get moving, to accept Catherine's death, to escape from his melancholy. During a Sunday evening dinner she had approached the subject, "Henry, I think it's time for you to do something," Muriel said serving Hank two smoked pork chops.

"I know but I can't seem to pull myself out of this mood. I know I'm depressed, but I don't know what to do about it. I miss Mother terribly," Hank said as he cut into a pork chop.

"I think you should go on that towboat trip that mister, what's his name? from Guttenberg offered you."

"Merrick, Thomas Merrick, but I don't know. I was excited at the time but now I've lost interest."

"Nonsense. It's absolutely what you need. You love the river. Now that you are retired, you have the time. Spring is almost here. It would be wonderful for you. I'll be all right here by myself," Muriel said placing her hand on Henry's arm. "I want you to call Mister Merrick tomorrow to make arrangements. Now that's a captain's order."

Hank had taken Muriel's suggestion. He had called Thomas the next morning.

____16

"ALL HANDS ON DECK! A mate's coming aboard," the grizzled captain yelled from the pilot house, "and step lively there because this gentleman knows the river. Treat him with respect!"

'Aye, aye, sir's' were shouted by deck hands from the first deck . . . sir . . . sir . . . sir echoing through the valley. Captain Merrick hurried down the steel staircase to greet Hank as he crossed the gangplank to the towboat. The captain stood at attention on the starboard deck, saluted Hank crisply, and greeted him loudly as Hank stepped aboard. "AHOY THERE, SIR! It is my distinct honor and privilege to welcome you aboard the Hawkeye State." Hank threw a wimpy open-handed salute back to Captain

Merrick; it seemed like the thing to do when boarding.

"Thank you, captain. I am indeed pleased to be aboard. Will we be casting off soon?" Hank asked, smiling at the captain as he dropped his duffel bag onto the steel deck, "AND STEP LIVELY THERE, MATES! BRING MY GEAR TO STARBOARD! or is it larboard?" Hank and Thomas both laughed, but the deck hands didn't know what to think of the comments and behavior between these two bearded old men. "Isn't that the way they did it in Mark Twain's day, sir?"

"Mate, I certainly believe they did, but sadly," both Thomas and Hank now absentmindedly tugged at their beards, "those ship-boarding greetings are a thing of the past. We still have a few formalities on the towboat—I get a little respect for being captain, mostly for passing out pay checks—but every hand has his job in order to push this tow downriver. But come along, sir, and I'll show you your quarters for the next two weeks. Step briskly now, mister."

Thomas had decided that Hank would board the Hawkeye State at Guttenberg's Lock and Dam No. 10. Before his boarding the towboat had already run upriver from Keokuk to St. Paul, and was now on its downriver run to St. Louis. As they reached the pilot house staircase, Thomas spoke of the river with its extensive lock and dam system. "Back in the heyday of steamboating, around the 1850s when our mutual 'friend' Sam Clemens was piloting these waters, there were no locks and dams. The river was wild and untamed, running its course wherever and whenever it wanted. Beacon lights, buoys and radar like we have today to guide us weren't in use yet. Instead, pilots navigated in the dark by guiding on prominent landmarks, and by moonlight if they were lucky. Lanterns were suppose to be hung on riffraff keelboats, packets and trading-scows, but many didn't use them. And the river kept changing course, also. As Sam Clemens wrote several times, it never could make up its mind where it wanted to flow.

From Guttenberg the river bends east for a considerable distance. I imagine it must meander at least sixty miles before bending back westward again downriver around Davenport; then it straightens out once again as it rushes past Muscatine. But you'll see that soon enough. All of the Iowa land in that sweeping Muscatine Bend—Maquoketa and Anamosa and Lost Nation and Oxford Junction—might have belonged to Wisconsin or Illinois today if the river had decided to make a cutoff straight downriver from Guttenberg to Muscatine instead of bending. But it didn't, and they aren't.

Our esteemed and enlightened Congress decided in the early Thirties to tame this great river by building a system of locks and dams to maintain a channel depth of nine feet. You know what Mark Twain said of Congress, don't you? I quote, 'Suppose you were an idiot. And suppose you were a member of Congress. But I repeat myself.' But you know that the system was built under F.D.R.'s Public Works Program, Henry; it's not like I'm imparting new information here, is it?" Thomas said as they reached the top of the stairs at the pilot house.

"Captain Merrick, you go right ahead. I'm on this trip to observe and to learn. I have lived my life *along* the river, but you have lived yours *on* it. You are the master, I am the cub," Hank said deferring to Thomas.

"Sir, with all due respect, I doubt that. I have read too many of your River Reflection essays in the *Times* to know that you are not uninformed about this river. I'm looking forward to hearing more about your insights. But as I was saying, Congress decided to corral the river, to make it more accessible to shipping by building this lock and dam system. Every thirty miles or so, up- and downriver, we have to break up the tow to navigate through the locks, only to reassemble on the other side. Most locks aren't long enough to handle the entire tow assembly at once, but some are. It takes about two hours to pass through a lock, but the system works. The locks and dams maintain a channel depth of nine feet and keep the river in place, mostly, but history has shown that you can't actually tame something as grand, something as independent, something as powerful as this river. We get lulled into thinking we can, but the river has, and will again, do what it wants to, whenever it wants to. You've lived with the floods we periodically get in the spring of the year. They're the river's way of reminding people that it's in charge, not congressmen."

"I can see that passing through a lock is a long process. I have watched it several times from on shore in Guttenberg and also in Lynxville, but never from on board a towboat," Hank said as he walked out to the pilot house railing to observe the process unfolding below him. Deck hands were scurrying around unhooking large cables and ratchet devices, unloosening barges from the towboat's capstans and timberheads while workers on shore operated the machinery controlling gates and water levels.

"Each individual barge is 175 feet by 28, and on this particular tow I have assembled twelve units, three abreast, four deep. Individual units are monstrous containers, Henry. When people see a loaded tow from shore, they are only seeing the tip of an iceberg. Much of the barge is actually below the water line. I like comparing them with coal trains you see rolling through McGregor and Marquette. Now, most people are impressed with the size of one coal car, but do you realize that just one of my barge units contains the equivalent of fifteen railroad cars? I'm pushing about two million dollars worth of tonnage to St. Louis. And when the river level is back to normal later in the summer I'll be able to add another three barges for a total of fifteen. We can then push three abreast, five long; that's equivalent to 225 railroad cars! With that tonnage you can see the importance of river shipping to this region and to the entire country. Fishermen sit on shore dangling their lines in the river, waving to us from lawn chairs thinking we're on a pleasure trip, but people in the know, men like yourself, know the facts. We are *not* on a pleasure trip here. But we need to share the river with pleasure boaters who frequently get in our way. They don't realize or appreciate the danger they're playing with around a tow," Captain Merrick said as he hollered below to the deck hands, "HOLD FAST THERE, BELAY! Don't let that barge drift out too far. Hard larboard now!" but the deck hand only looked up, wondering what the captain was shouting about.

"*Larboard?* Are you still using that term today? I thought it went out before the Civil War."

"You're right, Hank. I was only saying that to impress you. That deck hand down there doesn't know what in hell *larboard* means. You can see he didn't respond. PORT! LASH HER TO

PORT, I SAY! That ought to do the trick. My deck hands haven't read enough Mark Twain, if any, like you and I to know the romance, the language of the river.

How about a cup of coffee? We have another hour before getting through the locks."

"That would taste wonderful. It is brisk this morning, damp too. Coffee would be great.

I'm certainly looking forward to this trip. I . . . well . . . since I saw you last, my mother died." Hank leaned against the pilot house railing several moments watching the deck hands and lock attendants scurrying over the barges as the water level in the lock was gradually lowered. He realized this was the first time he had told someone else about her death. His tongue stuck to the roof of his mouth; his throat tightened. "She died the end of February and I've been in a dour mood ever since. It was my wife, Muriel, who finally told me to get out of the house, to take this trip with you. She said it would be good for me. Now that I'm standing here with you, I know it will be. I'm sorry to be speaking so personally, Captain, but . . . thanks for inviting me."

"I'm sorry to hear about your mother. My condolences.

I'm powerfully happy to have you along, Henry. I've been hoping for weeks that you would call. What with both of us being great admirers of the river, great admirers of Samuel Clemens— any man who makes his living on the river has to love Sam's writings—great admirers of Jack Daniels and Havana cigars, we'll most assuredly have a grand trip. I think we will have enlightening Twain discussions, also. I enjoy showing people the river, giving them some of its history, but I'm especially looking forward to hearing your insights. Now, here's a strong cup of coffee to ward of this brisk spring morning," Thomas said handing him a steam- ing cup, "and to my new friend and colleague, to a wonderful trip aboard the Hawkeye State, to the Mississippi." The two weath- ered, salty gentlemen clicked mugs, sipped the hearty brew, leaned on the pilot house railing together and looked far downriver in anticipation of their sojourn.

"Aye, aye, sir!"

The tow had finally been reassembled on the downriver side

of Lock and Dam Number 10, this being one of many such procedures Captain Merrick would supervise on the run to St. Louis. It seemed long and tedious to Hank, but the captain and his crew were used to it; it was simply a fact of river shipping. The captain carefully closed the gap between the towboat and lashed barges while calling out commands to the deck hands . . .

"Lash tightly there!

Pull hard on that capstan!

Butt that timberhead!

Tight on that cavel!

Half speed ahead!"

. . . until they were underway. Hank felt the power surge through the towboat as it strained to overcome the resistance of the tow and the river. There was such a tremendous weight stretched for two-hundred yards out front that getting the tow moving took considerably more power than keeping it moving once underway. Hank also knew that downriver steaming required significantly less power than upriver steaming, although downriver navigating made steering more difficult for the pilot. Getting the tow underway required the captain's total concentration, so Hank stood out of the way. The captain was looking to port, then to starboard hollering to deck hands, to the lock attendants on shore, to everyone. Deck hands were scurrying around carefully watching the movement until the tow cleared the lock and was safely into the main channel's deeper water. Captain Merrick supervised the entire procedure from high in the pilot house along with his second-in-command, Mr. Burnsley.

After they were underway in the main channel, Hank could see Captain Merrick relax. "That was some job of maneuvering back there, Captain. You certainly don't have much clearance between the barges and the lock walls. Congratulations!" Hank said as he now felt free to speak.

"It does take concentration, Henry. We're pushing such a tremendous amount of weight that there isn't room for a mistake, and I certainly wouldn't want to crash a gate. Under full power, I need to make decisions considerably in advance of the action I will take. You can't start and stop a tow on a dime, you know. Pleasure boaters don't realize that as they cut in front and around us, laughing and carrying on so. They can stop those little boats rapidly, but from the time I decide to stop this tow and the point where we actually halt is over a half mile . . . takes years to learn that."

"I can see that," Hank replied walking to starboard to get a view of the shoreline. "Even though I have driven to Guttenberg many times, even floated past here in a fishing boat, it looks different from this vantage point; of course, we're much higher than when motoring, or floating in a boat."

"That's true, Henry. We're standing at forty-five feet in the pilot house.

Later, when we're at full power, I'll take you down to walk out onto the barges. That's an experience I believe you'll enjoy. But now that we're clear of the lock, I'd like another cup of coffee. How about you?"

"Aye, aye, sir!"

"Two hot coffees coming up."

As the captain manipulated the steering sticks to make mid-channel adjustments, Hank stood to starboard watching Guttenberg recede in the distance. He felt the towboat shudder as it pushed and strained to get the tow up to full speed. The immense energy vibrated through his body. He recalled that from shore towboats looked peaceful, calm, romantic even as they churned downriver, just like Thomas said, but standing here on its deck, the immensity of the engine's power, even danger, was evident. The two diesel engines were also generating considerably more noise than what he had assumed—a persistent roar eventually melded with the flow of the river. As he looked toward the bow across the long expanse of barges, he was aware of a persistent slap of water lapping against them thrusting the deep blue waters outward in waves to the shore. He had experienced the energy in those waves many times sitting in a fishing boat, or standing on McGregor's dock as a tow churned past. He was impressed with the energy of the river, with the power of the Hawkeye State upon the river.

"How long have you lived in Guttenberg, Captain?" Hank inquired as he joined Thomas in the pilot house.

"First off, you can stop calling me *Captain*. We don't need formality between friends, unless you want me to call you *Mister Editor*."

"All right, *Tom* it is. I don't need *Mister Editor*, either," Hank said as he accepted a second steaming cup of coffee from the cook's assistant.

"As to your question, I've resided in Guttenberg for twenty years. It was in 1929 that I moved up here. I had lived and piloted out of Keokuk before that, but I prefer this upper river region. Guttenberg is a pleasant village to live in. When I'm not piloting, I relax around town talking to townspeople, fish when I feel like it, have a few beers at Moxie's Tavern on the main drag. Have you ever had poker beer, Hank?"

"Can't say that I have, captain."

"Moxie's has a potbellied stove in the corner around which the fellows sit telling yarns that spin on forever. We stick a couple of long-handled tongs into the fire, then when red-hot, stick it down into a full mug—beer sizzles creating a sweet taste—poker beer. If you come on down sometime, I'll take you over there to try it.

Guttenberg folks are friendly, fishing is great, hunting is great. I know you have pretty scenery up in McGregor, but we're partial to ours here in lower Clayton County.

Did you notice those huge stone warehouses back there along the shore? They've been there for many years. Even before the lock and dam system was constructed, stevedores—German immigrants primarily—loaded and unloaded steamboats then stored goods in the warehouses. One of your own, Diamond Jo Reynolds, had a warehouse here along the river, too. They could even store perishables because the heavy limestone kept them cool. It must have been quite an active, exciting place in those years. They cut the limestone out of these bluffs. There's a mid-nineteenth century stone school house still in use in Clayton, and an ancient stone church back up over those bluffs, too, maybe you've seen it . . . Pioneer Rock Church . . . built out of the same limestone—pitched roof, classic arched windows and doorway. It'll stand forever.

If you'll look downriver now, you'll see the confluence of

Buck Creek and the Mississippi. Most people wouldn't be aware of that, but a riverman would. It begins up in those westerly hills in Garnavillo Township, then flows through the village of Garnavillo before meandering to the river. In a few miles we'll also see the confluence of Miner's Creek and the Mississippi a short distance below Guttenberg.

You work with words, Hank, I work with water," Tom said as he maneuvered the steering sticks for a mid-channel adjustment. "It's interesting how we've chosen our professions. I know you enjoy a good word, a good sentence, a good story. I like easy water, deep water, cooperative water, waters of any size, any character, any color—trickling streams, circuitous creeks, raging rivers, winding tributaries, tumbling trout streams—be it the Wisconsin, the Ohio, the Missouri or the Great Mississippi. On a smaller scale, Buck- and Miner's Creeks are just as important as the Mississippi. They have a job to do, also. I know you're aware that the Mississippi Basin is the greatest and largest water drainage basin in the world carrying runoff from the Appalachian Mountains to the Rocky Mountains all the way to the Gulf of Mexico. Buck- and Miner's Creeks are part of that greater basin. Of course, you have Bloody Run and Sni Magill, a couple of nice creeks around Marquette and McGregor that do the same thing, even though people do think of them mostly as trout streams.

Other rivers contribute, also. For hundreds of winding miles throughout Clayton County, creeks join the Turkey River before it merges with the Mississippi downriver a few miles from here. We'll see the confluence of the Turkey and the Mississippi below Millville. It has always been one of my favorite rivers. How about you?"

"I don't know the Turkey as well as the Mississippi, but I have fished it around Elkader several times, and once at Osterdock. But I do know the Turkey has had a considerable impact on this terrain. It has been here for hundreds of thousands of years cutting deep ravines and valleys as it makes its way through the hills around Elkader, Elkport, Osterdock and Millville on its journey to the Mississippi. They have that bridge over the Turkey in Elkader, built before the turn of the century; Elkader folks say it's the longest stone arch bridge west of the Mississippi; of course, those Elkader folks like to brag a bit, but it's probably true."

"Aye, aye, sir! And they are sometimes a bit uppity anyway just because the county seat is there, even though we had it here in Guttenberg first, but we tolerate them; they do share the Turkey."

Hank was fascinated as he watched Tom steer the towboat through the expansive waters below Guttenberg. He had momentary visions of being in the pilot house with Mark Twain; in fact, Tom, sporting a long mustache and full beard, had a strong resemblance to Twain even though Tom was considerably larger than Twain. Nevertheless, he was magnificent standing behind the steering sticks in total command of the towboat. He looked like a captain. He was the captain.

The sun had burned off the morning fog by now; it was going to be a beautiful spring day. Later, however, during the summer months, humidity would rise along with the temperature in the valley. Waters brought humidity, you couldn't get away from that, but sultry weather had been such a part of Hank's life that he wouldn't have known how to live without it. "We're starting to head east now, Hank, as I indicated earlier. If the river had made a due-south cutoff below Guttenberg a hundred years ago, we could save a couple of hundred miles now, but it didn't . . . we have no choice."

For the next two hours, Hank was engrossed in the vast array of sights on and along the river. The Hawkeye State passed several villages doting the shoreline—Buena Vista, Balltown, Sherrill— before Dubuque's Eagle Point bluff loomed over the bow. The terrain certainly was beautiful along this stretch of river. It was obvious to Hank why he had chosen to live in this area. He realized most people were partial to their home states, to their home regions, and he knew he was biased, but he just couldn't understand why someone would chose to live anyplace else but here along the great Upper Mississippi Valley. The view from the pilot house deck was breathtaking as he peered downriver several miles observing the great expanses of verdant forests and rugged cliffs on the Wisconsin, Illinois and Iowa shores. Eagle Point's sheer precipice rose triumphantly in the distance, soaring hundreds of feet into the sky. The majesty of the terrain was overpowering.

"It's magnificent country, isn't it?" Tom shouted from the helm as he lit a Havana. "Care for a smoke?"

"Don't mind if I do, Captain, err . . . Tom. Yes, it certainly is. Regardless of how many times I traverse the river, I'm always in awe of its majesty," Hank said as he accepted a La Fendrich cigar and scratched a wooden match on the railing.

"Same with me. I've navigated these waters hundreds of times, but I never tire of it. The waters, the bluffs, the high flying bald eagles, the occasional deer swimming across the river, the timbered forests, the merging creeks and rivers are a part of my soul. We're rivermen, aren't we?" Tom said while adjusting the steering sticks for a hard-to-starboard maneuver, simultaneously scratching a match on his pant leg. "There isn't anything like it.

Dubuque is coming up fast and that means we will have to break up the tow again. Lock and Dam No. 11 is located just above Dubuque at Sageville; anyway, it'll give us a chance to relax as my watch is soon over. Mister Burnsley will take her through these locks. We can eat lunch soon. Are you enjoying yourself? Happy you came along?"

"Aye, aye! sir. I'm glad Muriel encouraged me. It's good for me."

"Great!

Being the historian you are, Henry, you know that Dubuque is one of the oldest cities on the Upper Mississippi River. Julien Dubuque, a French-Canadien, founded it in the latter part of the Eighteenth Century. He found lead ore around here which he began mining a couple of years after landing on these shores. There are ore mines east in Galena, Illinois also, but you know that."

"I've attempted to learn as much as I can about the river region, but you have a better perspective what with actually being *on* the river most of your life."

"I'm not so sure of that; be that as it may, Catfish Creek trickles into the Mississippi just below Dubuque, and that's where Julien first mined the ore. Dubuque became a flourishing town with the mining activity plus lumbering. And Sam Clemens stopped here periodically on his river sojourns . . . said Dubuque became a major steamboat port. Did you know that in 1840 it was the largest city in Iowa, eventually surpassed by Burlington due to a growing steamboat trade there? We'll be passing Burlington later.

You're obviously familiar with all the colleges they have here? After the citizenry realized Dubuque would become a legitimate city they desired *learnin'* places, as Sam Clemens would have said. Clarke College, the University of Dubuque and Loras College all began before the Civil War right in the heyday of steamboating. With these academic institutions established, the city also attracted preachers, and preachers attracted seminaries to these hills. Julien was Catholic which caused considerable numbers of crusading Catholics to be planted here, but the Lutherans staked out their own claims . . . started Wartburg Seminary to keep the area theologically balanced, you might say.

That creek where Julien found ore, Catfish Creek? Troublesome. It was about 1876, I believe, when it flooded—thirty dwellers drowned in that disaster. Then around the turn of the century, a fire wiped out much of the city's riverfront. Fires and floods have been troublesome in river towns; Dubuque certainly didn't escape them.

They have the Shot Tower, too, which was used to mold lead shot during the Civil War; and have you ever ridden the Fourth Street Elevator? It's still one of the oldest functioning inclined cable cars running outside of San Francisco. Am I giving you too much history, Hank? Once I get started, like this tow, I have a hard time stopping," Tom said as he slowed the towboat on its approach to Lock and Dam No. 11. "Down around this bend about a mile we'll pass Death's Head Bluff where some Indians were forced into starvation, or so the legend goes.

Do you see that fortress-looking structure up on that far bluff," Tom asked as he slid the steering sticks to port while pointing to the bluff. "That's none other than ol' Julien's grave. How would you like to be buried on a bluff like that? Good view for the rest of your days."

"That would certainly be fine with me. I *would* like to be buried along the river. We just buried Mother in the Pleasant Grove

Cemetery on a high bluff overlooking the river in McGregor. I suppose Muriel and I will be laid to rest alongside her. How about you?"

"*On* the river, Mate. I've been a part of these waters all of my life, so I want to be a part of them after life, too. Just cremate me, dump my ashes into the river. I won't raise the river level any, but I'll be a part of it, you can be sure about that.

Now that we're at the lock and dam, it's Mister Burnsley's watch; let's depart to the galley."

Later that afternoon they passed through Lock and Dam No. 12 at Bellevue, rounded the bend at Sabula, and passed through Lock and Dam No. 13 above Clinton before approaching Davenport. The river had taken them east then south and west as they pushed onward to St. Louis. With Mr. Burnsley holding the aft six-hour watch, Tom and Hank sat on captain's chairs on the aft first deck smoking cigars, sipping hearty whiskey, watching the river towns fade in the distance while chatting about life on the Mississippi. The roar of the engines, particularly on the aft deck, created a constant throbbing, a persistent vibration throughout the towboat. It took Hank some time to adjust to the decibel level, but he eventually became mesmerized by it. They watched the towboat's wake send rhythmic wavelets to the shoreline, momentarily disrupting docks and fishing vessels which settled back into their normal routine after the towboat's passing only to be disrupted by the next passing tow. After a long period without conversation, Tom broke the silence. "You know, Henry, we've both read so much about Mark Twain's escapades on this great waterway that I feel one with him on the river. He captured the essence of this river better than anyone I've ever read, although one of our fellow Iowans, William Petersen, did an admirable job with his *Steamboating on the Upper Mississippi*. Twain certainly had a way with words; he could absolutely turn a phrase, could he not? And it amazes me, even today, the perspective he held on so many things other than the river—Congress, Europeans, religion, growing up, editing. With you being a writer, you know that he thought author's vain when he indicated they valued compliments even from scoundrels. Yes, sir! He even mocked his own profession. What's your favorite Twain quote or story?" Hank didn't respond for several moments; instead, he watched the setting sun over the western bluffs, watched the wake rolling persistently to the shore over the beauty of the river. He blew a long column of smoke then watched it meld with the river before responding.

"There are so many I enjoy that it's hard to select only one. I have read and re-read both *The Adventurers of Tom Sawyer*, and *Huckleberry Finn*, but I also love his short stories. Did you read *The Old Ram*, or *The Man Who Corrupted Hadleyburg? Hadleyburg* is one of the most contrived, convoluted plots I have ever read. When reading it the first time, I wondered how he would ever resolve the twisted plot. How about *The Mysterious Stranger*?"

"I didn't read the *Stranger*, but did you read his story about the bluebird dropping acorns into a hole on the roof of a house, not figuring out why he couldn't fill it up? Interesting perspective on life," Tom said as he too stoked up a cigar. "Then he steamed up the Mississippi in 1882 on that final trip along these very shores to write an article for *The New Yorker* or *Atlantic*, I can't remember which. Actually, he used prior river writings then interjected observations from that 1882 trip, most of which became *Life On The Mississippi*. He wrote about river towns on his journey to St. Paul . . . talked about living and working as a printer for his brother Orion in Keokuk, and I believe he also lived in Muscatine for a short while. Of course, in those years, people probably thought of those towns as belonging more to Missouri than to Iowa. Twain mentioned the beautiful land around Dubuque, and he also mentioned Prairie du Chien briefly, but unfortunately for us, he didn't write about Guttenberg, McGregor or North McGregor. Our towns weren't much more than dock landings then. He did write, though, about the beautiful waters upriver in Minnesota's Lake Pepin, about Lake City and Red Wing. He was terribly impressed with St. Paul and Minneapolis. In typical Twain style, he interjected many a yarn about folks living along the river. He certainly could paint a word-picture of the valley. Yes, sir, Twain was a riverman . . . We're river men, too, aren't we?"

"Aye, aye, sir!"

After finishing their cigars and whiskey, Hank accompanied the captain up to the pilot house to assist Mr. Burnsley in navigating the locks at Davenport. A couple of hours later, after the tow was reassembled, Hank remained on the pilot house deck as they glided through olive-green waters toward Muscatine, Burlington and Iowa's final port, Keokuk. Although the sun had set beyond the western bluffs by now, a red luminescence remained on the horizon. Hank had certainly enjoyed it. The expanse of this valley and being in the main channel at sunset presented a different aura than when on land. In Marquette at sunset, the bluffs created a variety of hues and colors which filtered down onto the snug village, light reflecting off the mirrored river separating the sun's rays into vibrant rainbow reds, blues and yellows. But aboard the towboat tonight, the sunset had been even more magnificent, if that were possible. The river valley here had held the sunset momentarily in a golden bowl, not permitting it to escape to the far hills. Hank felt it had been a spiritual event. He had leaned against the railing not wanting the golden sun to slip from his grasp. He had wanted to bottle it, to reach out and put it in his pocket, to save it for another day, to save it forever. He had wished Muriel, Catherine and his father were here to share it with him. As he momentarily thought about them, he became melancholy again, but only for a few moments. Standing alone on the deck, watching the last remnants of the day's sun meld with the encroaching darkness, feeling water spray against his creased face, he had experienced a peace, a calmness, a solitude he hadn't known for several months. Tom, now smoking a pipe, maneuvered the steering sticks gently to port then to starboard, looked downriver past Hank with the presence of mind to leave him alone with his thoughts. Tom knew what a sunset on the river did to a man. He knew that words would be an intrusion.

Waves lapped against the barges as the towboat thrust persistently through the waters, waters that had been so much a part of Hank's life, waters that had carried Sam Clemens and Tom Merrick and Catherine Brandenburg and John Dalton, and generations of pioneers to these shores. The sun had fallen below the bluffs now, only a slight glimmer of soft shimmering red remained above the trees. He was aware of a calmness that had overtaken the river—fewer gulls swooped around the tow searching for fish, fewer pigeons fluttered around the barges in search of morsels, fewer deer, beaver and otters scurried along the shoreline. Even the fish had descended to the deep of the river, settling in for the night only to be awaked by a rising sun and warming waters. As his cigar stub began burning his fingers, he flipped it into the surging wake, watching it swirl in a whirlpool before being absorbed by the enveloping waters. He thought about the quickness of its disappearance. He thought about Catherine and John, and himself—how quickly their lives had passed, how quickly his own had passed. He, too, would soon pass into the life of the river just as quickly as the cigar stub had.

"Are you getting cold, Henry? Once that sun sets in the spring, it usually cools off on the river. Here's a cup of coffee to warm you," Tom said as he joined Henry on the deck.

"Thanks, Captain . . . err, Tom. Viewing sunsets on the river is certainly different than from on shore, but you know that; you've experienced thousands of them, haven't you?" Henry said, turning to accept the steaming coffee.

"Aye, aye! to that, but I never get tired of them. Each one is new, each one is different. Clouds, temperature, season, location on the river, level of the waters, speed of the current all have an effect. If I were an artist, I would paint it, but I'm not . . . just an old captain trying to make his way downriver," Tom said as he leaned against the railing and looked foreword over the strung-out tow, much of which he couldn't see in the encroaching darkness.

"Do you feel old?"

"Hard to say. My mind doesn't, but more and more, my body does. I've got some arthritis. I need to use glasses all the time now, but mostly, I feel ship-shape. How about you?" Tom asked turning to look directly at Henry.

"Generally all right. My right hip troubles me periodically, but like you, my mind feels young. But I don't mind getting older. I've had a good life."

"Aye, aye, sir!"

The two graying, bearded, wrinkled men leaned against the pilot house railing for another ten minutes . . . silent . . . watching the river flowing past as the Hawkeye State pushed toward St. Louis.

Hank tossed and turned throughout his first night on the towboat, because his bunk wasn't particularly comfortable; also, he wasn't used to the constant throbbing of the engines below him. At half past four he decided to get up; besides, the aroma of coffee filtering into his room from the galley below was attacking his nostrils. He slipped into a pair of khakis and light jacket, flipped on a braided captain's cap Tom had given him, then gingerly descended the staircase to the galley to retrieve a cup of hot, strong coffee. He walked to the aft deck and stood at the railing directly above the menacing propellers. The immense power and urgency of the engines flowed through the steel deck to his feet and body as they strained against the weight of the tow and the resistance of the river. In the darkness and thick fog of early morning, he knew that dormant fish and animals along the river would soon come to life once the sun broke over the bluffs to devour the fog. But the constant roar of the engines was too loud on the aft deck, too loud to hear the Mississippi's heartbeat. He walked along the side gangway to the fore deck, glanced to the pilot house to see Mr. Burnsley on watch, squinted through the darkness to locate the bow and wondered, for only a fleeting moment, if he would dare walk way out there without Captain Merrick's approval, or assistance. He stepped gingerly onto the steel gangplank joining the towboat to the barges, and within three steps had landed on the first barge. With only a faint moonlight guiding him, he walked carefully along the barge toward the blinking red beacon. He hopped onto the second barge, another wary trek and hop to the third, then a final hop to the fourth until he finally came within a few feet of the beacon at the bow. As he stood above the menacing, pulsating river, his heart raced, his face tingled. He grabbed his cap and steadied himself into the wind feeling an excitement, a vitality he hadn't experienced for many years. Even though it was extremely dangerous, he was terribly excited as he steadied himself by holding on to a cavel and spreading his feet wider for balance, letting the water and wind sting his creased, old face, letting the energy of the river drive life into him. At the bow he *heard* the river with its persistent staccato, thrusting, surging rhythm; its melody penetrated his ears, its harmony soothed his soul.

Rounding the bend south of Keokuk, the sun finally broke through the morning fog flooding the river valley with golden rays as the towboat invaded Missouri waters. Hank sipped the last of his cold coffee while attempting to absorb the sights and sounds unfolding around him. Even after seventy years worth of experiences, this was a new one—adventuresome, exciting, vibrant, dangerous. He was invigorated; his blood felt red hot, boiling in him like the churning river only a few feet below. He wanted to feel, to touch, to hear this river forever. He hadn't recalled ever experiencing such vitality, yet inner peace. In spite of the waves drumming against the bow like field artillery drummers advancing to battle, he sensed a silence—a dichotomy of thrusting, splashing waters superimposed over brooding solitude. The rising, mysterious and dissipating fog, the evergreens interlaced with golden maples and vibrant oaks embracing the shoreline made him feel separated, other-worldly. This moment felt like the summation of his life. He had an urge to jump into the river, to swim, to be absorbed totally by it. He wanted to re-vitalize his body, his mind. He wanted to feel even more danger.

From the pilot house one hundred yards to the rear Captain Merrick, now on the early morning watch, saw Henry standing on the bow. He was concerned. No one knew better than the captain the danger of the river, the danger of walking alone on the barges, but he also was wise enough to know what Henry was experiencing. Tom was only a few years younger than Henry, but had been invigorated by these waters his entire life. He held a sense of the waters Henry was experiencing at this moment as he stood so close to death trying to imagine death yet desperately hanging on to life. Tom didn't disturb him, didn't send a deck hand out there to rescue him. He respected Hank's solitude.

Hank certainly didn't know the breadth of the river as well as

Tom. He knew it best from La Crosse to Dubuque, but he judged they were in Missouri waters by now. He felt a stronger current beneath him which indicated the river was straightening out, heading due south. Back upriver yesterday navigating the Guttenberg Bend, he recalled a slack current, easy water, but here it was once again racing toward the Gulf. Even though he had only been on the towboat for twenty hours, he was beginning to recognize the river's signals, beginning to notice the same clues Sam Clemens said were so difficult for him to learn when he was a cub pilot in training. Hank was now able to pick out points on which to gain a bearing. He recalled this was the technique pilots in the early 1800s used to navigate this river, an era before beacon lights and buoys marked the main channel. Suddenly, he wanted another cup of hot coffee, but was enjoying his experience too much to walk all the way back to the galley.

A thin, silvery mist hung tenaciously over the river in spite of the rising sun. Gliding past steep and towering cliffs, he felt as if he were floating through a fleecy cloud. Gradually, however, the warming sun attacked the fog with its slicing lance, devouring it like a great white Knight until the valley burst into blinding brilliance. Jagged limestone cliffs and bluffs cradled the river on both sides as they penetrated Missouri waters.

With the spray of the river washing over his face, with the wind billowing his jacket, he reflected on his friends and acquaintances back home—how they too loved the river, how their lives had been shaped by it. Patrick O'Reilly died in these waters, Ludwig Biersdorf found life fishing in these waters, Ethel Matters found harmony in these waters, waters still reverberating with echoes of her throaty, earthy blues . . .

> *I woke up this mornin', with an awful achin' head,*
> *Oh, I woke up this mornin' with an awful achin' head.*
> *Oh, my man done left me,*
> *Just a room and an empty bed.*

He thought about Cletus, his simple life, his obsession with sweeping the streets and mowing the mayor's grass. He thought about Doc and Bruno and Charlie and Theodore and Peder and Samantha and Bernie, and how connected he had been to them for so long. And even though he was now two hundred miles below McGregor and Marquette, the river connected them; it was a lifeline to his friends.

Startled, Hank turned to see Tom standing several feet to starboard. Tom hadn't yet spoken. He, too, was absorbing the view. "Good morning, Captain. I hope you're not upset with me being out here by myself," Hank said as he carefully walked toward Tom.

"Good morning yourself, sir. It's certainly not something I recommend for yearlings, but you being past that stage, I figure you can make your own decisions. It's your destiny," Tom said as a light mist enveloped them.

"Where are we?"

"About ten miles above Hannibal. We should pass there in an hour."

"Hannibal? Sam's hometown. I'll be darned. You know, in spite of my affection for him, I have never visited Hannibal. It will be nice to see it, especially from mid-river. We're probably close to the waters on which Tom and Huck and Indian Joe floated timber rafts and scows. I am honored to be in Twain's waters," Hank responded as the tow suddenly dipped causing both men to reach for a cavel.

"The water is getting rougher in this reach. Probably reefs, sand- or bluff bars causing it. See those slanting lines on the water to port? . . . means there's a reef building underneath. And do you see that boiling water foreword about fifty yards? . . . means a reef is breaking up. The river is always changing, always creating new islands, new reefs, new bars, even new channels. Although the Army Corps of Engineers charts these waters, we still use steamboating-era techniques to read the river. Before it gets too rough, though, let's walk back for breakfast. You must be starved. Then we can come back out here tomorrow when we're in easier water," Tom said as the two men began their wobbly trek across the one hundred yards of barges to the towboat.

While eating biscuits with honey, sausage and eggs in the galley, Tom saw the village of Hannibal appear through the windows. "Hannibal off the starboard bow. Coming up fast." In the middle of a bite, Hank grabbed his coffee cup spilling coffee on his jacket as he rushed outside to the railing.

"The Mark Twain Mecca!" As the town slipped into sight, he was struck by the realization it wasn't some mythological town. It looked like McGregor or Marquette or Guttenberg or Clayton, just a river town that Sam Clemens had made more through his writings. He had put it on the world's map with his stories. Abreast of the wharf now, Hank could see all the way up Main Street. He imagined a young Sammy Clemens sitting on the wharf one hundred years ago waving to the Hawkeye State. Hank had done the same thing sitting on McGregor's levee waving to steamboats when he was a youngster. But even so, this *was* Hannibal, the only Hannibal. Too soon, they had passed by, the towboat thrusting persistently toward St. Louis. Hank craned his neck until Cave Hollow erased Hannibal from view.

By mid-afternoon a thunderhead began forming in the river valley. Ominous, gray clouds rolled in from the southwest causing the river to churn with anger. White caps appeared on its surface indicating agitated water. Although concerned at this sudden change in weather, Hank felt invigorated by the impending spring storm. The river had already presented many different faces on this trip—calmness, peacefulness, solitude—and now this. The bubbling, violent river was causing concern for Captain Tom, too, as he and Mr. Burnsley piloted the towboat through the growing turbulence. Suddenly, thundering peals echoed from bluff to bluff as a torrent of rain pelted the towboat in sheets of cold, piercing rain. A tempestuous wind brought rain in torrents, tearing at Hank's face as he grasped the pilot house railing, refusing to retreat inside in spite of Tom's pleadings. Hank was on this trip to experience the river. If a lightening bolt struck him, then that was Providence and they could just plant him on the river's shore, as Mark Twain would have said. Wind and water lashed his face, lightening cracked over the bluffs creating an echo that roared passed him to Hannibal and back. Tom handed him a slicker which Hank valiantly tried to put on in the wind and rain, but he didn't care about getting wet. His body was once again aching, his blood was once again red hot, boiling, surging through his old veins, pumping through them to their limit, but he was alive ... very alive. Passing Clarkesville, Missouri, the storm finally abated, the sun broke through the settling clouds creating a beautiful rainbow across the river. Yet once again, Hank was startled by the magnificence of the river. A golden arch with vibrant reds, blues and yellows bent from shore to shore as the towboat seemingly passed under it like a king promenading to his throne, distant thunder echoes heralding the king's arrival. Hank wanted to capture the rainbow, to paint it, to put it into prose, but he was left with only his eyes, his mind to remember it by. He would. He would never forget the storm and the rainbow on the river.

That evening, after Hank and Tom had finished dining on deep-fried catfish, they sat on the forward deck smoking La Fendrichs, sipping seven-year-old whiskey, and watching moonbeams bounce off the river's glazed surface. Two old men. Two men whose lives were as much a part of the river as the fish swimming below them, as much as the wildlife scurrying along these shores, as much as the soaring bluffs which had been cut by these powerful, majestic waters. They each puffed deeply, inhaling tart, acrid smoke into their ancient lungs. They sipped Jack Daniels like two master drinkers, sitting silent for a long time preferring to look out upon the waters as the towboat and tow sliced through the encroaching darkness. "This trip is going much too fast, Henry. I'm enjoying your company, immensely," Tom whispered as he lifted his cocktail glass in toast to Hank. "To a gentlemen, a scholar, and I must say, a shrewd judge of character . . . a riverman."

"Aye, aye! And to a captain of the waters, the captain of captains," Hank rejoined. By the time they had bunked down they were mellow with Jack Daniels, mellow with the ambiance of the river, looking forward to another sunrise.

The sunrise was as beautiful as yesterday's. Again, Hank had risen early to capture it as the sun sliced through the morning fog, gradually burning away the quiet lonesomeness of the river as they glided past Peruque above St. Louis. But he didn't walk out onto the barges this morning, electing instead to sit on the towboat's forward first deck. As he was enjoying his solitude, Tom descended the stairs to greet him. "Good morning, Henry. How are you felling this fine morning?" he asked walking toward Henry.

"Fine, Captain, just fine. I'm considering acquiring my pilot's license so I can continue this experience now that I've retired from the newspaper. Would you hire me aboard, sir, even if I am . . . over the hill?" Hank asked as he stood to shake hands with Tom.

"We will most certainly hire you, sir. I would be honored to have you aboard. Now, however, if you'll hike these stairs with me to the pilot house, I have something to show you." Hank's hip gave way, momentarily, as he climbed the staircase to the third-deck pilot house. Tom walked to the front railing and pointed downriver. "There's a significant historical marker upriver a few minutes from here that I want you to see. It's only a stone marker about ten feet tall on the Missouri side, but to a riverman like you and me, it's important. Shipwreck. One of the most significant losses in the history of river lore happened right up there a few miles. It was back in the summer of 1879, I believe, that the John J. Roe's boilers exploded one pitch-black night in mid-channel, opening her up as if you were gutting a walleye. She went down immediately taking ninety-eight passengers and two officers with her. The captain was a Mister LaPointe, and the cub pilot was Mister Dalton . . . John, I believe. The water is so deep here that they never raised her. She's still down there along with all those people in Davy Jones's locker. We ought to be approaching the spot in a few minutes." Hank's heart suddenly beat violently against his chest—pounding, racing, hammering—like a catfish trying to throw off a fishing hook. His head swirled. He thought he was having a heart attack. He reached for the railing to steady himself. Tom looked at him to see an ashen face. "Are you all right, Henry? What's the matter?" Tom said grabbing his arm.

"I . . . I'm . . . stunned. I'm woozy. What did you say the name of that steamboat was?"

"The John J. Roe. She blew with ninety-eight passengers, a pilot and a cub pilot in 1879."

"And . . . and . . . what did you say the pilot's name was?"

"Mister Cormack. Why? Are you sure you're all right?"

"And the name of the cub pilot? What . . . what was his name?"

"His last name was Dalton. I believe his first was John. Can I get you some water or maybe a shot of Jack Daniels?"

"I . . . I . . ." Hank looked to starboard. "How far until we reach the marker?" he asked as he staggered along the railing.

"Just around the next bend. What's happening, Henry? Do you know something about the sinking of the Roe?"

"I . . . how far now?"

"About two minutes until we're around the bend, then you'll see the marker on the starboard shore." It seemed like an interminably long time before they circumvented the bend. He grabbed the railing with both hands and peered into the ghost-like, ethereal floating mist.

"This is the place where my long-lost father rests, in this water chamber." Finally, the Hawkeye State cleared the bend.

"There! Upriver two hundred yards to starboard. Do you see that tall, gray, stone pyramid-shaped marker? Right out from it in the main channel is where she foundered. I shudder every time we cross it, because of all those mates down there. But it's a good place to rest, if you ask me . . . in these waters."

"I would take that glass of water now." Hank drank a half of the water then stared at the shore as the stone marker loomed larger. He fixed his eyes upon it, grabbing the railing to steady himself.

"We're just about over the spot now, Henry. Are you all right?"

"I'm all right, Captain. My father is down there . . . *John*. It's a shock to see this place, to float above him. I have spent my entire life trying to find out who he was. Only last Christmas did Mother share her secret with me, did she reveal his name. She said he died on the river, but I didn't know where, until now." The Hawkeye State was now directly abreast of the stone marker out in the main channel. Hank reached out with both arms, stared at the marker wanting to touch it, to connect with his father. The towboat was moving too rapidly. He looked around, desperately, searching for something on the deck, but nothing suitable was within reach. He looked at the stone marker again, thrusting his hands toward it, opening his mouth but nothing came out. He looked down into the deep blue waters, straining to see through the great river, deeper, deeper. He sucked deeply on his cigar, grabbed it from his lips, blew the smoke out upon the waters toward the marker then tossed it onto the undulating waters where it floated like a flower, like a wreath. It dipped, darted, floated for a moment until it descended into The River.

The End

Last Parade

A Short Story

"I DON'T KNOW WHY THEY GO TO ALL THE TROUBLE every year. I simply don't understand it. They get dressed up in their uniforms, even though they don't fit anymore, then they march down the street making a spectacle of themselves. Their potbellies hang at half mast over their belts, shirts popping buttons like Joe Polooka. They couldn't march in a straight line when they were in the Infantry; they sure can't when they've been primed with several beers. But most of all, I don't like them coming out here firing those damn rifles over my grave. I tell you, Clarence, I'm sick of it, sick of the annual Memorial Day Parade and services here in Everest."

The night air was cool and damp as moonlight peeked around the water tank on the hill overlooking Everest Cemetery. But the two skeletons sitting on their headstones weren't bothered by the damp air or the coolness of the night. They enjoyed the moonlight; in fact, many skeletons left their graves most evenings to sit on headstones, enjoying the peace of the evening. Few were bothered by the hot, muggy summer nights, bitter cold winter days of the Middle West. The climate made little difference to them, because they couldn't feel its effects in their bones anyway. Moonlit nights were special. Gazing at the blue-haloed moon was one of their pleasures as they whiled away the long hours, months, years, eternity in the cemetery.

This evening, Clarence and Elmer were gazing at the moonlight and talking about the upcoming annual parade in the village,

and the ensuing cemetery services. They weren't looking forward
to it . . . "I tell you, Clarence, the Memorial Day Parade has gotten
out of hand. I wish they would forget it and leave us here in peace.
Although we both died in World War Two, it's time for villagers to
forget us and get on with their lives. It spoils my whole year just
thinking about those drunken Vets marching up here firing their
damn rusting M-1 rifles over our graves. Why don't they really let
us *Rest In Peace* instead of just giving us lip service?"

"You got that right, Elmer. My grave is in the northwest
corner, but even being entombed way over there, I still get
disturbed when that whole parade gang traipses into the cemetery
. . . bothers me with those loud rifles blasting our peace, and snotty-
nosed kids reciting the Gettysburg Address. It's irritating. I'm so
sick of hearing . . . *Four score and seven years ago* . . . that I'd like
to pick up my casket and move to Elkader. I'd even consider
moving to Dubuque or maybe up to Effigy Mounds to *live* with
those old Indians. Maybe I could find real peace at the mounds.
Those Indians weren't dumb. They knew where to place their
burial grounds—quiet places where folks wouldn't bother them."

"I hear you, Clarence. Maybe we should seriously consider
moving our graves. Memorial Day is only a couple of days off now,
and I haven't had any rest for weeks just thinking about it. They'll
walk over my grave, tramp on the grass, sit on my headstone, and
plant those damn plastic flowers so I have to look at them for the
rest of the year. What do you think, Clarence, do you think we
ought to dig up our caskets and move up to Effigy Mounds?"

"I'd really like to, but we do have other things to consider."

"Consider? What on earth or under earth or in hell do *we* have
to consider?"

"Our living relatives for one thing. They'd be powerfully
upset if they came here for a visit and found us gone. I know they
think they're making us feel good when they come out to kneel and
pray and leave plastic flowers, even though it doesn't mean a thing
to us, but it makes the old folks feel good. I'd hate to disappoint
them by not being here."

"You have a point there. Even so, my unlife is more important
to me than their lives. Aren't we more important in our skeletons

than our relatives are in their skins? Aren't we, Clarence?"

"We are but you can't be so hard-headed about it. Life and death go together, you know. It isn't over just because we're dead. We still have responsibilities to our friends here in the cemetery, and to our living friends and relatives down in the village. They'll be coming up here someday themselves; we have to exercise patience. We have to help them feel good, so I don't know about moving our caskets, especially before Memorial Day. Folks will be up here trimming weeds and mowing grass and hanging red, white and blue banners on the fence, and Father O'Connell and Reverend Goodsell will inspect the cemetery to see that all is right, and that school teacher will bring one of her kids to practice that damn Lincoln address. You know, Elmer, I don't believe I can stand hearing that old Lincoln chestnut one more time . . . makes my skin . . . err . . . bones ache. On second thought, maybe we should move before Memorial Day.

Listen! Did you hear something over by the fence? Sounded like someone opening the gate . . . at this time of night?"

"I did hear something. Look! Over there by the fence under that big evergreen tree. Why, if it isn't ol' Sylvester Larson, drunk as usual. Now, why on earth would he come out here in the middle of the night? Maybe we should go talk to him." Clarence and Elmer raised their creaking bones off their headstones and clanked toward the fence. They walked as quietly as they could approaching Sly, of course that wasn't easy for a couple of skeletons, but he didn't raise his head. He was well into his second fifth of Seagram's Seven for the day and wasn't feeling any pain or hearing any clanking. Clarence and Elmer clanked to within a couple feet of Sylvester, now slumped against the fence, caressing the black bottle. "Hey! Sly. Sly Larson! Is that you?"

"Huh? Who's talking to me? Thu-rs no one he-re in the cem-ur-tury. Just dead people up he-re . . . they can' talk."

"Sly! Look up. It's Clarence and Elmer, your old buddies from the village and World War Two. Sly! Wake up and talk to us."

"Wh . . . Wh-at? Clar . . . Elm . . . can' be. You guy 's kill-ed on O-kina-wa. Hell! You've be-en dead for twe . . . twen-ty years. God! Must have got some ba-ad S . . . Seagram's . . . from the Liquor

Store. This stuff is ma-king my head cra-zy."

Clarence unhinged his knee socket and reached down to shake Sly out of his stupor. Sly looked up into Clarence's vacant eye sockets and almost jumped out of his shoes. "Damn! Who'r you? Why, you-re a skeleton? I've got to get the hell out of here. Wha-t am I doing in a cem-ur-tury?" Sly said attempting to get up.

"Sit down, Sly. We're not going to hurt you. This is your old war buddy, Clarence, and you remember Elmer, don't you? We fought together on Okinawa, only thing was, Elmer and I came back in boxes."

"Sure I 'member you, but you guys's de-ad, twenty-five years de-ad. Skeletons can' ta-lk, can' wa-lk, can' stand here . . . it's not right, not real. That damn barten-der must have sold me bad booze." With an exerted effort, Sly heaved the bottle into the night, hitting a headstone, crashing the eternal silence.

"Sly, you shouldn't have done that. Clarence and I live here, and we don't like a messy neighborhood anymore than you do. Besides, the Memorial Day Services are in a couple of days, and the Auxiliary will have to clean the cemetery before all you folks traipse up here."

"I'll go clean it up, Clarence," Elmer said. "It's by my grave and I don't want a littered gravehood. It's tough enough spending eternity here; I might as well have a clean grave. Be back in a few minutes." Elmer clanked off into the moonlit as Sly tried valiantly to focus his blurred eyes, watching in dumbfounded amazement as Elmer bounded off.

"Ho-w do you guys wa-lk? You only have bo-nes, no muscle. Ho-w do you make those things work?"

"Oh, it's not so difficult, Sly. You learn to adjust to many inconveniences after you die. We can't get around as fast as you can, but we can move around the cemetery, and once in awhile we walk through the village, too. Not too far, though."

"You guys wa-lk through the village loo-king like that? I've never se-en you. Do you me-an we've got dead p . . . people, skinny skeletons walking through our village? Whe-n do you do it?"

"We're careful because we don't want to scare any villagers, but we like to get out of the cemetery periodically. Graves aren't so bad, Sly, but they do get boring, this cemetery gets boring, so sometimes, about three or four in the morning, we walk when you're snug in your bed. We don't bother anyone."

"I'll be damn-ed. You guys wa-lking around at night? I never would have thought it."

"What are you doing up here, Sly? Why on earth did you walk to the cemetery tonight to drink your booze?"

"I don't know, Clarence. By the way . . . never figured to see you again after you ch . . . charged that bunker on O-kin-awa. You went down real hard . . . blood spurtin' all over . . . it's nice ta-lking to you. Wa-nt to sit down here beside me?"

"Don't mind if I do." Clarence clanked to the fence, balanced one spindly hand on Sly's meaty shoulder and slowly set himself down. Elmer returned from his corner of the cemetery to take up a sitting place on the other side of Sly.

"I don't know, fello-ws. I get to drin-king and wan-dering. Sometimes I don't know where I am. Drinking too much, for sure. If I don't stop, I'm go-ing to end up here with you fello-ws."

"That wouldn't be all bad, Sly. Dead isn't as bad as most folks make it out to be. We've got a place to live, don't need food, don't need water, don't pay rent or taxes, our graves are usually dry, so it's not such a bad deal. About the worst thing is boredom. Days get long, and we get lonesome up here, so it's nice to see you tonight. Maybe you should come out more often to visit."

"I never thou-ght about visiting skeletons. I visit mother's grave, but that's diff-erent from a-ctu-ally talking to dead guys. I didn't know I c . . . could. How come you and Clarence haven't told me be-fore?"

"You've got to come to us like you did tonight. We couldn't come to you. It would have scared the living life out of you, but now that you've wandered into our cemetery, you can see that we can talk."

"Yessir, I can se-e that for sure, but I'm still dumbfounded."

The night's spring air was getting cooler, and even though Sly was filled to the brim with Seagram's Seven, he was getting cold. He snuggled closer to Elmer who placed his bony arm around Sly to help ward of the cold, invading wind blowing in from the northwest corner of Everest. The remainder of Everest's residents were tucked in their graves dreaming or thinking or doing whatever it is that corpses do. By now Elmer was thinking it was a stroke of luck that Sly had unexpectedly appeared tonight. Sly was a Legionnaire. "Say, Sly ol' buddy. You know, it's fortuitous that you happened into the cemetery tonight."

"F . . . For-tu . . . For-tu-i-cous? W . . . Wha-t kind of word is tha-t for a skeleton to use?"

"It's a good word, but that's not the point here. Just before you staggered in, Clarence and I were talking about the upcoming Memorial Day Parade and services. You still march with the Veterans, don't you?"

"Darn too-tin'! Wouldn't miss it for the world. Look forward to it every year. I like to wear my old WWII uniform even thou-gh it doesn't fit good anymore, and I like march-ing to the river, then up here to f . . . fire my f . . . five volleys over you guys' graves. Yessiree. I like Memo-rial Day . . . wouldn't miss it for anything."

"Clarence and I take a different perspective on the entire proceedings, Sly. To be blunt, we don't like it at all. We'd just as soon the villagers, the mayor, the Legionnaires, the Girls Scouts, the Boy Scouts and everybody else stay home and not bother us. We don't like those guns firing over our graves; we heard enough of them on Okinawa. And we're sick to death of the Gettysburg Address. Another thing—we're tired of people walking on our graves. I'm telling you, Sly, it's a bad day for us skeletons. Oh, I know you living folks think you're doing us a favor by shooting and addressing and praying, but it doesn't do us any good. We like being remembered, but you could do that without all the rigmarole of the parade and cemetery services. Could you talk to the townsfolk to eliminate this year's festivities? We'd be mighty obliged to you. What do you think, Sly?" Elmer asked as both he and Clarence held Sly in a warming embrace against the fence.

"Think? I'm ha-ving a har-d time just thinking, but if I did think abo-ut canceling the para-de, I wouldn't think of it at all. You fellows'll just ha-ve to put up with our goodwill 'n' pray-ing 'n' remembrancing. Yessiree, you'll have to tolerate it whether yo-u like it or no-t. It's only once a year."

"But it gets tiring, Sly. We don't have much to look forward to except solitude. We want to enjoy it. Dead people like quietness. That's why we're here. We like to hear birds singing in the trees. We like to watch butterflies flitting silently over our headstones. We like to hear the grass grow above us. We like to hear soft southerly breezes blowing through the evergreen trees. There's no more pleasant sound than that to us, Sly, on earth or under earth. A southerly wind makes little sound until it reaches those long pine needles way up there. When it does, it whirls around the needles and cones of one tree before spinning on to the next. It whistles and sings and moans as it moves pines, cones and branches ever so gently, ever so melodiously. It's a lonesome sound to you living folks, but not to Clarence and I. And we like quiet, dew-laden sunrises and warm, golden sunsets. We don't like noise, Sly. We don't like children hollering, running and scampering on our graves. We hate plastic flowers, and to tell you the truth, Sly, we get especially exasperated with of all that crying folks do over our graves. We're dead. We're good and dead. Dead is dead. There isn't anything you or the Legionnaires or the Girl Scouts or Father O'Connell or Reverend Goodsell can do about it. We're gone. Clarence and I were finished, blown apart out there in the middle of the Pacific Ocean. You can't bring us back, so let us go. Give us our solitude and peace. Let us truly *Rest in Peace!*"

"Don't know about all of tha-t silent stuff, Elmer, 'cause I've never be-en dead, but you sure do ta-ke a different ta-ck on this parade thing. I've never talked to a dead person before tonight, so I don't kno-w quite how to handle this. I thou-ght we were doing you guys a favor by marching and parading and addressing and firing gun salutes in your honor. We figured you liked it, but now I'm hear-ing something contrary-wise. Maybe I could talk to the fello-ws at the club 'bout it. Yessiree, I'll do tha-t much for my Okina-wa buddies. I'll talk to the Vets at the next mee-ting . . . come to think of it, we have a mee-ting tomorrow night. I'll get back to you, fellows.

Well, I've ha-d enough talking for one night. Got to get ba-ck down the hill. Talk to you tomorrow night." Sly staggered to his feet, shook two cold, clammy skeleton hands, then wobbled slowly into the moonlight filtering through the lonesome, moaning ever-green trees.

"Bessie! Set up a double bo-urbon for me, will you? I've got a story to tell."

"Oh, Sly, you're one continuous bullshitter. I don't believe half the stories you tell."

"But this one's d . . . different, very differ'nt. Shoot! Make that a triple brandy. I'll need it to tell my sto-ry." Sly tipped the brandy snifter high letting the sweet taste warm his tongue where he held it momentarily before swallowing. Chilled from sitting on the ground in the cemetery and stumbling down the hill—sobering up slightly from the walk—he thought a few brandies would warm him and rekindle his glow. "Yessiree, ma'am, I've a hell of a sto-ry to tell. I'm glad you're still open even if it is nearly tw-o o'clock.

You see, Bessie, I was meandering around the village whe-n unbeknownst to me, I ended up in Everest."

"What would you be doing in the cemetery this time of night?"

"I hadn't planned on go-in' up, just found myself there when all of a sudden I . . . I . . . no . . . err . . . I guess you wouldn't believe it anywa-y."

"Believe what, Sly. Lay it on me what I wouldn't believe. Lay it hard!"

"You wouldn't believe that I . . . err . . . that . . . I . . . no, you abs'lut'ly wouldn't believe."

"Sly, you're drinking too much. You'd better go on the wagon, because you're nuts," Bessie snarled as she began vigor-ously wiping the bar, anticipating closing.

Sly sat at the bar tossing brandies into his immense body for a long time. He didn't tell his story to Bessie after all, because even with considerable Seagram's and Five Star brandies in him, he still had sense enough to realize she wouldn't believe such a tale. He would be the laughing stock of the village if he told it. Nobody would believe he actually talked with skeletons. Folks would laugh and point fingers at him as he walked the streets. Some thought he was a bit "off" anyway; they might run him right out of town if this story got out. They might lash him to a bass boat and launch him from the dock, letting him float aimlessly down the Mississippi. No, even though he was completely soused, he wouldn't tell about his encounter with Clarence and Elmer.

Peter Hartman sidled up to the bar, whacked Sly on the back spraying cemetery grass and dust across Bessie's newly polished bar, and sat down beside him to order a Grain Belt. Sly didn't even raise his blurry eyes. Instead, he stared straight ahead, mesmerized by the blinking Grain Belt sign behind the bar. "What the hell are you doing, Sly? You didn't even recognize me. You look terrible, too. Look like you've seen a skeleton or something. You seen a skeleton, Sly?" Peter taunted. Sly turned slowly toward him, head bobbing like a fishing cork out on Catfish Slough, eyes glassy trying valiantly to focus on this intruder.

"Ma-tter of fa-ct, I'ave. Saw two of 'em tonight. So , wha-t do you think a tha-t?"

"You're full of shit as always. You've had way too many brandies . . . seeing dead folks, skeletons. Huh! First thing I know, you'll tell me you were even talking to them."

"Wa-s."

"Bessie! Better give Sly another brandy here. Say's he's been talking to skeletons. You ever heard of such a thing?"

"I been thinkin', Pe-te, about the Memo-rial parade. Maybe we shouldn't march this year, maybe we shouldn't go to the cem-ur-tury. It's got to be too much of an effo-rt, sort a like me talking right now. Why don't we shut her down this year?"

"What? Cancel the parade? You're off your rocker. We can't do that. The Vets look forward to marching. The Boy Scouts and Girl Scouts look forward to it. We've finally got a high school marching band that can keep a beat and you want to cancel it? Hell! We aren't the marchers we were a few years ago, our uniforms have shrunk, but the villagers like seeing us anyway. And we've got our departed Army and Navy and Air Force veteran friends to think about. We have to march and show our respect for their service to our county."

"Don' know, Pete. Maybe they don't like it all tha-t much.

Maybe our deceast'd buddies would just as soon be left in pea-ce."

"You are crazy. Maybe you *have* been talking to skeletons."

"Maybe we got this thin-g all wrong. Maybe parading and firing guns is only for us. Maybe it only makes us feel go-od. Maybe it don' do nothin' for our buddies up in Everest. Maybe we're foolin' ourselves. Maybe, after we croak, we'd prefer marchers and bands and Gettysburg addressers staying t'home, not going to the cem-ur-tury. Maybe we should just have a few drinks here at the Club; our Master of Arms could read a couple o' chapters from Gideon so's we could remem-ber our buddies by. What do you think o' that idea, huh? Wha-t do you sa-y? Let's bring her up to the club meeting tonight. I say we should cancel her this year."

"You're sly, Sly, and nuts, too. I'm getting away from you. I'm finishing my Grain Belt. You are c-r-a-z-y."

Peter left Sly slouched at the bar staring past Bessie's concerned eyes, at the blinking beer sign. Sly knew he was confused, but he couldn't sort out his thinking. Clarence and Elmer had made sense to him earlier. They didn't want the parade, and now Sly, too, thought the Vets should cancel it. In his present state he couldn't determine how to do it. Peter had left in a huff thinking he was crazy. Soon, other Legionnaires would brand him, also. What on earth, or under earth, could he do. "Bessie! Fill my glass here. Damn thing's got a hole in it. I've got serious thin-king to do. And give me a glass without a hole in it, will you?"

"That's enough, Sly. Go home."

The meeting commenced at seven with the Pledge of Allegiance. George, Clem, Andy, Harold, Peter, Albert, Dillon, Walter, Karl, Doc and Matt were finishing the recitation when Sly staggered in. "Nice to see you could make it on time, Sly."

"Amen. I'm here, ain't I? I've said the pledge before. It ain't been changed, has it?" Sly retorted dragging a folding chair to the end of the table.

"Meeting will come to order with old business. Anyone have any?" Al intoned over the men sitting around the long folding tables. "We haven't finished work on the flags yet. How's that coming? Do we have enough for each street light on Main Street? Have you taken care of that, Doc?"

"Flags were shipped from Dubuque yesterday. They'll be here."

"Anymore old business?" Al asked. No one responded. He looked up and down the table at men in work clothes, pointed American Legion caps sitting awkwardly, cockeyed on graying, balding heads. "If there isn't any more old business, we'll move on to new business. Anyone have any?"

"I think we should cancel the Memorial Day Parade and complimentary services at Everest," Sly blurted from the end of the table.

"Cancel it? Cancel it? What the hell are you talking about, Sly? You've been drinking again," Karl hollered. Everyone turned to look at Sly slouched in his chair, sitting forlorn at the end of the table. They couldn't believe what they had just heard. Men began huddling, murmuring to one another, then they began laughing, slamming the table, shouting until Al banged his gavel on the table.

"Order! Order, please! I did ask for new business and Sly has just given us the business. I don't know where in hell he came up with the idea, but new business *is* on the table."

"Well, take it off the goddamn table then," Dillon hollered. "I've never heard of such a stupid idea. I vote to disregard Sly's suggestion about canceling the parade and services."

"We've got to follow Robert's Rules of Order here. We need to discuss it first, then we can vote on it. Who has something intelligent to say about canceling the parade?"

"I do. I've got an earful to say," Peter said angrily while rising to the occasion. "Sly suggested this to me last night, but I didn't really think he was crazy enough to put it on the table tonight. We can't do it. We've had a parade every year since I can remember. It's patriotic. We don't want to be unpatriotic. We'd be the laughing stock of Clayton County, of the entire state if we didn't hold our parade. Every community has one. I say we keep it. Sly can go to hell!" Peter hollered as he sat down trying to keep his cap from falling off.

"Anyone else have something intelligent to say?" Al snarled.

"I've wondered myself, from time to time, whether the parade is a good idea. Sure, we do it, but I'm not certain who we're doing it for," Walter said softly, staying seated. "I guess we do it more out of habit than anything else. I enjoy coming to the club early before the parade to sip a few beers with you guys. We all get a little tipsy, then go out and try to march in straight lines and keep in step, but maybe we're only doing that for ourselves. Maybe we aren't doing the community much good, and I don't know if we're doing our deceased brother veterans any good at all," Walter suggested.

"We aren't." Sly barked.

"What do you mean, we're not. How would you know?" Doc snapped.

"Talked to 'em. Talked to 'em last night. That's how I know," Sly retorted.

"Talked? Who did you talk to?" Karl asked.

"Clarence and Elmer."

"Clarence and Elmer were killed on Okinawa, you dumb shit," Walter responded angrily.

"I know that, but I still talked to 'em. They don't want the parade, don't want the cemetery service. They said to forget it— let them *Rest in Peace*."

"Doc, go over and take Sly's pulse, will you? He's not feeling well. Talking about conversing with two dead guys? I've never heard of such a thing. Sly, you're crazy," Peter snapped.

"I make a motion to continue the parade and cemetery services," Dillon hollered.

"I second the motion," Walter responded.

"All in favor say 'Aye.'" The table erupted in a raucous volley of Ayes.

"Opposed?"

"I'm opposed. Damn right I'm opposed. I'm opposite the entire thing," Sly shouted while standing, tipping beer on his pants. "Clarence and Elmer don't want the parade. This is a mistake!"

"Motion carried. Parade and cemetery service continue as usual," Al said slamming the gavel on the table knocking several gum wads loose. "Now let's retire for poker and beer."

Memorial Day morning broke hot and muggy in the valley, long pillows of steam wedging between the embracing hills. Even though it was only the twilight of May, the Iowa corn-growing humidity had already begun, but the morning was cloudless, a good day for a parade. By eight o'clock most Legionnaires had assembled at the club for pre-parade "services." They couldn't march through this humidity without first watering their systems; besides, it was a tradition to sip and retell war stories and reminisce about their departed military friends. Over the years the stories had become increasingly extravagant. Everyone was a hero. Men looking like Pillsbury Doughboys cinched belts, polished brass buckles, snapped bolts on M-1s, blackened shoes, sipped boiler-makers, sucked in paunches, straightened ties, and set helmets at the proper, jaunty angle just like they did in 1943, all the while talking about historic escapades on Guam or Okinawa or Pearl Harbor or Iwo Jima, about naval and air battles in the Pacific. Most had seen action in World War II and even though the war was terrible, the stories and fellowship had kept them going for twenty-five years. They wouldn't have missed this early-morning rite for anything, Sly's admonition notwithstanding. By nine o'clock they and their rifles were well lubricated—all was ready to assemble.

In rout-step, Karl acting as point, the bedraggled squad searched out the parade assembly area at the high school where the marching band was already in parade formation, as were the Girl Scouts, Boy Scouts, American Legion Ladies Auxiliary, and other participants from various clubs and organizations. The Veterans assembled at the head of the parade directly behind the leading color guard. Reluctantly, Sly had agreed to carry the American Flag in the color guard as he had done the past fifteen years. When he awoke this morning, the pull of marching, of participating was even too strong for him. He reasoned Clarence and Elmer would simply have to understand.

A whistle pierced the hovering steam, drums snapped and rolled releasing the parade from the assembly area. By the time the color guard had marched one block, most Vets were in step, all that is except Sly. He never did get in step, and he didn't care. Carrying the American Flag on it's gold-tipped eagle standard was important, being in step wasn't. The parade proceeded toward the river while passing villagers lining the street waving tiny flags. They hooted and shouted and waved and cheered the Legionnaires, the band, the scouts and every marching mother and child. By the time the assembly reached downtown, tan Legionnaire uniforms were soaked with beer sweat making the Vets look like they had swum ashore at Okinawa, but they marched proudly, nonetheless. This was Memorial Day. At the riverfront a young girl floated a wreath onto the river in remembrance of the service men and women who had lost their lives in any war. Taps floated mournfully over the river as the wreath floated gently out into the main channel. Then the band and Legionnaires boarded buses for the short trip to Everest.

"Four score and seven years ago our fathers brought forth on this continent a new nation, conceived in liberty and dedicated to the proposition that all men are created equal . . ." Johnny Swiggart intoned from a grassy knoll between the band and the Legionnaires, both standing at parade rest, although for the Legionnaries *rest* was the dominate position as they swayed like top-heavy wheat stocks in the humid breeze. Their early morning rite was having its effect; even standing at parade rest, much less attention, was proving to be difficult. And they had heard the Gettysburg Address hundreds of time. *". . . that this nation, under God, shall have a new birth of freedom—and that government of the people, by the people, for the people, shall not perish from the earth."* Father O'Connell intoned a few prayers for the departed service men and women. Finally, it was time for the Legionnaires to fire their salute. They fumbled in their pockets for blank cartridges, loaded M-1s and waited for Al's command to fire . . .

"Ready, aim, FIRE!" . . .

BOOMB!

"Reload. Ready, aim, FIRE!" . . .

BOOMB!

"Reload. Ready, aim, FIRE!" . . .

B-O-O-M-B!

The volleys echoed through the pine trees, throughout Everest. Children grabbed mothers' skirts, covering their ears as the volleys bounced off the tombstones. It was a terrible sound for a cemetery. As the echoes bounded through the cemetery out across the road into the surrounding hills and wheat fields, silence once again enveloped Everest. All stood quietly as they listened to the echoes rolling through the lonesome valley to the river. The congregation stood motionless for an eternity around the graves of their countrymen, wiping tears with white handkerchiefs fluttering like spring butterflies. Sly lifted his head slowly to look across the tombstones, followed by Peter, Doc, Dillon, Walter, Karl, Al. They gazed into the far corner, startled to see two skeletons, coffins on shoulders, trudging through the gate and down the road.

"Lord! Sly was right!"

Overture
For A Band

A Creative Memoir

O LD MAN WINTER WAS MAKING HIS FIERCE presence known this morning as I sipped coffee at the Marquette Hotel pondering what selections our band would play at the approaching spring band contest. Heavy, wet flakes were sticking to swaybacked electric wires, forlorn telephone poles and road signs while blizzard winds swirled under the high bridge, wind tornadoes twisting, dancing along the icy river creating a surrealistic scene. The decision would be difficult because so much was riding on it. My personal preference for band literature certainly wasn't the only consideration; I also needed to consider the band members' desires, what selections would impress the three judges, and what compositions would highlight our band's strengths while hiding their weaknesses. We would need at least eight weeks to prepare. From out of nowhere, a butterfly landed on my coffee cup.

Gazing at the frozen river through a cracked window, I slurped coffee and pondered as a snow plow created a maelstrom on the street imprisoning my car against the curb.

It's Friday and the weekend is approaching. I'll listen to recordings and study scores Saturday and Sunday. I'll have made a decision by Monday so the band can begin rehearsing as soon as I purchase the scores and parts. Maybe I'll even drive out of town Saturday to reflect on my choices. I want to play something meaningful for our students and myself, because these Mar Mac students are good instrumentalists. Maybe we could begin with a Karl King march. Iowans consider him to be the march king even though most of the world thinks John Philip Sousa is. And King was from Fort Dodge, too. We might be ready for his famous circus march, Barnum and Bailey's Favorite, *as our opening number, although it would be difficult. I'll have to give that more thought. Yes, I'll rise early tomorrow morning for a drive if this storm doesn't get too bad. I'll slip a tape into my cassette player, then see where the music and spirit take me. Maybe I'll drive north toward the Minnesota border as I haven't been up that way for awhile. Maybe something I see or hear will inspire me.*

"Arthur, my check, please. I have to leave . . . can't stay here drinking coffee all morning when I have music to teach. What do I owe you for the eggs and coffee?"

"If I had your money I'd throw mine away, mister music man. I'd take it all, but I'll settle for a dollar and a quarter, and you're getting off cheap at that," Arthur hollered while extracting his hands from soapy dish water.

"I can see you're really going broke in this joint charging me over a dollar for such a measly breakfast, but I'll pay today . . . not sure about tomorrow, though," I said slipping my topcoat over my shoulders, preparing to venture into the snowstorm.

"You'll be back and you'll pay tomorrow, too, music man. You don't have anyplace else to eat, and you sure can't cook for yourself. You'd burn water trying to boil it. You'll eat my food and pay my prices, because I need the cash. Being poor ain't no disgrace, but it sure is unhandy, I always say," Arthur snapped as he bellied up to the counter tossing the coffee-stained check in my face.

"You're probably right about that, but I need to leave, though . . . have to teach these kids some music today."

"Here's your hat. What's your hurry?"

"I'll see you tonight for dinner. What are you serving?" I asked opening the front door to a bitter, brisk winter wind.

"Salisbury Steak. It'll be good. Buck eighty-nine. Take it or leave it."

"That's what you served last Friday evening, and if I remember correctly, it wasn't anything to write home about."

"Don't let the door hit you in the ass on the way out!"

Friday would be a nice day at school. They usually were, because the students would be in a good mood even though they were anxious for the weekend. I began with two hours of teaching individual clarinet and flute lessons, then an eighth grade general music segment on early American music—William Billings, Charles Ives, Civil War bugle calls, Stephen Foster songs—before preparing for band rehearsal over another cup of coffee. I pulled out the scores we were currently rehearsing for our Mid-Winter Concert in two weeks—arrangement of *America The Beautiful* by Carmen Dragon, transcription of J. S. Bach's *Jesu, Joy of Man's Desiring*, Nicolai's *Overture to the Merry Wives of Windsor*, and Sousa's *Washington Post March*. We had considerable rehearsing yet to do.

Studying the scores, I soon began daydreaming about the significant progress the band had made throughout the past several years. I had arrived at Mar Mac from Minnesota four years ago having accepted this position without knowing what I was getting into. On my interview day, it appeared to be a nice place to teach and live. The Mississippi River was inviting, beautiful and entrancing in this quadrant of Iowa, not unlike the river area upstream in Red Wing and Goodhue County, Minnesota. Towering bluffs and woodlands guarded Marquette and McGregor with maple, oak and walnut trees while wild flowers accented the hills with golds, rusts, yellows and ambers. A fawn, lone rabbit and meandering flock of wild turkeys crossed my path on the outskirts of Marquette. It had felt comfortable. And the people I had met at the grocery store, the drugstore, and the Marquette Hotel cordially welcomed me with big handshakes and whacks on my back. As I drove back upriver to Minnesota that day after the interview, I had a good feeling about the community. What I didn't know about was the status of the band. I hadn't heard any recordings, or seen any accounts of its past history: concert programs, band activities, contest results, membership, instrumentation. The superintendent had been elusive or uniformed about the band, but he said they were good students and would work hard for me. I phoned him

Monday morning to accept the position for the coming year, informing him that I would arrive a week before school began to locate an apartment and to prepare for the year. I felt good about the decision even though I would be moving to Iowa, leaving my beloved Minnesota behind. "Hello, Hawkeyes. Good-bye, Gophers."

The euphoria of signing that contract quickly evaporated when meeting the "band" at my first rehearsal. Thirteen assorted, scraggly river rats walked in lugging dusty, tattered instrument cases from their grandparents' attics. A motley crew, to say the least. Thirteen! I wondered how I ever got myself into this. There were three flutists, two clarinetists, two cornetists, one trombonist, one immensely dented Wayne King vintage C-Melody saxophone (the instrument, that is), and four would-be drummers. I assumed they were drummers in that they totted sticks looking somewhat like drum sticks, although several looked as if they had been used to pry open cellar doors. That was it. Thirteen. And they just sat looking at me. They didn't take their instruments out of the cases, didn't blow a note . . . just sat. A couple of drummers banged away on the bass drum with their snare drum sticks, and the trombone player tried valiantly to open his case, upside down, slide eventually bounding across the floor toward the drummers, but the remainder only stared, expecting magic from the wayward baton I held. But there wasn't any magic that day; in fact, there wasn't any magic for a very long time.

I can't begin to describe the sounds of that first rehearsal, but to this day I hear them clanging in my head—noise, not music, escaped from dusty, dented, moldy, acrid-smelling-broken-down instruments—a cacophony of sound that will be with me to my dying day. I'm glad we didn't have a tape recorder then. I'm glad there is no permanent record of those first rehearsals and of the music we tried valiantly to make. But I persisted, we persisted. A humble beginning it was, those first days and weeks four years ago. But the superintendent had been right—these were good students. They listened to me, usually; practiced hard, usually; attended rehearsals, usually, so that over the weeks and months of that first year we were eventually able to get from the beginning of *Activity*

March and the *Star Spangled Banner* to the end without breaking
down. We were improving even though we couldn't play Karl
King or John Philip Sousa or Richard Wagner or Franz von Suppé
or Ludwig Beethoven. The parents, the school administrators and
the villagers were happy even though we didn't march for the
Clayton County Veteran's Day Parade that first November, a fact
which caused considerable consternation in the community, particularly at the Legion Club, but I asked everyone to be patient. I
promised them that next year the band would be able to both march
and play at the same time. Cynics had their doubts.

By the end of the first year we were still learning notes,
rhythms and fingerings for *Activity March* in Bennett Band Book
No. 1 with nineteen players. By the end of the second year we were
polishing *Activity March,* trudging through a transcription of
Suppé's *Light Cavalry Overture*, and generally succeeding with a
watered-down transcription of the *Second Movement* to Beethoven's
Fifth Symphony with twenty-four players. By the end of the third
year we had worn out *Activity March,* having replaced it with Karl
King's *Iowa Band Law March*, and were struggling through
Richard Wagner's *Overture to Die Meistersinger* with twenty-nine
players. Mark Twain once said, "Wagner's music isn't as bad as it
sounds." He never heard our band tackling Wagner. By the end of
the fourth year we had forty-three players and were well on our
way to developing a respectable, balanced instrumentation. We
even had our first oboist and bassoonist, giving the band a much
needed double reed tonal quality. And we had two tuba players,
two snare drummers, nine clarinetists and a reasonable number of
saxophonists and trumpeters. We were finally sounding like a wind
band. We received our first Division I rating at the spring contest
in Fredericksburg that year, and were on our way to developing a
quality band program for the students, school, parents and community.

But as I attempted to refocus my attention on today's rehearsal, I was still in a quandary about selections for this year's contest,
compositions to keep this hard-won momentum going. It wouldn't
be an easy decision—King, Sousa, Bach, Suppé, Wagner? Could
we do justice to any of these composers? Could we prove Mark

Twain wrong and make Wagner's *Prelude to Act Three of Lohengrin,* or the overture to *Tannhauser* sound better than it was? *I'll have made my decision by Monday's rehearsal.*

March 1 broke clear and bright along the upper Mississippi, arriving like a lamb after yesterday's lion snowstorm. It would be a fine day for driving, listening to tapes, selecting contest compositions. I filled up at the Sinclair Station then drove north along the river. Although the sun was an hour above the Wisconsin bluffs already, it hadn't warmed enough to burn off the thick, ice-tinged fog shrouding the river valley nor the crusted ice on the roadway. I knew, though, that the persistent fog would dissipate once the relentless, bright March sun attacked it. As I approached the suspension bridge at Marquette, a fifteen-unit tow appeared around the bend in the main channel pushing ice floes to the shore like winter months toward spring. How did I know it was fifteen? Since my childhood days along the Mississippi up in Minnesota, I always counted the number of barges and box cars on the railroad paralleling the river. Don't all children count box cars? This tow was probably running from St. Paul to New Orleans carrying Minnesota grain bound for Russia or China, countries and people needing Midwest grain.

I had elected to drive along the river this morning even though the Great River Road was more winding than the inland state highway. I wasn't in a hurry; besides, I did some of my best thinking while driving or sitting along the river. Watching the mighty waters flow by put me in a decision-making mood. I had made the decision to teach at Mar Mac while sitting on the levee up in Red Wing. I had made the decision to enter graduate school in Cedar Falls while sitting on the Marquette dock. I had made the decision to play *Activity March* while walking along the river's shore below Point Ann. And today I would hopefully determine our contest selections along a river's shore.

I saw fishermen rowing out onto the river for a day of bass and crappie fishing. Later they would drink beer at one of the innumerable stilted bars skirting the river.

Maybe I'll have a beer myself tonight at the hotel when I get back. This valley stirs my soul . . . so much to see, to hear, to feel: egrets standing on one leg (why do they do that?), waiting, dipping, darting; eagles soaring lazily over the bluffs before diving swiftly like World War Two dive bombers to the river in search of prey; large-mouth bass exploding through the placid river's surface to capture much needed spring air; tree buds sprouting in the warming March air, and even though I can't see them from the highway, brook trout swimming up the waters of the Yellow River.

Crossing the Yellow River bridge and rounding the sweeping curve at Effigy Mounds National Monument, I flipped the cassette over to hear Franz von Suppé's *Morning Noon and Night in Vienna* overture.

That sure is a fine composition. I wonder if the band is capable of playing it this year. But that long opening clarinet solo certainly is exposed, and those up-tempo woodwind passages would take considerable rehearsing. It would be a fine challenge for the band, though.

Effigy Mounds faded in my rear view mirror as I recalled how, upon its dedication two years ago, our band played for the ceremonies. That was a feather in our hats, particularly a monument dedicated to native Indians in this region.

This ancient Indian burial ground is sacred ground. They lived in these bluffs, along this river hundreds of years ago, but are now long gone. Only their burial mounds—bear, eagle, wild turkey—remain. They developed a culture here long before McGregor and Marquette were founded. I'm glad the government protected the area with a national monument. I'm glad our band performed at the dedication ceremonies. Is there any Native American music we could play? That surely would be appropriate for the Mar Mac Band. But I don't know of any Indian music for wind band. They had developed their own musical system over centuries, one considerably different from our European tradition, so it would be difficult to transcribe Indian music for wind band. Maybe I could arrange something for next year. Or maybe we could play The Mississippi Suite *by Ferde Grofé? No, I don't think our band is ready for that yet. Grofé will have to wait.*

As the rising sun broke through a cloud bank spreading golden rays across the valley, I passed Smoky Hollow to crest a ridge before turning onto Highway 364 which took me toward the river and Waukon Junction. Soon, everything appeared old—old rocks, old outcroppings, old trees, old people, Old Junction. I quickly entered an area of brackish water, sloughs meandering among varied islands, and more decrepit house trailers than I could count. Paint Rock Road slithered through sheer sandstone cliffs like a water snake, exposing layers of slab rock dotted with evergreen trees reaching skyward.

I approached the Yellow River Forest beyond Waukon Junction. Coming over a rise at the summit, I entered another long valley suddenly understanding why Indians had chosen this land. The Mississippi had provided a constant source of food, the bluffs, hills and valleys had provided protection from the fierce upper Midwest weather, and the vistas had provided them with serenity for their spirits. It made sense to me. Had I been an Indian five hundred years ago, I would have chosen this country, too. The Yellow River Forest area extended for ten miles northward along the river providing modern-day Americans opportunities to camp, hike, ride, run, walk, contemplate—a wilderness for urban people escaping the city. I periodically escaped to this place myself. Because McGregor and Marquette are villages, sometimes folks can get too close. When there is only one main street, a fellow can't even purchase groceries, attend church or guzzle a beer without folks knowing it. If you don't want people to know what you're doing, don't live in a village. Sometimes a guy needs to get out of town. The Yellow River Forest was a good place to do that.

I can't stop today, though . . . have to keep moving, thinking about contest. What about Wagner? His music works well for wind band, although he wrote long, languid passages requiring extraordinary breath control. His staged music dramas go on forever; however, his overtures are shorter. Maybe we could play the overture to Die Meistersinger *this year. Although stretching it somewhat, there might be a musical connection between Wagner's Bavarian Forest and Iowa's Yellow River Forest. That connection could be a good musical experience for the band.*

As I left the northern boundary of the Yellow River area, I approached Harper's Ferry through Harper's Slough near Lock and Dam No. 9 where the continuous life cycle of the river was displayed directly in front of me. New trees struggled for life among decaying trees, trees that had lived their life, had served their purpose, now laying motionless like prehistoric dinosaurs among the new growth. Shacks, lean-tos, log cabins, faded aluminum-sided mobile homes occupied every seemingly available spot along the shore—people drawn to the water, toward life. Soon, I was past Andy Mountain Campground entering a wider delta plain—Harper's Ferry. There are two Harpers Ferrys in the country, but the one most Americans know is over in Virginia—the Civil War Harper's Ferry—but a war wasn't fought in Iowa's Harpers. Sure, the fellows lining the bar at Pete's Tap get into fist fights periodically on Saturday nights after fishing all day, but that doesn't amount to much. They spend the night in the jail, then make up to become friends again the next morning. River towns and river people are like that. They're different from prairie towns and prairie people out in western Iowa. Mississippi River towns are more open, more free, more exciting, more alive. As the country was becoming established, rivers provided transportation to undeveloped, wooded lands in Midwest Territories. Rivers offered food from their bellies, wild animals and vegetation from their banks; it was logical immigrants would settle first along their shores instead of out on the wind swept, barren prairie. With thousands of pioneers migrating by steamboat, settlements grew along the river while simultaneously attracting an assortment of river characters. It took years for river towns to become cultured, if they ever did; it took years for river towns to appreciate the finer things in life, for men to learn manners—how to behave around women, how to use cuspidors, how to be law abiding citizens. They're still working on it, even today. It was the same, even worse, in Alaska. Law was a long time coming to the Klondike; it was a long time coming to Mississippi river towns. But you can't hold that against river folks. Tom and Huck down in Hannibal didn't wear shoes, seldom attended school, attended church under duress, cussed, spat and swam nak'd in the river. Why, Aunt Polly spent her life trying to get Tom to be civiliz'd. And that wayward Huck never did. Hannibal folks were so happy Tom and Huck survived five days in that cave that they showered accolades on the pair for weeks afterward. Those boys found Indian Joe's money, but Huck couldn't tolerate what the money brought him—civilizin'. He left Aunt Polly, tramped to a river shack to live like he had been before he and Tom found the treasure. River folks are like that. They were in Hannibal. They are today.

I pulled over for a cup of coffee and Hostess doughnut at Irene's Cafe in Harpers then walked to the levee to watch shore fisherman at their trade. "How they bitin'," I asked sauntering up to the trio of men sitting in tattered, blue K Mart-webbed chairs, knowing full well I shouldn't have asked such a stupid question. Folks always ask fishermen "How they bitin', but anglers have never given an honest answer in their lives. But I didn't stay long. I had an objective. The sun had risen to the ten o'clock position, and there were places to go, decisions to make. "Nice talking to you, fellows. Hope you have a good day's catch."

Continuing northward out of Harpers on the rutted Great River Road, I drove through startling land, a land unseen by most travelers, because while the Great River Road meanders around bluffs skirting the river, the more traveled main state highway takes a less circuitous route farther inland. This land is pristine, almost untouched. Even the piercing glances of generations of people have not eroded the jagged, jutting cliffs which dominate the land overpowering sculptured hills, backwaters and marshes of the Great River. I was by myself on the road, one devoid this morning of John Deere tractors pulling grain wagons, for this was not farming country. This land belonged to nature, to the Indians who had lived here hundreds of years ago, to the wildlife living here today. To the east I saw the expanse of the river. To the west lay grand valleys with groves of evergreens interspersed with wild meadows, a veritable patchwork of nature. The evergreens were still green (that's why they're called evergreen, you know), but it was too early for maples, oaks and walnuts to bud. Ice crystals fluttered through the air, glistening in the bright March sunlight, bending blues, reds and yellow into a thousand prisms. South of

Lansing, I stopped below Big Rock Bluff, standing alongside the road drinking in the fresh river air, absorbing this land, peering, gazing without adulterating it.

I continued around numerous bluffs, slowly climbing inclines then rushing into valleys around contoured patches of prairie grass, spreading sumac bushes, birch, burr oak, even a few aspen trees near Heytman's Landing where ancient steamboat parts—decaying paddlewheels, rusted boilers, broken filigreed staircases—lay decaying along the shore.

What is a paddlewheel without its boat?

Soon, I reached Bosco Bluff anchoring the dichotomous angular and curvilinear bridge at Lansing. My objective during this drive was contemplation of contest selections, but I was having difficulty concentrating because the land was so awe-inspiring. In Lansing I could see several miles across the river into Wisconsin; I thought I might have even seen Minnesota's golden hills through the rising morning mist. Suddenly, Suppé's *Light Cavalry Overture* burst into my ears with its opening trumpet fanfare as I inserted the third cassette tape of the morning.

Maybe we're ready for Suppé. I don't know if the band could play the original score, but we could probably play a watered-down transcription. On the other hand, Suppé is sometimes corny, trite; besides, it's been played so much by other bands. The judges may be tired of it. Suppé? Wagner? This isn't getting any easier.

The Mississippi's main channel narrowed at Lansing, but it was still wide compared to other rivers, rivers less grand, less majestic. Its headwaters begin three hundred miles north in Minnesota's Itasca State Park as a stream, a creek so small that one can literally step across it as it trickles through the underbrush searching for a path, a route to begin its journey through the heartland of America. By the time it reaches northern Iowa, it has already gained considerable momentum, having accepted the waterways of numerous tributaries through Minnesota and Wisconsin.

I could cross the river here and drive into Wisconsin. No, I don't think so. I'll stay in Iowa today, head west toward Decorah then make a loop southward back to Marquette. That'll make a good drive, and it isn't even noon yet.

I drove west through Allamakee County toward Waukon, Frankville, Ossian and Calmar. As the river faded from view in my rear mirror, I left the towering, jagged bluffs to enter sculptured hills and valleys left untouched by the voracious glaciers which scored this lazy, driftless land millions of years ago. Although I had never been to Austria, I imagined Innsbruck and Vienna to be something like this. Thinking about Haydn, Mozart and Beethoven, I peered to the top of the hills expecting to see alphornists in lederhosen trumpeting their spinning, lonesome harmonics, welcoming me into this valley. For the next ten miles, I slipped around hills, rising to their summits only to rush downward toward a creek—Village, Clear, French, Silver—child-like streams seeking the Father of Waters like a great magnet. Ancient limestone houses, barns, grist mills, the Wexford Stone Church and Cemetery dotted the valley, relics of immigrants who had settled here one hundred years ago. Higher, on Mullarkey Hill, there was an absence of buildings, a crest left untouched by the pioneers. With Haydn's *Military Symphony* resounding in my ears, I passed Wexford Hollow Road, a serpentine filament wiggling its way through a steep ravine, a ravine devoid of buildings, of man's presence.

How wonderful that there are still places like this where man's presence is lacking, were nature presents only itself.

Beethoven's *Song of Joy* ran through my mind in counterpoint to Haydn's *Military Symphony* creating cacophony in my consciousness.

Thrusting westward, the embracing countryside gradually became more gentle, though certainly not prairie. Rock-strewn bluffs constrain the majestic Mississippi, but several miles inland they begin loosing their grip. Bluff land isn't farming land, but I began seeing more wooden, gabled barns and wood-staved silos tucked into the hills and valleys, museum structures dating from the 1880s when hopeful immigrants crossed the Mississippi determined to tame this land, determined to carve out a new life for themselves west of the Mississippi, determined to put even this land under the plow as they had done in Ohio and Pennsylvania. Little did they know that this river land was untamable. I began seeing periodic farmers rushing spring plowing as they turned the earth along the precarious hills. But northeast Iowa is difficult land to farm. If a fellow is serious about farming, he needs to live in central Iowa around Mason City, or in western Iowa around Red Oak. That's farm land. Northeastern Iowa isn't. A man on a John Deere can only farm about one hundred acres out of his three hundred twenty in northeast Iowa, because the remainder is too wooded, too steep. But Iowa farmers are persistent wherever they live, and they're particularly tenacious up in this quadrant.

Snare drum paradiddles snapped in my ears like Civil War Harper's Ferry musket shots as the *Military Symphony* came to a rousing conclusion as I slowed to a tractor's pace behind a trudging Allis Chalmers and New Deal grain wagon entering Waukon where flags were flying everywhere from two-story-frame-hip roof-front-porched white houses. This is Middle America where people are proud of their American heritage, proud of the country even though they do get tired of the shenanigans in Washington. But they stick by it. They fly the flag every day.

Out by the Waukon Conoco station, I veered west toward Decorah thinking I would visit the Norwegian Vesterheim Museum and Luther College for musical inspiration.

Maybe we could play a Scandinavian composition. There are hoards of Norwegians in this part of the state, and just maybe, one of the judges might be Norwegian. Playing a Norwegian composition would impress him, wouldn't it? What composers do I know? Let's see, there's Edward Grieg. Could we play anything from his Peer Gynt Suite? *And there is Sibelius. Was he Norwegian or Finnish or Swedish? Sibelius is ponderous, though, worse than Wagner.*

I began seeing *Velkommen* signs on mail boxes along the road, *Velkommen* signs on front doors, barn doors, chicken coop doors, *Velkommen* all the way into Decorah. Those folks sure like to welcome you, that's for sure ... "Vell, you betcha, you yoost batter come right in und sit down und have somme Kaffe und Kaker. Ja, vee yoost *velkommen* you."

I drove down *Velkommen* Street past one hundred bright red and blue *Velkommen* signs pondering how I had been welcomed into Iowa myself a few short years ago.

Uff da! *I'm not Norwegian, not even Lutheran—although I had known some in Minnesota—but Iowans accepted me, nonetheless.*

Leaving Minnesota hadn't been in my plans, but moving to Iowa had turned out to be a good decision. The students had responded positively as I taught them music, as we built a respectable band, as the community became increasingly proud of us. Personally, I participated in community events—Kiwanis Club, church suppers, church bingo games, poker games in the hotel's back room. Sure, McGregor and Marquette were sleepy little hamlets—no bright lights like Chicago, Kansas City, Minneapolis or even Iowa City—and the winter months imprisoned the valley in a vise grip, but by March, renewed life again appeared making the communities and valley more hospitable.

I'm glad I came to Mar Mac, but I have felt some restlessness lately that I don't want to recognize. For these past years, I've thought of nothing but the band, the students, the wind band music we've played, getting better, getting bigger, but I have noticed recently that fleeting thoughts of moving on have entered my mind during unguarded moments. It scares me. I don't want to move. I don't want to leave this band, these students, this valley, this river. I don't think there is another place as Velkomming.

I was startled out of my reverie as the Vesterheim Museum loomed directly in front of me, Vesterheim flag flying from a third-story veranda of the grand, restored structure which shed its imposing facade on downtown Decorah. The building was ornate, almost Baroquish with carved arches above every window, filigreed balcony above three ponderous ten-foot doors, even decorative carved blocks under the vast cornice. I paid my fee to the matronly woman bedecked in a colorful, festive costume to browse among reconstructed ancient fireplaces, baskets, rosemaling crafts, model ships, church relics, wooden skis, heavy winter clothing, and a fiddle or two, literally thousands of immigrant artifacts while wondering about their struggle for a better life here in the New World, hoping desperately that Iowa would prove to be better than the troubles of the Old World. Although I enjoyed learning about the Norwegians' western home in America, I found nothing to inspire me musically, nothing that would provide a connection for our band. Oh, a couple of nineteenth century foot-pump reed organs were roped off along a darkened back wall with folk song books on their music desks, but music of the masters was conspicuously absent.

Uff da!

Leaving the museum, I drove past The Church of Our Lady of Perpetual Help—*Help me, Lady, with my contest selections*—past the statue of the leaning Norwegian where two white-haired bachelors sat smoking and talking in the brisk spring sun, probably about good times back in the old country. I waved, hung a left by Knute's Market—large wooden *Velkommen* sign enticing sausage and ludefisk buyers inside—and was soon heading toward Luther College where I hoped to find musical inspiration. It was already noon and although I had been brainstorming all morning, I wasn't any closer to determining contest selections. The day had been enjoyable, but was dissipating much too rapidly.

Before arriving in Iowa, I had heard of Luther College, because a high school colleague had attended Luther. Being a good German Lutheran, he was mystified by the Rule of the Norwegian Lutherans, so he returned to his German Lutheran community in Minnesota after only one year. But he had said that Luther College had a wonderful music school which I soon confirmed upon my arrival in Iowa. Unfortunately, the music school was bound tightly this Saturday, not a single, wayward note escaping.

Half past one. I sped toward Calmar down Highway 150 south, inserting a new tape to hear Karl King's *Iowa Band Law March* pouring through my speakers.

No, I don't think we'll play Grieg or Sibelius. A King march would be good to open with. He has so much meaning and importance in Iowa, having written that march to commemorate the first state in the country to levy a community tax for band. That says something about Iowa, doesn't it? Yes, an Iowa composer's march would be a good opener.

Ten miles south of Decorah a T-intersection jutted to the west. A faded, leaning sign twisting slowly in the breeze proclaimed:

HOME OF BILY CLOCKS

TURN RIGHT, RIGHT HERE

THREE MILES TO SPILLVILLE

SUMMER HOME OF

ANTONIN DVORAK (1893)

It caught my attention. I slammed on the brakes, fishtailed on the gravel shoulder creating a column of dust, and made a hard right to pull up alongside the battered sign. I had heard villagers speak of the Bily Clocks, but I didn't know Dvorak had spent summers here. No one had mentioned that to me.

H'm, Dvorak? What do I know about him? Wasn't he the Yugoslavian or Hungarian or Turkian? No, not Turkish. I think he was a Slovak. Polish? Czechoslovakian? That's it. Czechoslovakian. Now I remember; we played a Dvorak selection when I was in Seventh Grade. What was the name of that piece? World? World Symphony? *No.* New Music from the Old World? *No. New something.* New World? New World Symphony? *That's it. We played the finale´ to his* New World Symphony. *I didn't like it then, and I think we murdered it anyway. Poor Dvorak. But this is interesting . . . think I'll drive into Spillville to check out the Bily Clocks and see what I can find out about Antonin. What else did he write? Maybe Dvorak is a possibility for spring contest.*

After driving through rolling, wooded hills for a couple of miles, I came to the crest of a long ridge, layers of limestone guarding my ascent like Roman centurions. In a valley a mile below sat a tiny village tucked into the hills reminding me of a mountainous Italian village. I pulled over to admire the view for a few moments before descending.

What a wonderful place to create, to compose, here in the solitude of this valley. Dvorak found a home far away from his Czech home.

I slowly descended and was soon in the center of the hamlet where a tall town clock loomed over the square, a statue on the opposite side.

H'm, must be the standard Union soldier statue.

There couldn't have been more than one hundred people populating Spillville, maybe seventy-five, but it had a warm feeling, probably because of its size, although I sensed there was more to it than that. Parking my car near the clock tower, I sat for a few moments then walked into the square. A couple of old-timers looking like Laurel and Hardy were sitting on a bench, just talkin' and spittin'. They waved and hollered . . . "How you doin' there, young fella? You're new to these parts, ain't you? We ain't seen you around Spillville before, have we?" The fat one fired three questions at me before I even had a chance to answer the first, but I knew he was only being friendly. Folks in small towns are that way. I walked over and struck up a conversation. "Just passing through, fellows, just passing through."

"It's hard to just pass through Spillville. We ain't on a main road or nothin' like that, so maybe you're lost. You lost, fella?" the white-bearded man in bib overalls said as he puffed on the biggest cigar I had ever seen.

"No, sir, I am not lost. I've driven down from Decorah . . . saw the road sign back at the intersection about Bily Clocks and Antonin Dvorak—could use some paint and fixing up—so I thought I would drive in to see the clocks. You gents know anything about them?"

"Sure. Hell! We know everything about Spillville, don't we, Jan? [Jan nodded.] Jan here don't talk much. He lets me do most of the talkin', doesn't you, Jan? [Jan nodded again.] But he's a good fella anyway. What's your handle? I have a hard time talkin' to a guy if I don't know his handle," the loquacious one asked as he spat a stream of tobacco juice to the grass.

"It's Jim. I'm from McGregor, downriver."

"Howdy, Jim. This here's Jan, but I've already told you that, and I'm Karel. Karel Hrdlicka. Now that I know your handle, I can talk to you straight like. Why don't you sit here on the bench with us. I know it's a tad nippy today, but Jan and I sit out here most of the time, don't we, Jan? [Jan nodded.] We don't get many strangers through here in the winter months, mostly summer and fall when the leaves turn into colors. Your comin' through is sort of a treat, John."

"Ah, not John, Jim. Jim Franklin."

"Okay, Jim. Sorry about that. I ain't too good with names. Teeth are good, though. I got all of 'em yet, and my sight's pretty good, too, ain't it, Jan? [Jan nodded.] My hearin' lacks a little, though. I can hear that big Billy Clock over there when it clangs the hours, though, can't I, Jan? [Jan nodded.] You said you wanted to know about Billy Clocks and Dvorak? That what you said, sonny?" Karel shouted as he reached into his bib pocket pulling out another cigar, scraping a farmer match across the sole of this boot before bringing the flame to the cigar. He sucked deeply, coughed two or three times like a sputtering John Deere then blew a long, twisting spiral of smoke skyward adulterating the fresh spring air. "You want another cigar, Jan?"

"Nope."

"Jan don't talk much, but I already told you that. Clocks? Dvorak? Hell! I can tell you 'bout the clocks, but I don't know much o' nothin' 'bout old Antonin standing over there on the other side of the square. Guess he lived here some summers writin' music back before they turned the century, but that's all I know 'bout him. Don't know much about fancy music. Know what I like, though . . . like Old-time music—polkas and schottisches and mazurkas and waltzes and ländlers. Jan and I here are Czech, you know. You must know that if you sauntered into Spillville. This whole valley is Czechoslovakian . . . guess Antonin come here 'cause of the colony, but I told you that already. They got Amish down to Olewin and Kalona, and those True Inspirational Believers are down there in the Amana Colonies, got Bohemians down there in Cedar Rapids, too, but this is the best Czech place in Iowa. Spillville's small but we like it that way. And we're not bothered by strangers either, mostly, 'cept in summers and when fellas like you get lost, 'cause of bein' hidden up here in these hills and draws, off the beaten path so to say. Most locals either come from the old country, or their parents or grandparents did. But I was tellin' you about polkas and schottisches. See that old granary building over there past Pavel's Shoe Shop. We have dances there ever' Saturday night. Got one tonight. You ought to stay around, young fella. You'd have a hell of a time," Karel said wheezing from cigar smoke.

"Thanks for the invitation, Karel, but I'll need to be driving back to McGregor before dark. I don't know my way around these hills. I might really get lost," I responded while shifting for more room on the bench. "What's the story about the Bily Clocks?" I asked, trying to get Karel back on track.

"You want the long version or the short one? Well, hell! I'll just start talkin' here, won't I, Jan?" [Jan nodded.]

Seems like 'bout 1920 a fella sauntered through here one day just like you're doin' today, kind of lost like? Was a carpenter, mostly, but was out of work and down on his luck; his saw was dull, don'tcha know. The story goes that he was sittin' here in the square just like you, ain't that right, Jan? [Jan nodded.] when old Mrs. Masaryk happened by carrying a broken mantle clock. She set down right here on the bench to catch her breath, started up a conversation with this fella by the handle of William. She told the fella that she had taken her broken clock to the repair man behind the shoe shop, but he was sick so she was out of luck. William said he knew a little 'bout clocks, asked to see it, fiddled with the innards a few minutes—get that, sonny, a few minutes?—found the problem and within five minutes had Mrs. Masaryk's clock ticking right then and there. She was so dumbstruck that she asked William to stay 'round the village for awhile. Well, he did. Not only did he stay 'round, him being down on his luck and all as I told you, but he began fixin' clocks for other folks; before long he was even making them from scratch. Being a carpenter, he made beautiful cabinets, too, and began learnin' how to forge metal, wheels and gears for the clock innards. Mrs. Masaryk rented a shack to him out on the edge of town up that draw over there past St. Wenceslaus. From that little shack his handle and fame spread.

Folks here in Spillville began buying his clocks—used to be called Spielville, ain't that right, Jan? but locals couldn't spell good so they simplified it to Spillville. City slickers from New

York and Chicago, Bohemians mostly who summered here back in the Thirties and Forties, saw his clocks, bought gobs o' them so's now William's fame spread outside o' Spillville. Locals started calling him *Billy* 'cause *William* was too stuffy, too high handed for this place. Hell! He built the best clock innards and carved the cases by hand, too. He was a craftsman, that's for sure, wasn't he, Jan? [Jan nodded.] Jan don't talk much. And he was a musician, too. Billy played accordion . . . played with the Polka Czechers over there to the Granary House, Saturday nights. You could stick 'round tonight, young fella. Hell! He could play polkas and schottisches that'd make you sweat right through your overalls. He sure could do that, couldn't he, Jan?" [Jan nodded.] He made hundreds o' clocks when he weren't playin' accordion. Sold them to Iowa and Minnesota folks, folks who'd come over from the old country, mostly . . . sold them to New York and Chicago city slickers, too, but I already told you that. He kept making them until the day he croaked. Let's see, that was back 'bout 1950, wasn't it, Jan? [Jan nodded.] I think Billy died in '50, but folks still drive up here to see his clocks, don'tcha know, even though he ain't here no more. Of course, he's buried out there in St. Wenceslaus Cemetery under one of those cast iron crosses that's so heavy a fella'd never get up, top of that ridge over there; you oughta stop by. We got his clock museum right over there next to the Shoe Shop. Ain't open today, though . . . don't 'cept Sunday's during winter months. Grouchy, ancient Gretchen Sedlacek runs it and she runs it on her own time. That's a joke, young fella. Clocks? Her own time? Get it, son? Hell! You're too slow for my jokes. Your clock's runnin' way to slow. Anyway, she's real testy 'bout Billy, but she runs the museum for free so we can't complain. Just 'bout everybody 'round here has a Billy Clock in their house, and most of the merchants 'round the square here have a couple. You could see one in Vaclav's Meat Market or Pavel's Shoe Shop or at Jaroslav's Drugstore. Well, John, I'm kind of tirin' myself out here with all this talkin'. You want to tell mister John more 'bout the Billy Clocks, Jan?"

"Nope."

"Jan sure ain't a talker, but I make up for it, don't I, Jan?" [Jan nodded.] Karel leaned back on the bench, sucked several long breaths of smoke to the bottom of his lungs, hitched up his britches, coughed, belched and blew smoke toward the Bily Clock tower as it chimed three times.

"Wow! That's a beautiful chime. Did Bily make that also?" I asked Karel, turning to look at the clock.

"You can bet your sweet Czechoslovakian ass he did. But you ain't Czech, are you?"

"No, sir. I'm Irish and Austrian. I don't have any Czech in me whatsoever, although I did play polkas, waltzes and mazurkas for Minnesota dancers. They were mostly German, though, not Czech," I answered still looking at the clock.

"Well, I won't hold that against you, but we ain't much for Germans 'round here. They got enough of them down there in Clayton County, your neck of the woods, and down in the Amanas, too. They got a smattering up there in Decorah, but Jan and I don't go to Decorah very much, do we, Jan?" [Jan nodded.] Jan smiled his plastic, toothless smile. I could tell he was a gentle man, even if he didn't say so himself. He looked like a rail sitting next to fat Karel, Jan in his stained pea hat, tattered denim coat, bib overalls and airy boots. These two men were characters, that was for sure, but they were my first Spillville contact. Karel had been talking for almost an hour, but I still hadn't pried any information lose about Antonin Dvorak, the real reason I detoured into town. I prodded Karel. "Where can I find out more about Dvorak? You said there was a Bily Clock Museum. Is there an Antonin Dvorak Museum?"

"'Course there is. You should know that by now. Did you get off the train yesterday or somethin'? It's in the same building that holds Billy's clocks down the street there. And they's a Humorous Memorial over in Riverside Park to Dvorak. Only thing is, I don't know nothin' 'bout it. Locals say that he never penned no polkas and I figure any guy not writin' polkas ain't much of a musician? Don'tcha think?"

"Polkas aren't so bad, Karel, but I like other types of music better. I'm a band director in McGregor; in fact, that's why I'm in Spillville today. I'm trying to decide what music to play for spring contest, so I'm driving around northeastern Iowa to generate ideas.

I thought something I saw or heard today might inspire me. Dvorak interests me," I said pushing and scooting over for more room on the bench.

"Hell! You want ideas? You're a band director you say? Play polkas. Locals here like polkas, don't they, Jan? [Jan nodded.] You can't go wrong playin' polkas. You could play a mazurka, too, couldn't he, Jan? [Jan nodded.] You don't need to go no further. I've got the answer for you. Stop being so stubborn and listen to me—polkas, schottisches and waltzes."

"I agree that they're fun, happy, danceable music, Karel and Jan, good for your Saturday night dances, but not appropriate for a contest selection. I need something more serious, more classically oriented, more musically structured, more harmonically advanced. Now, I'd like to find about more about Dvorak. Can you direct me?"

"Well, if you're gonna be stubborn 'bout your fancy pants classical music you need to talk to Olga Komensky. She's the director o' the Dvorak Museum. Doubt she's open today, what with this bein' Saturday and all, and the middle o' winter, too. Those Dvorak fancy pants come in here ever' summer. I don't know, they make music and upset the whole apple cart here, if you ask me, don't they, Jan? [Jan nodded.] They give concerts here in the square and over to the Inwood Pavilion, but I don't come 'round to hear 'em. They don't play no polkas, just that classical stuff that Jan and I don't like. We go to the polka dances, but I already told you that," Karel said as he belched and spat a sputtering stream of brown tobacco juice toward the sidewalk. "Olga lives up that draw on the other side o' the square—big two-story house. Biggest one up that hollow. You could walk up there to talk with her, you bein' persistent 'bout it. She's quite a wind bag, and once she gets to talkin' 'bout Dvorak, she'll bore a fella to tears, but then you bein' a music-type yourself, you'd probably like her.

Well, Jan and I got some pool playing and serious drinkin' to do, don't we, Jan? [Jan nodded hitching up his trousers.] We got to meet some fellows over to Josef's Tap for a few games and beers. Nice meetin' you, John. Go up and talk to Mrs. Komensky then stop back at Josef's for a couple of beers if you ain't bored out of your skull with Olga by then. If not, come on back to Spillville during the summer months. Take 'er easy now. Come on, Jan, let's shoot pool and drink beer."

"Yup."

I said good-bye to Karel and Jan as they traipsed across the square headed for Josef's, then looked over my shoulder toward the big house, an imposing structure even from this distance. I could see a rotunda on the second story, and white columns supporting the porch skirting two-thirds of the house. It was an impressive house, suitable for a famous composer.

I walked to the far side of the square toward the statue. Coming around in front, I saw that it was a bigger-than-life bronze statue of Antonin Dvorak towering twelve feet into the Spillville air. Dvorak was full-faced, bearded wearing a long, split-tailed coat, and holding a music manuscript in his right hand. Actually, he looked somewhat like Karel, though shorter, lighter without a pot belly. There was an inscription on a plaque below his feet:

ANTONIN DVORAK
1856-1910
FAMOUS WORLD-RENOWNED
CZECHOSLOVAKIAN COMPOSER
BROUGHT HIS FAMILY TO SPILLVILLE IN 1893
FROM NEW YORK CITY TO SPEND THE SUMMER WITH
US AMONG OUR MAGNIFICENT HILLS IN OUR BELOVED
CZECHOSLOVAKIAN (BOHEMIAN) COMMUNITY.
HERE, HE COMPOSED HIS AMERICAN STRING QUARTET
AS WELL AS OTHER NOTABLE QUARTETS. IT IS BELIEVED HE
ALSO SKETCHED IDEAS FOR MANY OF HIS SLAVONIC DANCES
IN OUR LOVELY HILLS AND ALONG OUR REFRESHING STREAMS.
SINCE 1899, MUSICIANS FROM AROUND THE WORLD HAVE
GATHERED HERE EVERY SUMMER FOR
THE DVORAK MUSIC FESTIVAL.
FOR FURTHER INFORMATION CONTACT
OLGA KOMENSKY(INQUIRE AT VACLAV'S MEAT MARKET)

I stood in front of the statue for a long time contemplating his deep-set, piercing eyes, wondering how he had felt arriving in Spillville so long ago. In 1893, Iowa must have felt like wilderness to him. I even had that feeling in 1960. Suddenly, I felt a need to know more about Dvorak, his journey to Iowa, his life in the old country, his feelings about music, his compositions. And I began thinking about my own musical journey, how I had arrived in Iowa on a circuitous but noteworthy route, nonetheless. Dvorak and me. What was there about Iowa that drew us? I felt a kinship for him at that moment, a feeling heretofore absent. Yes, I had played his finalé to the *New World Symphony* as a boy, but that's all I knew about him or his music. I must have studied Czech music in my college music studies, but I didn't recall it. We studied Mozart, Haydn, Bach, Beethoven, Charles Ives, Aaron Copland, but Dvorak? Gazing at his face, I realized that he had been a real person, not simply a dusty, dead composer living between the pages of a stuffy music history text. He had walked, admired and composed music in this valley. There were similarities between us. I immigrated to Iowa as he did. I am a musician as he was.

I want to find out more about him, about his music, about our Iowa connection.

As the sun skittered behind a sudden, swirling March squall sweeping over the steeple of Saint Wenceslaus Church, I pulled my topcoat tighter around my shoulders, walked to a bench near the statue and sat on a cold wrought iron bench. Two squirrels scurried around the statue, a boy with a squashed loaf of Wonderbread under his arm rode past on a fat-wheeled Schwinn, a lone canting, rusted pickup bounded slowly around the square, a red neon Dubuque Star Beer sign flickered in the window of Josef's Tap in the encroaching twilight; otherwise, there was little visible activity. A sense of peace and tranquillity enveloped me matching the solitude of the village. I looked up into Dvorak's deep-set eyes guarded with heavy, imposing eyebrows, now blurred to my vision through the lightly falling snow, and thought about my own music experiences—love of music from childhood, first clarinet lessons, late Saturday night radio listening excursions on clear channel WXLE Del Rio, Texas reaching me all the way up in Minnesota's tundra. I recalled my first meager attempts at playing jazz—I thought then that it was jazz, but it was mostly sweet dance music: Glenn Miller's *Moonlight Serenade*, Lawrence Welk's *Bubbles In The Wine*, Six Fat Dutchmen's *Blue Skirt Waltz*—then my journey to college to play unknown concert band compositions, march on bitter northern Minnesota fall Saturday afternoons, struggle with string instruments in orchestra rehearsals, then choir rehearsals, clarinet lessons, music theory and history classes. Music History was the most difficult. Oh! so painful because my classmates and I knew little or nothing about history, nothing about Greek music nor Palestrina, Bach, Mozart, Haydn, Beethoven, Wagner, Stravinsky or Copland. Everything, every composer was new to us and so terribly difficult to assimilate. And we certainly didn't study much, if anything, about Dvorak. But here I sit in front of his snow-covered statue contemplating his life, my life . . .

I was drawn to music because of its art—melody, harmony, rhythm, texture, themes, structure, aesthetics. They drew me like a powerful magnet; still do. Music is a force, a creative energy needing resolution in my soul. I want to share it with my students. I want them to feel what I feel, enjoy what I enjoy. I know how music will enrich their lives as it has mine. Building the band program at Mar Mac has been gratifying for me, and I hope, for the students. We work hard, practice hard, rehearse hard, perform hard and the better we get, the more musical joy we experience. Sure, moms and dads are proud of their children's developing musical skills, but music is more than demonstrating newly-acquired technical skills on a saxophone or trumpet. It's more than a Division I rating at Spring Contest in Fredericksburg or Guttenberg, although we do want that. A Division I is a measure of accomplishment, but the joy of making, experiencing music daily is the most important thing we do.

I remember our first concert and how meager it was, but the audience liked us nonetheless. Our intonation was horrible, our precision ragged, our rhythms ill-defined, our musical lines less than effective, but we didn't break down. We didn't have to stop in the middle of a composition to start over. No, sir, we didn't have to do that. Although we had only nineteen band members on the stage, their parents were as proud as if we had had one hundred. I was proud of us. The students were proud of themselves. They walked down the street the next day with heads held high, and rightly so. That was four years ago—thousands of notes have been played since. Our second concert was better, the third better yet. We're still getting better.

I wonder what Dvorak's childhood music experiences were? I wonder if he played in a wind band or orchestra or string quartet in Czechoslovakia. I think I'll walk up to Mrs. Komensky's to see if she is at home. I want to find out more about Dvorak.

By the time I reached the twenty-first step leading up to Mrs. Komensky's mansion, I was breathless. The Spillville hills and her stairs tested my endurance. I was wheezing, leaning on the door jamb as I spun the handle on the ancient silver door bell . . . "Hello, Mrs. Komensky?"

"Yes? Are you ill, young man?" the tiny, shriveled old lady asked peering over wire-rimmed glasses, around the half-opened door .

"No, ma'am. Your steps are quite steep. I'm just out of breath." Several deep breaths later, I announced, "My name is Jim Franklin. I was wondering if I could talk to you about Antonin Dvorak."

"I am not certain. It is becoming late in the afternoon, and I have a pot roast cooking. Dinner is at six."

"I wouldn't take much of your time. It's just that I stopped into Spillville about an hour ago to inquire about the Bily Clocks, but mostly about Dvorak. I've been talking to a couple of fellows down at the Town Square, Karel and Jan, and . . ."

"Heavens! Those two no-good scoundrels? They are trouble, and imbibers also," Mrs. Komensky said as she opened the door several more inches, a wince spreading from the corners of her mouth stretching dried, aged skin tightly across her dull gray teeth.

"I agree they're characters, if not scoundrels as you say, but they did tell me you are the director of the Dvorak Museum. Is that correct?" I asked politely.

"That is correct; however, we are not open today, and I have that pot roast on the stove. I also must cook beans and greens. This is not a proper time to speak with you about Antonin," Mrs. Komensky responded in a testy tone, taking a step backward into the house while closing the door slowly.

"I suppose I'll need to come back another day then. Would next Saturday, say about noon be a better time for you?" I asked peering around the nearly closed door, feeling disappointed; I had that decision to make.

The door reopened slightly. "What did you say your name was?" she asked straightening her hair net.

"Jim Franklin. I'm the high school band director in McGregor. I'm searching for a composition to play for the upcoming spring contest. Dvorak intrigues me. I was hoping that . . ."

"Oh, come in, young man," she said opening the door fully and stepping back into the spacious foyer. "I suppose I might spare you several minutes even though the museum is not open; it is Saturday you understand, and I have dinner to finish," she said as sternly as a bespectacled one-room school teacher. She invited me in from the imposing column-lined porch to the spacious but stifling parlor—over-stuffed chairs and heavy wood-engraved couches filled the room which flowed into the formal dining room—imposing with its dark, heavy decor. Nonetheless, it was a grand house; I could tell that immediately. And the pot roast aroma filtered throughout the house, too. I hadn't eaten since breakfast.

"Let me have your overcoat, mister Franklin. Please sit here on the davenport. May I serve you a cup of tea?" she asked hanging my hat and coat on a brass hall tree. She was a tiny, severe looking woman—maybe Karel was right—reminding me of that lady in Grant Wood's *American Gothic* painting. Her hair was packed tightly in a bun; she wore turn of the century gold, wire-rimmed glasses which she peered over instead of through creating a sternness in her demeanor. I began wondering if this were a good idea.

"That would be wonderful, Mrs. Komensky, but I'm beginning to feel guilty. I believe I'm keeping you from your dinner preparation."

"You need not concern yourself with that. What did you say your name was again? John?" she asked as she hobbled toward the kitchen.

"Jim," I hollered. "Jim Franklin from McGregor."

"Of course, mister Franklin. I will try to remember, although my memory is not good anymore; however, I can remember everything about Antonin Dvorak. Did you say you want to know more about him?" she hollered from behind the swinging kitchen door. What do you want to know?"

"I'll wait until you come back into the parlor, Mrs. Komensky It's hard to talk with you being in the kitchen," I yelled as I searched for a comfortable place on the hard davenport.

"Of course. I will return momentarily, after I boil more water. Please make yourself comfortable."

It was hard making myself comfortable, though. The house reminded me of grandmother's back on her Minnesota farm, although it certainly wasn't as grand as this. Houses like this are overwhelming for many people, particularly young fellows. They have shadowy corners, imposing photographs of angry looking men and women in heavy, walnut-stained wall frames, dusty planters in the four corners, formal crocheted doilies on menacing, carved end tables. And they're closed in, too, dark because women like Mrs. Komensky and Grandmother Franklin like to keep window coverings shut so folks—busy bodies—can't peer in, although I don't see how anyone could with Mrs. Komensky's windows, the house sitting so high on this hill. I saw a classic windup Victrola in the corner. I walked over to look at it more closely. A thick 78 record was on the turntable, but I hesitated to pick it up, choosing instead to bend down and scan the faded label. I could barely read, *Dvorak, Slav . . . o . . . D . . . ces No. 1 & 2.*

I'll ask her to play it when she brings the tea.

Above the Victrola hung two daguerrotypes that looked like Dvorak, if the town square statue was a fair representation. He had been a chunky man, maybe five-foot-nine with a dour expression covering his bearded, haggard face, heavy eyebrows and deep-set eyes. But old photos all look the same. He could have been one of my uncles, or Ulysses S. Grant, or the minister at the Methodist

Church, because the photo looked remarkably similar to those on Grandmother Franklin's walls. Another photo showed Dvorak, his wife and children sitting outside a cabin. It must have been taken around 1900 judging from the styled clothes they were wearing. I circled the parlor past the sentinel ferns in the corner and realized there was an antique reed pump organ against the far wall. A yellowed, tattered music book was on the music desk, a transcription of Dvorak's *American Suite* for organ. I wanted to sit down and attempt it, but the organ looked delicate, severe and frail, just like Mrs. Komensky. I thought better of it. Other heavy-framed photos filled the walls, but I didn't notice any of Mrs. Komensky, or what would have been her family.

"Here is your tea, mister Franklin. I have chocolate chip cookies for you also," she intoned returning from the kitchen carrying a silver serving set. "Let us sit here on the davenport so that you may ask me questions about Antonin."

"Thank you for the tea and cookies. But are you sure I'm not taking up too much of your time?" I said burning my tongue as I gulped the hot tea. But it tasted good. I was still chilled from sitting in the square.

"Silence yourself, young man; I will monitor the time," she said, also sipping her tea much more gracefully than me.

"As I said to you at the door, I'm the high school band director in McGregor and Marquette. Have you ever been to our villages?" I inquired hoping to soften her a little, hoping to make her feel more comfortable with me.

"Yes, many times, mister Franklin. It is a pretty area of Iowa along the river. Of course, Spillville is considerably prettier," she responded as she bit into her cookie.

"We have the state spring contest in May, and I'm trying to select a meaningful composition for our students, something that would have a connection to this part of the state. We'll probably play a Karl King march as our opening composition, but I've been searching for our main selection. I had been driving through Harper's Ferry and Decorah today when I came upon the Spillville sign out at the intersection. The reference to Dvorak caught my attention, so here I am. Karel and Jan didn't know much about him, but they, I should say Karel, talked extensively about the Bily Clocks," I said sipping more tea and tasting the moist homemade cookie for the first time.

"Heavens! Those two cronies do not know a thing. They are two drunkards, no-goods, if you ask me. I would not believe a thing either of them said. Karel is known as the biggest braggart, biggest liar in the village. He undoubtedly told you a far-fetched story about the Bily clocks, did he not?"

"Well, he did ramble on some about how Bily got started here and how his fame spread to New York and Chicago, but it seemed plausible to me. They were cordial, and they said you would be the person to talk to about Dvorak."

"That is correct; however, he has the story of the Bilys wrong, because he reiterates the same convoluted tale to any person who will listen to him. I have heard it all before. I will now correct his story. First, the spelling is B-i-l-y, not B-i-l-l-y, and there were two brothers, Frank and Joseph, not one named William. They were reared here, farmers who began crafting clocks during the long winter months around World War One. They were not strangers passing through. The first clock honored the twelve apostles. This was followed by one showing tribute to Lindbergh, then a clock depicting the Little Brown Church. But I am the village expert on Antonin, not Bily Clocks, although Annabelle is quite well-versed on Antonin though not as thorough as myself," she said with a pompous air.

"Did you know Dvorak?"

"Not what one would call personally, but yes, I knew him. I was a girl when he first arrived in Spillville. He gave me piano lessons; however, he was all business, not personable, though kind. I feel I have gotten to know him better throughout the years as I have read his letters, studied his writings and manuscripts, and listened to his symphonies, overtures and string quartets. I am eighty-five, you know, but I can still get around well enough with help from my cane. I read, listen to music and remember most things, John."

"Jim."

"Heavens, yes, *Jim*. I have been directing the Dvorak Museum for fifty years. We do not get many visitors like you stopping in unannounced during the winter months, mostly summers when we offer the Dvorak Music Conference. We utilize the Inwood Pavilion for concerts, recitals, master classes and seminars, as well as log cabins along the Turkey River to house guest conductors, teachers and performing artists. We house conference participants in local homes; I myself accommodate eight to ten in this big house." Mrs. Komensky turned toward me on the davenport, one still hard and stiff, but I could tell she was used to sitting up straight, proper-like for a proper lady.

"You certainly have a nice, big house, Mrs. Komensky. Was it in your family?"

"Goodness gracious, no! We did not have that much money. Father was a Dorchester grocer from north Allamakee County, and Mother was reared on a struggling farm—if one could even call it that—on hilly bluff country between Dorchester and New Albin near the Mississippi River. That is not farming land, you must know. Real farmers moved to western Iowa where the land is tillable, but my grandfather was stubborn. He ferried across the Mississippi at Lansing and put down roots on the western shore saying he was going no farther. No, we only scraped by, especially during the Depression. This house was built by Antonin, did I not tell you that? He became quite wealthy directing the New York Conservatory of Music. Also, his compositions began selling well throughout America as well as in Europe. He built this house his second summer in Spillville then lived in it for two more summers before returning to Prague. Heavens! I could never have afforded something this grand."

"How did you acquire the house then?" I asked, realizing immediately that my question might have been too personal.

"How did I acquire this, you ask? Why, Antonin willed it to me providing I direct the Dvorak Festival and Museum. I was never so surprised in my life. He eventually tired of living in New York, subsequently moving his family back to Prague, permanently. He wrote me later indicating he would not be returning to Spillville. He willed the deed to me, I presume, because I had been supportive of his work here, and also his best piano student. He said

I should use it as I see fit. Heavens! You can imagine my surprise. Annabelle, my friend, was aghast and I must say, put out. She took violin lessons from Antonin, but Annabelle plays only mediocre violin. Antonin did not encourage her; that is probably the reason I received the house rather than her. However, mister Franklin, please do not say a thing about that to her. She got over it, eventually, so we are still friends. She is arriving soon for dinner. Maybe you will have an opportunity to meet her. Would you care for more tea? I will heat more water."

"That would be lovely. Are you sure I'm not taking up too much of your time?"

"Do not continue creating a fuss about that; besides, I do not receive many visitors during the winter. Summer brings more people than I can tolerate these days; however, winters are long and lonely in our sequestered valley. You are not such a bad fellow to converse with, better than those two inebriates in the town square," she said wobbling on spindly eighty-five-year-old legs to the kitchen with the silver serving set.

"Please make yourself comfortable. I will return with hot tea and more cookies in a few minutes."

That's amazing. She knew Dvorak . . . played piano for him. I'm impressed. I've never met a real, live, world-renowned composer. She actually played music with Antonin.

Waiting for more tea, I walked through the formal dining room and the spacious foyer, admired the long, curving oak staircase leading to the second and third floors, looked at the pictures lining the walls—more photos of Dvorak and his family. I spotted a picture of Antonin with a young girl at a piano. She was about thirteen, in pig tails. Could that be Olga? It was signed, "Best wishes to my piano princess, Antonin."

"Here is your tea, mister Franklin."

"Thanks. I was admiring these photos. May I be so presumptuous as to ask if that is you at the piano with Dvorak?"

"That is correct. I was fourteen when that daguerrotype was taken. He thought I would become an outstanding piano player, but he was only partially correct. I have played throughout my life; however, my fingers do not work as well anymore. I have acquired creeping arthritis. I actually became a better organist than pianist, playing organ for Sunday Mass at Saint Wenceslaus for forty years on our magnificent 1876 Pfeffer pipe organ. St. Wenceslaus Church was built in 1860; you probably didn't know that. I played Antonin's compositions, presented recitals at the church, even at Luther College. Music is as important to me now as it was when that daguerrotype was taken. It is good that you are a musician, John."

"Jim."

"Of course . . . Jim. I am pleased that you are a musician."

Once Mrs. Komensky began talking there was no stopping her. Although she was eighty-five, she could talk nonstop. She was almost a bigger talker than Karel. I listened intently, sipped tea and ate tasty chocolate chips for two hours enthralled with her stories about Dvorak's compositions, viola playing, organ playing for Mass at St. Wenceslaus, conducting, participation in summer string quartets and chamber recitals in the town square. She told me about him hiking through these hills developing theme ideas for Humoresque, finalizing ideas for his *New World Symphony*, sitting on the banks of the Turkey River in Riverside Park composing the *American Quartette* and *String Quintet*, inspiring her musically, and lovely summers when New Yorkers and Chicagoans came to Spillville to make and enjoy music. She told of how she became director of the museum after Dvorak no longer returned to Spillville. She talked on and on until her lips were stretched and dry, until the parlor had become dark, until she was interrupted by the loud musical ring of the doorbell.

"My goodness, now who could that be?" Olga said as she slowly rose on her brittle legs to wobble to the door. "Annabelle? What are you doing here at such an hour?"

"I've come to dine. Don't you recall?" Annabelle responded tartly. "I don't know what I am going to do with you, Olga; your memory is failing rapidly," Annabelle admonished as she brushed past Olga into the foyer.

"You hold your tongue about my memory, Annabelle. I can remember anything that is important to me. Some things simply are not," Olga said leading Annabelle by the arm into the parlor.

"I'm not important, Olga? Your best friend in the world isn't important to you? Hrumph! I think I'll turn around and go back home."

"Annabelle, I want you to meet a nice young man from Monona. His name is John Franklin," Olga exclaimed escorting the spinsterly, gangling lady to the davenport. I stood in anticipation of the introduction.

"How do you do, John. I'm Annabelle," she said thrusting her slim violinist's hand toward me.

"Pleased to meet you, Annabelle. I'm Jim."

"She said you were John. Olga?"

"That's all right, Annabelle, but it's really *Jim*, from Mc–Gregor," I responded.

"McGregor? She said Monona. Olga?"

"That's all right. Monona sounds a little like McGregor; besides, it's just up the road a few miles. Anyway, I'm pleased to meet Olga's best friend."

"Hrumph! I don't know if we're best friends anymore. She didn't even remember I was coming to dine."

I attempted being a peacemaker by telling Annabelle how I had intruded on Olga late in the afternoon, how she had been telling me about Dvorak, and how the time had slipped away. And Olga did have a pot roast on, after all—we could all smell the tantalizing aroma drifting into the parlor. Dinner would be served soon.

I hope Olga invites me.

I stayed for dinner. The three of us dined at the long, cherry wood table with Olga's (or was it Antonin's?) finest china and silver serving set. We dined on pot roast, boiled potatoes, whole kernel corner, rice pudding, wheat bread and coffee. We talked—Olga and Annabelle talked, I listened—for two hours. They spoke of their experiences with Antonin, recalling the pleasant summers shared making music. By the time Olga's (or was it Antonin's?) grandfather clock struck eight, I was stuffed with scrumptious home cooking, much different from my usual fried fare at the Marquette Hotel, but my ears were tired. I had done considerable listening this day, first Karel then Olga and Annabelle, but it had been a pleasant and informative day. I had acquired several contest ideas, and was confident of finding a suitable selection for our band.

"Olga, this has been wonderful. I have enjoyed, so much, our conversation about Dvorak, and your dinner was simply out of this world. Now, I must be leaving. It's gotten dark and I don't know my way around these hills. It's an hour's drive back to McGregor, so I best bid my adieu . . . Olga . . . Annabelle," I said as I excused myself from the table, extending my hand to the ladies.

"Do not rush off; however, if you must, do be sure to return. I have not had an opportunity to show you the Dvorak Museum near the Square; however, you do not live far from here. We can do that another day," Olga said as she escorted me through the foyer, retrieving my hat and coat from the hall tree.

"I'll certainly accept your offer to return. It has been such a pleasure. So nice to meet you, Annabelle." I slipped into my topcoat and hat, then stepped onto the porch into a brisk wind blowing down the hollow.

"Drive carefully, mister Franklin," Olga hollered as I reached the bottom step.

"Good-bye, ladies. Thanks for dinner," I shouted back up those long, twenty-one steps.

Although it was late, dark and cold, I felt a need to stop at the square before driving home. I swung around the square, parked my car and walked over to the statue. It had begun snowing lightly again; I pulled my hat lower, tugged the collar of my topcoat around my neck, slipped on my gloves then sat on the cold iron bench. The Dubuque Star sign was still flickering at Josef's Tap, a lone street light winked through the falling snow as the town clock chimed the half hour. As I looked into Dvorak's snowy eyes, I thought about our music program, about our contest selections, about my life in music.

I thought about how much I had loved bands throughout my life—jazz bands, concert bands, marching bands, Dixeland bands, military bands, maybe even polka bands, *Just a little, Karel*. During the Forties, children hadn't broken away from their parents' music yet. Their music was my music. Those were pre-Rock and Roll days, a style of music I never identified with. Rock and Roll passed me by, fortunately. I was maturing during the Swing Era, before Rock & Roll raucously invaded our music culture. The first live bands I heard were at Gorman's Dreamland Ballroom in downtown Goodhue before I was old enough to gain admission—Jules Herman, Whoopee John Wilfart, Frankie Yankovic, The Six Fat Dutchmen, The Polka Dots—and even though most were old-time bands, they did play modern swing music about every third set. Outside Dreamland, sitting on the back stairwell, I would listen intently to saxophone voicings, the crisp articulation of muted brass, the constant, reassuring thump of the upright bass and the striding of the pianist on that ancient, out-of-tune upright piano. And I heard national name bands on the radio when I pulled in a distant station on my Philco on clear evenings. Cloudless nights were best for receiving clear-channel stations from Texas, Colorado, Chicago, occasionally New York City, St. Louis or Kansas City. If I were lucky, I would pick up Benny Goodman's Let's Dance broadcast from New York City, or Earl Hines' broadcast from the Grand Terrace Ballroom in Chicago, or Count Basie stomping through One O'clock Jump from the Vine Street Cabaret in Kansas City. Listening was heaven as I reclined in bed dreaming of being a jazz musician myself some day. Those rich saxophone voicings, those clarinet leads over lush sax harmonies, those biting, muted trumpet tones are reverberating in my head to this day.

But we didn't have a jazz band at Goodhue High School, none in the village, and few villagers knew much about jazz. Everyone liked to dance, though, you can be sure of that. The dancing craze swept the country during the late Twenties, Thirties and Forties, the Midwest notwithstanding. Every little burg around Goodhue County—Bellechester, Zumbrota, Belle Creek, Hay Creek, Lake City, Red Wing, Oak Center, Welch, Oronoco—sported a dance hall. Why, you couldn't drive twenty miles across the county on a Saturday night without running into a dance hall. Those folks had put in a difficult work week plowing or cultivating or harvesting or milking; Saturday night was a chance to kick up their heels, drink beer, laugh, shout, dance. Saturday night dancing was part of their life; it was part of mine.

It was unfortunate Goodhue High School didn't have a jazz band, though, but I made up for it later. Sure, an upperclassman tried to organize a dance band one summer just like those at Gorman's Dreamland. He recruited high school concert band players, purchased arrangements, called a couple of rehearsals in his mother's living room, but it turned out poorly. He nor any of us knew enough about music theory to make it a success; we didn't know what E-flat or B-flat or C or F meant. The E-flat alto saxes ended up with B-flat sax parts. The B-flat tenor saxes played the E-flat alto parts. The B-flat trombones were playing in the key of C. We murdered Glenn Miller's arrangements. We wanted to sound like Miller, but sounded more like a poor excuse of Spike Jones and his City Slickers. We never played at Gorman's Dreamland Ballroom.

My chance to play in a jazz band came, though, when I entered college. I played in The Moonmisters jazz band (it was really a dance band), concert and marching bands. We purchased stock arrangements from a New York publisher, wrote arrangements, played music of the big bands for high school homecomings, proms, autumn nocturnes, spring flings, and Ancient Arabic Order of Nobles of the Mystic Shrine beer busts. And I played for many years after college while beginning my teaching career . . . bands, bands, bands where I taught children to play, to experience the love and joy of making music.

I shifted on the cold bench and thought about how much pleasure I continued to realize teaching music at Mar Mac, working hard to develop a fuller instrumentation, advanced instrumental skills, the ability to play faster, higher, lower, more express–ively, more sensitively; how we rehearsed to develop better tone quality, better sonority. This challenge of making music drove my life. I pulled my scarf tighter as the evening's chill descended into the valley, as that rusted pickup backed slowly away from Josef's Tap, creaking and listing around the square, the driver waving to me with his Pioneer Seed cap. He probably thought I was crazy to be sitting in a snowfall. I waved back. Dvorak's statue was accumulating considerable snow on its head and shoulders. The pickup, pigeons and squirrels had gone home for the evening, Karel and Jan were nowhere about leaving me alone with Antonin.

As the snowflakes became thicker and wetter, covering my hat and coat, I thought about how I planned on teaching at a bigger high school or college someday. Oh! it would be wonderful to be Director of Bands at the University of Iowa or Iowa State.

I'll keep working hard, studying and practicing my conducting. I'll do it.

"Jim! Jim Franklin."

"What? Who is it? Karel? Jan? Where are you two? I can't see you in this snowstorm," I said, startled out of my reverie.

"It's not Karel or Jan. It's me, over here," the heavily accented bass voice said.

"Where? I don't see anyone. Who am I talking too?" I said nervously, looking left then right seeing no one in the square.

"Over here. It's me, Tony."

"Tony? I don't know any Tony in Spillville," I answered to the melodious wind.

"Tony Dvorak. The statue!"

"Tony Dvorak? The statue? Statues can't talk. I don't believe it, a talking statue," I said to no one in particular as I rose, taking one hesitating step toward the statue.

"But we can, at least I can. Come over here closer so I can see you. I've heard you thinking about music sitting on the bench; I would like to talk with you."

"I don't believe this," I whispered to myself as I looked sheepishly around the square to see if anyone had heard me. But I took several more hesitant steps toward the statue to stand in front, looking up into Dvorak's eyes.

"There, that's better. Now I can see you," the statue said in that low, guttural voice. "Hello. I'm Tony Dvorak. You were down here earlier in the day talking with a couple of friends of mine, Karel and Jan. I was listening to your conversation about the Bily Clocks. Excuse me for eavesdropping, but it's hard not to when I'm here all day."

"I . . . I don't know what to say. I can't believe I'm talking to a statue," I said glancing over my shoulder toward Josef's Tap to see if anyone saw me talking. That larboard-listing pickup was circling slowly around the square, once again parking in front of Josef's. "And you're calling yourself Tony. It's *Antonin*, isn't it?" I asked meekly.

"It was when I lived here in 1893, but this is 1965, Jim. Antonin sounds too old-fashioned, too old-worldly. I would rather be called Tony. Call me Tony, will you?"

"I . . . well . . . Anto . . . n . . . Tony. I suppose I can, but I'm talking to a statue. It's a little difficult getting used to that," I said through the swirling flakes.

"It will be all right, Jim. You will get used to it in a few moments."

"All right, I'll try. But listen, Tony. Have you talked with Karel and Jan before. They didn't say anything about a talking statue."

"No. I'll only speak with musicians like you, people interested in and dedicated to music. I do not waste my time talking with others or itinerant musicians. Karel and Jan enjoy their polkas. I hear Karel rambling about it continuously, but polkas bore me. Do they you?"

"As a matter of fact, they do. I played polkas ad nauseam in Minnesota with The Kufus Brothers, and the Polka Dots, but that was when I was first getting started in music. It was a way to make money for college. I tired of it real fast."

"Excellent! I experienced the same thing in Czechoslovakia. As I was growing up, being a child prodigy in piano, violin and composition, townspeople and relatives always wanted me to compose trite little two-beat polkas for their accordion and concertino bands. It grew increasingly tiresome. They did not understand that I desired to write symphonies, string quartets and overtures, but I persisted. You have to tolerate intrusions if you are going to develop your art," Tony said as a pigeon intruded his space, landing on his left shoulder.

"Do you mind the birds much?" I asked as the pigeon's landing created a swirl of snow around Tony's face.

"No, they don't bother me excessively. Pigeons are all right because they possess a melodious, tonal coo in their voices. I like the meadowlark's five-note melody also, though they seldom fly into the village, preferring open fields and fence posts instead. Sparrows are the most exasperating. I dislike their singing because of it being harsh and out of tune. Sparrows are not musical birds."

"Have you *talked* with Olga Komensky? I had dinner with her and Annabelle this evening. They didn't mention talking to you, but then, I guess, most people wouldn't admit to talking to a statue, would they?"

"You are correct about that, Jim. And I must say, you are courageous to stand here in the snow on a cold night conversing with me when you would probably prefer the warmth of your McGregor home."

"It's all right, Tony, but how do you know about McGregor?"

"I know everything that goes on around here, though I don't focus on anything other than music. But I know what you've been doing with those band students. I can hear your rehearsals all the way up here in Spillville."

"You can? Oh, my God! We sound bad sometimes, and you being a world-famous composer. I'm embarrassed," I said sheepishly.

"Do not be embarrassed. You and your band students are doing fine work. We all must begin somewhere. We all must produce those first meager tones. You should have heard my first violin attempts. That would have been approximately 1873. They were not good either, so do not be embarrassed. You could rehearse somewhat harder on intonation, though; occasionally it grates on my ears, sounding like these sparrows."

"I'll try harder, Tony, now that I know you're listening. I'll try very hard.

Tell me, do you hear other bands and orchestras?" I asked as I became more comfortable talking to . . . Tony.

"That is true. I can hear all of them. I have selective hearing. I can turn on and turn off what I want to hear. I am an excellent musician, you must not forget."

"Oh, I know that. In fact, that's why I'm here today. I became curious about you and your music when I saw the sign out at the intersection. I'm looking for a composition to play for spring contest. I thought maybe I might play one of yours. What would you think about that?" I asked tentatively.

"I would be honored. I know you have been considering it, mind reader you know, and I was hoping to have an opportunity to converse with you. I even have several suggestions," Tony said as the pigeon, obviously bored with the conversation, took flight leaving a swirl of snow around Tony's face.

"That would be great, but first I want to ask more about your listening skills. You say you can hear any music ensembles in the area practicing and performing? Did you say that?"

"Yes, Jim, that is correct. I hear bands from Monona, Postville, Garnavillo, Guttenberg, Strawberry Point, Elkader, Decorah and West Union on a regular basis. I usually tune in to each at least once per week to remain abreast of their progress. I also hear Luther College rehearsals, though the University of Northern Iowa is on the fringe of my listening range; I do not hear them often. And Iowa City is too far south. I cannot receive the Iowa Band at all—hearing deteriorates with age, do not forget, and I am one hundred twenty-five."

"One hundred twenty-five? But . . . but you're not alive. You're a statue, Tony."

"Yes, I am a statue. Your music history texts will say that I died in 1910. I don't compose any more; however, my spirit lives on here in the square. Do not forget that composers have special skills. People know us through our music; however, we have additional talents," Tony responded as snow accumulated on his head and shoulders. "Are you becoming chilled? We could continue this conversation on a warmer night."

"Yes, I am cold, but I'm too intrigued to leave. Tell me more about these special talents. Can you talk to other composers?"

"Indeed. I converse with Bach and Mozart frequently, though Bach is a stuffed shirt, pompous, one who thinks he's the only composer who ever graced this earth. Mozart is a jolly fellow, though, and Schoenberg is considerable fun, though I never cared for his extended tonality," Tony responded, a wayward, squeaking, out-of-tune sparrow circling, searching for a landing place, "because his music is dissonant, harsh. I prefer tonal music, pleasant, lilting melodies and harmonies."

"I can't believe I'm even talking to you, but to hear you say you talk to other composers. Why, it's unbelievable! Can Bach hear our Mar Mac band practicing, too?" I asked nervously.

"Certainly; however, I doubt if his does. Bach does not care for wind bands. He devotes his time to organists, church choirs and chamber orchestras. You need not concern yourself with Bach tuning in. He would not be interested."

"I asked you earlier if you have talked with Olga Komensky? She was a good musician, wasn't she?"

"No, I have not. I have considered speaking several times when she walks around the square on her sojourn to the market; however, I reasoned she might have a heart attack or stroke if I attempted it. Although she directs my museum, she never comes here, and I cannot be shouting throughout Spillville. That would upset these fine villagers; I do not choose that. Spillville is a pleasant village, a suitable home, an excellent site for my statue. In fact, Jim, before conversing with you this evening, I had not spoken with anyone since 1931. A composer by the name of King, Karl King from Fort Dodge sojourned through here that summer. He was a good composer of marches, therefore we conversed late into the evening. Pleasant gentlemen, good composer, not Sousa, but good, very good."

"You talked with Karl King? I'll be darned."

"Composers are common people. You young musicians shower us with excessive adulation. You read about us in music history texts, and listen to our compositions, frequently placing us on pedestals like I am standing on now; however, we were only common people, like you and everyone else. We faced similar problems. You are attempting to determine what to perform for contest, where your next teaching position will be, what college band you will be conducting. We had similar problems. As a composer, I was continually contemplating where my next meal would come from. Composing is not a high paying career, do not forget; however, we love it. Most importantly, we leave a legacy and aesthetic enlightenment behind after we are gone."

"That's for sure," I said stomping my feet to increase the blood flow. "I'll have to admit, Tony, that I'm not well versed about your compositions, but I do know *The New World Symphony,* and I've heard some of your *Slavonic Dances.* I'll do more listening now that I know you . . . err . . . personally."

"Excellent, though you need not be embarrassed because of your unawareness. I composed in excess of three hundred compositions. Not all were of equal quality. I discarded many and several should never have been recorded. Take your time. Purchase a recording periodically to become familiar with more of my compositions. Certainly, I am partial to them; however most are excellent, Bach and Mozart notwithstanding."

"Tell me about the *New World Symphony.* I played the Fourth movement in grade school, and I know the Second movement has been popularized as *Going Home.* In fact, you're probably aware that because of your summers here before the turn of the century, the Iowa State Legislature has adopted *Going Home* as its state hymn."

"That is correct. I am exceedingly proud and honored. Indeed, I feel at home both in Iowa and Czechoslovakia.

But more about the *New World.* Growing up in Czechoslovakia, I was surrounded by Old World traditions. Europe is considerably older than America, the traditions longer, the music older. Upon receiving the opportunity to direct the New York Music Conservatory, I accepted it forthwith. I became impressed with your new country, so different from my old Czechoslovakia. I heard the music of your people—Appalachian folk songs, cowboy saddle songs, Negro spirituals, Mississippi River ballads and rags, steamboat calliope songs. I wanted to incorporate that folk culture into a composition the result of which was *The New World Symphony.* It is not programmatic in that it is a musical description of your country; however, it has the spirit of a new world. It is my compositional impression of America."

"It certainly has been popular all of these years. You did a good job on that, Tony."

"Thank you."

"Tony, I hate to mention it, but I'm pretty cold. Would you

mind if I walked over to Josef's Tap to warm up. I'll come back and talk some more."

"That would be fine. I know you are chilled; however, I am acclimated to it. Go warm up for awhile. I'll be here."

"See you in a few minutes."

"What in hell you doin' here?" Karel hollered from the bar as I stomped into Josef's, snow clinging to my coat and Lester Young-styled porkpie hat. "I thought you hightailed it to McGregor hours ago. You look like you're frozen to death. Get over here, and give this man a shot and beer to warm him up, Josef. Hell! Give everyone a boilermaker, Jan and me, too."

"Hi, Karel. Hi, Jan," I said brushing snow from my hat.

"This here's Josef. He owns the joint," Karel said as I placed my coat and hat on a bar stool.

"Good to meet you, Josef. That beer sounds good, but do you have any coffee? I've been walking and need to warm up," I asked Josef as he set a Dubuque Star long neck and shot glass in front of me.

"Coffee? Sure. Got some burnt grounds left over from this morning, but it's hot," Josef answered as he sidled to the far end of the bar in search of a mug.

"You been walkin' in this snowstorm, Jim? Did you hear that, Jan? Don't know 'nough to come in out o' the storm, does he? [Jan nodded.] Jan don't talk much."

It felt good getting inside after talking to Tony. My feet were frozen, my fingers were frozen, my cheeks were stinging, my nose was red and running, but I would warm up soon with hot coffee.

Although this was my first visit to Josef's Tap, it was similar to any other neighborhood bar in lonely whistle stops across Iowa, Minnesota or Wisconsin. It wasn't any different than the Corner Bar up in Goodhue, or assorted dives across the river in Prairie du Chien. A bar is a place to be, to sip, to chat, a place for Karel and Jan. The glowing red Wurlitzer jukebox in the corner was belting out Hank Williams' *Your Cheating Heart*. I didn't appreciate it very much, but tolerated it because of the hot coffee.

"What in the hell would you be doin' walking 'round Spillville freezing your ass off for? Why would a guy do that, Jan?" Karel snarled as I cradled the hot cup in both hands letting the warmth caress my fingers. I didn't answer for a moment, being mesmerized by the Hamms Bear circling the blue lake above the bar. "You gonna talk or not? Your tongue frozen, too?" Karel barked growing impatient with my reticence.

"Sorry, Karel. I was enjoying my hot coffee. Walking? After you two gents left the square, I walked up to talk with Olga. She invited me in, served dinner, then talked for several hours about Ton . . . y . . . Antonin. After I left I felt like walking around your village to absorb more of Antonin's presence. It wasn't cold when I started, but it's gotten colder, snowing heavier, too," I said while gulping burnt coffee.

"If that don't beat all, does it, Jan? Dumb fool walkin' 'round town on a night like this. You gonna drive through these hills in this snowstorm all the way back to McGregor tonight then?" Karel asked as he drained the bottom of his long neck Star.

"That's my plan. I'll be all right once I get out to the intersection at the main highway."

"You're a crazy musician, that's for sure, just like that Dvorak fella. Damn fool, if you ask me, ain't he, Jan?"

"Yup."

"And there's 'nother fool 'round here, too. I saw some fool standin' in the square over by the statue 'bout an hour ago in this storm. Couldn't make out who he was, though, through Josef's frosted windows, but I don't know what a guy would be doin' standin' in the park on a night like this, do you, Jim?"

"Beats me," I answered reaching for my Star.

"He even looked a tad like you, but you ain't that dumb, are you?

That old bat Olga give you the stuff you wanted 'bout Dvorak?"

"She was very accommodating and informative after she warmed up to me. She knew Dvorak as a girl, took piano lessons from him in fact, and loves to talk about his music, his life and what he did for Spillville. She was very helpful."

"That's surprisin' 'cause she ain't good for much o' nothin' else 'round here . . . don't drink no beer, don't talk to Jan and me, don't come into Josef's. Belongs to the Women's Temperamental Union; drives me crazy. She brings all those longhairs to the Dvorak Music Conference in the summertime. Too many funny looking people, ain't there, Jan?" [Jan nodded.]

"She's not so bad, Karel. You ought to give her a chance. Talk with her sometime when she comes downtown. You might even get to like her."

"That'll be the day. Huh! That'll be the day."

"You can say that again," Jan whispered.

"That'll be the day . . . Jan?"

"Well, fellows, I've warmed up, so I had better be getting back to McGregor before this storm locks me in. It's been nice seeing you again, and thanks for the coffee and beer. If you two ever get to McGregor or Marquette, just ask for me at the Marquette Hotel. They always know where I am, even when I don't want them to."

"Hell, don't go away mad, Jim, just go away. You come back any ol' time. You ain't such a bad fella, is he, Jan?" Karel said as Jan nodded. I slipped into my coat, set my porkpie on wet hair, tugged on gloves, and ventured into the swirling snow. Josef's windows were completely frosted, so I didn't worry about them seeing me trudge back across the street to the deserted square, only the diffused light from that lone street light breaking the darkness. I plodded straight toward Tony. His head, arms and shoulders were completely covered with snow when I returned.

"Hi, Tony. Are you cold?"

"No. I don't get chilled anymore. I like this snow. It's a nice change for me.

Did you see your friends?"

"Yes, Karel and Jan were there. They sure are characters, aren't they?"

"Absolutely!

I have been pondering your contest selections while you were away. I think you should open with a Karl King march, possibly *Barnum and Bailey's Favorite,* or the *Iowa Band Law.* Follow that with *Going Home,* the second movement to my *New World Symphony*, then finish with my *Noon Witch Overture*. That would be a fine programming combination, and it certainly would provide you with the Iowa connection you are seeking."

"That sounds good, Tony, but I don't know your *Noon Witch Overture*. Tell me about it," I said brushing snow from my eyelids to see him better.

"The *Noon Witch* is actually a fairy tale from my childhood that had been passed down for generations. The story says that children are to be cautious when leaving their homes at mid-day during the winter months, because that's when the wicked witch appears unexpectedly to capture them, flying off to her wicked, haunted house at the mouth of the Moldau River. I composed a theatre work about it in 1900, though it was not successful; the overture was popular, however. It is in three-part form, fast, slow, fast; therefore, it would make a good overture for contest. It is melodious with nineteenth-century tonality and not exceedingly difficult. I composed it for orchestra; however, there is a band transcription. Try it. If you don't like it, you might consider my *Slavonic Dances* which are always popular. I think my *American Suite* would be exceedingly difficult for the Mar Mac band at this time."

"I'll do it, Tony, first thing Monday morning.

I hate to leave, but this storm is getting worse. I'll have to go now," I said, sadly.

"I understand. I do not want you to leave, either. I have enjoyed speaking with you. I haven't conversed with anyone since Karl King. I like standing here, though I do get lonesome occasionally. Will you return?" Tony asked as a large piece of snow and ice slid down over his right eye. It looked a little like a tear.

"I certainly will, Tony. I won't forget you."

"I will appreciate that, Jim, and remember . . . I will be listening."

The roads were more snow packed than I had anticipated; consequently, my drive was exceedingly treacherous and slow. I slipped and spun up the long valley out of Spillville to the intersection of Highway 150, fishtailed right, gingerly drove to Calmar then onto Highway 52 through Ossian, Castalia, Postville, Luana, Froelich and Giard until finally reaching the treacherous hill down into McGregor and Marquette. As I slowly descended, I realized that all the way back I had been mulling over Tony and the other-worldly experience of *talking* to him. Staring through the windshield at the frenetic swirling snow for the past hour had put me in a daze. Was my encounter with Tony real, or had I only been imagining it? How could I have been *talking* to a statue? Were Karel and Jan real, or was I imagining them, also? Maybe I wanted to know about Dvorak so badly that I imagined everything.

It was half past ten when I slammed into the curb in front of the Marquette Hotel, snow falling so heavily that I couldn't see the high bridge, but I was safely back. I needed a night cap. As I entered the hotel bar, a couple of familiar faces stared at me; Patsy Cline's *Crazy* was playing on the jukebox.

How crazy *am I . . . talking to Antonin Dvorak?*

"How you doing, mister music man? And *what* are you doing out in this storm? Your face is redder than a turkey's ass in pokeberry time," Arthur snarled as I sat on a bar stool.

"Hi, Arthur. Well, it's nippy out there. I've been in Spillville today tending to music business. My heater isn't working so well."

"Spillville? Shoot! There isn't anything going on in that dried-up ghost town. I need Spillville about as much as a tomcat needs a marriage license. They did have that dusty European composer there years ago, though. What was his handle? Darwin? Debussy? Dvorak? That's it; crusty old fart, they say. Want a beer?"

"Just one. Yes, you're correct, Arthur, there was a T . . . Ton . . . ah . . . Antonin. Antonin Dvorak was his name. Not a bad fellow, they say."

March soon transformed itself into April, the weeks flying by much too rapidly. We started rehearsing our contest selections, just like Tony suggested, a week after I returned from Spillville. The band was initially disappointed in the Dvorak pieces–they liked the Karl King march immediately—but as we rehearsed over the following weeks, they grew increasingly fond of Dvorak, enjoying the haunting, lyric quality of *Going Home*, and the technical challenges of the *Noon Witch*. They liked it even more the day I reiterated the story behind the composition. I didn't go into detail about having *talked* with Tony. I didn't even say I knew him, but they enjoyed the story's Iowa connection. The *Noon Witch Over–ture* was giving us considerable trouble, however. The middle section was mostly playable; we were able to handle the technical demands, but the first and third sections were extremely demand-ing. I divided those sectional passages into smaller segments to rehearse slowly, gradually increasing the tempo as we developed facility. The composition really was too difficult for us, but I reasoned that it would be a wonderful learning experience for the band as well as an opportunity to expand our musical knowledge. By April 15 I felt confident about *Barnum and Bailey's Favorite*, and I knew we could play *Going Home*, but I was loosing sleep over the *Noon Witch*. I was perturbed with Tony for talking me into that overture. Additionally, after five years of teaching at Mar Mac, those periodic disturbing thoughts of moving on caught me during unguarded moments, interfering with my contest focus. If I were to resign, I certainly didn't want to leave town with a Division II rating for the students or myself.

Tony, why did you get me into this? You had been listening to us from Spillville. You knew the level of our band. You shouldn't have recommended the Noon Witch.

During rehearsals I was so involved that I didn't worry. During the nights, though, I would awaken, sweat beads running down my temples. But we were making progress . . . then the flood came.

The Mississippi River is a magnificent river, although it certainly has a mind of its own. It can be as calm and peaceful as a lamb, as violent as a lion. It certainly roared on May 1, two weeks before contest. We had had considerable snow throughout the winter—that storm I experienced in Spillville was one of many ferocious storms throughout March. In fact, the entire Upper

Midwest had been slammed hard. Most rivers in Minnesota and Wisconsin flow to the Mississippi; consequently, its banks couldn't hold all the melting snow rushing from St. Paul and La Crosse to Lansing, Harpers Ferry, Marquette, McGregor and Dubuque to the Gulf. In McGregor water attacked Main Street like Grant at Vicksburg, all the way up past the Scenic Hotel, a distance of a quarter mile. In Marquette water invaded the benches threatening homes like Confederates at the Battle of Harper's Ferry—Virginia, that is. Bloody Run became a lake. McGregor was shut off from Marquette. Marquette was shut off from Prairie du Chien. School shut down, towboats shut down, fishing shut down, traffic shut down, everything shut down. Certainly, the disaster of that flood was more important than winning a Division I rating, to most people, but that year, to me, no! Oh, I filled sand bags, patrolled the dikes at three in the morning watching for breaks like the little Dutch boy while drinking coffee and chomping doughnuts, but my mind was elsewhere. The band was loosing valuable time because of this violent, uncontrollable, angry river. I had to do something. I did. I got on the phone, called each band student, told them to be at the band room at seven the next evening, swim or sink. They came, each one of them. Some hiked over the bluff from Marquette, some sauntered from houses fortunate enough to be on high land, some rode high-wheeled tractors in from their farms, and some arrived in fishing boats. There was even a story floating throughout the communities of our first flutist, a young Marquette girl, breast-stroking down the swollen river to rehearsal, flute gripped tightly between her jaws, but that was never substantiated. We rehearsed that evening and every evening until the waters receded. The flood had left its debris—bottom mud, old shoes, skunk carcasses, rodents, snakes, a submerged 1947 Chevy released from its deep grave by the surging waters—but the band was on schedule. Tony might be right after all.

Only one week remained before contest at Elkader High School. *Barnum and Bailey's Favorite* was ready needing only an increase in tempo of ten beats per minute. We were currently playing it at a metronome marking of 110, but needed to achieve 120 to render a proper march style. We would make it. *Going Home* was ready also, but we still needed to improve our intonation—*You could work harder on intonation, Jim*—and the musical line needed shaping. We would make it. Part II of the *Noon Witch* was in the same condition as *Going Home*. We would make it, but the opening and the finale´ still needed attention—wrong notes, faulty intonation, flute and clarinet facility lacking, uneven harmonic balance. We would ma . . . k . . . e . . .

Five days.

By the final days of preparation the river had receded to its proper, respectful place, although mud still filled the gutters and sidewalks of the villages releasing an odor heretofore known only to deep-scavenging catfish. High-water marks engraved most buildings on Main Street permanently recording this flood, but signs of spring sprouted throughout the valley, nevertheless. Crocuses were breaking through watery patches of mud, Kentucky blue grass was sprouting up through water-logged lawns, buds were breaking out on Lilac trees, Forsythia bushes began transmitting their sweet aroma to counter the musty flood odors, and robins were bringing fresh spring songs back to the valley. Even Old Buck reclining in front of the bank had an extra spring to his step, whenever he did get up to walk, that is. It was a nice time to be in this valley.

I just wish these disturbing thoughts would leave me alone. I don't want to think about them. I'm happy here, aren't I? I don't want to leave, do I?

But those thoughts wouldn't disappear in spite of my best efforts to suppress them. And their timing was horrible. I wanted *all* of my concentration focused on preparing for contest and the May Concert at the end of the school year, but I finally had to deal with the intrusions. Three days before contest, at dusk, I decided to face the monster. After school, instead of stopping for dinner at the hotel, I drove up the long, circuitous bluff road to Pike's Peak State Park. I liked going to the towering Peak when I needed to think; it truly was God's country because no one or nothing else could have made something so grand. I walked to the edge of the precipice while lights flickered far below in McGregor, Marquette, and across the river in Prairie du Chien. For miles up river and down river, I could see the river's expanse and the confluence of the Wisconsin and Mississippi rivers. Alone on the overlook, I peered into the river valley just as Effigy Mounds Indians had done hundreds of years ago. I wondered if they, too, had stood on this very cliff to decide their futures. Where did they go? Why did they leave this region, these bluffs, this river, this valley? Why would I leave? Am I any different than them? Couldn't I stay to be buried here like they were?

As a river tow sliced through the darkness, sounding its bellowing horn far below me, I thought about my students, my friends, my band director colleagues throughout Clayton County and Iowa.

It has been a special time, but I have so much ahead of me. Do I want to teach high school students the rest of my life? Have we reached our *high-water mark at Mar Mac like the recent flood waters?*

I walked away from the precipice toward a trail heading upriver as the fading sun escaped beyond the evergreen trees. Rabbits and squirrels scurried across the path in front of me, a deer hurtled across the trail into the brush. I hiked the trail along the bluff in creeping darkness, lit only by the Indian moon . . . thinking . . . pondering about music, about life. I walked for half an hour on the high path abreast of the river, stopping periodically to look down into the auburn valley, this river valley that had provided peace and tranquillity to me for several years. It would be a shame to leave it, but I have other *musical* bluffs to climb, other *musical* rivers to ride. "Tony, you're probably listening to me at this moment. What would you do?" I whispered to the singing wind. Tony didn't answer. I was left alone with my predicament, but I *was* facing the monster.

That river, that river,
Rolls, rolls endlessly along . . .

One final day for polishing before Saturday's ride to Elkader. *We'll make it. I'm confident now. I faced my monster on Pike's*

Peak a couple of nights ago, and we'll face this one.

On Friday I worked especially hard during rehearsal to be positive with the band students, trying to build confidence in their musicianship and preparation. Polish, polish, polish. Tomorrow.

By eight o'clock we were on the buses, out of McGregor and up that long, steep hill that I had slid down two months ago when returning from my "Tony encounter," but today, heading to Elkader instead of Spillville. Our scheduled performance time was eleven o'clock, but we would have an opportunity to warm up prior to that. The students were excited—jittery, hyper, laughing, jostling, noisy—expending considerable excessive energy as we drove over high, rolling plateaus past newly-planted fields of Grant Wood corn beyond Garnavillo and Monona. But I was calm as our buses sliced through limestone walls descending into Elkader's picturesque valley. My work was mostly done, although I needed to conduct well this morning. Soon, we were off the buses, into the rehearsal room, instrument cases flying open—blowing, blaring, squeaking, but no catapulting trombone slide this time. I stood on the podium . . . silence . . .

"B-flat major scale."

Do, re, mi, fa, sol, la, ti, do. Do, ti, la, sol, fa, mi, re, do.

"Again. Slower."

Do, re, me, fa, sol, la, ti, to. Do, ti, la, sol, fa, mi, re, do.

"Faster, with eighth notes."

Do do, re re, mi mi, fa fa, sol sol, la la, ti ti, do do.

"Descend." Do do, ti ti, la la, sol sol, fa fa, mi mi, re re , do do.

"Get up our warmup Bach chorale, *Come Sweet Death* . . . first sixteen measures. Tune up. Here's a concert B-flat pitch." Thirty minutes of nervous energy. By now, I was nervous; the students were nervous.

"Everyone take several deep breaths. Get up *Going Home.*" We played without stopping. It was fine.

"The *Noon Witch Overture*, Part I." I gave a brisk downbeat into Tony's composition. Ragged.

"Start again, please. More precision, more bite to the initial attack. Get ready for that first chord, trombones. Again." Crisp downbeat.

"Better!" Through measures 12, 16, 24.

"Stop. Ragged entry, trumpets. Be prepared, please. Measure 32. Ready?" Downbeat. Good. They were relaxing, beginning to focus only on the music which is what I wanted them to do. I didn't stop this time. We played for sixty-four measures before stopping.

"Excellent! Part III, Finale´." This was the hardest section in our entire contest repertoire. Suddenly, that long-dormant butterfly flew out of my stomach and landed on my quivering, raised baton. It hung on through a speeding downbeat. Furious opening woodwind passage . . .

"Stay with it clarinets. Be ready, flutes. Good! That's it. You're on top of it today." Cut off.

"We're ready. Relax for half an hour, get a drink, be back in thirty minutes, dressed, ready to perform. Good job."

My back was to the band as I squinted toward the deep recesses of the auditorium waiting for the signal to begin our performance. Three judges huddled there in darkened conclaves like sixth century Benedictine monks toiling over music manuscripts. An announcer stepped to the side of the stage, "Contestant number seven, Mar Mac High School." I turned, stepped onto the podium, breathed deeply, smiled at the band, raised my baton (blew that pesky butterfly off), recalled the march tempo then struck a sharp downbeat into *Barnum and Bailey's Favorite*.

Good start, crisp rhythms, sharp attacks. The band is energized, playing well. At the Trio now. That's it, nice, lyrical, watch the intonation, clarinets. Too much trombone, hold it down a bit 'bones. Now, to the dogfight. Good. Crisp! Bring up the volume, everyone. That's it, we're on a roll. Cutoff. Great!

Going Home. *Let's show these judges how beautifully, how lyrically, how expressively a wind band can play. Ready, Tony?*

Lush beginning, haunting, plaintive theme . . . *Going home, Going home . . . to Iowa.*

Band is playing exceptionally well today. Does it have something to do with Dvorak? Now, finish with a delicate pianissimo. There. That's it. Smile. Great!

This is it. The Noon Witch. *Watch your opening tempo, Jim. Not too fast. Concentrate for the woodwinds' sake.*

Onto the podium, baton high in the air (no butterfly), fifty-five pairs of eyes focused on the tip. Now! A rushing woodwind passage cracked the monastery's stale air, hopefully startling those monks out of their contemplation. Energetic, crisp, decisive passage.

We're out of the starting gate. Stay with it, clarinets. Be prepared for that entry, flutes. Ready, trumpets? Intonation. Intonation. Tony is listening! I don't think I've ever heard our band play better. What is happening to them today? Just listen. They're inspired. Middle lyrical section now. Be prepared for the ritard. That's it. Nice, gradual. Now, let's play with more expressiveness than we've ever played before.

We did. I had tears in my eyes by the time the finale´ approached.

Not long now, band. Here we go. Stay on top of it. Fanfare in the trumpets. Crisp counter-rhythms in the percussion. Magnificent chord in the lower brass. Come on, woodwinds, show them your stuff.

Suddenly, much too suddenly, it was over. I was perspiring profusely, droplets dripped into my eyes, the baton slipped from my hand to the podium. I looked at the band. They looked at me. I nodded. They nodded. We knew. I turned to see angelic smiles on the faces of the *monks,* then I looked toward the heavens . . .

We did it, Tony.

The Division I rating posted in the school cafeteria was a forgone conclusion. We knew we were Division I sitting back on that stage, but we all shouted and cheered when they posted it, nonetheless: Mar Mac Band, Division I.

The bus ride home was the best I ever had even though it was in a rickety, drafty, tank-sprung school bus. But a Rolls Royce bus couldn't have ridden better that day. The students were singing, laughing and joshing, but I stared straight ahead down the highway as we wound our way through the hills of the Turkey River and ascended, once again, to the high prairie. I was pleased for the students, pleased for myself. The Division I was more than a rating, more than a plaque. The walnut-stained-wood plaque, Iowa Music Association emblem gracing its face, would be placed in our school's trophy case for many years, collecting dust like other high-water memorials of past generations, then years later transferred to the McGregor Historical Museum, taking its place alongside photos and awards generated by Harvey Haltmeyer, the magnanimous gentleman of music education in McGregor and Marquette long before I wound my way downriver into this valley, but the feelings generated by today's musical success would last a lifetime. I was proud to have a part in that, pleased to have brought music to these students, so they could carry it through their lives, so they could share the joy of music with their future families, and maybe someday, their own students. That's what teaching music meant to me . . . sharing the joy.

An hour after arriving back at the high school they were all gone. Lonesomeness spread over the empty bandroom as I sat on the podium looking at empty chairs and music stands in disarray . . . thinking, pondering. I had been so focused, so caught up in the day's activities that I realized, at that moment, I hadn't thought about my personal quandary. But now it came rushing back *prestissimo* as a quiver flitted across my temples, as my face became flushed. I looked up to see that butterfly flitting lazily across the bandroom.

Is this the time?

Darkness had enveloped the river valley as I walked to my car. I didn't stop at the hotel for dinner; rather, I drove along the river upstream past Marquette, past Effigy Mounds, past Yellow River Forest, across rolling hills of Waukon, Castalia, Ossian, Calmar to the T-intersection, then left into the Spillville Valley. That forlorn light bulb was still shedding its measly glow on the square. Josef's Dubuque Star sign was still spilling red neon light onto the deserted street. I pulled slowly up to the curb, sat for a minute, then walked over to the statue, pulling my topcoat higher.

"Hi, Tony. It's Jim."

"I know. I heard you coming all the way from Marquette,

selective hearing, you remember. I have been awaiting your arrival," Tony said as a squeaky, out-of-tune sparrow fluttered past his right ear.

"We did it, Tony. We played your *Going Home* and the *Noon Witch Overture* just like you suggested. We earned our Division I rating. And we really played well today. I'm so proud of those Mar Mac students. Here I am talking to you, a world-famous composer, but I'm telling you, we played exceptionally well," I said excitedly.

"You certainly did, Jim. I am proud of you and your students, also. I don't know if I have ever heard *Going Home* played more musically, more from the heart. I certainly felt the Iowa connection, even up here. I had tears in my eyes. I am going to rust this old statue if I am not careful."

"Thanks, Tony. That's a wonderful compliment. How do you think we did on the *Noon Witch*?" I asked nervously.

"Good. Not perfect, though good. Some intonation problems in the trumpets, slight chord balance problems in the lower brass, periodic raggedness in the woodwinds; nevertheless, a fine performance for a high school band."

"Thanks for being honest with me. I'm proud of our performance, but I know it wasn't perfect. Not many things are, I guess."

"That is correct. Few things are. All we can do is try our best with the talents we have. That is what I have attempted with my compositions. Even Beethoven composed under less that ideal conditions when he was becoming deaf. Nothing is perfect," Tony said with a tender, compassionate voice as that same white pigeon returned to roost on his shoulder.

"The problem is, I'm searching for perfection. I guess that's part of being a musician. We're always looking for the perfect performance, but it never happens. I'm looking for the perfect job. Is this it? Is this the most perfect place there is, Tony? Should I be staying here, or should I be moving on to further my career? It's a difficult decision."

"You will have to make that decision yourself. I see and hear what you have in your heart. I know and see your love of the band students and of the community; however, there are other students who need your help, other communities who would benefit from your musicianship. I made a similar decision when I resigned from the New York Conservatory to return to Prague. Believe in yourself and you'll be doing the proper thing. Have the courage of your own convictions," Tony responded as a few rain drops began falling. I pulled up the collar of my topcoat and stepped closer to the base.

"Mind if I sit here for awhile, Tony . . . just want to think for a moment."

"That will be fine. I will be here when you are ready to talk."

It began raining harder, but I wasn't concerned about it. My thoughts were on the day, on my future . . . to stay or leave. To resign when the band was on a high note, when another director could take them even further would be a good professional decision. I decided to walk. I shuffled to the end of the square past Josef's Tap—Karel and Jan slouched over the bar, Karel's mouth beating like a snare drum, Jan nodding like a metronome, Josef listening, bored—but I didn't go in, preferring at this moment to stay with my own thoughts. I walked around the corner of Josef's then up the hill toward Olga's mansion, high and majestic above the village. A soft, Tiffany lamp light filtered softly through the red and green stained glass dining room window. I walked past to the top of the hollow to look down on the singular twinkling street light of Spillville, the shadowy outline of the meandering Turkey River disappearing into the night—another decision along a river— before walking back down to the square, filled with joy for the day, anxiety about my future. By the time I returned to the square, I had made my decision. I walked back to Tony as the rain continued its downpour . . .

"Tony?"

"Yes?"

"I've decided what I'm going to do. You've helped me so much these past few weeks. You've been an inspiration to me. I realize now how much direction your presence has given me."

"Yes?"

"I'm going to pursue my goals. I'm going to gain experience now at a larger high school, then study for another degree to obtain that college job. I'll be leaving Mar Mac this spring."

Tony didn't responded for several minutes. I thought maybe he hadn't heard me. The pigeons and sparrows flitted around his shoulders and head, rain streamed down his cheeks. I looked up and realized it wasn't simply rain tumbling over his cheeks; it was more than that. I thought I saw his lips quiver, his shoulders shudder, but I must have imagined that. Statues don't cry.

"Tony? Did you hear me?"

"Yes, I heard you. It's just that . . . well, I want what is best for you; however, I know you will be moving away from here, and I won't be able to converse with you because you will be beyond my listening range, and I had not spoken with anyone since 1931 before you came along . . . and . . . oh, I wish things could be perfect," Tony said as a trinity of pigeons now roosted on him—one on his head, one on each shoulder.

"I'll be back, Tony. I'll be back," I said as I realized rain was also streaming down my cheeks.

"Please, do not forget me," Tony whispered.

"Thanks for everything, Tony. I'll be seeing you around."

"Good-bye, and remember, Jim, I will be listening."

Going home, going home . . .

Dancing Along
The Upper Mississippi

Separating Fact from Fiction

Dancing Along The Upper Mississippi is a work of historical fiction both in main characters portrayed and story line. The early citizens, North Iowa Times editors, businesses, buildings, streets, dates and events portrayed in the primary setting of McGregor, Marquette and Prairie du Chien are, however, historically accurate. Considerable research was undertaken to provide a true portrayal of the villages and Upper Mississippi river region.

The following people are historically accurate: Alexander MacGregor, Gregor MacGregor, Diamond Jo Reynolds, Colonel Richardson, F. W. D. Merrell, Colonel Otis, Samuel Clemens (Mark Twain), Horace Bixby, Julien Dubuque, Walter Family Band, Doc Evans Band, Bix Beiderbecke, Frankie Trumbauer, Buddy Bolden, King Oliver, Jelly Roll Morton, Bessie Smith, Billie Holidy, Julia Lee, Count Basie, Benny Moten, Walter Page, Andy Kirk, Jack Daniels, Father Marquette, Joliet, T. J. Pendergast.

These businesses existed at one time in McGregor, some even today: North Iowa Times, Pocket City News, McGregor News, Lewis Hotel (Alexander's Hotel), American House Hotel, H. D. Evans Dry Goods Emporium, John Hagensick's McGregor Brewery, Athenaeum Opera House, Sullivan's Opera House, Ramage & Peterson Drugstore, Ann Street Public School, McGregor

Hospital, Pilkington's Mortuary, White Springs Restaurant, Klein Brewery, Rob Roy Ferry, G. Hawley & Son's Carriage Works, and Amos Pearsall's Livery Stable. In Marquette: Marquette Hotel, Burke Hotel; Chicago, Milwaukee, St. Paul & Pacific Railroad. In Prairie du Chien: Villa Louis, Spit & Whistle, Kaber's Nightclub, Dousman Hotel. In Cassville: Denniston House Hotel. In Guttenberg: Moxie's Tavern, Pioneer Rock Church. In Kansas City: The Reno, The Subway, The Chesterfield.

And the following sites exist today: McGregor (MacGregor's Landing), Marquette (North McGregor), Triangle Park (Diamond Jo Triangle Park), Spook Cave (Spook Hole), Beulah Falls, Bloody Run, Sni Magill and all rivers and creeks, Buell Park, Old Military Road, Fort Atkinson, Effigy Mounds, Pike's Peak, Indian Isle (Bergman's Island), Pictured Rocks, McGregor Heights, Methodist Hollow, Walton's Hollow, Pleasant Grove Cemetery, Lock & Dam No's 10, 11, 12, Wyalusing Park, Clarke College, University of Dubuque, Loras College, Wartburg Seminary, Shot Tower.

Flemming's Sawmill and the pontoon railroad bridge are gone.

River points still guarding the Great Waters: Point Ann, Fire Point, Eagle Point, Barn Bluff, Maiden's Rock, Chimney Rock, Horseshoe Lake, Sturgeon Lake, Death's Head Bluff.

Steamboats that plied the great waters: John. J. Roe, Ida Fulton, Belle of the West, Paul Jones, Gem City, Diamond Jo, Keokuk, Hawkeye State, Effie Afton, Delta Queen.

Watch For These Forthcoming Books

from

Popcorn Press

Last Waltz In Goodhue
Creative Autobiography
Publication, Summer 1997
Jim Franklin

County Road No. 9
Novellas, Stories, Personal Essays
Publication, Summer 1998
Jim Franklin

Ragtime Along The Upper Mississippi
Historical Novel: 19th Century Steamboating
Publication, Summer 1999
Jim Franklin

About Popcorn Press

*Our publishing plans and the answer
to the question . . . Why did you call your
book publishing company Popcorn Press?*

Dancing Along The Upper Mississippi is the first book
published by Popcorn Press: Upper Mississippi River Book
Publisher, an independent, small press publisher. The com–
pany is new with the publication of *Dancing Along The Upper
Mississippi*, and *Last Waltz In Goodhue,* but the writing has
been going on for ten years. One doesn't want to rush things,
you understand. It's our intention to bring out a new book every
summer for the next several years, thereby establishing a catalog of books for your reading pleasure.

Last Waltz In Goodhue was actually the first book written,
a manuscript which has been completed for five years. Its publication coincides with the Centennial celebration in Goodhue,
Minnesota during the summer of 1997. We've been patiently
waiting for that centennial to arrive, but folks up in Minnesota
think it's about time this book was published. They don't want
to wait another one hundred years.

County Road No. 9 has also been ready for several years,
but it needed to wait its turn after *Last Waltz In Goodhue.* We
will see its publication during the summer of 1998.

Ragtime Along The Upper Mississippi is the newest book
in the Popcorn Press Catalog. Actually, it's not in the catalog,
because it hasn't been written yet, although it has been plotted
and researched. We'll have it for you in the summer of 1999.

Our writing focus at Popcorn Press is on the Midwest, at least the first four books are set in that region, but we are not limiting ourselves to only Midwest writing. What the heck, though; it's a good start.

Other authors may appear in our catalog as the years pro–gress, as well as out-of-print books of special interest. Also, we hope to be offering selected musical items: jazz books, tapes and paraphernalia.

As a boy back in Minnesota, my older brother and I oper–ated a popcorn wagon in the village. We parked it next to the hardware store on Saturday nights to serve popcorn, soda and candy bars to the folks watching the free movies projected onto the side of the railroad station. Then on Sunday afternoons we pulled it to the dusty old ball diamond to serve the local clien–tele as they lounged under the spreading elm watching their heroes play ball. And we would pull it out County Road No. 9 to serve popcorn and pop to folks attending a farm auction at Walt's or Carl's place. Popcorn Press. It fits.

We'll also be publishing a newsletter for people wanting to stay abreast of what is happening at Popcorn Press. It will con–tain news about forthcoming books, tapes, and tidbits about the Midwest.

We are projecting the publication of *The Upper Mississip-pi River Journal*, winter 1998, a periodic literary potpourri of short stories, essays, history and opinion.

Go ahead and fill out the form on the last page to place your name on our mailing list for our catalog, direct mail notic-es of forthcoming books, newsletter, and *The Upper Mississippi River Journal* updates.

So, don't put it off, then.

Colophon

Typeface: Times Roman
Paper: 60# Booktext Natural, Acid Free
Cover: 10pt. C1S, Film Lamination-Matte
Designer: Popcorn Press &
Chris L. Shelton of Infinite Visions
Printer: BookCrafters
Composed in Pagemaker on a Macintosh Computer

Order Form

Please send me the books I have checked below.
Telephone orders:(319) 873-2546
FAX orders: (319) 873-3816
Mail orders: Popcorn Press, 126 Main Street
                 P.O. Box 237, McGregor, Iowa 52157

☐ *Dancing Along The Upper Mississippi* by
   Jim Franklin. An historical novella set on
   and along the Great River in 1949. 272 pp.
       (No.)_____ copies at $16.95: $_____
☐ *Last Waltz In Goodhue: Adventures of a Village
   Boy* by Jim Franklin. Relive your childhood
   with this creative autobiography. 328 pp.
       (No.)_____ copies at $18.95: $_____
              Subtotal books: $_____
              Sales Tax: 6%, IA residents only $_____
              Shipping: $1.75 first book.
              $ .50 each additional book. $_____
              TOTAL to Popcorn Press $_____
Payment:
☐ Check
☐ Visa. No._____ Exp_____
☐ Mastercard. No. _____ Exp_____

Name:_____
Address:_____
City:_____State:_____Zip:_____

☐ Please place my name on the mailing list for the *Popcorn Press
   Newsletter*, announcements of forthcoming publications, and
   updates on *The Upper Mississippi River Journal*. FREE.

Popcorn Press
126 Main Street
P.O. Box 237
McGregor, Iowa 52157
(319) 873-2546